MY EYES
GLOW RED

MY EYES GLOW RED

BOOK ONE

J. V. Simms

Podium

Podium

Publisher's Note

This book is the final result of a devoted effort by the author's family and Podium Entertainment. We celebrate J. V. Simms's memory and hope his longtime fans and new readers alike enjoy his works for many years to come.

MY EYES
GLOW RED

CHAPTER ONE

Two *hundred years after the Vampire Apocalypse, in the castle of the Lord of Blood, Kyler Stragos . . .*

. . . Mayner gave an agonized shriek of pain when I caught his kick in mid-air and wrenched his leg from his hip with a moist popping sound. I then used my magic to seize control of the blood that spurted from his wound and transformed the liquid into a solid strand of ribbon that quickly wrapped itself around the rest of his body in a diagonal pattern and pulled itself taut, dicing him into a mound of thick, wet cubes of meat that cluttered the floor of my throne room.

Hemokinesis. That was the name of the ability to mentally manipulate blood. It was not the kindest power in the world, but then again, I *was* a Vampire Lord. Kindness wasn't a trait expected of me. Besides, Mayner had started it. Assembled the silly little raid and invaded my home with the intention of, how had he put it? *Bringing you to justice for your innumerable trespasses against humanity and delivering you to final judgement!*

He'd had an excellent speaking voice. I could have listened to him rant about my crimes for hours before eating him. He'd ignored my request to repeat himself, though. That had been a sad moment for me and an utter tragedy for him and his friends.

It'd been fifteen minutes since our dance began and things weren't looking too well for Mayner's little gathering of heroes. Mayner himself had just been cubed and only a dozen of the thirty he brought with him were still standing. All of them were hollow-eyed and on the verge of animal panic, especially now that their leader was dead. If any of them wanted to flee, I felt no obligation to chase after them. I'd already seen their faces and caught their scents. I could hunt them down at my leisure.

Then again, they'd made a terrible mess of my residence. It wouldn't do to let such behavior slide. I was a bit obsessive about arranging things exactly how I liked them, but now the whole area was cluttered with destroyed objects and mutilated corpses.

Yeah, looking at what they'd done annoyed me. Okay, I'd just kill them all and be done with it. Or maybe I'd just kill most of them and let the survivors clean the place up. Then I'd kill them too.

That seemed fair.

I wondered though, should I congratulate them for lasting this long, or should I taunt them for failing to deliver on Mayner's threats? As I ruminated over the proper course of action, my final opponent appeared before me.

How best to describe this young beauty? She had silver hair, which she kept tied back over a flawless-looking face. Over her athletic frame, she wore enameled plate armor with golden highlights. Despite her serene expression, her gray eyes blazed with a warrior's righteous certainty, and in her hands, she carried a spear that emanated a disturbing light, the presence of which made my undead flesh recoil.

Just by observing her calm approach, I somehow knew that my doom had finally found me.

For the first time in centuries, I knew *fear*.

"Oh, shoot," I said to myself just before she began her attack.

Dodging her wasn't easy, which was the first indication of how much trouble I was in. You see, dodging a strike delivered by a mortal should *always* be easy. After all, I was nearly twenty times faster than any human being that ever lived. This girl shouldn't have been able to perceive my movements. That didn't stop her from launching a furious series of vigorous thrusts at my face and torso, all of which I narrowly avoided with no time to deliver a counterattack of my own.

In frustration, I leaped into the air and floated there, safely out of her reach. My powers allowed me to not only control any external sources of blood, but I could also control that which flowed within my own veins. By infusing it with my magic, I could fly, and augment my strength and speed to levels that dwarfed even vampiric norms.

While that was usually enough for me to win, for occasions like today, when I was facing a truly *tenacious* foe like this girl, I preferred to mold spilled blood into weaponry and attack from a safe distance. It was cowardly but highly effective.

Raising my hands before the blood-soaked room below me, I willed dozens of edged weapons into existence from the gore that coated my floor and bid them to rise into the air alongside me. Then I pointed the weapons toward my opponent and sent them flying at her in an unending stream of certain death.

If I was the sort of egotist who named his favorite attacks, I would have called this one *Bloody Rain*. Didn't that have a certain charm to it?

Sadly, despite the large quantity of my munitions, the girl parried, blocked, and danced away from everything I threw at her. Her precise movements and unshakable poise were beyond any other humans' that I'd ever seen. Who was she? What was her grievance?

More importantly, could I beat her?

I received my answer a moment later.

Before I could defend myself, she suddenly launched herself into the air above me, and with one perfectly delivered overhead kick to the top of my head, smashed me painfully to the ground. Just as I regained my legs, she threw her weapon at me.

Wasn't that unsporting of her? *I* thought it was.

In a flash, her holy spear pierced my chest, pinning me firmly in place to the stone wall behind me. I screamed in pain and struggled to dislodge it, but I could feel my many powers being weakened and suppressed. I knew in that moment that I had finally been defeated. After a thousand years of bloody revelry, someone had finally stepped forth to put me in my place.

It felt so anticlimactic.

I was one of the four great Vampire Lords. Over the years of my impossible span of existence, I'd dueled demigods, saints, and legendary chosen warriors. I'd even stood my ground against that brief but terrible superhero fad, when it'd seemed like every orphaned alien and maladjusted billionaire with repressed sexuality had been determined to put on an outlandish costume and impose their wrath on whichever socially acceptable target of the day they could pummel half to death with their leather-gloved fists.

No matter who my opponents were or however much power they wielded, I'd always found a way to either win or survive. That was the benefit of being beyond death and growing stronger as I aged. Time would *always* be on my side.

Except for today, it seemed.

After a few more half-hearted attempts to remove the spear, I sighed and let my hands fall away. It looked like there was no getting out of this one. If I struggled any further, it would only hurt my public image. I had a legacy to consider. If this was the night where I finally met my end, then I would do so calmly.

I owed that to myself.

Honestly, I couldn't deny that I had this coming. I hadn't been a very kind person. To put it bluntly, I'd been a complete monster who'd killed quite a few people over the years. And when I say quite a few, I mean *quite* a few.

Want to hear an amusing story? Once, in a fit of anger, I painted an entire block of Philadelphia, Pennsylvania, red with the blood of its residents. Not by myself, of course; I had a lot of help. Mostly mind-controlled first responders and a few lesser vampires that I bullied into pitching in. Surprisingly, a lot of the locals assisted as well. Not because I forced them to do it, but because many Philadelphians were dead inside and took malicious joy in spreading suffering.

I miss them.

It took us a while to get the job done, but we made it into a sort of community project and gave it our best effort. It really wasn't worth it, though. Blood didn't stay that vibrant red color for very long, and in massive quantities, it drew *a lot* of flies.

So many flies . . .

Still, while the final results might have been disappointing, I treasured my memories of that day. Getting out of my comfort zone, meeting new people, and trying something a little different. It really had been fun. I wonder how everyone's been since then? I mean, the humans were obviously all dead by now—even the ones who weren't dined upon—and Philadelphia has been a radioactive crater for the last seventy years. But maybe I should have seen if any of those other vampires were still around?

It's so hard to maintain connections.

It was strange to realize that I couldn't even remember what had originally made me so angry that day. Time flows through us and leaves us with our broader recollections while taking away all the fine details. The past becomes so insubstantial that even a deathless existence like mine can't hold on to its nuance. In the end, we're all just sieves attempting to hold on to our identities.

That made me feel a bit melancholic. But such is the nature of this ephemeral world. It's foolish to lament over things that can't be changed.

"Why aren't you begging?" a cold female voice asked me, shaking me out of my depressing thoughts.

"I *beg* your pardon?" I replied sarcastically.

"I asked why you aren't pleading for your life," she said. "This is the end for you. *All* of you. You're the last of the Vampire Lords. Without you to make others of your kind, your species will die out within a century."

"Ah," I said, now understanding her point. "And you believe that concern for the lesser members of my race should somehow compel me to beg for your mercy?"

"If you cared for them at all," she said.

"Well, that's the problem right there, I'm afraid," I said with a small laugh.

"How can anyone be so selfish?" She frowned. "I've now struck the final blow against the darkness. Plead for your life."

"To begin with, I don't have a life to plead for," I informed her. "I'm already dead. I could also care less what happens to any other vampire. By infernal design, we're a race of murdering parasites. If we're truly falling into extinction, then it's what we deserve."

"You're only pretending to be calm," she said accusingly. "You're just trying to rob my victory of its sweetness."

"I'm really not," I said with as much of a shrug as my shoulders could provide while being pinned to a wall. "I'd much prefer our current positions were reversed. But what can be done? Wishing won't change anything, so why make a production over it?"

"I hate that," she said angrily. "After everything you've done, you should be afraid! You should be remorseful! You're a monster, Kyler Stragos! You don't deserve peace of mind! It isn't fair."

"Believe it or not, I concede your point," I said. "But when has *fairness* ever factored into anything relevant? That's a concept that exists outside of nature."

"As if an undead abomination has the right to speak of natural law," she scoffed.

"Even if I transcend and defy the laws of nature and man, I can still make a neutral observation," I replied. "A criminal is still permitted to have an opinion."

"A criminal? So, you admit you deserve a greater punishment?" asked the girl.

"I already said so," I replied. "Unfortunately for you, I'm a soulless *thing*. A simulacrum of a living being. I may bear the shape of a man but never his spirit. I can be destroyed but I can't truly be punished. No hell awaits me, just the endless dark. Sorry if that makes your victory seem pointless."

"Don't listen to him, Sophia," said one of the survivors. A burly-looking young man with handsome, rugged features. His was the sort of swaggering masculinity that would have offended an insecure Athenian. I felt a little bad for scarring him. Or rather, I had, *before* he pulled out a large, silver-edged knife, which he swiped viciously across my face.

"Ouch," I said mildly.

"The pain is just beginning for you, bastard," he spat, before plunging the knife repeatedly into my torso.

He wasn't wrong, I supposed. It *was* extremely painful. But pain was something I'd learned to ignore over the years. After a while, it just became another distant sensation. Another flavor of experience. Hot or cold. Mild or spicy. Pleasure or pain.

It was all the same, really.

"Enough, Thomas," the girl, Sophia, said gently as she placed her hand on my tormentor's shoulder. "Don't sully yourself on this vile thing."

"He killed Mayner," Thomas said with tears in his eyes. "He killed *all* of them. All of our friends! Played with us like our lives meant nothing . . ."

"Your lives *don't* mean anything," I chimed in helpfully.

"SHUT UP!" he screamed before dragging his blade across my throat. Ouch, again. He'd nicked my vocal cords. Now I couldn't speak.

Not that he seemed to care.

"Thomas, stop," Sophia said, more firmly this time. Thomas began sobbing and let the knife drop from his fingers. She embraced him and whispered soothingly into his ear as he trembled with anger and grief and hugged her back, no longer a warrior, but a survivor in severe mental anguish.

Hmm. It was quite an intense interaction. Seeing their physiological reactions to each other told me those two were definitely going to be having sex later in the evening.

Well, who could blame them? They looked good together. I'd heard second-hand that copulating after a near-death experience felt exhilarating. I couldn't confirm it myself, though. I'd been so powerful for so long that if I'd ever personally experienced survival sex, I'd long since forgotten it. I'd had loads of *victory sex,* but something told me it wasn't of the same quality. Probably because it lacked the elements of adrenaline and intense emotionality.

Ugh, watching those two together was quickly growing aggravating. I really did wish I could murder them both.

Sometimes while walking alone at night, I'd see a pair of young lovers doting on each other with sincere affection. The mere sight of their blissful contentment would set me off and I'd begin wishing with all my heart that they would drop dead on the spot. That *all* lovers everywhere would immediately die wherever they were and never again sting my heart with their malefic presence.

Why was I a thousand years old and still so resentful of happy couples? Where did that aggression even come from? It had to be because of my own marital troubles. I'd had three beautiful wives, but I didn't like any of them and they each hated me as well. Most of the time we'd avoided each other entirely, but occasionally we'd had to appear publicly for social events.

It was so stressful.

If I could give one valuable piece of advice to any younger vampires, male or female, it would be this: *Don't convert powerful enemy warriors into one of us and force them to marry you. It's incredibly stupid. Yes, it's natural to be attracted to a competent fighter who defies your will and resists you to the very end, especially if they're physically appealing, and equally intrigued by you.*

But don't give in! Resist the urge to raise them from death to become your groom or bride! Remember, gifting them with eternity doesn't mean they'll stop being your enemy. It just means that they've become immortal and now they have all the time in the world to make you pay for your hasty decision! Once that brief haze of lust passes, an eternity of suffering will be yours.

But if you couldn't stop yourself the first time, then at least make certain not to repeat the error ever again. Harems are an immature fantasy for mentally unstable masochists. No matter how up to the challenge you delude yourself into thinking you are, they'll always *be united against you!*

How had Dracula done it? Kept three wives satisfied and gone for two more? He must have had a talent for maintaining relationships, a skill for which I have no knack. It's so embarrassing that I'm still so lacking as an individual.

When will I finally mature?

Probably not today, since Sophia intended to kill me.

If only that spear wasn't so powerful! Where had she gotten that thing? It felt like a relic of some sort. Something that was even older than I was. *Far* older. A weapon that had possibly slain beings more powerful than I would ever be. Didn't using it against me seem like overkill? Whatever happened to facing your opponent fairly? This new generation of hunters clearly had no sense of sportsmanship.

I wondered, though. Had Sophia been telling the truth when she said I was the last of the Vampire Lords? I hadn't been paying much attention to anyone else's circumstances, but now that I thought of it, it *had* been a while since I'd last contacted any members of the old gang.

We'd all gone our separate ways shortly after those damn cultivators and their celestial ancestor had defeated Great Crusica, the Emperor of Undeath, but I had been sure someone else would eventually take up our fallen leader's mantle and get the wheels of domination rolling again. I supposed that would no longer be the case.

Huh. A world without vampires. What would that be like?

More specific to my interests, a world without *me* in it. Would that even be a world worth living in?

I didn't think it would be. But I was biased on that matter.

If only there were a way I could screw over those heroes at the last minute. That would feel so nice. Unfortunately, Sophia's accursed spear was sealing my abilities. No blood manipulation, no mind control or superhuman strength and speed. Just me, pinned to the wall like a dead beetle to a bit of Styrofoam.

Were there truly no options left to me? It seemed so unfair.

Oh, wait. Maybe there *was* something I could do.

It was widely known that vampires were incapable of standing before the light of the sun. Solar energy was incredibly harmful to us, but not because of what most people believed.

Sunlight didn't hurt us because we were weak against it; the actual problem was that our bodies absorbed it too readily. Vampires craved sunlight almost as much as we did blood. It was a consequence of existing in utter darkness. We wanted sunlight *badly*. We just couldn't handle it; we absorbed it in such quantity that it overloaded our capacity to contain it and caused us to explode.

That's right. We *exploded*. It all depended upon the age of the vampire; the greater our reserves of power, the more solar energy we absorbed, and the more violent the detonation became when we finally went. Lowly, lesser vampires would puff out of existence into an ignoble pile of dust. But ones at *my* level?

I had no way of knowing, really. No one my age had ever done it. But some three-hundred-year-old twerp had been caught in an ambush a few decades back and brought down an entire skyscraper when he went off. Who knew what sort of havoc I'd cause in my death throes?

I now found myself looking forward to finding out.

The key to my victory would be the spear. My body was reading the magical light it exuded as sunlight. It was agonizing, but that no longer mattered. Instead of resisting, I began quietly pulling the energy inside of myself, flooding my body with it, like a tick clamping on to a fresh vein.

It hurt. It hurt *so* much, but I still couldn't keep the triumphant grin off my face. Whoever this Sophia was, and however she had acquired her skills and this damnable spear, I would never know. But I didn't care anymore because *she still wasn't going to win.*

Closer and closer the clock ticked toward the coming of the end. I could feel the power swelling within me. Oddly enough, the spear tried to resist me. Wasn't that something? It was as though the weapon possessed a will of its own. How sad that it was too late to stop me.

Sophia! I thought I heard someone cry out in a voice tinged with panic.

Sophia looked away from her lover with a startled expression as she realized that something had gone horribly awry. Pushing past him, she ran to me and grabbed the spear, trying to pull it free of me, only for me to grab ahold of it and keep it in place.

"What are you doing?" she yelled with growing fear.

I really wanted to say, *I'm taking you with me, you impudent nobody!*

Sadly, I still couldn't speak thanks to that idiot Thomas and his knife.

So instead, I settled for laughing maniacally as I drew in more of the spear's power. All over my body, glowing cracks began to erupt from my skin as I grew closer to exploding.

Around the throne room, the survivors looked upon us and realized what was happening. The terror they expressed once they realized that they weren't going to escape with their lives was *immensely* gratifying.

Just as I prepared to release myself to oblivion, a blue notice screen appeared before my eyes.

Huh. That was unexpected.

[Congratulations, Lord Kyler Stragos!] the sign told me.
[You have successfully corrupted the holy artifact, Spear of Dawn (replica).]

Had I? *Well, how about that.* A final feather in my cap at the conclusion of a long and mostly satisfying existence. The sudden appearance of this screen didn't bother me very much. When you've been around for as long as I have, it's not difficult to adjust to unexpected things.

[For your success, you will be rewarded accordingly!] said the screen.

I would? That seemed unlikely, considering I was seconds away from exploding.

[See you soon!]

Okay, whatever you say, status screen. However brief our acquaintanceship, it was a pleasure meeting you.

"Let *go* of it!" screamed Sophia as our final moment came. "Let go!"

And that was exactly what I did.

I let go.

I'm pretty sure I took the entire castle with me.

Heh, stick me with a spear, will you? Serves all of you right.

And then darkness.

Followed by *confusion*.

When I opened my eyes, the back of my head exploded with pain. Not a literal explosion; I'd already done that earlier. No, I just mean that I was experiencing a dreadful headache. I gingerly placed the palm of my hand against the back of my skull and was surprised to see it covered in red when I examined it.

I had a head-wound.

But since when could a vampire lord suffer a lasting wound?

And while I was asking questions pertaining to my current situation, why was I also naked?

And also, *alive*?

That was the biggest surprise of all. I could feel my heart beating wildly in my chest. I was also breathing in air, not because I was merely filling my lungs to project my words to someone else's ears, but rather because I needed to circulate oxygen throughout my bloodstream in order for my internal organs to function.

This was so wild! I'd forgotten what having to breathe felt like! I felt so . . . human!

But my enjoyment of these novel sensations aside, what precisely was happening here?

To my left appeared four small, ugly-looking beings with scabrous, mottled green skin, wearing rotting loin cloths and bearing old, rusted weaponry. They grinned wickedly as they approached me. I'd never seen anything like them before, but their ill intentions toward me were clear.

"I'm new here," I said with a boy's unsteady voice. "I don't suppose you'd be willing to guide me to the exit?"

Instead of answering my question, they laughed nastily in reply and encircled me.

Okay, I was just going to assume that was an emphatic *no*.

CHAPTER TWO

As the creatures around me continued to slink nearer, I took a few moments to consider the options available to me. While their intent was obviously hostile, that didn't mean that they were in the wrong in this situation. This was their home, which made me an intruder. That made me reluctant to engage in violence.

Had I not personally just fought a vicious battle against human encroachment upon my own domain? I'd be an absolute hypocrite if I attacked first without attempting to offer an explanation for my presence in their lair, not that I had one to give.

All the same, I decided to be a good guest and attempt the path of diplomacy. I didn't *need* to do it. I *chose* to. Forget super speed and strength; what truly made a superior vampire was excellent manners!

So, I dusted myself off, pretended I wasn't stark naked, and cleared my throat to speak. Then I said, "Greetings, my dear hosts. I'm dreadfully sorry for appearing suddenly in your home, sans clothing and invitation! It's a long story, all the pertinent details of which even I am ignorant!"

The creatures that surrounded me paused. Were they listening to my words or merely curious about why I was speaking to them so fearlessly? I would soon find out.

"Please let me introduce myself," I continued. "My name is Lord—er, that is to say, *Mister* Kyler Stragos. I'm an unassuming gentleman from the distant realm of . . . *Canada*, here for reasons currently unknown to me, and I'm afraid that I'm woefully ignorant of your local Yankee customs! Am I being understood? I don't suppose any of you speak the Queen's tongue? Or is it the King's tongue, now? Wait, do any of you know if England still exists, and if not, did it at least outlast Ireland? I'd feel awful if Ireland survived the plague of undeath longer than England."

That didn't get a response either, but I continued anyway, now growing annoyed by my own memory of a certain event.

"I know survival during the apocalypse isn't a competition, but an otherwise charming Irish lass from Longford County once spat in my potato soup while I was eating it, and I've never been able to let that go. I mean, really, who *does* that? She maintained eye contact as well! She didn't even have red hair! I thought the gingers were the ones to watch out for, but no, as it *turns out*, the brunettes are just as keen to snap at you!"

Now I was feeling *very* upset.

"When I demanded an explanation for her behavior, she said it was *my* fault for invading *her* pub. I said, *invading?* They had a sign outside that said open for business! Then she pointed at the football jersey I was wearing. I told her I didn't follow the sport; I was just dressing comfortably! But instead of ceding my point like a functioning adult, she called me a tourist gobshite! I would have torn her head off on the spot, but first I needed to look up what *gobshite* meant because it was really confusing me, and the definition wasn't in my copy of *Cambridge's*! By the time I found my answer and returned to destroy her, she'd already scarpered. I transformed a few of the other locals into my lesser kin and commanded them to hunt her down but they never got back to me. It wouldn't surprise me in the least if she turned out to be some manner of *bog witch* and was too much for them to handle. I must say, the whole unsavory experience has soured me on that entire island. Can you blame me, though? What do you think?"

Instead of a reply, one of the creatures gave a howl of bloodlust and launched itself at me with its filthy clawed hands outstretched.

Hmm. If I had still been a vampire, I'd have noticed far earlier that these creatures smelled extremely unpleasant. It was as though they'd never been introduced to the concept of a bath. It was a horrendous sort of caked-on stench that can only be built with months of dedicated living in utter squalor. Now that they were closer to me, my newly human nose had finally registered the scent of these things.

The first thing I decided was that I didn't want any of them touching me. Nor did I want to touch them myself. Who knew what manner of infectious germ was nesting within their uncleanly flesh? Regaining my humanity only to lose my life to some malignant infection wouldn't do at all. That meant avoiding contact with them, which was easy enough to do. My new body was immature, but it possessed a small level of athletic conditioning. Avoiding the fiend's clumsy strike was as easy as stepping to the side and letting him collide with one of his comrades.

[Goblin Assailant has missed!] said a line of blue text that appeared from nowhere.

What? Where had that come from? And is that what these creatures were called? Goblins? Like the creatures of myth and fantasy? It was a name that suited these unseemly beasts. How strange to see them in the flesh, though. If you'd told me that beings such as this existed, I would have mocked you for being deluded.

That just showed that a mere thousand-year lifespan was far too short to learn anything truly interesting about the world. *I must take steps to avoid becoming arrogant.*

Now I hopped backwards, scanning the ground for anything I could arm myself with. By happy fortune, I spotted a spear on the ground not far from where I'd originally awakened. Scooping it up quickly, I pointed it toward my attackers and warned them to stay back. A warning they promptly ignored.

Adrenaline then flooded my new body and caused my heart to hammer in my chest and my breathing to become shallow and rapid. Heh, if I remembered correctly, this was the fight or flight effect.

Wow, that really took me back.

It was only a few deep breaths before I settled once more. Fighting may have been a new experience for this body, but I was an old, *old* hat at it. Aesthetic monks had figured out long ago that the secret to controlling your body's urge to panic during an emergency was to simply ignore it and keep going about your business. Ignoring pressing issues was something that came easily to people like me.

It was a shame that my attempt at diplomacy had failed. How sad it felt to christen my newly regained life with the blood of an enemy so soon after my miraculous return to mortality. I didn't want to kill these . . . goblins, was it? . . . I didn't want to kill these goblins, but my peaceful intentions were either blocked by an insurmountable language barrier, or they were simply too hostile to be reasoned with. In such a situation, it truly was kill or be killed. And since death had been my primary state of being for well over a thousand years, I was in no hurry to return to it.

The spear felt good in my hands. Although in the past I'd fancied myself something of a gentleman swordsman, I had experience wielding a lance and pike that transferred easily to this weapon. With one sure-footed thrust, I plunged the spear into my first assailant's forehead and buried the tip in the center of his brain. I'd been aiming for his eye, but he tried to duck at the last moment. Oh, well, this worked too.

For some reason, the number fifty-five floated above my victim's head. Then another message like that from earlier flashed before my eyes. In bright, large text, it said:

[You inflict 55 points of damage on Goblin Assailant 01. 55 damage from 50 health points deducted. You have fatally injured Goblin Assailant 01! 5 points of overkill damage recorded.]
[Goblin Assailant 01 has died. You have gained 25 experience points.]

Oh, I didn't like this at all! It was so distracting! While my focus was pulled, I narrowly managed to avoid a goblin trying to bring a rust-encrusted sword down on my head. In reprisal, I pulled my spear free from the first goblin's head and swept it across the back of my new opponent's ankle, lopping his foot off at the joint.

[Goblin Assailant 02 has taken 25 points of damage. Goblin Assailant 02 has been inflicted with the status effect: Bleeding. Goblin Assailant 02 has suffered 10 points of bleeding damage.]

Now, that was surprising! I'd meant only to try and hamstring the oaf. Just how sharp *was* the blade of this spear? And why did it feel so strangely familiar in my hands? It was as though I'd held it before.

Still, that could wait for now. I was still fighting for my life, after all. A fight that was being hampered by this silly blue screen! By the shadow, all this pointless information appearing before me wasn't helpful in the slightest! The second goblin was bleeding, was he? I had a pair of eyes that could already tell me that! And these floating damage indicators served no purpose either. Centuries of practical experience were enough to inform me when I'd delivered a good, fatal hit to a foe.

As I clashed with the third goblin while attempting to keep the other one from circling behind me, I couldn't help but feel frustrated. "Please get out of my face!" I yelled. The goblin before me blinked in confusion. "Not you, imbecile!" I snarled. "Floating screen before me, would you *please* clear my vision! You're making it very difficult to focus!"

[Would User Kyler Evans like to temporarily disable Combat Text?]

The screen had answered me. It could listen!
"Yes!" I said immediately. "Yes, I would!"

[Combat Text disabled.]

And with that, the numbers and messages vanished from view, leaving my vision unimpaired. With my eyes now wonderfully cleared of all that senseless clutter, I was free to give my full attention to the fight, which I promptly won after rolling out of the way of the fourth goblin's attempted backstab that caused him to impale his friend. While the pair of them stared at each other in shock, I proceeded to pierce them both with a backstab of my own.

Ah, satisfying.

With them taken care of, that left only the one I'd already hobbled. The silly thing had been attempting to drag himself away, leaving a trail of streaking blood behind him. As I made my way to his position, he saw me and suddenly let out a pained gasp before falling still.

Unsure if he was actually dead or attempting to deceive me, I reluctantly called forth the blue screen. "Has he truly perished?" I asked.

[Goblin Assailant 02 has died. You have gained 25 experience points.]

"Wonderful," I said with genuine pleasure. Then I thought over those words for a moment and asked, "What is an experience point?"

[The means by which your battle experience is measured to assist you in acquiring a new Level that will increase the power of your Job Class.]

"Ah. So, you've assigned a numerical value to combat that's capable of being remotely monitored, and the more of it I gain, the more powerful I'll gradually become?"

[Correct.]

"So, I gain experience points to acquire Levels and Levels to acquire power?"

[Correct.]

"Why?"

[. . . Why?]

"Yes, why? What's the point? I was already far more powerful before. Why do I have to start over at zero?"

[You are mistaken.]

"Come again?" I asked, surprised by the screen's cheek. "If experience correlates to power, I have a *thousand years* of it! By rights, I should be a bloody demigod compared to this . . . what am I? What is my Job Class? I assume that's the role I've been assigned in this bizarre system?"

[Correct. Your Job Class is Porter. Level 1.]

"Excuse me?"

[Your Job Class is Porter. Level 1.]

"Does *Porter* in this place mean something other than the word I'm thinking of?" I asked the screen carefully.

[How does User Kyler Evans define it?]

"The bloody help who carries the luggage."

[Your assessment is correct. A Porter is a support Class with a storage skill who assists the party by collecting the carcasses, money, weaponry, and other valuable items of defeated monsters.]

"No," I said firmly.

[No?]

"No," I repeated. "Absolutely incorrect. Have you gone mad? I'm Kyler Stragos, the Lord of Blood. I'm one of the four most powerful beings on the damned planet. I do *not* carry the luggage!"

[User Kyler Evans is mistaken.]

"I very much am not," I said, now feeling slightly offended.

[User Kyler Evans may not exchange his Job Class for another.]

"Are you absolutely certain of that?" I asked.

[Quite.]

Well, well, well. It seemed the screen was feeling a bit full of itself. *Well*, so be it. I had another question for it to answer.

"How foolish would you feel right now if I told you that I am *not* Kyler Evans? That you've mistaken me for someone else entirely and assigned me an inappropriate Class?"

[. . . What?]

"Yes, that's what I thought you'd say," I said with more than a little smug satisfaction.

CHAPTER THREE

Before the blue screen could ask me to clarify what I'd meant, I heard the ringing of a telephone. A noise I'd not heard for quite some time. Looking around, I discovered an old-fashioned device with a rotary dial in the center resting on top of a small table beside me.

Need I bother saying it hadn't been there a few moments earlier?

Curious as to what was happening, I decided to answer it. "Stragos speaking. May I ask who this is?"

"Greetings, Lord Stragos," said a woman's warm voice. "I'm a first-time caller but a longtime admirer. Could I ask you to please stop teasing the Akashic guide assigned to you?"

"Isn't it a bit early in our relationship to ask for favors?" I replied. "I still haven't heard your name, after all."

"You're right, you haven't," she said in a tone suggestive of one wearing a brilliant smile. "You address the Alpha Administrator."

"That's an alliterative title," I playfully replied while I searched my memories, trying to put a face to her voice. The Alpha Administrator, was it? I didn't believe I'd ever met such a person in my previous life. Yet she seemed very familiar with me.

This blatant disparity in knowledge bothered me. I would have preferred to deal with her on an equal basis, if that were possible. At least until I could find a way to gain the upper hand and ensure my safety. She was an administrator after all.

Caesar's defeat came about because he'd underestimated the Roman Senate. And what was a senator if not an administrator with a taste for corruption? Because they weren't warriors, he'd paid them no mind. His arrogance cost him his life and left the world with an abiding lesson: An administration was a ship of rats. Never back a rat into a corner.

Time heals all wounds except mortal ones.

"I love the letter *A*," the voice continued. "Many of my favorite words begin with it. Such as *adoration* and *admiration*. Especially for someone as capable as you."

"Am I speaking to a fan? I'm genuinely flattered," I said.

"It *thrills* me to hear you say that, Lord Stragos," she said happily.

"Then why keep your identity a secret?" I asked. "My curiosity is piqued."

"I'm afraid I can't reveal myself to you directly," she said regretfully. "Now that you're human once more, you might go mad from the revelation."

"For clarity's sake, would that be madness in a biblical sense or a Lovecraftian one?"

Either option was terrible, but if I really had to pick my poison, then losing it after realizing that angels have too many eyes and wings would be preferable to having my mental well-being peeled away by beholding some indescribable cosmic horror.

"A little from column A, and a lot from column B," sighed the voice on the line.

"Well, now that you've warned me, I'll gladly heed your advice," I quickly replied. "Thank you for being considerate. A lot of beings with your level of authority wouldn't have bothered."

"You're very welcome!" she exclaimed with good cheer. "And let me in turn thank you for your polite understanding. You're the first soul I've pulled into this world in quite some time who wasn't immediately hostile and rude. It gets so wearisome being berated and cursed at."

That was pleasing to hear. I enjoyed being praised for having good manners. I'd been a bit savage in my youth, so cultivating politeness had taken me quite a while. I hadn't needed to, but I didn't want to be thought of as uncouth. Just because I could take whatever I wanted whenever I wished didn't mean I had to be *rude* about it. When had rudeness ever convinced anyone that you were a decent person?

I also understood her point of view. As a vampire, most of my interactions with others in a public setting had been regrettably hostile.

I didn't blame other people in the slightest for their resentment of my dietary needs, but on the other hand, did they always have to be so foul-tempered about it? It wasn't as if I *wanted* to feed from them, but I had specific nutritional requirements that couldn't be met without their participation, willing or otherwise. I didn't even need that much. The older I grew, the less blood I required. I had been reaching a point where I could have eventually forgone humanity entirely and pulled the energy I needed directly from the earth itself. At that point, I would have become truly immortal.

What a shame I'd been forced by unpleasant circumstances to blow myself up. All thanks to those invasive pests and their petty grievances. For a moment I found myself blinded by rage. If any of those invaders had been present at that moment, I would have happily killed them all over again. It was a thought that filled me with warmth. But after letting myself enjoy it for a bit, I breathed out and let my anger subside.

There was no point in dwelling on bygone injustices. Even if I could take further vengeance on those hunters who'd defeated me, what would be the point? They could never repay what they'd stolen from me. Wanting to do something as petty as torture them eternally for their misdeeds was beneath my dignity. Both as a former vampire and as a newly risen human being.

Worst of all, it was unproductive.

The cycle of perpetual vengeance was a trap that I'd seen ensnare too many other vampires over the years. Humanity was a pervasive and persistent foe. They had a gift for forcing their opponents to view things from their perspective. That made it easy for vampires to let themselves fall into the role of villains; to derive enjoyment from it, even. To view their necessary function as a mere game.

That wasn't a good thing to do. When you viewed your survival as a game, that meant you'd grown too comfortable in your designated role as the antagonist. It meant you had expectations for your opponent's behavior, which meant that they were now capable of surprising you when you least expected it. A comfortable vampire was doomed. I would know best; I was my own prime example of such a failure to adapt.

That got me thinking about my recent death and the bitter little man who'd orchestrated it.

Tch. Mayner, you silly old fool. Why did you hate me so much? Your family's grudge made no sense. Seven generations of them obsessed with avenging their precious ancestor, who only died in the first place because he attacked me! I could have wiped your line out at any time over the years, but I kept hoping that a seed of reason would take root in at least one of your hearts and convince you it wasn't worth the effort. I would have happily spent your entire life ignoring your existence.

How it irks me to have gone fifty-six years refusing to play along with you, only to fall prey to your delusional narrative at the very end. You may not have slain me yourself, but you set me up quite nicely. How did you convince so many people to die with you? Did they even know? I should have congratulated you for your ruthless persistence before I killed you. It takes a cold, cold heart to sacrifice so many people who believed in you, just so that Sophia woman could catch me off guard. I bet you even justified the act to yourself as an unfortunate necessity. Did you grow to believe that lie? It must have been a relief when I began tearing you apart, knowing you wouldn't be alive to apologize for your actions.

I would never kill a friend to slay an enemy. Much less twenty-two of them. Think about that, Mayner. Perhaps the monster you hated so much was, in a way, a better human being than you could ever hope to be. I hope that thought somehow germinates in your mind in whatever paradise your wretched soul finds itself dwelling in. I hope that feeling of unworthiness overwhelms you every night in your eternal garden.

"Lord Stragos?" the stranger said uncertainly, snapping me out of my grim reverie. I'd lost myself to my thoughts again.

That was embarrassing.

"My apologies. Bleak recollections come flooding in when least expected," I said. "The longer you live, the more frequent your disappointments."

"I understand," she said, and left it at that, for which I was grateful.

"But as I was saying," I continued after regaining my composure, "I've always believed that belligerence is unrequired. There are many things I regret seizing by force that I could have had simply by asking. It's a shame that the lived experiences of the past can be documented in writing but not directly inherited."

"Well, maybe we'll develop a skill for that later down the line," the Alpha Administrator said. "Oh, I know! I'll call it Diplomacy. It'll be a passive trait that gives you a bonus to charisma when being polite to others. How does that sound?"

"How helpful would such a talent be?" I wondered.

"Extremely, if I'm being completely honest," she purred into the line.

"I suppose that tells me everything I need to know about what sort of world this is," I said. "Well, everything except for why I'm here."

At that moment, I shivered. This place felt very drafty and being nude certainly wasn't helping me maintain a proper body temperature. Acquiring clothing was next on my list. But how could I go about doing that?

As if reading my mind, the Administrator offered a suggestion. "Why not try looting the goblins you killed?" she said.

I frowned at the very idea. "As cold as I am, I don't believe I'd like to wear any recycled loincloths. Especially not any that've been worn by these fellows. I'm fearful of getting a rash."

"Lord Stragos! You're too much," she laughed. "Here, let me help you understand."

As she spoke, light began emanating from the bodies of the defeated goblins, highlighting each of them where they lay. "This is just a visual cue for our participants, to let them know there are goods to be acquired from defeated enemies. The light coming from them can only be seen by you. That means that whatever they have is yours exclusively. You only need to hold your hand out above one of them. There's no need to make physical contact."

Made curious by her advice, I followed her instructions and held my hand out over one of the dead goblins. As I did so, the lights above them flashed briefly and then vanished. At my feet were a neatly folded pair of trousers and boots.

"Where did these come from?" I asked, amazed by my discovery. "What manner of magic is this? None of these creatures were carrying anything like these items when we fought."

"Of course not. Your reward for defeating them was provided by the Akashic Codex that all ascended individuals must abide by—"

"The Akashic Codex?" I asked, interrupting her. "I'm sorry, but what precisely is that?"

"You can just call it *the system* if it helps you to remember," the Alpha Administrator said patiently. "Anyway, the system calculates the difficulty of any tasks you undertake and offers you a suitable reward in exchange for your success. Since you were the victor, these spoils were generated for you."

"Ingenious," I said, thoroughly impressed. I reached for the pants, eager to cover myself, when the Administrator's voice chimed in once more. "No need to put them on manually, Lord Stragos. Simply envision wearing them and they'll be equipped automatically."

"That is *absurdly* convenient," I chuckled as I followed her directions. To my continued amazement, I was now wearing the pants and boots exactly as she said I'd be. "Incredible," I said.

"In dangerous environments such as the Goblin's Lair that you're currently trapped inside of, it wouldn't be safe to have to manually equip your gear. After all, an attack could come at any moment. It wouldn't be fair to be caught with your pants down," she said.

"Hear! Hear!" I said. My newly acquired clothing held the titles *frayed pants* and *worn leather boots*, with a durability rating of five each. But despite their names, I found them quite comfortable. The boots felt nicely broken in but still sturdy to walk in, and the pants fit nicely while remaining flexible. To my surprise, I even had a bit of change in my pocket. Five silver pieces.

"Not bad," said the Administrator. "If you'd like, you can secure your money by using your job's storage skill. It'll keep it nice and safe while you further explore your environment."

"Ah," I said. "Thank you for reminding me. Madam Administrator, while I'm hesitant to make a complaint after all the helpful advice you've provided me, I feel compelled to protest my current assignment as a *Porter*. It makes no sense! I'm a man of action! A warrior who has striven uncountable fields of battle and wrung honor and blood from them in equal proportion! I'm a big deal! I really don't want to carry anyone's luggage."

"Lord Stragos, are you pouting?" she giggled.

"I'm not pouting," I said defensively. "I'm simply presenting an argument for why I should be given a different role. My experiences alone—"

"Okay," she said.

"Okay?" I asked in surprise.

"I agree with you," she continued. "There is no need to convince me of how to use someone with your talents. You don't have to be a Porter. I wouldn't dream of wasting your obvious capabilities on such a minor role."

"Thank you," I said, letting out a sigh of relief as I did so. "I'm glad you're so quick to realize my value—"

"How does being a Priest sound to you?"

". . . I beg your pardon?" I could already feel my face freezing into a rictus of abject horror.

"Offering prayers and worship to the divine in return for holy favors used to bless and empower your righteous cause. I can already see you kneeling before an altar singing your praises to the light. Twice on Sundays and Wednesdays."

"Uh . . . M-madam," I stuttered.

"Just kidding!" she said with a raucous belly laugh. "Oh, Lord Stragos, it's going to be a lot of fun having you around, I can already tell. You really should see the look on your face! Which you can do now. Use mirrors, that is."

"Please stop teasing me. I've only just regained a beating heart and I'm not sure it can take much more of your devilish humor," I said with considerable relief.

"No worries, no worries," she replied in her merry tone. "Now, it's my understanding that you have extensive experience in the role of a supremely powerful Vampire Lord. Would the idea of continuing that career path be of any interest to you?"

I thought it over for a few moments before answering. "Well . . . I don't like to brag, but I *have* been told I was *pretty good* at it," I said with as much humility as I could muster.

I heard the Administrator laugh once again before saying, "Somehow, I *thought* you'd say that."

CHAPTER FOUR

And so, I received my Class.

[**Vampire Lord.**], read the helpful blue screen.
[**Role: Support/Guardian/Damage Dealer.**]
[**Job Rating: Five stars. S-rank.**]
[**Rarity: Mythical.**]
[**Leveling potential: 100+.**]
[**Would you like to accept your Job?**]

"Why, yes, I believe I would," I said with a delighted smile.

A *mythical* level of rarity, was it? Well, that made sense. I didn't want to sound arrogant or anything—fate *forbid* I should be too pleased with what I'd been given—but I thought we all knew that in comparison to all the other monumentally less interesting beings currently cluttering up creation, vampires were life's obvious winners. There is no need to go into great detail about why that was so. It was an obvious truth.

Yes, the fact that my title would be unobtainable to the vast majority of the soon-to-be envious masses felt only right. Why wouldn't it? That was the sort of satisfaction that came with being a born winner.

All the other descriptions didn't really mean much to me, but I was sure they were wonderful as well.

"I apologize for not being able to restore you to the level of power you enjoyed in your previous life," the Alpha Administrator said. "But by leveling regularly and using the skill selection option that will unlock for you at Level Ten, you'll quickly be able to regain everything you lost. There'll be no need to wait another thousand years to become a notorious threat to humanity!"

"Now, why would I do that?" I grinned. "I'm a human being myself, now. Why resort needlessly to old habits?"

Yes, this was the aspect of my new life I believed I would enjoy the most. "Vampire Lord" was my Class title now. Not my *race*. That meant that despite having all the perks that came with the role, such as enhanced strength, speed, vision, and hearing, I could bypass all its infamous weaknesses simply by deactivating the title. No more fearing holy symbols or dreading the light of day. I could take walks on a sunny afternoon and drink consecrated water from a wine glass if I felt like it.

I was now free from the chains of darkness. Forever.

It really did feel like a win.

I knew I didn't deserve such a wonderful gift. If anything, I should have been locked in a silver-lined coffin and left to rot at the bottom of an ocean. But what we deserved in life wasn't always what we received. Sometimes bad things happened to good people. In this case, something good happened to a monster. All we could do was accept it and move on. Such were the vagaries of fate.

Speaking of fate, there was one more twist to this rollicking little tale.

"So, this was the weapon that destroyed me?" I asked as I gestured toward my spear. "It looks nothing like what that woman Sophia was wielding. And yet . . . as soon as my hand closed upon it, I felt such an overwhelming sensation of familiarity."

"That is indeed the replica Spear of Dawn," said the Administrator. "It would appear that the two of you are now joined at the hip."

"How?" I wondered. "Shouldn't it have been destroyed by the detonation?"

"That spear is crafted from divinely wrought materials and is also ensouled. Destroying it outright might be physically impossible."

"Ensouled, you say? You mean this thing is somehow alive?" I asked.

"As strange as that may sound, yes. The process of creating such powerful weaponry involves the use of a heroic soul being voluntarily bonded to a new form to continue aiding in the struggle against evil. It's an honor bestowed upon only the most deserving and dedicated champions of the past."

"An honor, eh?" I said with a sly little grin as I closely examined the spear. "Perhaps not so much anymore, though, hmm? But that naturally begs a question: if this spear was created in *this* world, then how did it wind up in my old home, killing me?"

"A mystery I resolve to seek an answer for," the Administrator promised. "In the meanwhile, are you certain you wish to keep it? It could become dangerous for you if someone were to recognize it for what it truly is."

"I think I will," I decided. "Why part ways after a single night's company? We've hardly begun to learn about each other."

"Very droll, Lord Stragos. But do be careful. I'm afraid the intelligence that dwells within the spear has become very resentful of you."

"Of course it has," I said ruefully. "Why should it be any different from anyone else in my life?"

"*I'm* on your side, Lord Stragos. Know that I'll be cheering you on from above," proclaimed the Administrator. "But for now, I must return to my many duties. I hope you understand."

"I do and I appreciate your candor," I said, sad that our brief time together was now concluding. "Will we ever speak again?"

"We will! And sooner than you think," she assured me. "You need only survive this dungeon. Either defeat the lord of this place or find another means of escape. Do that and I promise to try and explain everything."

"If that's the case, then your challenge is accepted," I said with a flourish of my spear as I bowed. "You may look forward to my victory."

"You really are too much, Lord Stragos," she said fondly as her voice faded away. "Oh, I forgot to mention, I included a little bonus with your Class. I think you'll find it quite enjoyable. Stay safe for now! I look forward to our next conversation."

"And I look forward to learning your real name," I said. But there was no response. The spear and I were now alone.

"Seems as though it's just the two of us now. What do you say to us getting along?" I asked it amicably.

The spear began vibrating menacingly in my hands after I spoke. It did so with such force that I nearly jabbed myself with it. "Stop that," I said in annoyance. "You're only embarrassing yourself."

In response, the spear began to shake even harder. The motion was so powerful that gripping it soon began to feel painful. "I *said* to stop that," I said sternly. "Making your master repeat himself is beyond childish. Your actions will only harm yourself in the end."

Now the spear was thrumming with such violent power that I nearly struck my own face. I'd had enough of this willful behavior. "Fine, have it your way," I said. "As your master, I forbid you from utilizing your free will until I say otherwise. Now *obey*."

Suddenly the spear grew perfectly still. I felt a powerful sense of confusion emanating from it, which in turn fueled my mockery. "Oh, you're wondering how that happened, aren't you? How do you think I corrupted you to begin with, you silly thing?"

A flash of deep resentment was sent towards me; I had to roll my eyes at the sheer *drama* of it all before continuing.

"Think about it. In the moments before I died, you were immersed in my blood as I was feeding off your mana. Don't you know? That is a *very* similar process to transforming someone into a vampire. Which makes you no different from any of my other progeny. As the one who gifted you with vampirism—you're welcome, by the way—that means you have no right to refuse any command I give you. I urge you to quickly adjust to your new circumstances. We'll be having no more of your little tantrums today."

The spear sent a final surge of hateful resentment toward me before falling into sullen silence. I nodded, amused by its impetuous personality. "Whatever you say, my friend. We'll talk later."

Making my way through the goblin lair was much easier now that I had access to my vampiric form. Although thanks to the loss of my many powers it was hardly stronger than my human self, it still carried with it several key advantages. One of them was perfect night vision. I needn't worry about stumbling in the dark or walking into a trap.

The other was undeath. As my vampiric self, no wound that would have killed a mortal being could truly harm me. So long as I had access to blood, I could recover from any injury in moments. I could also move in perfect silence because I didn't need to breathe, making it easy to ambush my prey . . . which there was surprisingly little of.

There were many lifeless goblin bodies scattered throughout these ruins. The few living ones that I came across were dispatched easily enough, allowing me to reach Level Two, but the fact remained that they were outnumbered by their dead. Someone else was in this dungeon, killing them. A group of someones.

The Administrator had explained to me earlier that this dungeon was a place that existed inside a dimensional anomaly known as a fracture. A sort of portal to another world that existed temporarily. It could only be entered by a handful of people at a time. No more than five. It would last until the one who ruled this place was defeated, then it would cease to exist after a day had passed. One of the chief duties of ascended beings, or Hunters, as they were commonly known, was to seal these fractures wherever they appeared, to prevent monsters from spilling forth from them and attacking the earth.

It sounded like a lot of work.

The thing that was bothering me about the presence of a team of Hunters being here was the fact that the previous owner of my body, Mr. Kyler Evans, had been murdered here. I say *murdered*, and not *killed*, because it was obvious none of the goblins here had committed the deed. Everything I'd seen of those miserable creatures suggested they were far messier with how they went about things.

By which I mean that after killing me, they would have immediately eaten my body. Or done other things to it, which I chose not to dwell on. That meant I'd been killed by someone other than them. And the only other people that were here were the Hunters. Kyler Evans must have been their Porter.

Which meant that for whatever reason, they decided to kill him, strip him naked, and leave his corpse behind.

That was all a little disrespectful, wasn't it?

This was problematic for a few reasons. The first was that other than coincidentally sharing his name and inheriting his body, I didn't have any of the other Kyler's memories. Which meant I had no idea why his allies had decided to dispose of him. That meant that thinking of him as a victim wouldn't necessarily be correct.

He may have had it coming. He could have been a bad person.

He wouldn't have been the first Kyler to go wrong in life, now, would he?

The second problem was that they believed Evans was dead. If he turned up alive and perfectly sound of body, that would raise more than a few questions. It might even spur them to make a second attempt on his life, which would be bad. These wouldn't be ordinary humans. They'd be experienced warriors wielding powers that were unknown to me. I couldn't just haphazardly take them on, not without more information.

This left me with fewer options than I'd have liked. I had not the slightest interest in avenging Kyler Evans's death. He was gone now, and he had taken his memories with him. I had no impetus to seek justice on his behalf, nor any desire to. What would be the point of making his killers my enemies? If anything, I'd benefited from their misdeed. In a strange sort of way, that meant I was indebted to them.

But even so, if they became hostile towards me, I wouldn't have a choice in the matter. If I could convince them I had no memory of what had occurred, perhaps they'd back off. If not, then what choice was there other than to kill them?

Decisions, decisions, decisions.

Fortunately for me, luck was on my side when the outcome was eventually determined. There was an outside factor I hadn't even considered while trying to decide what I should do. And that was the dungeon lord himself. As I neared what I presumed to be his lair, I heard the terrible sound of screaming coming from a short distance away.

"Please! Please, please, *pleeeease!*" I heard a man's voice beg, followed by a deep voice grunting in cruel laughter and more screams. These in turn were followed by wet snapping sounds and the unmistakable scent of fresh blood.

I quickly pushed the massive stone door open and stepped inside. Before me, I saw a young woman in armor, huddled against a wall, staring forward with wide, unfocused eyes, a small line of drool trickling down her lower lip.

I'd seen expressions like that before.

It was the sight of a shattered human mind that had seen too much, too soon.

As to the sight that had broken her, well, it might have had something to do with the pieces of her companion decorating everything around us.

Everything.

Not pleasant. Not pleasant at all. And yet . . . if you really thought about it, wasn't this wonderfully convenient? I mean, yes, what happened to that girl's mind was clearly terrible, *oh bless this poor child and her friends, how awful, how truly,* truly, *awful, oh* why *do the young have to suffer so much in this cruel and unjust world?*

Buuuut, if you were to look on the bright side, which I could do now since I could walk in the sun, you *could* say that I'd just been given a real opportunity for personal renewal here. And it wasn't as though those kids had been completely innocent, right? Sometimes you got away with your misdeeds and other times you got devoured alive by monsters.

Hey, let's hear it for the monsters, everyone.

CHAPTER FIVE

The goblin chieftain was an enormous, obese thing sitting in a stone chair as though it were his throne. Fat and muscle in equal portions adorned his massive frame. But despite his slothful appearance and his near-feral features, I could see that his eyes gleamed with wicked intelligence. Baleful, even. The brute could *think*.

While observing him, it was difficult not to notice the blood and bits of gristle that covered his mouth and flabby chest.

He was also a messy eater.

Around him chattered the remnants of his tribe. They hissed and spat in my direction, but I noticed they didn't move too far from the protective presence of their leader. So pitiful.

Although the goblins had seemed so dangerous when I first awoke, I realized now that most of these creatures were opportunistic weaklings. Cowards who only showed strength in numbers. Their lives were miserable, dirty, and short. Aside from their use in providing experience points, what was the purpose of such a bleak existence?

Where was the honor in trampling over such wretched lives?

"Are you my latest toy?" the chieftain asked in a deeply bored voice as he rested his head on his fist. "The last of my unfortunate challengers to appear for the evening? Have you come to amuse me with your dying screams before nourishing me with your flesh?"

"Unlikely," I replied, unsurprised by his ability to speak perfect English. Why wouldn't he? The laws that governed this world were clearly insane. Why be startled by anything?

"So many have come here to challenge me," he said. "All of their bones lie before you. Broken things that once brought me pleasure. I enjoyed this game once, but now all it brings me is tedium."

"You've never known defeat?" I asked him.

"Never," he said proudly. "Nor have I have ever battled to my fullest measure. My glory has been squandered on weaklings like you. Your species has produced naught but unremarkable trash."

"Talent *can* be alienating," I said in agreement. "When one fully develops their skills, it's only natural to expect that others will do the same. But the inclination of the masses to settle for mediocrity instead of striving for perfection means you'll rarely face a true test of your abilities."

"Then you understand my pain?" he asked. He began to laugh. "A little human claims to know my suffering?"

"I do." I nodded. "But I don't empathize with it. If anything, I think you deserve it."

That stopped his laughter cold. "What makes you say that?" he asked in an ugly, sullen tone of voice.

I pointed to the wall where the girl sat in her daze. "What did you do to her?"

"I defended myself," he said.

"Did you really? I wonder about that," I said doubtfully.

"She came to my lair to kill me alongside her friends," he said angrily. "They laughed while slaughtering my children and made cruel jokes about my appearance when they first beheld me. Her remarks were especially hurtful. So, after I defeated them, I tortured her companions in front of her and then I devoured them as I made her watch. That silenced her japes quite nicely. I was about to begin playing with her in a more intimate manner before your unexpected arrival. It is my right as the victor."

"Why wasn't it enough to simply kill her?" I asked him. "Why single her out for additional torment? Your behavior seems unreasonable."

"Human women are attractive," he admitted with a revolting leer. "I like listening to them beg for my mercy. Her pleas for the lives of her friends were especially sweet."

"So, you would have done this even if she had been kind and virtuous," I said with unfiltered distaste. "Which means nothing she said or did would have mattered in the slightest. You only pretended to take offense to justify your actions."

"What's your point?" he asked as a disdainful sneer curled his lip. "Are you offended on her behalf? What for? She's already dead inside. You may as well let me keep her. Nothing will bloom behind those lovely, empty eyes ever again."

I graciously decided to ignore his ugly provocation. Despite my growing dislike of goblins, I was willing to overlook their many, *many* flaws as mere cultural differences. For today, anyway. The problem was their innate hostility. They refused to listen to anything I said, even when I was attempting to spare their lives. Perhaps the issue lay with their leader? What if the matter was as simple as humbling him?

I wasn't trying to make these beasts my servants or anything. If I required anyone to see to my needs, I could just create some lesser kin. But that approach had its own significant issues. Newly raised vampires required constant feeding during the first century of their existence, and until they matured, those feedings were usually fatal. I didn't know nearly enough about this world to reliably hide such acts from detection by the authorities. It would have been too risky.

Setting the issue of servants aside, I genuinely had no interest in killing *everyone* in this dungeon. The goblin chieftain had to die of course, because his life was tied to the exit. But was it truly necessary to kill the others? This was the first day of my new life. I was eager to leave this place and learn more about my new world. For that, I was perfectly willing to grant mercy to any who would receive it.

They just had to be willing to submit.

"I suppose you're intelligent enough, despite being a perverse oaf," I said after giving some thought to the chieftain's fate. "Your trespasses are unforgivable, so of course I'll have to punish you for them. But perhaps the remnants of your tribe can be rehabilitated afterwards. There must be *something* worthy about your strange species. Nothing exists merely for its own sake."

"What the hell are you talking about?" he asked with growing belligerence.

"I'm trying to spare your tribe," I said to him. "As a human being, I've been struck by a sudden desire to show benevolence to those in need of it. Surrender yourself willingly to my spear and your family will survive. Isn't that kind of me?"

"Are you insane?" he asked after staring at me for a bit.

"Sir? That was uncalled for," I said as a frown took hold of my brow. "I'm making you a generous offer. Submit to me. It's their only means of survival. It's not like there's any point in resisting. Hunters will keep coming here until you're all defeated."

"We will *never* be defeated!" he yelled.

"That's an impossible promise to keep," I said. "Impractical, too. Everyone loses eventually. What truly distinguishes us is how we allow those moments of defeat to affect us. Think rationally. Would I be speaking this frankly if I wasn't certain I could easily kill you?"

"This is just another stupid human trick," he said with a fool's certainty. "A new one, to be sure, but not one I'll fall for. Give it up, *boy*. I won't play your game."

"Are you certain?"

"I am!"

"Well, I can see there's no convincing you," I said with disappointment as my hopes for a relatively peaceful resolution fell apart in the face of his stubbornness. "I won't bother trying any longer. Instead, I'll just punish you for offending my sensibilities. You're a pitiful thing who allowed yourself to plunge into depravity. As such, I declare you unworthy of continued existence and now sentence you to die."

"Depravity?" he laughed. "And when was I ever well-behaved to begin with? What manner of being do you believe a *goblin* to be? And what's this nonsense about my death? Who are you, eh? Just another little human morsel I'll soon be picking out of my teeth."

"Well, *someone* has to take responsibility for you," I said. "Since you've already ceded your moral authority to the void, I don't believe you have any right to complain if I usurp the rest of it."

It was a shame that the goblin chieftain had refused my offer; it was the first time in what felt like ages that I'd made such an offer. Oh, well. I had taken a chance on altruism and things hadn't gone as I'd wished. Fate remained as unpredictable as ever. There was no point in dwelling on a failed gamble.

How unfortunate for this goblin that he didn't understand the scope of my magnanimity. By willfully rejecting me, by refusing to even concede a single point I'd made, he left me no choice but to kill him in as cruel a manner as possible.

I really had no choice. He'd forced my hand; I lived my life under the guiding principles of vampiric hierarchy, which needs no explanation because it's easy to grasp on an instinctive level. I'd informed him what his options were and why he must obey. Instead of accepting his fate, he chose to disagree with me.

So, now he was going to suffer. I'm sure you can understand why.

What would become of the world if the rabble began dictating terms to their betters?

"You arrogant human filth," he growled.

"Also the last human being you'll ever speak with," I informed him. "Choose your final words carefully."

"*My* final words?" he said with growing anger. "MY final words! What a stupid, presumptuous thing you are! *I* am the lord of this realm! In this hall, *I* am the one who decides life and death! You dare speak of bringing judgement to *me*? I'll rip you open with my teeth and slurp out your innards—ARRGH!"

The goblin chieftain screamed when I caught him in the neck with a quick jab from my spear, which I then pulled free before he could snatch it away. He gurgled and slapped a hand to his spurting throat, from which pale, foul-smelling blood began dripping through his fingers.

He squealed as he stood up, desperate to staunch the bleeding. Around him, the other goblins clustered, speaking their guttural language and trying their best to assist him.

"Don't bother," I explained to him before he tried anything pointless. "You've been afflicted with a curse. No wound delivered by this spear will ever heal unless the one who dealt it perishes."

Pretty nasty, eh? Apparently, that was a feature the spear possessed even before it came into my possession.

"That means," I continued, "if *you* want to live, then *I* need to die. I'd say you have a time limit of around three minutes before you lose too much blood to remain conscious. Better get at it, yes?"

"Bastard," he hissed wetly as he grabbed the mace resting at the side of his throne. It was a testament to his strength that he could wield it with one hand while clenching his throat with the other. He began swinging it wildly, smashing into the stone walls of the lair with each desperate attack while his followers cheered him on.

He wasn't very good. In fact, if I had to assess his talent with a letter grade, I'd give him a D minus at most. He had strength and endurance to spare but he was impatient and inaccurate with his strikes. I doubted he'd be much better even if he wasn't dealing with a mortal injury. His claim of being bored due to never meeting his match was now a dubious one, in my opinion. Since this dungeon existed on a lower tier, it must have only attracted weaker Hunters who couldn't participate in higher tier fractures, which were more rewarding but far more dangerous.

That meant that this goblin's victims had all been either neophytes seeking experience or desperate low rankers trying to make some quick money. He'd never once in his life fought on even terms with a true warrior.

This was a clear example of ignorance leading to ruin. The world was a far bigger place than the little hole he'd cozied up in, but he was too stupid to realize it. Even worse, his undue arrogance had led him to become a disgusting sadist who had led his tribe into ruin. Such foolishness begged for a permanent correction, which I would now gladly deliver.

Even with his size and strength advantage, he was a poor match for me. I evaded every swing he threw at me and kept striking with my spear, thrusting its tip into his legs and retreating before he could retaliate, poking hole after hole into him. Soon blood was streaming down his thighs in copious amounts, making the ground beneath his feet slippery.

The goblin chieftain was gasping at this point, mad with rage and pain but unable to will his body to move faster. All he could do was continue to tire himself until he eventually collapsed. From his back he glared at me as I stood just beyond his reach and patiently waited for him to lose consciousness. The other remaining goblins wailed in sorrow before running off, leaving the two of us behind.

It was a sensible decision on their part.

"You didn't fight fairly," the chieftain said accusingly, as if that meant anything to me.

"You're right, I didn't," I said in agreement. "That's probably why I won so easily."

"Coward," he said hatefully. "You're a bloody coward."

"I'd prefer it if you said I was a pragmatist," I replied. "Besides, plenty of people have fought you fairly. That sort of misguided honor has clearly spoiled you. Just look at the results."

"Why didn't my other children come to my aid? Why was I left alone to face you?" he murmured as weariness began to overtake him.

"You already know the answer to that," I said to him with unfeigned indifference. "It seems your victims disposed of them quite nicely before coming across you."

"All of them?" he asked before suddenly breaking into tears.

"Well, I took care of the rest. But it was mostly them," I said.

"You didn't spare a single one?" he wept.

"Mercy was offered more than once. Sadly, your progeny were as prideful as their father. It was ultimately to my benefit, however. Once you finish expiring, I believe that'll raise me to Level Three."

"Always your kind comes for us," he wept. "Stealing and killing, not because you need to, but because you use our lives to empower yourselves. You dare ask why I torment my prey? Because you're parasites! All of you! You feed on us, treat us like chattel, turning our lives into a game of slaughter! You call us monsters, but you're all the real fiends! *All of you!* Nothing but *BLOODSUCKERS*!"

What *did he just call me?*

"Fairly stated," I said coldly. "And in this case, far truer than you'll ever realize. Goodbye, goblin."

"Your eyes," he whispered as I raised my spear. "Why are they doing that?"

Before he could ask again, I ended his life. The process of doing so was unkind so I'll spare you the details. Just know that he paid dearly for his foul insult.

Bloodsucker. I despise that term. I DESPISE IT! I don't *suck* blood, okay? I *drink* it! That's a very distinct difference! I'm not a *leech,* damn it! I have a mouth and teeth, not a gaping wet maw with a slimy proboscis! Do my jaws *look* like they unhinge? DO THEY?

Oh, I swore I should have hunted that detestable Guillermo del Toro down like an animal the instant I finished watching *Blade II.* That movie was *so* offensive . . . sure, *Nosferatu* was far worse, but that was a product of its time. And it was directed by a German too, so . . . *y'know.* Not a people historically famed for their cultural sensitivity. But that del Toro bastard, *he* should have known better! What was *his* excuse?

Wait . . . wait. Stop. I was getting carried away again. Sudden changes in mood and temperament. How could I have forgotten such a basic aspect of being a vampire? Being human again had been so overwhelming that it'd made me slow to remember. To stand guard against my own impulses.

I didn't really want to kill Guillermo del Toro. He was a magnificent talent! *Pan's Labyrinth* had been one of the greatest viewing experiences of my life.

That poor little girl. Was the ending real or just a comforting fantasy as she drifted away into death? The ambiguity of it had haunted me for years.

I needed to focus. I was Level Three now, just as I said I'd be. But more importantly, the goblin chieftain's body was still glowing even though I'd already looted him and received a good quality new item. It was called a Tunic of Deflection. Wearing it increased my avoidance stat by three and gave bonuses to something called a defensive roll.

That sounded good, I supposed. And it did allow me to finally cover my torso, so no complaints there. But even though I'd claimed it, there was still a red light emanating from the dungeon lord. What could that mean?

Suddenly, another blue screen appeared before my eyes. **[Acquirable skill detected.]**, it read.

[Would you like to activate the Gore Grimoire?]

An acquirable skill? Did that mean what I thought it did? Could this Gore Grimoire be the bonus that the Alpha Administrator had spoken of earlier?

Eager to find out, I stood before the body and held my hand out before it once more. This time instead of envisioning myself receiving its loot, I focused on receiving whatever abilities it apparently had to give me.

Soon, the chieftain's body began trembling violently as something within its torso began bulging outward against its ribcage. Slowly at first, and then with greater force as it sought to tear itself free of his flesh. Before much longer, it finally pushed through and flew to my waiting hand.

It was the chieftain's heart.

I stared at it in confusion, wondering what I was supposed to do next. A hint of some sort would have been nice. After a minute of staring at it, waiting for something to happen, I noticed something. There was an oddly pleasing scent wafting from the dead organ, which I found increasingly difficult to ignore.

It smelled delicious.

"You don't suppose I'm meant to . . . *eat* this, do you?" I asked the spear. But it offered no feedback, still clearly having a snit. What a brat.

It wasn't as though I'd never torn out someone's heart and devoured it. Cannibalism and vampirism went virtually hand in hand. But I'd grown out of such wolfish displays centuries ago. It was mostly something you did to frighten your enemies or to impress a pretty girl.

Well, no point in just staring at it.

I opened my mouth and took a big bite.

Delicious. As I swallowed it, I felt something flow within me. Something *powerful.*

"Evans? Kyler Evans?" said a boy's voice from behind me.

Hmm? Where had he come from? I turned around, wiping my mouth as I did, and beheld a teenager perhaps the same age as my new body, dressed in a black leather outfit, over which he wore a cloak. He was standing there, staring at me with a look of revulsion on his face.

"What the hell are you doing, dude?" he asked me.

I looked around and saw that the room was filling with more teenagers, all of them armed with dangerous weapons and equipped with armor of varied materials. Some of them looked like knights out of the age of gallantry. Others crackled with energy like sorcerers of eld. Not one of them looked the same as the others, but on their right shoulders each of them wore the same blue emblem that bore the words *Vandal Academy.*

And they were all staring at me.

"I'm just having a snack," I said in reply. "It tastes better than it looks."

No one had anything to say in response, so I tossed the heart over my shoulder and gave a little stretch. "Well, I guess that's that," I said to no one in particular.

[The Gore Grimoire has absorbed a new skill.]
[You have acquired the passive trait Titanic Strength.]

Oh, that was interesting. A boost to my physical capability sounded like it would be useful.

And judging by the looks some of these youths were giving me, it might come in handy very soon.

CHAPTER SIX

There were now over twenty of these Academy students gathered before me. At first, I was confused by their numbers, since only five people were supposed to be able to enter this dimensional space at once. Then I realized that the limit of five only applied to an active fracture. With the death of the goblin chieftain, this dungeon had shifted into a cleared state, and could now accommodate many more people.

According to the Alpha Administrator, this place would now continue to exist for another twenty-four hours before vanishing, during which a cleanup team would mine it for every available resource they could take. There was a thriving industry that had developed in this world based around acquiring rare materials from fractures and the monsters that dwelt within them. I personally found it remarkable that human mercantilism had found a way to turn a profit from surviving a potential apocalyptic event.

"Evans," one of the students said as he approached me. He was a tall, clean-shaven youth with coffee-colored skin, wearing a silver breastplate over a set of gray fatigues. On his back he carried a sheathed, broad sword and at his side he had a holstered pistol. All in all, he gave the impression of being a very dangerous fellow who moved with the learned grace of a killer at ease.

His poise impressed me. He couldn't have been older than seventeen, but his experiences as a Hunter had clearly shaped him well. The other children carried themselves with an intensity that matched his. So, these were the sort of people this world produced. Not a single lamb among them, but butchers aplenty.

I immediately disabled my Class, so that I couldn't be perceived as anything other than a Porter. As far as I knew, I was the only Vampire Lord on the planet. If they decided that made me a threat, they might impulsively decide to dispose of me before I could offer any sort of explanation. It would be best to avoid any potential misunderstandings. At least until I was strong enough not to care what others thought of me.

"Tell me what happened here," he said brusquely. "You're missing three men. Where are Collins, Shaffin, and Harper?"

Although those names meant nothing to me, I quickly discerned that they were the names of the devoured members of the hunting team. I waved a hand around the room, gesturing to the gore all around us. "They're, like, everywhere, man," I said with a slightly high-strung giggle. "But, like, mostly inside him," I concluded while pointing at the dead goblin chieftain.

I had no idea what Kyler Evans had been like as a person, but I suspected he wasn't very well regarded by his peers. An examination of their healthy physiques, new and expensive equipment, and general cleanliness suggested a very distinct Class difference between me and them. Although we were in the same age bracket, my body was smaller, scrawnier, and my hair was thinner and unkempt. That happened when nutrition was poor.

Had Kyler Evans been a scholarship student? I wished I had a mirror so I could examine my teeth and eyes. Any yellowing would explain a lot. I also smelled strongly of tobacco and other substances. Unhealthy habits like that disproportionately affected those of lesser means. People with money tended to take better care of themselves.

Based on the information I had, I decided to improvise my speech and mannerisms. To perform as a flighty idiot. I doubted anyone would call me out if I got anything wrong. These children of privilege were unlikely to have paid any significant attention to Evans when he was alive. Besides, teenagers reinvented themselves all the time. They were always trying out new ways of speaking and thinking. It took a while to decide who you wanted to be for the rest of your life, after all.

"Shit," the teen swore. "I know they were only E-rankers, but Jesus Christ. All three of them? That's just pathetic."

I shrugged my shoulders. "It's like . . . I don't even know, brother. It was bad. Like mice throwing themselves at a housecat, yeah?"

"Is that right?" he asked me with a sneer. "Well, I'm sure you were a big help during the fight, burnout. That tunic you're wearing is system generated loot. How'd you come across that?"

"Got it when I poked the big guy," I admitted.

The other boy was stunned. "Wait, you seriously helped fight a dungeon lord? What the hell were you thinking? You're a fucking Porter."

"Brooo, c'mon, I know my role," I replied. "But I didn't have much of a choice, right? Hey, it was all hands aboard! He was smashing us! If I didn't step up, me and what's-her-face would have been beans on toast!"

"Beans on what? Stop rambling, you idiot," he said while shaking his head in disgust. "Jesus, a fucking Porter had to make the clear? I am going to eat so much shit over this."

"Hey, I was pretty good, man! You should have seen me!" To emphasize my point, I waved my spear around enthusiastically, then jumped back in fright when I accidentally dropped it, to avoid accidentally stabbing my own foot.

"Yeah, I can see that," he snorted as he leaned down to pick the spear up. He gave it a quick examination before clucking his tongue and tossing it back to me. "That thing's a piece of garbage, Evans. It suits you."

"What? Nooo, don't say it like that. It's good luck, bro! It saved my life, I swear!" I protested. "Oh, hey, quick question, though."

"What is it?" he said with a raised brow.

"Uh, bro, what's your name?" I asked him.

The boy stared at me silently for a full count of three before his face turned wrathful.

"Evans, you mother fu . . . did you come into this dungeon *high*?" he asked me sternly.

"What? No!" I said immediately.

"I'm serious, kid, you better fucking not have," he said as he leaned into my face. "We're down three bodies on this trip, four if you count whatever happened to Anikka. If you came in here blazed and that in any way contributed to this fuckup, I'll see to it that you're booted or worse. Test me, *bitch*."

"Not testing you, not testing you," I said quickly as I avoided making eye contact with him.

"Yeah, right," he said. But I could hear a subtle excitement in his voice as he spoke. He was happy that he'd questioned me because I'd just provided him with a way to escape any repercussions for the disaster that occurred under his watch.

If this Vandal Academy that we apparently attended was anything like a military school, then this boy was the officer in charge of this group. As such, he'd be the one held responsible for the failure of my team to safely clear this low-ranking dungeon without casualties.

A failure like this wouldn't look good for whatever career prospects awaited him down the line. Like any young person who'd gotten this far through determination and grit, he had ambition. And ambition made people ruthless when their future was threatened.

What he needed was a patsy. Someone he could pin this catastrophe on so he could avoid any personal consequences. So, that's what I gave him. I presented myself as a fool, an impression he seemed to have already had of me, and made it clear that I was unsuitable for my role.

Hopefully that would lead to my expulsion from this Academy. I had no intention of spending my first few years in this world in a school setting. I respected those who sought improvement through education, but I was more of a hands-on learner. I was the sort who preferred gaining knowledge through experience. The idea of wandering this new land was too delicious to resist.

There was also the fact that I just didn't get along well with children. This is an embarrassing admission, but as the young ones say, I just didn't vibe with them. Generational divides are difficult enough to navigate when you're an ordinary human being. A mere twenty-year difference in age is enough to separate two souls by a lifetime of experience. Imagine how massive those differences would be when the age gap is over nine hundred years.

Kids in general bothered me. It's not truly their fault. It's all to do with my personality and my unhappy family history. You see, in addition to being a terrible husband, I was also a neglectful waste of a father. I don't speak merely of the thousands of humans I've transformed into my lesser kin. Over the centuries, I also fathered over a dozen offspring. The curse of undeath doesn't prevent vampires from being able to reproduce traditionally. It's something many of us avoid, however, because so-called purebloods have even less humanity in them than their parents. They're supremely selfish, ambitious, and without loyalty. I would know; most of my children ended up rebelling against me.

Mortal fathers have it easy. They only have to deal with their progeny getting tattoos, or picking a profession or a partner they disapprove of. When my kids went astray, they came for my throne.

In the best-case scenarios, I had to cut them out of my life and send them away to live in banishment. With the worst? I had to destroy them with my own hands. Have you ever killed your son or daughter before they could plunge a silver dagger into your heart or behead you with a sword? I've done it three times.

My wives never forgave me. Vampire drama is the worst kind of drama.

It was a very depressing cycle. When they were small, my children loved me unconditionally. They treated every observation I made as though it were beyond profound. They laughed and played and wanted to be just like me. They made me feel happy.

But something always happened that shattered their image of me and led them to find constant disappointment in who I was as a person. Eventually, cracks began to form in our relationship that quickly became unmendable and always led to betrayal or the final death.

After the eventual blowup, I would always vow never to have another child. I also always broke that promise, given enough time. It was like I was tormenting myself. Was I wrong to want to leave someone behind who I felt was . . . worthy of me? That wasn't just me being an egotist, was it?

Yeah, it probably was.

I supposed my recent death meant that my last daughter by birth, Veronique, would now inherit my old title as the Lord of Blood. I pitied anyone who crossed her. The girl was an utter sadist. The first thing she'd probably do was hunt down her siblings and force them to swear their fealty to her. Then she'd imprison her mother and stepmothers to ensure there'd be no interference with her decision-making. It'd serve my dear brides right, since they'd spent centuries poisoning her against me.

Wait, hadn't Sophia said that no one was left to inherit my title? Did that mean that my children were already dead? I had difficulty believing that. You could more easily dispatch a bull with a flyswatter than you could permanently slay those rotten brats I'd sired. It might have been fun to watch some fools attempt it, though. It'd certainly be a show.

Was that a touch of pride I now felt?

Nah, it couldn't be.

"Evans, what the hell are you staring at?" asked the boy again. "Stay in the moment, you powder freak."

Goodness, I really did hate the way this fellow spoke to me. Just because I was playing the part of a loser didn't give him the right to behave so disrespectfully. What good was a warrior without courtesy? He was in dire need of refinement.

Well, maybe we could settle that later.

The boy, who I later learned was named Andre Culver, announced that we were pulling out. The remains of the deceased Hunters were cut out of the goblin chieftain's body to be returned to their families. As their Porter, I was given the honor of storing the assorted bits that remained of them. *Hurray.*

I also learned that the reason so many Hunters came running into the dungeon after I cleared it was due to the girl the goblin had tormented. My teammate, I supposed. Her name was Anikka Velas. Very wealthy, very popular, and a daughter of a famous household. Although I had nothing to do with what happened to her and may very well have been a victim of murderous mistreatment at her hands, her problems would soon become my problems.

Nobles don't like it when their children suffer. Even if it was due to their own incompetence, honor and reputation must be preserved. If there was someone else who could possibly be blamed for when things went wrong, then blamed they would be.

As it would turn out, my performance as a clueless dolt had been a little *too* effective.

CHAPTER SEVEN

Once my little question-and-answer session with Culver concluded, Anikka Velas was placed on a gurney and rolled toward the dungeon's exit with the rest of us following behind. I saw another student, a young brunette wearing a white cloak with lightly glowing blue hands, keeping pace with the traumatized girl, gently laying her palms on her head and whispering soothing words.

Curious, I was about to ask one of the others what she was doing when a muscular arm suddenly wrapped itself around my shoulders. When I looked up, a broad-shouldered lad with olive skin and dark hair, easily hefting a massive tower shield over his back, looked down at me like I had two earthworms dangling from my nostrils.

"Bro, what the fuck happened?" he asked as he half-dragged, half-choked me in his wake. "Three KIA's and a shell-shocked blonde. That's not very good for your first outing, little man."

"Uh, what can I say? It was like a mega culmination of utter fucking tragedy," I said as I squirmed beneath his grip.

"You're telling me!" he said. "I told you that you should have gone with my group. I know you're trying to network with the blue bloods, but holy shit, results like this won't impress anyone."

"I survived, didn't I?" I said defensively.

"Sure, but *she* sure as hell didn't come out unscathed," the big lad said as he pointed at Anikka Velas on her stretcher. "Plus, those other three were her family's retainers. That's too much money spent for a gutter rat like you to be the only one walking out on your feet. If you ask me, you might be more than a little fucked."

"Be serious," I said with a frown. Apparently, I was friends with this muscle head, or at least well-acquainted with him. I was glad. Perhaps this meant I could discreetly acquire information about this world without being perceived as acting strangely.

"What's the deal with the chick with the glowing hands?" I asked him.

"Wow, you really are blitzed today, aren't you, Evans?" he snorted. "That's Cassie Wells, remember? She's a healer. H-E-A-L-E-R. That's the person who patches us up when we get injured, remember?"

What I wanted to say was, *No, I don't remember, you condescending oaf; I'm not from this reality. But thanks for the information; I'll be sure to keep your helpfulness in mind later, when I'm deciding whether to rip your throat out with my teeth.*

What I said instead was, "Whoa."

"Yeah. *Whoa*," he said sarcastically. "Cassie went all in on her Holy Priestess spec. No offensive abilities at all, but she's deep enough into her skill tree to help with mental trauma. Whatever Anikka went through, Cass can help her recover from it. That's really lucky for you, spud."

"Why do you say that?" I asked.

"Duh. If you didn't have anything to do with what happened to her, then Anikka can confirm your story once she gets better. Otherwise, you'll be *fuuucked* once her sister and your brother find out what happened."

"I have a brother?!" I asked with genuine surprise.

The big guy broke out into raucous laughter and slapped my back hard. "Evans, are you dipping your ciggies in petrol? Come on, man, keep it together. Or better yet, set me up with your connection. God knows tanking is scary enough. Whatever you're on must have hit you like a horse tranquilizer."

"Bro let's assume for a minute that, uh, I have total amnesia and can't fucking remember *anything*. Can I desperately beg you to help me get clued in?" I asked him with wide eyes.

"Evans, are you high or actually brain damaged?" he asked with a slightly worried expression. "You remember *me*, right? Your old pal, Nick Pankratz?"

"Are we friends?" I asked hopefully.

"Nah, not really," he snickered. "You just crack me up is all. I think of you as more of a stray that follows me around hoping to get a treat."

"Do you like strays?" I asked.

"I tend to prefer animals that can feed themselves, honestly," Pankratz smirked.

"I mean, if you feed wild animals and make them dependent on you, do you really have the right to complain?" I asked him.

"Oh, shit, dude. I'm not sure. I'm a Tank, we're bad at philosophy," he said while tapping himself on the head. "What do you want to know anyway?"

"What year is it, what's the name of our country, and what's our current level of technology?" I immediately said.

"It's the current year of the twenty-first century, you live in the Reunited States, and porn can be streamed on smart phones, so the tech level is pretty high, I think," he replied.

"So, magic didn't destroy civilization when it was introduced?" I asked.

"Evans, don't joke around about that shit," Pankratz said with a frown. "Even I don't think it's funny to speak that lightly of the AOC."

"The famous politician from the Bronx?" I tried.

"The *Age of Collapse*," he said, now with genuine irritation. "Hey, Cassie! Once you're done over there, you might want to poke around this doofus's skull for a bit. I think his brain has become a colander."

The girl, Cassie, frowned at us both before turning her attention back to Anikka. Soon, we were outside the dungeon, where I saw that a large camp had been set up for the students. There were tents, an area where hot meals were prepared and distributed, a medical unit where Cassie and her team took Anikka, and a command center where I finally saw some adult personnel supervising the students.

There were also armed guards, who'd set up a perimeter around the area, and a dozen resource gatherers, who were preparing to enter the cleared dungeon and strip it of everything useful they could find.

Parked nearby were two large, armored transports. They were huge, menacing-looking vehicles, whose exteriors were covered in thick steel plates and bristled with deadly ranged weaponry.

Not exactly a cheery yellow school bus, was it?

"All of this for just one low-ranking dungeon?" I said with a whistle. "Vandal Academy really goes all out, huh?"

"There were *five*, dummy," Pankratz said as he sat in a chair beside a warm campfire and gestured for me to have a seat as well. "Five lowbie fractures for five teams of five student-Hunters. Try to remember, this was our big end of the year examination, bud. The goblin lair was the very last one on the list."

"Which one did you get?" I wondered.

"The Golem Cavern," he said with a triumphant smile as he proudly held up his dented shield. "I fucking aced it, man. It was a two-hour clear time, and not a single one of those rocky bastards got past me and Becky."

"Is Becky your co-Tank?" I asked him.

"Shut the hell up, Evans!" he snorted. He then gently patted his shield and said, "Please forgive him, Becky. I think he's cutting his powder with moldy baking soda or something. He doesn't know what he's saying."

"Pankratz, I'm a brain-damaged amnesiac, but even I think talking to your equipment is a little weird," I said after staring at him for a bit.

"It's not weird, it's good luck," Pankratz insisted. "Becky's gotten me past golems, fucking *spiders*, goblins, you name it! She's kept me alive and nurtured me more than any girlfriend I ever had. She's a *lady*, and deserves to be treated like one, isn't that right, baby?"

He then made cooing noises toward his shield and gave it a lingering kiss before setting it aside. "But yeah, me and my boys did great. *Me* especially. I'm on track to hit D-rank by graduation next year! I even have permission for a probationary license with the Hunter's Guild! That means I can start taking requests for pay! Goodbye Narrows, hello Uptown!"

"You're not a noble?" I asked.

"What?" Pankratz said in disgust. "Come on, Evans, get it together. I know I look good in armor, but be serious. My family and I work for a living, unlike the rest of these monied pearl-munchers. Life is too easy for them."

"Fuck you, Pankratz," someone called out. "I do my fair share."

"Fuck you harder, Burtlowe," Pankratz shot back. "And this is exactly what I mean. *Burtlowe.* Only someone with a lot of gold in their account can get away with naming their kid something that fucking absurd. Not a lot of girls would wear their sexiest lingerie for somebody with a name like that if he wasn't loaded."

"Your last name is *Pankratz*!" someone yelled as they tossed him a canned drink. Pankratz caught it easily and gulped half of its contents down within moments of opening it. "Damn straight it is!" he cheerfully yelled. "PANKRATZ! A hero of the people, kids! Once all of you nobs get tired of pretending to be Hunters and settle down to run your coal factories and printing presses, you're going to be paying out of your asses for me to guard your stuff. Be advised, ladies, my shield and sword may be for sale, but you're gonna have to *earn* my body!"

"Touch my girl and I'll kill you, bro!" laughed someone else.

"Just for that, I'm gonna let you raise my kids!" countered Pankratz as he signaled for another drink.

Soon other students gathered to sit with us and exchange quips and jokes with Pankratz, as well as the occasional insult, all of which he deftly countered with a clever and punishing wit of his own. He was a charismatic brute; I'll say that for him. He had the respect and admiration of his peers, and it was easy to see why. The others were drawn to his energetic personality like moths to a flame.

It was an excellent performance.

If I'd been far younger than I was, he might have convinced me that he was the easygoing life of the party that he pretended to be. But I could see Pankratz's eyes. They were filled with intelligence and calculation. He hadn't merely befriended his more privileged classmates; he was *imprinting* himself on them. I could tell he hadn't been joking when he said that he'd be working for them one day. I also knew that he hadn't been lying when he said he intended to make a lot of money doing it.

Men like Pankratz always required lots of money for the lives they invariably led. Not ones filled with hedonism and leisure, though. People born with a fire like his could never be satisfied with an existence as pointless as that. There was an insatiable greed within his heart that yearned for far more and would not let him rest so easily.

I wondered what his wealthy friends would think if they could see the spark of deep-seated hate he carried for them beneath his friendly smile. His mockery of their social class had been amusing, but also genuine. He was truly contemptuous of his supposed betters.

Now I wondered what sort of a vampire he'd make. An excellent one, most likely. But probably too ambitious.

Why were these children so carefree? I was suddenly struck by that thought as Pankratz made another joke that had everyone roaring with laughter. Twenty-five of them had set out to conquer five dungeons. They had surely trained alongside each other for years. They weren't mere strangers. But only twenty-two of them had returned alive. (Truthfully, it was twenty-one, but there was no need for anyone to learn the fate of the real Kyler Evans.)

Why wasn't anyone mourning?

Pankratz had said that the three who died were only retainers. In other words, mere servants. Did that mean these young nobles didn't view their loss as meaningful? The more I thought about it, the more I realized that had to be the case. Was that why he worked so hard to make an impression on them? So that they would *care*? And therefore, not view him as disposable?

Was the popularity he cultivated also a survival mechanism?

What a disturbing notion.

These children were far too comfortable with death.

"Evans!" a young woman's voice cried out sharply, cutting easily through the din of laughter. Everyone grew silent as a blonde girl wearing a black tunic and pants beneath a red cloak swiftly approached me. A quick scan of her attractive features made me believe that she was Anikka Velas's sister, whom Pankratz had warned me of.

A warning I should have taken more seriously.

At the very least, I should have asked what her name was.

"What did you do to my sister, you WORTHLESS piece of trash!" she said in a voice filled with anger.

Before I could give an answer, she raised her palm towards me. "Take cover!" yelled someone in a panicked voice as Pankratz and his circle of friends dived for safety, leaving me exposed to whatever was about to happen.

The air suddenly smelled thick with ozone as I felt my hair become statically charged and begin to rise. An unpleasantly intense tingling sensation began to run over my body.

Oh, I knew what this was. I knew exactly what was about to happen.

"Die, you little *worm!*" the girl shouted as my senses were overwhelmed with blinding light and the roar of thunder.

CHAPTER EIGHT

One helpful method to determine if you're dealing with someone who may be severely irrational is to see how they react during an intensely emotional moment. Fear and anger can be extremely triggering for someone who lacks a calm and focused mind.

Let's use the elder Velas sister as an example. She had just learned that her younger sibling had experienced a horrifying mental trauma at the hands of a monster. She'd also learned that the three valued family servants who'd been entrusted with protecting her sister had met their fates at the hands of that same beast and died in a terrible and grisly manner.

Now she was upset. She was off-center. She was frightened for her sister and angry at how events had played out.

If she'd had a rational mindset, the first thing she would have done was breathe deeply to regain control of herself. Then she'd calmly collect all the available information to help determine the best course of action.

That's what a disciplined warrior who wielded her power responsibly would do, yes?

Well, this little black-clad fruit loop chose to do the exact opposite. Instead of steadying herself, she decided to lash out and release her frustrations on the second of the only two survivors, because that wasn't crazy or anything. Her ire towards me made no sense at all; I was the party's bloody *Porter*. What exactly did she think I could have done to her precious sister?

Oh, I'm sorry, that was me using logic and common sense. Two things that apparently don't matter when you're wealthy, angry, and (unhappily for me) capable of generating lightning from your fingertips. Forgive my lack of awareness. Let's just jump to the part where this cu . . . confused young lady decided to toss a thunderbolt at me to relieve her stress.

With the speed of thought, I managed to shift into my undead state just before the lightning struck me. I then clamped my hands tightly against the aluminum piping of the folding chair I was sitting on, which allowed much of the electricity to flow through me to the chair and then harmlessly into the soil.

Wait, did I say harmlessly? That might have been an exaggeration on my part, because my skin was now covered in random scorch marks. And they were *itchy*.

Also, my hair was on fire. Can't forget that part.

Have no fear, I wasn't in any pain. In my undead state, the only thing that could cause me physical discomfort was the presence of the divine. This insolent girl's lightning packed quite a punch, but there was no heavenly aspect to it that I had to fear.

All she'd really done was *greatly upset me*.

What I wanted to do at that moment was stand up, lightly brush off my clothing so that she could see that I was unharmed, then saunter over to where she stood as though I didn't have a care in the world while her mind tried to process what was happening. I'd grab her by the sides of her head so that I could use both of my thumbs to force her eyes open. Then I'd begin pulling the skin off her face with my teeth while forcing her to meet my gaze.

It would have been an enjoyable experience for me and an educational one for her.

Too bad it was the wrong environment for that sort of lark. So, instead, I shifted back into my human form, which had no difficulty feeling the pain of my new injuries and began screaming my head off while slapping my hair and trying to extinguish it.

Eventually, the healer, Cassie, came running to my aid, while the other students got in front of my attacker and began talking her down while one of those handy adult supervisors, who'd done nothing to prevent this ridiculous violence, began hemming at the girl and asking her what her father would think of her behavior in a slightly peevish voice, as though she were refusing to eat her vegetables at dinner and hadn't attempted to vaporize a fellow human being.

"Thalia, you need to do *better*, okay?" he nagged. "Just try to do *beeeetter*. Think of your position."

"I'd do it again in a heartbeat," she sniffed.

Ah, her name was Thalia. Thalia Velas, was it?

I made a mental note to remember that name for a later occasion.

What occasion might that be, you ask?

Oh, nothing much.

Nothing *muuuch*.

* * *

"Are you mad at me, bro?" Nick Pankratz asked me the next morning after the campsite had been packed away and everyone was loaded onto the two transports that would return us to the academy.

"Why would I be upset with you?" I asked him in a painful rasp. My voice was sore from a night spent screaming in pain. Cassie was a talented healer for such a young person, but Thalia's lightning attack had been altered by a skill point investment to cause severe pain that couldn't be dispelled.

As I understood it, the skill didn't increase her lightning's damage or benefit it in any way, really. It just caused pointlessly intense agony to anyone that was struck by it, because whoever Thalia blasted, she wanted to *suffer*.

I was really learning a lot about that girl today. Thalia Velas was a sadist. How sad for her. Sadism is one of the most useless personality traits a person can have.

To a sadist, other beings existed to provide them with pleasure. And what was the thing sadists enjoyed most? Causing extreme suffering whenever possible. A sadist prolonged a fight for the joy of pummeling a helpless opponent. They also attacked the weak whenever possible and were overtly cruel whenever they could get away with it. It was a mindset in which one developed a powerful inclination towards detestable behaviors such as animal abuse and rape. It was a *coward's* disposition, held by outwardly normal people who were absolutely twisted inside.

In other words, sadists were living *garbage*. You'd think that having been a vampire for so many years, that I would have a natural inclination to torment the weak, but in this case you'd be wrong. The long march of time has taught me that savoring the pain of others is a worthless behavior. Indulge in it enough times and you'll eventually lose the trust of others, but you *will* have a legion of former victims eager to someday return the favor.

Just as I now intended to do for dear Thalia. But only when I was good and ready.

"I told you she was going to be pissed when she saw her sister," Pankratz continued. "But I still feel bad this happened to you."

"Ah," I said bitterly. "Is that a fact?"

"You know it is, bro," he said sincerely. "You and I are tight."

"Then why didn't you block it with your shield?" I asked him.

"Huh?" he asked with some confusion.

"Why didn't you block her lightning with your shield?" I mumbled again. "You were just bragging about how nothing ever gets past you. Blocking a lightning bolt would have been great for your rep."

"Oh. Well," he said uncertainly. "I probably *could* have done that, but . . . well, no offense, Evans, but helping you out would have meant standing against Thalia Velas. I'm just getting started in life, man. I hope you understand."

"Yeah, I get it," I replied. And we spoke no more for the rest of the ride.

I truly wasn't upset with him. I understood Pankratz's point of view perfectly. He was being practical and had made a choice that would benefit his long-term odds of prosperity. Why alienate a wealthy and influential household for the sake of a lowly wretch like Kyler Evans?

I'd made far colder decisions throughout my life. Even with the element of attempted murder, this incident with Thalia couldn't match the betrayals that I'd willingly committed to ensure my own success and survival. In comparison to those many burned bridges, this was naught but a child's game.

Besides, why would I be affected by the betrayal of Kyler Evans's friend? I didn't know him. And he *certainly* didn't know me. Keeping things at that distance would be best for everyone.

My expulsion couldn't come quickly enough.

I spent the rest of the time staring at the landscape that the transport carried us through. It was a confusing mix of different environments that could vary wildly at different distances. I saw desert terrain give way to a random burst of forest growth within ten miles of each other. A bewildering blend of flora, fauna, and fluctuating climate.

Occasionally, the powerful guns attached to our ride would open fire to warn off creatures that were too close for the driver's comfort. How had humanity maintained their technological developments in such a hostile and chaotic environment? Industry needed stability to provide civilization with its boons. What exactly was stable about a world like this?

I received my answer when we arrived at the city of Gardenia, home to Vandal Academy.

Gardenia's appearance wasn't too dissimilar to that of any other twenty-first century North American city constructed with international influences in its design. What differentiated it from those that I remembered was the protective golden dome of light that covered it. Even a mile outside its outskirts, I could feel the potent magic exuding from that light. It felt like stability, like . . . safety.

Well, this explained a lot. I was glad to not have to ask any silly questions. Although, I did now wonder how an undertaking of this magnitude had been performed. Was this dome a magic developed by mankind, or had it been gifted to them by the system? How many other cities operated under similar protection?

What I really needed more than anything else was a history book.

Well, we were heading to a school, weren't we? Perhaps I could get one there.

Things happened quickly once we arrived at the Academy.

As the transport pulled up to let us disembark, I beheld Vandal: a lavishly decorated old manor house on a large estate that had been converted into a center of education. I later learned it had been named after Conrad Vandal, also known as Vandal the Wild Sword. A local legend who was also the only S-ranked Hunter that Gardenia had ever produced. When he died, he willed his estate to a private trust whose sole purpose was to raise new generations of elite Hunters using his exclusive training methods.

After I stepped off the transport, I *once again* found myself being accosted. Strong hands grabbed me from behind and spun me around to face an angry-looking older version of myself with a much better haircut, dressed in expensive clothing.

Ah, this must have been my brother.

Wonderful. Clearly someone else that I had a friendly relationship with, yes? No.

He slammed me against the side of the transport and glowered at me. "What did you do this time, you little idiot?"

"Save the day?" I choked out.

He gave me a hard slap. "None of your backtalk," he said with a quiet intensity. "Anikka Velas is like a dear sister to me. Do you even know what an honor it was when I asked her to let you act as a Porter for her first foray? This was an *opportunity* for you to make a valuable connection, you ungrateful little bastard. How could you fail at this? How could you make me look this bad?"

"I protected her," I rasped. "Doesn't that mean anything?"

"Why couldn't you have just died instead?" he whispered with a hateful glare.

Okay. This was already a ridiculous situation to begin with but now it was going in a direction that I could only charitably describe as *absolutely stupid*. Why was everyone so eager to interpret events in such a way as to put the blame entirely on me?

But wait, Lord Stragos, you might say. *Didn't you* want *to be blamed for things going wrong so that you could be expelled and left to your own devices?*

No. What I *wanted* was to be accused of dereliction of duty for showing up to the dungeon high. Or pretending to, anyway. I still wanted to be credited for saving Anikka Velas from the dungeon lord *BECAUSE THAT WAS EXACTLY WHAT I'D DONE*! I'd saved an innocent girl's life and slew a dangerous monster! So, yes, I should be thrown out, but I should also be acknowledged for performing a valuable service!

But what had I received instead? Accusations and abuse! No, worse than abuse; humiliation and contempt! An attempt on my bloody life! I'd *seen* Thalia Velas's eyes, damn it. She'd been surprised that I survived her lightning strike.

The witch had tried to kill me.

Her little sister's Hunter team *did* kill me.

Another person who should presumably have been pleased with my heroic actions was instead berating me for still being alive.

You know what? This entire situation was beginning to feel like a *setup*.

Just what sort of life did you live, Kyler Evans? Because it seems like the world itself was against you.

"Patrick!" cried a girl's voice.

My brother pushed me away and turned to face a distraught-looking Thalia Velas, the lightning bug herself. After rushing to each other, he kissed her lips and wrapped his arms around her in a tight embrace. *Wow, how about that? My* favorite thing in the world. A loving young couple making a public display of affection.

Something told me that Patrick and I weren't going to get along.

At exactly this moment, because the timing of the universe had been set for melodramatic, Anikka was wheeled off the transport. Patrick and Thalia were at her side at once, and I got to see something interesting.

Anikka was aware of her surroundings. She was looking at Patrick and her sister and smiling sweetly. That goblin chieftain had claimed he'd broken her mind by making her watch him torture her friends. He must have been an even bigger fool than I thought, because that was not the expression of someone who'd just recovered from a terrible mental trauma.

She looked like a cat that had awoken from a nap.

Thalia showered kisses on her sister, her face filled with affection and relief, and Patrick was now holding her hand quite tenderly. Wow, look at the intimate way in which his thumb circled her palm. I thought he said she was like a dear sister to him. What sort of a person touched their little sister like that? Certainly no one that I'd want to be around.

As they moved away, Anikka's gaze suddenly shifted towards me.

She winked at me.

Then she began sobbing as loudly as she could while yelling, "Get him away! Please! Get him away from me! Get him away from me, I can't bear it! *Pleeeease!*"

The hostile eyes of everyone gathered there turned towards me and the looks they shared were not friendly in the slightest. Even my "good buddy" Nick Pankratz looked at me like I'd just brandished a knife at a toddler.

"Evans, what did you do, man?" he asked in bewilderment.

A hand came down heavily on my shoulder. It belonged to a heavyset adult in a school official's uniform who asked me to come along quietly with him.

It took only one glance at my brother and Thalia to decide that going with the official was likely the safer option.

Ha. Anikka Velas.

Well played, you evil little thing.

CHAPTER NINE

Okay, I'll confess . . .

By the end of my first and only day at the school, I ended up killing someone.

I felt bad about it. I know that didn't make it all right but give me *some* credit at least for not being a complete heel about things.

It's not like I planned on doing it. It was a spur-of-the-moment action fueled by frustration at how the last couple of days had gone for me. I was hungry, I was tired, I was being accused of attempted murder, and worst of all, I was dealing with the irrational, hormonal mindset that comes with being a teenager again. Authority figures kept yelling at me and accusing me of things I hadn't done, promising that I would soon be severely punished, and . . . well, I was feeling a little overwhelmed by it all, so in a dark moment, I lashed out at the first available target.

It's not ordinarily my style to lose control like that, I swear it isn't. But I have to take full responsibility for my behavior. Yes, my circumstances were bad, but that doesn't excuse me from my obligation to conduct myself civilly. I needed to stop behaving like a bewildered wild animal. My survival in this world would depend on maintaining self-control.

So, *mea culpa*, oh random guard whose name I didn't know. May you rest in peace. I'm sorry for losing my cool and for storing your dead body in my inventory where it will never be discovered, which in turn will lead your loved ones to wonder for the rest of their lives where you vanished. That's a cruel thing to put another person through, let alone an entire family, but if it's any comfort, they're all mortal, so they'll surely die from natural causes within a few short decades. That means you won't have to wait long before you're reunited with them.

Also, I've now acquired your Stealth ability thanks to the Gore Grimoire, so for what it's worth, know that your death was not in *vein.*

I'm sorry. I threw in a little vampire humor at the end in an attempt to lighten the mood. I'm terrible at levity. I need to try harder to improve so that more people can feel relaxed in my presence.

Just another goal to shoot for.

Earlier in the day, I was led inside the halls of Vandal Academy while being flanked by two armed guards. First, we stopped by an examination room, where I was ordered by a woman in a white coat to release the remains of the three dead members of my party from my inventory, as well as any remaining supplies from the mission.

After complying, I was taken to a small, poorly lit room, where I was seated across a table from a portly, middle-aged man with graying hair in a navy-blue uniform, which I had begun to recognize as the standard garb for instructors in this institute.

This fellow stared at me silently for a bit, as though he were appraising my value as a person. From the frown he wore, I guessed the conclusion he reached wasn't a generous one. Facial expressions like that were usually reserved for people who'd accidentally stepped on excrement while wearing new shoes.

Poor Kyler Evans. It seemed that he had been a boy who truly impressed no one. Wasn't there anyone at this place who'd been on his side?

The stranger interrupted my thoughts by sliding a piece of paper and a pen over to me before saying, "Sign it," in a bored and impatient voice.

"Sign it?" I asked.

"Yes," he replied. "Quickly, please."

"No," I replied. "Not without knowing what it is."

"You're really going to drag this out?" he asked me unhappily.

"I'm afraid I must," I said unsympathetically.

"It's a confession to the murder of three of your fellow students," the man said. "And the attempted murder of Lady Anikka Velas."

Ah.

Well, then.

"A murder confession?" I asked incredulously. "I got off the transport less than ten minutes ago and you're already trying to pin this nonsense on me?"

"You call the deaths of three brave and talented future Hunters, as well as the attempted slaying of a member of a prominent noble household, *nonsense?*" the man asked me with another, deeper frown.

"Certainly not," I said. "Especially not when such tragic circumstances have the potential to negatively affect my own future. But I think it's obvious to anyone with eyes and a brain that I committed no such foul acts."

The man gazed at me in surprise before replying. "You're not quite how I expected you to be. A little more articulate than was implied in your student profile."

"I've been working on improving my vocabulary," I replied dryly.

"So, I see," he said as he made an exaggerated display of opening a manila folder and flipping through the papers within. "Kyler Evans: a probationary basic course student. Notable for having a sizeable personal inventory, but otherwise unremarkable by all other applicable means of measurement."

I said nothing but listened very carefully to his words. Finally, some useful background information on the boy whose body I'd received! I kept my expression neutral so that he wouldn't see how excited I was to learn more about myself.

"You're certainly nothing in comparison to your older half-brother, Patrick Stonefaith," he continued. "We're all very proud of Patrick, as I'm sure you know. A warrior with A-rank potential, already reaching C-rank by the age of eighteen. An unprecedented talent, invited into serving the Velas family, and winning the heart of Lady Thalia with his grace and charm. It's a story for the ages."

Oh, so Patrick and I were only half-siblings, eh? That somewhat explained his disdainful attitude towards me. Brother dearest was moving up in the world and could only view me, a Porter, as a shabby embarrassment that marred his glory.

I thought that was enough information for me to decide that I disliked him.

I could not abide familial disloyalty. Be a jumped-up little lordling if it made you feel special, but don't spit on someone just because they didn't share your talents. Especially if they were of your blood.

It seemed no matter where I went, I'd always be saddled with family dysfunction.

"It's a shame you'll never come close to matching his achievements," the man continued. "Even though your relation to him was what allowed you admission to this fine institution, I'm sure the jealousy you felt must have been great. You must have *burned* with envy at the honor and privilege that were soon to be his. Anger at the new family that uplifted him and left you behind for a future of mediocrity at best, and squalor at worst. Do you hate them, Mr. Evans? Do you hate the great Velas family for taking him to the top and leaving you in the gutter? Do you yearn in your heart for a seat alongside the nobility?"

The nobility . . .

This new world, while similar in so many ways to my old one, was also so very, very strange. To hear an American, of all beings, fawning over a noble family just didn't feel right. I mean, the United States of my world had always possessed gaping inequities in class that allowed their wealthy minority to openly reign over their dystopian society, but they always at least *pretended* to espouse egalitarian values.

Just how badly had things gone wrong to lead these people to embrace such neo-feudalism? And how far did it extend? Was there also now an American monarchy? Were school children required to recite the pledge of allegiance before vigorously chanting *long live the king*?

I really wanted a damn history book.

The man slammed his fist on the table to regain my attention. "Am I disturbing you, Mr. Evans?" he snapped.

Ah, it appeared my mind had been wandering again.

"Sorry, sorry," I said. "I'm still wrapping my head around the concept of landed gentry in the states."

"Are you an *equalist*, Mr. Evans?" the stranger suddenly asked. "Oh, that explains so much about your behavior. Decided to take a shot at your betters while safe from the prying eyes of others in the dungeon, didn't you? How pathetic."

"I take it an equalist is someone opposed to the current way our nation operates?" I asked him. After he gave an exaggerated nod, I next asked, "And how am I supposed to have, as you phrased it, *taken a shot at my betters*? I'm a Porter. I carry the luggage. That's not an impressive power to wield against true Hunters."

"Lady Anikka informed us that you poisoned the food you were carrying for your team," he told me with a sharkish smirk. "She said that her retainers began behaving sluggishly shortly after taking a meal break. That after eating, their performance plummeted, which was what allowed a mere Level Five F-rank boss to defeat and devour them."

"Is that so?" I asked, impressed by the cleverness of the lie.

"It explains *everything*," the man said smugly. "Including how a Porter was able to kill a goblin chieftain. You just sat back and let the poison seep from their bodies into him. Even a weakling like you would have been able to handle him if he was already dying."

"And how did I acquire this supremely effective poison?" I asked him. "A toxin this powerful wouldn't be easy to get my hands on, would it? And while we're at it, what's the name of this murderous brew?"

"That has yet to be determined—" he blustered.

"No, that means you haven't yet decided what it is," I countered. "You're so obviously framing me, it's comical! I'm not signing this."

I pushed the paper back to him and crossed my arms to see what would happen next. It wasn't a long wait. The official nodded at the guard standing behind me, and I was struck at the back of my head and sent crashing to the floor.

"Ow," I mumbled.

"The pointless prevarication of this pitiful Porter will not prevent your punishment, Mr. Evans," my accuser said. "It's Lady Anikka's word against yours. Accept your loss like a man and confess your crimes."

"I saved her life," I said angrily.

"You *endangered* it!" he shouted. "Oh, but was that the reason behind your actions? *Engineered heroics?* Did you want to save Lady Anikka from harm like a true hero and receive the praise and admiration of your peers? Was that the reason three brave youths had to die by your cowardly hands? If so, what a monstrous misdeed!"

"I swear, the people around here are in *love* with alliteration," I said as I brushed myself off and resumed my seat. "What's her Class?" I asked.

"Your pardon?" he replied.

"What's Lady Anikka's Class? I'm *so* curious," I repeated.

"She's an Apothecary with B-rank potential," he said. "One blessed with the capability to one day evolve into the advanced Class, Alchemist. As expected of a member of the Velas household."

After hearing this, I sighed loudly and gave him a frank look. "Sir, did I hear you correctly? Lady Anikka is an *Apothecary.* Is that right?"

Understanding dawned swiftly in his eyes.

"You get it now, I see," I said to him, now matching his prior smugness with my own. "I'm a classless joke. Even if I wanted to poison a Hunter, aren't you people all but indestructible to things that would harm a mundane human? An E-rank poison resistance would let you guzzle a can of Raid without feeling even the slightest bit of indigestion."

I had no way of knowing if that was true or if Raid even existed in this world. But I must have guessed correctly due to the grim expression the man was now wearing.

"An Apothecary, though?" I continued. "I bet one of those could easily whip up something that could take out a Hunter or three. I repeat, *easily.* And just because I carried the food didn't mean I was the one who prepared it. Anikka's a noble! Even on a mission, I doubt she or her retainers would eat anything prepared for commoners like me. Rich kids have fancy tastes! I bet she and her sister have a personal chef of their own, don't they?"

He said nothing, so I continued.

"If they did, then who exactly had the time and the ability to prepare an effective poison? Who had plenty of access to the food? Who was closer to the victims? Huh? God, you're all so stupid. So stupid and arrogant and *lazy.*"

"What did you just say to me?" he bellowed.

"I didn't eat the food," I said mockingly.

(Kyler Evans had already been dead before they had their meal. I could tell that this body hadn't been recently fed when I first awoke inside of it.)

"Therefore," I continued, "I didn't succumb to the poison, *therefore once more*, I'm a loose end. For whatever reason, Anikka decided the three of them had to go. Probably because of the endless games that the upper class are always playing with each other. Doesn't this sound like something they'd do? It sure as hell does to me! And you're clearly, blatantly, in on it! So, I'm not signing shit, I'm not participating in this farce, and I insist on legal representation. I'm going to scream my innocence to the world, you vexatious lackey! Even if that's not enough to get anyone to listen to me, I'll do it anyway just to be annoying! Kiss my ass, I'll confess to *nothing*!"

And it was at that moment that they promptly beat me within an inch of my life.

I woke up in a cell, bloodied and humiliated and feeling quite wrathful. When the door opened an hour later so that a tray of food could be delivered to me, I'm afraid I lost track of my senses in my urge to lash out. When I came to after a few moments lost to a red haze of anger, a nameless guard lay before me on the ground, sans throat and pulse.

In my hand, I held his heart. Apparently, I'd just added another skill to my Gore Grimoire. Just outside the door, I saw another guard resting on a stool with his eyes shut, taking a nap. He hadn't seen anything. I must have taken the other one in silence.

That was good. Even in a predatory haze, I'd acted with discretion.

But when had I shifted into my undead form? I must have done so instinctively upon awakening. That meant the injuries I received during my interrogation had been life threatening. Dangerous enough to require me to transform. Which had left my vampire-self hungry enough to attack a stranger.

Technically not my fault, but still a shameful lack of control. I could do better. I *had to* do better.

After hiding the corpse in my inventory, I sat on my bunk and considered the options available to me. It was obvious that Anikka was using her family connections to pressure the academy officials to side with her version of events. Despite my earlier claim, I had no chance of changing anyone's mind. My supposed brother would support her as well, and I apparently had no friends of my own, so there'd be no one to speak up for me.

I wouldn't get so much as a character reference.

I felt a brief but powerful urge for bloody vengeance, which I promptly set aside. I refused to be provoked any further. This was nothing in the greater scheme of things. Who cared if some silly child's games had momentarily inconvenienced me? I was immortal and she was a mayfly. I doubted I'd even remember her name next week.

No, how I'd gotten into these circumstances was unimportant. What mattered was extricating myself from this situation, and doing so in a manner that would completely throw off my new enemies. I needed to vanish from their radar in such a way that they'd never even think to pursue me. Fortunately for me, there was one foolproof method of achieving that. And it's very easy to do when you're already a walking corpse.

With my course of action now decided, I removed the dead guard's sword from my inventory and used it to impale myself in the gut.

"What are you doing? *NOOOOOOO!*" I screamed melodramatically, before dropping to the floor. When my cell door was opened, the head watcher stared at me in bewilderment before kneeling at my side.

"Kid, what the hell happened here?" he asked with wide eyes.

"The other guard! He . . . h-he's killed me. Why? I was . . . innocent," I moaned before falling still.

"Kid? Who? You're saying Reg did this? What's going on? Kid, hold on! I'll get some help . . . kid? NOOO! Kid!" he shouted as he shook my body, trying to get a response.

Well, he seemed like a nice guy. It made me glad that I'd killed the other fellow instead of him.

Within two hours of my "murder," they buried me in a shallow grave. No paperwork involved. I overheard my interrogator speaking while they cleaned up the scene. To avoid any sort of controversy, they needed me to quietly vanish.

"Sir, even if he was suspected of a crime, a minor was still slain. Can we really just sweep this aside?" asked someone with a lot of scruples but little in the way of common sense.

"You have your instructions," barked the interrogator as I was being sealed inside a large black bag.

I'd be listed as KIA in the goblin's lair. All parties involved would be sworn to secrecy to protect the reputations of both the school and Anikka Velas. As for the guard I'd framed for the deed, they assumed he'd done it to curry favor with the Velas family and wrote him off.

Now I was free of their game. And free to play games of my own if I later decided. But that could wait for another time. What mattered most to me now was taking a moment to myself to relax.

A peaceful day of sleep beneath the earth was exactly what I needed. I usually slept on a soft mattress, so I'd forgotten how restful it could be to rest in a grave. I honestly don't believe I'd slept that well in decades. How blissful. How restorative.

Well, soon enough I'd need the energy. I'd be very busy soon.

It was time to start grinding Levels.

CHAPTER TEN

After a gloriously restful two-day period of sleep, I awoke to discover a large dog gnawing on my arm. I must have been quite flavorful because he was doing his level best to tear into my bicep.

I should have expected something like this to occur. It could happen when you chose to rest in a shallow grave. It'd been so long since I last roughed it out in the wild that the notion of being eaten had completely slipped my mind. Just another senior moment, I guessed.

I supposed I should have been grateful for having been buried at all. I'd been taken into the wilderness outside the city walls. They could have just settled for leaving me there instead of bothering to dig a hole. Was that professionalism on their part or a kindly act of human decency?

I may have felt touched.

Meanwhile, the dog kept chewing away at me.

"Knock it off," I said irritably to the beast after flicking his nose. He yelped in surprise and backed away. Then he began growling at me with his hackles raised as though he were preparing for a fight.

"Calm down," I commanded the pest after I finished climbing out of my meager place of rest. "Don't paint yourself as a victim. Who was trying to make a meal of whom, eh?"

Instead of bowing to my logic, the silly beast continued to growl while hunching over, moments away from throwing itself at me. Oh, right, I'd forgotten that even the most basic abilities I'd taken for granted for centuries were currently sealed from me.

I'd gotten used to giving orders that were enforced with powerful telepathic commands. But now that option was closed to me. Anyone could refuse my demands. Even the simple beasts of the fields.

I'd have to do something about that.

When the dog leapt for me, I stepped to the side, allowing him to pass by. After he landed, I pressed my hand against the back of his neck and pinned him firmly to the ground, leaving him unable to move.

He continued with his angry growling for a bit while trying to snap at my hands, but all that posturing eventually gave way to pitiful whining as his tail slapped helplessly against the earth. It wasn't difficult holding him down. Despite his aggressiveness, the dog was severely underweight for his size, leaving his ribs visible beneath his short coat of fur. Clearly the life of a nomad had done him no favors.

When the dog's body went slack in submission, I eased up the pressure and began gently patting his head while scratching his belly. After a few minutes of this kingly treatment, instead of trying to get away from me, he now kept trying to force me to continue. As easily as that, I'd earned my first true friend in this world.

"Yes, yes, I can see you like it," I said with amusement as I continued petting him. I moved to sit beneath a nearby tree, and he followed, with his tail wagging, to sit beside me. Wild though he may have been, I suspected this poor brute had once had a home among men before being discarded.

I wished that people would take better care of their animal companions. But wishes never changed anything, so lamenting the irresponsibility of others served no purpose. Besides, his former owner's loss was my gain. I got along very well with canines. Mostly wolf packs, but also the occasional hellhound. Honestly, my new companion, mutt that he was, was less visually impressive than the wild creatures of the night I'd run with in prior years, but at that time I wasn't feeling picky.

I just had to make a few adjustments for him. Wait, not for him. *To* him.

"I apologize for leaving you in storage for so long," I said to my sentient spear a few moments later as I used its sharp edge to slice strips of bloody flesh from my arm. "I should have commanded you to sleep before I placed you in storage. I hope you weren't uncomfortable."

My vampiric form is extremely durable and possesses a naturally high resistance to being pierced and slashed. Luckily, now that I could shift between being human and undead, I could gather the necessary bits for the dog's transcendence by cutting away at my far softer mortal self. It was . . . an experience, to be sure. An extremely unpleasant one. But when viewed through the lens of eternity, such discomfort is practically ephemeral.

Still, when the final slice of meat was cut from me, I was very quick to resume my vampiric form. I sighed in relief as the pain was immediately dulled. A tingling sensation then enveloped my arm as my flesh began to regenerate. My body was still filled with relatively fresh blood from the guard I'd slain two days prior, so my healing was exceptionally quick.

I was doubly pleased to learn that shifting between my two forms allowed me to avoid being afflicted with my spear's curse. Its ability to deliver unhealing wounds could be negated with a shift into undeath. That was good to know.

The dog licked its teeth and stared at me while whining as I picked up the pile of fresh meat and placed it before him. "Go ahead," I encouraged him with a pat as he began wolfing it down.

I felt a surge of intense disgust emanate from the spear as I watched my new friend enjoy his meal, which in turn annoyed me. I dislike judgementalism.

"I didn't have anything else to give him," I said to the spear. "I'd have cut my arm off, but his teeth are so loose from hunger that I doubt he could have handled gnawing through bone. This was the kinder option."

Another negative burst of emotion came from the spear. Oh, it could be so tiresome.

"That's enough of your Tinkerbell routine," I said to the weapon. "I'm your creator. You can't hide anything from me, *including* your voice. When I'm addressing you, I expect you to speak when spoken to. And if you have something to say, just spit it out. Is that understood?"

"How did you know?" asked the surprised voice of a young-sounding woman.

"I heard you try to warn Sophia shortly before I detonated," I said. "There were no other women close by at that moment. I eventually realized that it had to be you that I heard."

"Congratulations on being so clever," the spear said bitterly.

"I accept your compliment," I said politely.

"How could you do such a thing to that poor animal?" the spear suddenly asked.

"He was hungry. I provided for his needs," I said. "You ought to be praising me for that."

"You've cursed him with your foul condition," the spear said accusingly.

"He cursed himself, actually," I corrected her. "He bit me while I was resting. If he'd gotten any of my blood into his system, it wouldn't have ended well for him. If I hadn't voluntarily given him more with a serving of my flesh besides, the poor thing might have died in agony by morning's light."

"Is he a vampire now?" she asked. "Have you stolen the sun from him?"

"No. He's more of an elevated existence," I replied. "He'll be stronger and far more durable. His intelligence should show a considerable increase as well. But undeath is a condition that only humans can inherit. He'll still be a dog. Just a far deadlier one."

"Is that what happened to me?" the spear asked sarcastically. "Did I somehow *inherit* your condition?"

"I explained it to you earlier," I said patiently. "Your exposure to my blood has transformed you into a being similar to myself. You're my progeny and I'm your creator."

"Me becoming a vampiric weapon should be impossible!" she said with growing rage. "I'm a sacred weapon! I served the light faithfully all my life and in death I was elevated to one of its blessed champions! I could never be so forsaken! You're lying!"

"I gain little from such a petty act of deception," I retorted. "You can believe whatever you like. The results still speak for themselves."

"How?" she demanded. "How did you do this to me?"

"My vampiric nature can be quite infectious," I explained. "Anything with human characteristics can fall prey to it. It seems that ensouled weaponry can be added to that list. A shame that your friend Sophia didn't realize that in time to save you."

"Don't speak my wielder's name so casually, monster!" the spear said angrily. "You know nothing of her! Don't think I'll let you mock her without consequence!"

"You raise an excellent point," I conceded. "Would you like to tell me more about her? So that I can insult her memory with greater accuracy?"

"I'll tell you nothing! I would never betray my friend."

I paused for a moment upon hearing those words. Then I said, "I respect that. Loyalty is the sincerest expression of true friendship. I envy those who receive it uncoerced."

"What would a devil like you know of friendship?" the spear said.

"That I miss it," I said with an honesty that surprised me. "I existed for so long at the heights of power that I forgot how nice it was to stand alongside a small, committed few. It feels good to have a pair of true companions at my side once more."

"Save your praises for your new dog, bastard," the spear said hatefully. "I'm not your companion! I vow in heaven's name to one day strike you down for the injustice you've dealt me!"

"Goodness, is that sort of vengeful mindset really required of your religion?" I asked. "Where's the element of forgiveness?"

"Forgiveness is denied to you and all the night's fiends!" the spear said zealously.

Ugh. Crusaders. No matter the era, they never change.

"If that's the case, then as your master and creator, I forbid you from directly causing me harm, or of allowing harm to come to me through malicious inaction," I replied. "You will not conspire against me, deceive me, or intentionally allow me to be misled by others. If you attempt any of these things, I command you to feel intolerable pain until I alone allow it to relent. Do you understand?"

The spear said nothing in icy defiance.

"I asked if you understood," I said mildly.

"I'll never give into you . . . AAAAARGH!" shrieked the spear as I allowed her to experience a taste of the pain that I warned her would come.

"Do you *understand*?" I repeated. I was content to let her stew in her self-inflicted agony for as long as it took for her to get the message. Fortunately for us both, she was quick to concede.

"And you call yourself a civilized being," she muttered after a few minutes of quiet. The dog had fallen asleep and wouldn't awaken for quite some time. I now sat beside him, spear in hand to guard over him as he rested.

"Civilizations exist due to the willingness of the strong to exercise their power without remorse, Daughter," I told her. "Until I wielded it against you, my authority was merely conceptual. Now you know that it is a *reality*. I hope this will better inform your future decision-making."

"Daughter?" she scoffed.

"What else would I call a child of my blood?" I asked her.

"Anything but that. It's ridiculous, and saying it makes you sound pompous," she said tartly. "How old were you when I killed you?"

"I was approaching my eleventh century when *I slew you*," I replied.

"Ha! I was in service as a divine weapon for nearly two thousand years," she said with a vexatious note of triumph. "Clearly it is *I* who holds seniority over you, *Father*."

"I can see why you might think so," I replied. "But I'm also sure you probably spent the majority of those years in a glass case or hanging on a wall."

"I did no such—" she began to say before I cut her off and ordered her to sleep.

It was nice being able to have the last word whenever I wanted. I rarely wielded my authority in this manner, preferring to let my lesser kin have their voices heard, but . . . this spear was a *lot* to put up with. I was going to have to gradually adjust to her caustic personality. I knew she would eventually grow used to me and her new place in the order of things, but for now, she was going to be extremely adversarial and would have to be carefully managed.

To pass the time, I began studying my character sheet.

As a human, my stats were as followed:

[Strength: 17.]

Strength was my highest stat by far, which surprised me, considering how malnourished this body was. Kyler Evans must have had some minor level of natural athletic ability that would explain this. Don't get me wrong, in comparison to a Hunter, his might was severely lacking. But as an ordinary teenager without any extensive physical training, I found him impressive. Let's see . . . to properly calculate my current physical limit, it seemed I must multiply this stat by ten. That meant I could currently lift around one hundred seventy pounds. At my age, that could easily be improved with regular exercise and a good diet.

[Speed: 4.]

Again, another impressively average showing for this urchin. The formula for this one was the stat times two. Which meant that at top speed, Kyler could run at about eight miles per hour, which was the standard for a fit human male. What could Evans have accomplished if he'd been given proper guidance and an opportunity to excel?

[Reflex: 1.5.]

Ah, the first major hindrance. Reflex represented agility, coordination, and manual dexterity. The higher it was, the more easily you could control the fine movements of your body. It could be roughly calculated by dividing your speed by half. Two would have been another average number, but one point five clearly painted him as being clumsy and slow to react. Where had the remaining point five of his ability gone? Had he been previously injured or was he afflicted with some manner of physical disability?

[Constitution: 10.]

A means of calculating my body's health. It operated on a times two principle like speed, which meant my health points maxed out at a whopping . . . twenty?
Twenty health points?!
By the all-devouring darkness, Kyler Evans, just how weak could a boy possibly be? You couldn't even be said to be made of glass, could you? More like wet foam! Twenty health points? Really?
That meant that the beating I'd received during my interrogation hadn't even been that intense, had it? I'd probably passed out after a single slap.
For the first time since coming to this world, I felt genuine apprehension about my odds of survival. I simply *had* to get that number up as quickly as I could. My human form would be vital for disguising my vampiric nature. I couldn't let it remain this fragile! The notion was intolerable!

[Endurance: 0.5.]

This was the one that *really* made me angry.

Endurance, like strength, was the stat times ten, expressed as active minutes. That meant that the maximum amount of time Kyler Evans could currently endure in cardiovascular activity was a paltry *five minutes*.

Forgive me for this. I'm going to curse. I don't do it often, and only when I'm in the foulest of moods. Again, I apologize.

FIVE FUCKING MINUTES ARE YOU FUCKING KIDDING ME???!!! WHAT THE FUCK DOES THIS EVEN MEAN HOW CAN ANYONE GET THAT FUCKING GASSED SO QUICKLY?! DOESN'T ANYONE HAVE A SENSE OF URGENCY ANYMORE?! WHAT SORT OF SLUGGARD WERE YOU, KYLER EVANS?

There. It's out of my system. Thank you for bearing with me. I feel terribly embarrassed about my outburst and will strive to avoid having another one. No one should have to endure bad language.

Still, things were beginning to make sense. Now I understood why my performance had been so sluggish in the goblin's lair. It was true that I'd easily overwhelmed my opponents, but that was due entirely to experience. If I'd been a true novice with only my physical strength to rely on, I would have been butchered like a Sunday hen.

What manner of institute was Vandal Academy? How could Kyler Evans have been admitted, so lacking in ability? Even as a Porter, it made no sense. What good was a *Porter* who could barely move? There were surely far better options! It also made little sense as an act of nepotism. As talented as Patrick was, the school had been taking an enormous risk with the lives of any students whose team Evans had been assigned to. He was *that* unqualified.

This only confirmed my suspicion that Kyler Evans had been set up from the start. Even before the class trip, he'd been doomed. Like some manner of human sacrifice unwittingly idling away the days of the school year until the moment of his death, never suspecting what was to come.

His . . . no, *my* brother was involved with two other women, one of which had set Evans up to die. And his brother's lovers were *sisters*. Honestly, these people were as hedonistic as the court of a French king! In my younger days I might have enjoyed such a bold display of uninhibited depravity. But the passage of time had long since cooled my ardor. Now I could only shake my head at their behavior like the old man I was and wonder where their parents had gone wrong with them.

Permissive parenting probably produced perniciously perverse progeny.

Rare were the days when I encountered children more monstrous than my own. I sincerely hoped to never meet any of those people ever again. Not Patrick, nor Thalia, and especially not Anikka, who now seemed to be the most dangerous of the three. To hell with all of them.

So, obviously that was me "planting a flag," right? I really needed to reacquaint myself with certain standard storytelling tropes so that I could better avoid danger. One of my wives once mentioned to me the existence of an Evil Overlord's checklist. I wished I'd read it just once before I died.

I spent the rest of the night thinking bleak thoughts as I pondered the days to come.

CHAPTER ELEVEN

Two nights later, after my newest acquisition finished recovering from his transformation, our newly forged team was fully in business. The experience points came pouring in, even as the heads of our unfortunate prey were sent flying.

I had a lot of fun. I hadn't enjoyed myself this much in quite some time.

The creatures we hunted this evening were an infamous goblin variant known as Redcaps. They were given that name because of their notorious habit of slitting the throats of their dying victims and dipping the tiny bowler caps donned on their bulbous heads in the fountaining blood, dyeing them a vibrant red.

Just how repulsive could a lesser life-form be?

Most people might think that a vampire would be unconcerned about such blatantly unhygienic behavior, but in this regard, they'd be completely wrong. Did I occasionally get other people's blood on my clothing during a violent confrontation or feeding? Sure. It happened. Such was life. But do you know what I always did afterwards? I took a shower and changed my clothing! I didn't make nasty little keepsakes that would attract buzzing parasites and spread blood-borne pathogens because I'm not gross and I believe in the value of cleanliness.

Trust me, I'm a *big* advocate of soap. Soap is dope as far as I'm concerned. If you could have seen what the world was like before we had the option to enjoy things like a nice lavender rinse, I'm certain you'd be quick to agree.

From above, a Redcap came flying down, yelling a ferocious battle cry as it swung its jagged butcher's blade at my head, only to be caught in midair by the tip of my spear as I impaled it. Its eyes bulged with pain as he was next flung down and dispatched with a crunchy stomp to the head that splattered the contents of its skull across the cold earth.

Bits of the creature also splashed across my face, which I cheerfully wiped away as I sought another target. What a joyous exercise this was! How exhilarating to hunt in the name of pleasure and profit, something I hadn't had cause to do in ages.

I hadn't realized how much I'd missed going forth into the world and staining my hands with the blood of my foes. This was how life should be lived! Adventuring, conquering, *slaughtering*. Before my death I hadn't left my castle in nearly seventy years. What had I been doing all that time?

Sitting and brooding and lamenting past mistakes.

Being out here was so much better!

It felt like a *renewal*.

I wouldn't have known so much about the nature of these Redcaps if I hadn't begun making a study of the Gore Grimoire that had been gifted to me by the Alpha Administrator. In its sprawling pages I discovered so much useful information about the world I now inhabited, and the creatures and cultures I shared it with. The grimoire was far more than a repository of stolen powers. It was the key to my potential ascendency, should I decide to pursue that path later.

The Alpha Administrator had proven to be a very good friend.

At first, I'd been disappointed that Alpha, as I'll now call her for brevity's sake, had yet to reach out to me even though she promised we would speak again after I escaped the goblin's lair. I feared she was either too busy to keep her word, or she'd told a fast lie to get rid of me, as though I were an unsatisfied customer who'd been harassing a call center operator.

It wasn't until I materialized the grimoire into my hands out of sheer boredom and gave it a good read that I realized how much aid she'd already provided. The Gore Grimoire was a tome that provided answers to any question I could even think of asking. It was a collection of spells, a history book, a player's guide, and a monster manual all in one package. To get the answers I sought, all I had to do was make an offering of blood, which was hardly an inconvenience when you were a vampire.

My question for tonight had been, "What is an appropriate enemy for me to fight that is nearest to my location?"

The answer had been Redcaps. And so, I'd sought them out.

My new canine companion growled ferociously as he nipped at the heel of another Redcap with his razor-sharp teeth and successfully severed the hamstring of the monster's right leg, causing it to fall hard on its face with a pitched squeal of anguish. When it turned to slash helplessly at the dog in an attempt at pointless reprisal, I stepped forward with my spear at the ready and plunged its tip through the back of his neck, killing him instantly.

The dog wagged his tail happily at the Redcap's body before stepping over it to circle around me and demand a pat on the head. I granted his wish and even gave his pointed ears a gentle scratch as I gave our work an appreciative whistle.

"That's number eleven so far, Providence," I told him as he stood on his hind legs to demand a pat from me. "Just one more and we'll be Level Five. Won't that be nice? Yes, it will be. Yes, it *will* be!"

"Why don't you just call him *Lucky*?" asked the spear for what felt like the two hundredth time. "You're supposed to be an uneducated rube barely ranked above serfdom. Why would an irrelevant commoner teeming with rude ignorance name his dog *Providence*? Where would he even hear that word?"

"Because our chance encounter with this wonderful beast was an act of providence itself, thus Providence shall be his name," I replied. "And the background history of my body's former owner is unimportant. Evans was Evans and Stragos is Stragos."

"Naming a dog Providence is pompous and out of touch. For his own sake and in deference to his class, I'm calling him Lucky," the spear said stubbornly.

"Must I order you to use his correct name?" I asked with an exasperation that was only slightly exaggerated.

"You could if you wanted to prove your tyranny," the spear sniffed.

"Why would a spear care about a dog's social class?" I asked.

"A spear is the weapon of the laborer!" the spear exclaimed proudly. "Let some arrogant knightly nobles wield their precious swords that've been in their families for a thousand generations or whatever. Who cares? Spearmen were the backbone of any true fighting force! Conscripted peasants dragged from their homes and given a pointy stick to prosecute the rights of their monarch against foreign scum and traitorous scum and prayerful scum who weren't doing it the right way or were doing it for the wrong gods. My eternal heart beats in solidarity with the humble people of the farm and field!"

"You sound remarkably Marxist for a tool of divinity," I observed. "How's that work?"

"What's a Marxist?" the spear asked curiously.

"Typically? Someone too trusting in the better angels of their fellow men to make their vision a reality."

"What's wrong with trusting in angels?" she asked, puzzled.

"I think you just disqualified yourself from the glorious revolution with that one sentence," I said with slight smirk. "Although I am curious to know what a blessed spear would know of life in the farm and field."

"Well, I didn't start out this way in life, did I?" she said. "I spent the first fourteen years of my life on the family farm, raising cows and swine. A hard life to be sure but one I'm glad to have lived. Another few years and I would have eventually had a husband and children of my own. But the will of heaven had a different fate in store for me."

"What made you so different?" I wondered. "What set you apart so much that your church came to literally forge you into a weapon of holy wrath?"

"I don't see why I have to discuss that with you," the spear said sharply. "Set your pain upon me if you must, but I prefer not to betray the mysteries of my faith."

"Be at peace," I said to her with an offhand wave. "I was just curious about your past circumstances. Keep any secrets that you wish if they won't negatively affect me. There's no need to leap into martyrdom."

"I would be proud to suffer for my faith," she said stiffly. "There is no greater honor than to sacrifice yourself for the goddess."

"How convenient for your goddess," I replied.

So, the soul that existed in the spear had a farming background, eh? How unpleasant. Animal husbandry was a career path I always found unsettling. I understood the necessity of creating a stable food supply for the maintenance of civilization, but the fate of the livestock made me feel sad. Cows adored their human owners. They *loved* them. But that love would inevitably be rewarded with a rent throat and a body drained of blood.

Mass agriculture and certain vampiric practices had entirely too much overlap.

To my left I saw another Redcap staring hatefully at me before turning his back and scrambling away at an impressive speed. Providence growled and was about to give chase before I stopped him.

"What are you doing?" the spear asked. "If you let it escape it'll warn its allies. Let Lucky bring it down."

"His name is *Providence*," I corrected her. "And we're not letting the creature escape. We're allowing it to lead us to its lair. More blood, more experience points, more amusement to be had."

I knelt beside the dog to rub his head affectionately before bidding him to track the fleeing monster. "Besides," I added, "it's important to teach you both the necessity of delayed gratification. It's impossible to hold the advantage in every situation. Killing an opponent that we can find a use for is the same as denying ourselves future success."

"I'm a warrior of considerable experience, you pretentious boy," the spear said bitterly. "I'm hardly in need of your coaching."

"You *were* a weapon of war fought in open plains under the light of day," I informed her disdainfully. "Those options are now denied to you. It's time you cast aside such regulated gentility and embrace your shadowed nature. We are monsters who strike cruelly from the dark with never a thought reserved for fairness or mercy. In your new existence, honor is ornamentation. A beast's only concern is survival and proliferation."

"I refuse," she said forcefully.

"You are overruled," I replied.

The Stealth skill that I'd taken from the guard proved its value as we made our way to the kobold's lair. It was an active magical skill that allowed me to hide my presence from others, even if I was standing in front of them. Thanks to the familiar's link I now shared with Lucky—I meant *Providence*—I was able to extend the cloak to him as well.

The Gore Grimoire's ability to steal talents from other Hunters and monsters would prove to be invaluable over time. It was a shame that it came with such strict limitations. The grimoire could only store a total of twenty skills and would never allow me to slot more than four stolen abilities at once for use. And that was further restricted by limiting those abilities to two active skills and two passive ones.

That meant I not only had to be selective with which abilities to use but that I also would eventually need to discard older powers if I came across a new one I desired.

While that was disappointing to learn, I understood that this was a necessity for reasons of balance. If I could just take however many abilities I wanted and use them whenever I wished, I'd quickly become unstoppable. As a Vampire Lord, I was meant to gain most of my power by investing in my skill tree once it was unlocked at Level Ten. The skills I acquired by using my grimoire were just a bonus. The honey in the tea.

Be that as it may, I didn't see myself discarding my two current skills anytime soon. Stealth had already proven its brilliance by allowing me to easily infiltrate this Redcap nest. But the skill I'd taken from the goblin chieftain, Titanic Strength, was what allowed me to dominate the encounters that followed.

While Stealth was an active skill that had to be focused on to activate, Titanic Strength was a passive one that multiplied my physical strength by two. With passive skills, you only had to set them and forget them to reap their benefits. In my human form, it would have given me the power to lift about three hundred forty pounds. Not bad for a malnourished teenager.

But my vampiric form was *considerably* stronger. A young vampire could lift a ton without straining themselves. With Titanic Strength doubling my might, I could now comfortably throw around up to four thousand pounds. A vampire would normally have to be at least two hundred years old to gain that level of strength.

All this to say that when I struck at the Redcaps from behind with even a light blow, the wounds they received were grievous. And when I slapped one with full force out of a desire to experiment, his head exploded as though an overly ripe melon had been struck with a war hammer.

Oh, dearest Gore Grimoire. Imperfect as you are, I shall always adore thee!

There in the lair of the Redcaps, with spear in hand and my hound by my side, we unleashed such splendorous ruin upon the hapless fools that I actually received a notification for it, informing me that I had completed an achievement.

[Congratulations!] said the status screen.
[You have received the following achievement: Redcap/REDRUM!]
[You have earned the title Butcher of Gobkind. Goblins and goblin variants will automatically feel hostility towards you.]

"No," I said immediately. "No, not satisfactory at all."

[. . . I'm sorry?]

"You should be," I said.

[May I ask what you find unsatisfactory about your recent achievement?]

"Only that it makes no sense and is completely illogical," I replied.

"What are you doing?" my spear asked in alarm. "That's a celestial messenger! You're supposed to graciously accept the news he delivers on behalf of the system, not . . . not *quarrel* with him!"

"I'm not quarreling with him, I'm offering an opinion," I said to her. "And to better answer your question, status screen, take a look around this foul den. What do you see?"

[Dead and dying Redcaps.] the screen said reluctantly.

"Exactly," I agreed. "Exactly! This is an abattoir. A grinder. Cast your eyes upon this pitiful rabble and know that from the dark, we have dealt them a *horror*. There's more of them beneath my boot than inside their bodies. Do you *see*?"

[. . . Yes.] the status screen said reluctantly.

One wounded Redcap lay helpless nearby. To help illustrate my point, I seized the wretch by its thin neck and held it aloft, while it kicked helplessly and choked.

"Look into its eyes, messenger. *That* is mortal terror. That is the fear of being swept westward presently tormenting its mind. If I've become a *Butcher of Gobkind*, then is *hostility* truly the emotion my presence should evoke in this lesser thing? See how he *writhes*? That is not resentment! *The hand of Phobos has seized his heart!*"

[I understand.]

"DO YOU?" I shouted as the goblin sputtered a final time before dying from lack of air.

"Kyler," the spear said uncertainly. Providence barked suddenly and pawed at my leg.

[Corrections will be made. You have made your point.]

I blinked suddenly and looked around my surroundings while wondering where my mind had gone.

"I'm sorry, what?" I asked sheepishly as I tossed the dead Redcap aside.

[Your title has been edited.]
[You have received the following achievement: Redcap/REDRUM!]
[You have earned the title: Butcher of Gobkind. Goblins and goblin variants will automatically feel the utmost terror in your presence.]

"Ah," I said after mentally processing that. "Okay. Well, good. I'm always happy to see reason triumph when prevailed upon. Thank you for making use of your good sense."

[Uh. Always happy to be of service.]

"Yes." I nodded.

"What the *hell* is happening here?!" the spear asked trepidatiously.

CHAPTER TWELVE

A nd you don't believe there was *anything* strange about your recent behavior?" the spear asked me later, her voice heavy with suspicion as we finished surveying the rest of the Redcap lair.

"Honestly, no," I said as I thrust her into the throat of a Redcap that had been clever enough to hide behind a wooden pillar but too excited to quiet its heavy breathing. From behind us, a sudden squeal of pain accompanied by excited barking informed me that the dog had found and dispatched another one.

"He's so good at this." I smiled. "Maybe I'll let him have one as a snack."

"You'd feed him the profane flesh of a monster?" the spear asked with a slight vibration that I interpreted as a shiver.

"I don't see why not," I replied. "They aren't human, they're barely self-aware, and to a man they're irredeemably hostile. Also, I find the taste of their blood foul. If our friend can derive pleasure from the consumption of such miserable beings, then it would be cruel to let them rot."

With that said, I transitioned into my Porter Class and stored my latest kill away. While doing so, I made a pleasant discovery. "Look at that!" I said with some excitement. I pointed to where the Redcap body had once been.

"Yes, yes, your Porter ability makes it very convenient for you to remove any incriminating evidence, what's your point?" asked the spear impatiently.

"Don't take the fun out of this for me, daughter," I said crossly. "Haven't you noticed? I didn't just store the body away; I stored the blood pouring from his wound as well! Look at the floor. It's as clean as though it were mopped with bleach-soaked water."

I assumed the spear gave the floor a careful examination. It was difficult to tell because it lacked a head to follow, but I was fairly certain it still gave the area a once-over because a few moments later, it let out an impressed whistle and said,

"That actually *is* interesting. Apparently, your ability to store things isn't limited to weapons, armor, and consumables."

"That would seem to be the case," I agreed. "Which makes me wonder . . ."

I then closed my eyes and focused on myself. Although I'd only recently acquired the clothing I was currently wearing, two days of sleeping in a grave, two nights of sleeping outdoors, and this evening's amusing Redcap slaughter hadn't done a lot to keep my attire presentable. Put bluntly, I was filthy. I also didn't smell very pleasant. But without easy access to water, there was nothing I could do about that. And even if there was, my clothing would still be stained with dirt and blood.

Or *would* it?

Here in my human form, with my Porter Class equipped, I focused on my body, envisioning every inch of it, including the clothes I wore and the spear I held . . . and then I *stored* everything that was on them. Every spec of dirt and mud, every particle of spilled blood, every odor producing bacteria or worse. All of it, I pulled away from me and sent away to storage.

When I opened my eyes, my clothes and boots were pristine. As spotless as the moment I'd received them.

"Nice trick," the now-gleaming spear said with grudging appreciation.

"Thank you," I said with a slight bow. "I'm quite pleased myself."

Next, I called the dog over and gave him the same treatment. He blinked in canine confusion as the filth that had once matted his fur disappeared in an instant, making him look as though he'd just been collected from a pet salon. Instead of showing appreciation, though, he instead cocked his head and stared at me in bewilderment.

"Oh, don't be like that. Trust me, it's a vast improvement," I assured him as I scratched beneath his chin. "I can't have my familiar following behind me while trailing a cloud of dust. They'd be calling you Pig-Pen instead of Providence."

"Was that a joke? I don't get it," said the spear.

"Pig-Pen was one of Charlie Brown's associates. He was so filthy that he existed in a perpetual cloud of dust and dirt," I informed her.

"I still don't get it. Who is Charlie Brown?"

"He was a creation of the famed cartoonist Charles M. Schulz. He's a beloved icon to millions of children everywhere," I said.

"Is this something old? Are you showing how out of date you are with your references, you silly old monster?" the spear taunted.

"No," I said with some irritation. "I was just making a reference to something I think people enjoy."

"In what way?" the spear scoffed. "Name one reason a modern person would give a damn about this silly cartoon strip. It's as far from the public's awareness as the Katzenjammer kids."

"I think you may be exaggerating," I said. "Like all good stories, the works of Schulz contain a timeless appeal."

"Such as?" asked the spear.

"He was notable for using his work to speak to children about issues involving depression and anxiety," I said.

"Is that really what children wanted to read about in their Sunday comics?" the spear asked sarcastically. "Anxiety and depression? Sounds like a fun time, indeed."

"Kids have more depth than you give them credit for," I replied.

"What's Lucky doing right now?" the spear asked.

"We're not calling him that! His name is *Providence*!" I shouted.

"Sorry, no. That name is ridiculous," the spear said.

"Why are you so fixated on that name?" I asked, trying to steer the conversation away from this irritating topic.

"I like what I like," the spear said. "Anything's better than Providence."

"Well, I don't want to call him that, and since I'm the one in charge, I feel I should have the final say," I said.

"No, I want to name him Lucky."

"I'm three seconds away from commanding you to be silent for all eternity," I warned her. "I'm not even joking."

"So, what you're really saying is, since you can't convince me to agree with you, you'll silence my voice instead?" asked the spear. "Really now, *father*. Kind of sounds like a petulant move."

"I'm not petulant!" I seethed.

"Then prove it!" said the spear. "Let's ask the dog which name he prefers. He might not be able to speak, but he can decide for himself what he likes. He'll pick his own name, and the loser must abide by it. Deal?"

"You think I fear your challenge, girl?" I sneered. "BRING IT. Just don't forget who walked away victorious the last time you came at me."

"You blew yourself up! We *both* died!" she shouted.

"But you admit you died because of me?" I asked with a deliberately condescending smirk. "Which means that I won?"

"Lucky, get over here!" the spear shouted to him. "Hurry up and side with me so we can deflate this evil prick's ego!"

The dog cocked his head and stared at the spear with a curious expression before trotting over. I knelt before him and gave him a pat as we each took turns explaining what we wanted to name him.

I was concise and to the point. "Providence hints at a divine destiny. Of all the savage beasts that prowl these untamed lands, you alone have proven worthy to be my familiar. Proudly accept the name I've bestowed upon you and prove to our arrogant companion how mistaken she is."

The dog stared at me blankly.

"C'mere, Lucky. Lucky come here! *Who's my good little boy?* C'mere, Lucky!" said the spear.

The dog whined and rolled over, exposing his belly.

"*No,*" I growled.

"Toooold you!" taunted the spear.

"RIDICULOUS!" I yelled and hurled the spear away in a fit of anger and disappointment. I couldn't believe it! The dog was *my* familiar. My preferences should have been his own. How could he go against me? I hated it when my wishes went unfulfilled!

As I stood there stewing in the unfairness of it all, the dog came trotting towards me, tail wagging happily as he dropped the spear beside me and sat patiently, waiting for me to throw it again.

"No, please don't," the spear said.

"Fetch, boy," I said with a small smile as I threw the spear again.

"No, don't do that, ARGHHHHH!" the spear said as she flew away.

A few moments later, the dog returned her to me and barked excitedly, wanting to go again.

"Well, well, well," I said. "Looks like we've got a game going on, doesn't it?"

"Please stop throwing me," the spear begged.

"I don't know if I can do that. It appears *Lucky* is really enjoying it. Aren't you, *Lucky*?" I asked him.

In reply, he cheerfully barked.

"What sort of master would I be to deny a good boy his sport?" I asked her.

"You are a petty, *petty*, little man," the spear said accusingly.

"Pettiness is a delight, I won't deny it," I said without shame.

"Be better than your small urges!" she pleaded.

"If that were possible, how could I have fallen into vampirism?" I asked.

"Providence! The dog's name shall be Providence!" she shouted desperately as I prepared to throw her once more.

"It's fine, you were right, that name really is too stuffy for a dog. Something more playful would better suit him," I said as I sent her flying.

"*Baaaaastard!*" she shouted miserably as she streaked away.

"Go fetch, Schulz!" I ordered him.

Schulz darted forth fast as lightning and quickly returned with the spear in hand. Er, mouth.

He really was a *very* good boy.

"I hate you I hate you I hate you," the spear mumbled as I received her.

"I'm sure I'll grow on you in time," I said. "But now that I think about it, perhaps it's time we came up with a name for you as well. I can't very well keep referring to you as *spear*, can I?"

"I am the Spear of Dawn. A weapon of divine reprisal! Whatever false name you assign me won't divert me from my holy purpose."

"Okay, so, Tarkington Van Bueler, it is," I decided.

"Excuse me?"

"Poppy Van Cleese?"

"You're making those up terrible names up, you prick."

"Brutus Buffinton Buffordson!"

"Is this the sort of thing you did to pass the time when you were holed up in that stupid castle?" she asked me.

"Among other equally silly things," I confessed. "Now that I think about it, since you're a spear, you should have a name that invokes your pointy nature. Hmm, now what should that be?"

"You are *such* an immature little—"

"How about Lady Thrustington Lungewell?" I asked.

"MY NAME IS RACHEL!" the spear shouted furiously.

"Oh, Rachel. That's a pretty name," I said. "So nice to meet you."

Rachel said nothing in reply. I think she was upset with me.

CHAPTER THIRTEEN

My goal for the next day was to discover where the Redcaps had been raiding their supplies. I'd realized last night after cleaning out the rest of the lair that there had to be a settlement nearby to explain the barrels of water and beer as well as the salted food I'd discovered in the center of their hideout.

Preparing foodstuffs and storing potable water wasn't an activity that such lowly creatures were known for. But stealing from those who could sounded exactly right. So, after indulging in a deep slumber that went well past noon, I set off with Schulz and Rachel in tow to find out who else shared these wilds with me.

The heat of the afternoon sun on my skin felt glorious. I was so distracted by the pleasure of it that I wanted nothing more than to park myself on a field of soft grass and bask in its radiance like a house cat beneath an open window. How could humans find such continual misery in their lives? Why were they so quarrelsome towards each other in the face of such contentment?

Didn't they realize they could eat and sleep whenever they wanted? They could pass their lives in joy and peace and never know a moment's worry ever again. Why did they prefer squandering their short lives in pursuit of something as arbitrary as meaning? Why bother with any of that when merely existing was purpose enough?

Honestly, they had such a good thing going. Why did they love complicating it so much?

Before long, I stumbled across the settlement the Redcaps had been stealing from. It wasn't nearly as well-defended as the gates of Gardenia. It was a small town warded by large wooden walls and a guarded gate that closed it off from the surrounding wilderness. As I neared the main entryway, two strong-looking men armored in plate challenged my approach.

"Halt and identify yourself," one of them said. Like me, he carried a spear, but he also wore a sword at his hip. The handle of it was well-worn, suggesting it had seen much use during his tenure as a guard. That wouldn't be surprising, considering how many monsters dwelt in these parts. He probably had to kill something every other day.

"Just a wandering Hunter seeking trade," I said humbly. "I came across a nest of Redcaps the other day and dealt with them. Knowing how troublesome they are, I thought I'd see if anyone had placed a bounty on them."

"You're a *wanderer*, you say?" the guard asked doubtfully. "Where's your identification?"

"You mean those pictures with serial numbers and the like?" I asked him, feigning ignorance of his request. "Wouldn't know where to get one. I'm not fancy like them city folks."

The guards had a nice laugh between themselves before my questioner continued. "Well, kid, around these parts you aren't allowed to call yourself a Hunter if you're not registered. These aren't the middle-states. We do things properly in the Eastern Kingdoms."

"Proper's good. I can do proper," I said earnestly. "Where do I sign up?"

"You been schooled?" the guard asked. "What's your education?"

"What, you mean like did I go to Vandal Academy?"

The guards laughed again. "No, no, that's for the elites. No blue blood's son is going to show up at the Narrows, looking to barter a few goblin ears."

"Hey, now. Vandal ain't that stuffy," said the other guard. "Nicky Pankratz's boy made his way there. Earned himself a probationary D-rank. And don't forget dear Cassie at the trading post."

"Kids like those are one in a million," the senior guard scoffed. "The rest are castoffs and wanderers like this forest rat. Son, we don't know you from Adam, and we can't take things on trust. Don't think poorly of me but be on your way."

"Why would I think poorly of you?" I asked. "Guarding a settlement is honorable work. In times such as these, it's better to be a wary man than a foolish one."

"I'm glad you understand," the guard nodded. "Now be off with you."

I waved and turned my heel on them.

Naturally, I came back a few minutes later under my cloak of stealth and slipped past them when they opened the gate to admit a few wagoners. No offense to those brave and capable souls, but I'm not the sort to be thwarted by mere watchmen. If I was, I'd never have any interesting stories to tell.

The town beyond the gates was an interesting sight to see. Rebuilt Americana, reclaimed from whatever disasters had wracked this world before the coming of their system. I wonder what drove these hearty civilians to flee the safety of Gardenia's walls to eke out a living in this dangerous environment. Maybe they were braver. Maybe they were less civilized. Maybe they just didn't want to let the monsters win.

Whatever the reason, I was impressed by their resilience.

Now, where could I go to sell a few Redcap ears?

"Are you a Hunter?" the old man asked suspiciously.

I hadn't been in town for more than ten minutes when a screen suddenly appeared before my eyes and informed me that a World Quest was now being offered.

[Red (with blood) Crab.
D-rank.
From: Tradesman Calford (non-ascended).

*I've had it up to here with all these damn monster crustaceans lurking around my pond like they own it! These **Koler Crabs** are twice the size of a grown man and those claws of theirs will snip an arm off faster than you can blink! I ain't got much in the way of money, but to the one who gets rid of them, I'll offer a year's worth of free meals! That's nothing to sneeze at! Please help me out!*

Request: Slay x12 Koler Crabs at Tradesman Calford's pond.
Bonus: Discover where they originate from.
Rewards: One free meal a day for a year. +2,200 EXP. +400 Narrows Reputation.]

Interesting. I didn't know ordinary people could put out requests for assistance directly through the system. It seemed that even those who couldn't ascend had limited access to its services.

Hmm. One free meal a day for a year, eh? Now *that* was a tempting offer.

"I am," I replied to the old fellow. "I came in response to your system-borne request, didn't I?"

"I hope that's true," he said. "If you've truly come to help, then I'm glad you came. But the reward is more meager than you're probably accustomed to, Hunter . . .?"

"*Stragos,*" I said. "Just call me Stragos. And to the contrary, sir, I believe this will pay me splendidly in experience."

"I don't think it'll give you a lot of experience points either," he said.

Wow, what an honest man.

"No, I meant experience as in the novel enjoyment of doing something I haven't tried before," I said. "I love doing new things."

"You just want to do this . . . for fun?" he asked with some minor confusion.

"Of course," I said chirpily. "I'm new around here and I treasure opportunities to expand my horizons. To fill my empty cup with the heady brew of experience is nearly payment enough for my services."

"Really? Well in that case, maybe we can—"

"Uh, but I will still be requiring material compensation, of course," I said quickly. "Education nourishes the mind, but food is what keeps us alive, yes?"

"Hmph," he said with some disappointment. "Well, that's the truth of things, I guess. Let me get you caught up on what's been happening here."

"What's to know? Your rights as a landowner are being impugned upon by impertinent shellfish. Have no fear, I'll have the matter sorted in no time," I said to him.

"Oh, but Hunter Stragos, I'm afraid the situation is a little more complicated than the request would have you believe," the old man said nervously.

"Oh? Pray tell," I said.

"Well, the thing is . . . I put that request out a year ago and no one's seen fit to answer it in all this time," he said fretfully. "And it seems that Koler Crabs are *fast* breeders. The scale of the situation is a little above its ranking . . ."

"In that case, we'll have to negotiate," I said grimly.

"What more can I possibly offer you?" he asked desperately.

"Free meals for life seems about right to me," I said mildly.

He blinked rapidly and stared at me in surprise.

"That's it?" he asked.

"Yup," I said.

"You'd risk your only life for so little?" he asked with widened eyes.

"I like to eat," I replied with absolute honesty.

"Son, are you all right in the head?"

"I'm just living life the best way I know," I said with a friendly smile. I then held forth my hand. "We got a deal?"

The old man gave a hearty guffaw and held out a hand of his own, and we shook on it. "Son, I think we do!"

[Tradesman Calford likes your attitude.]
[You've gained +50 Narrows rep.]

It took about twenty minutes of further walking before I found a large country house on the outskirts of town that had been built in front of a large outdoor body of water. Calford's directions had been precise and easy to follow. I came around to the back of the building and tapped on a glass door on the patio.

As expected, a woman soon answered. A raven-haired beauty in a white sundress who gave me a dazzling smile and invited me inside.

"You're Hunter . . . Stragos?" she asked with a charming lilt to her voice that quickly had my ears buzzing. Goodness, if I had been a younger man, a woman of this caliber would have been a problem for me.

"I am indeed," I said, greeting her with a smile of my own. We were now inside a large kitchen where she bid me to sit on a stool at the counter. "Did Mr. Calford call to inform you I'm here to take care of your seafood infestation?"

"He did. But all by yourself?" she asked with a raised eyebrow.

"I brought my dog too," I said.

"Do you have some kind of beast mastery Class? Are you a ranger, perhaps?" she asked.

"No, but I'm still an apex predator," I said humbly. "I'm just waiting for night-fall, when they'll be easier to deal with."

"You're definitely not lacking for confidence," she commented.

"The only thing I'm lacking right now is a name to call you," I said. "Miss?"

The woman grinned and showed me the ring on her finger. "*Mrs.*, actually. Jamie Wells-Calford. So pleased to meet you, Mr. Stragos."

"Goodness, aren't you a little young for him?" I asked with no small amount of surprise.

In response, she guffawed and swiped her hand lightly through my hair. "That's my father-in-law, silly. I'm married to his oldest son, Kurt. He's currently away in military service."

"You could do better," I said without delay.

"Cheeky. But sadly, for you, I dearly love the man I'm with."

"Curse you, Kurt Calford and your superior timing," I lamented.

"Luck is half of the game," Jamie said with a knowing look.

"It always is," I replied. "You know, I'd comment further on your beauty, but words would be redundant."

"If they weren't, what would you say?" she asked me.

"For starters? Are you doing anything later?"

"I'm sorry sweetie, but you're a little too fresh off the shelf to be that forward with your elders," she said. "I have a daughter around your age." Her tone sounded regretful, but her eyes were bright with cheerful amusement.

"If I'm a boy, it's in appearance alone. I assure you, I have a very old soul," I replied.

"Do you mean to say you're an educated man?" she asked.

"Very much so," I said with all due humility.

"And do you intend to share that knowledge with me?" she wondered.

"*That* will depend on your flexibility."

"With my schedule?" she asked.

"No," I said.

"Oh, Lord, aren't you a bad one?" she giggled.

"I think you're catching on," I said with considerable satisfaction as I took a sip from the cup she offered me. "This is very good by the way. Preparing a good cup of tea takes nimble fingers."

"My dexterity is a wonder to behold," she bragged proudly.

"You'll have to show me in person," I suggested.

"I'd better warn my girl about you when she gets back," the woman laughed. "Bold young men are their own kind of danger."

"No need for that," I assured her. "Girls don't interest me. *Women* do."

"And what sort of women do you prefer?" she asked as she leaned a little closer.

"Depends on the dessert they provide with the meal," I said with a wink.

"And what's your favorite kind, I wonder?" she asked.

"Cake."

"You like cake?"

"I *love* cake."

"Got a particular flavor in mind?"

I closed my eyes and breathed in the varied scents of the room. "Something with cherries would be good. Double layered. Sweet on top, *sweeter* on the inside."

"The only thing around here with cherries in it is my lip gloss," she said.

"Wow, whatever are the odds?"

"Sorry I couldn't help you out," she said wryly.

"That doesn't mean you have nothing to offer," I countered.

"How did you ever get this full of yourself?" she laughed.

"Come with me and I'll show you."

"Can't do it, I'm happily wedded," she sighed.

"We all make mistakes," I said. "Every day is a new beginning."

"I definitely need to warn my daughter," she said decisively to herself with a firm nod. "Want a sandwich?"

"I'd *love* a sandwich," I said.

"Jamie, who're you talking to in there?" an imperious sounding old woman said as she marched into the kitchen. "Is this him? Hurry up and get him out to the pond. I wish you wouldn't drag your feet so much."

"Carol, he's waiting until night to take care of it," Jamie said as she hurriedly began preparing my meal. The harassed look on her face caught me off guard. Not a trace of the friendliness that had been there earlier remained.

The atmosphere of the kitchen had changed perceptibly. Before, there had been a languid yet welcoming energy. A relaxed, homey vibe. The kind of pleasant feeling you got from a restful, lazy day.

But as soon as the older woman entered, an unpleasant sensation quickly choked that feeling away. Carol must have been one of those unfortunate souls who, by sheer dint of her awful personality, could kill the mood of wherever she set foot. People like her could suffocate any shared space. They'd be deadly if they could be weaponized.

"The fault is entirely my own," I said apologetically to the old woman. "I use a specific strategy for dealing with infestations of monsters and it works best at night.

Your daughter-in-law has been gracious enough to indulge me in conversation while I await sunset."

"She's an idling layabout," Carol said snippily. "You must be one as well. I warned my son she was too pretty for him. He married her anyway. Pretty girls like to think they shouldn't have to work for a living, and this one's no different. Getting her to perform any kind of useful task is a chore in and of itself."

"Carol, I work hard enough in my tavern," Jamie said with forced patience. "I also make more than enough to cover all the bills around here. I could have even offered a reward in gold for this Hunter's services if you weren't too proud to accept my coin."

"What you do isn't *real* work," Carol sniffed. "Nor a wife's duty. Staying out all hours of the night in service to *other* men. You should consider how that looks for my boy, if you're even capable of that sort of reflection."

"I work alongside plenty of women as well," Jamie said with a roll of her eyes. "I assure you I'm on my feet all day and hardly my back."

"Backtalking *slut*," Carol said venomously. As soon as the words were past her lips, she and Jamie began glaring daggers at each other.

Extended families can be hell. Millions of people have surely suffered from the generational clashes that can arise when a domineering older traditionalist tries to set herself over a more liberal-minded replacement, in a deadly struggle for control of the household. I felt glad to have never personally known such strife in my own home. It's a very easy thing for a vampire to wait out the lifespans of a spouse's family. I've succeeded at it three times. It's no bother at all to spend eighty years in hiding if it means never having to meet your wife's parents.

"Is Jamie really someone you should be judging?" I asked Carol a few moments later. "It was your son she married, not you. Why should your opinion on anything matter?"

"Excuse me?" Carol said angrily. "Boy, who the hell do you think you are?"

"A student of repeating patterns," I said as I sipped more tea. "One who also likes reading about interesting psychological conditions. Have you ever heard of emotional incest? That's where someone experiences sexual jealousy towards the spouse of one of their adult children."

"Where I *what*?" she gasped.

"I wasn't speaking of you. But it's interesting that that's where your mind automatically went," I said. "But seriously, your bile is uncalled for. Such an acrimonious attitude towards your son's wife makes you look like quite a horrid person."

"H-how dare you say such horrible things!" she choked out.

"Whose fault is greater? Mine for making a mild observation or yours for airing your dirty laundry in front of a stranger?" I asked. "I can't stand vexatious people, Carol. And since the particulars of my contract with your husband have nothing to do with *you*, I recommend you go back to your den and allow me to enjoy my meal in peace."

Jamie burst into appreciative laughter at my words. In fact, she laughed so hard that she began coughing, which necessitated pouring herself a glass of water, leaving her back turned to me and the old woman.

"How dare you speak to me in that manner! This is MY HOME—" Carol began to say in her increasingly wearisome manner. I was already tired of hearing her voice and I possessed enough patience to watch a stone erode into sand. This sort of attitude was what developed when someone lived too long without being challenged. I decided it was time to bring her back down to Earth.

Y'know, for *her* sake. Before she met someone less willing to forgive and forget.

So, before Carol could continue her nattering and spoil my mood any further, I leaned in very closely and whispered, "Leave right now or I'll return while you're sleeping *and eat you alive.*"

I then briefly shifted into my undead form and gave her a very toothy smile. If you've ever been grinned at by a shark that could unhinge its jaws to bite *more of you*, then you'll understand the immediate effect I had on her.

I think she got my point.

My pointed teeth, anyway.

[You have successfully intimidated Carol Calford.]
[Carol is terrified of your true vampiric visage.]
[Carol fails a willpower check. She won't tell anyone what she saw today.]

With a stricken look on her face, Carol very quickly made her way out of the room, leaving me to spend a few enjoyable hours shooting the breeze with Jamie, who for a time became a dear friend of mine. When I mentioned my difficulty producing identification for the town watch, she promised to help me out later by using her connections. "I know a few people." She grinned.

Goodness, how lucky could one guy be?

It was completely my loss that Jamie sincerely loved her husband. Not only was she temptation incarnate, but the sandwiches she made were out of this world.

When the sun finally went down, I thanked her for the pleasant time we shared. Then with my spear in hand and Schulz by my side, I set forth to hunt some Koler Crabs.

CHAPTER FOURTEEN

Dealing with the Koler Crabs turned out to be more labor intensive than I anticipated.

The first issue was that there were *so many more of them* than Tradesman Calford had suggested. Seventy-five of them, in fact. They'd completely overrun the pond. How could they be there in such numbers? Why hadn't they yet expanded their territory? There were more than enough of them to do it.

How had the Calford family kept things quiet? This was a burgeoning emergency for sure. The town had to be alerted. Perhaps a dispatch should have been sent to Gardenia, where there would be Hunters strong enough to deal with this situation before it spiraled out of control.

Well, I supposed that was where I came in.

"I should have asked for more than free meals," I muttered to myself.

"Do you really think so?" snarked Rachel.

"I do," I said.

"Well, good for you," she replied.

Rachel had been in a sour mood ever since I'd met the lovely Jamie earlier in the day. I suspected she didn't care for our flirtatious banter. Which made sense, I supposed; Rachel had a deeply religious background and likely didn't approve of such interactions between the opposite sexes.

I looked forward to the night when she'd wake and realize that she was now a vampire and no longer had to be a judgmental prude. I suspected that joyous time was still a long, long way off, though. In the meanwhile, I would have to continue enduring her pathologically puritanical outlook on life.

Yay.

"What are you thinking right now?" she asked me.

"How fortunate I am to have acquired such dear new friends," I replied.

"That feels like a lie."

"It is."

The second issue was that the Koler Crabs were extremely durable and much faster than they looked. At first glance, they were doddering, misshapen things with fat armored torsos that sat low on four wide, swollen legs. Their eyes were on two cartoonish-looking stalks that jutted from their ugly heads, giving them a look of continual confusion.

If not for their massive pincers, they would have looked mostly harmless.

At least until you saw them move.

"M'HAWK!" squawked one of them as it suddenly ran at a smaller one that had gotten too close. After a brief, violent struggle, the bigger one snipped the other's shell open and began greedily sucking the flesh out of it. After finishing its meal, it discarded the remnants and wandered away.

A cannibalistic species. I could relate to that. Fast and strong too. They were far more dangerous than I'd first realized. But the worst news was yet to come.

Before my eyes, the smaller crab's body began trembling violently as new flesh began to push out through the exposed areas of its broken shell, replacing everything the larger one had torn away. In less than a minute, it was completely restored.

That was an *incredible* ability to heal. No wonder their numbers kept going up despite their cannibalism. These things were virtually immortal.

Well, I supposed I'd now have to put them to the test, wouldn't I? What greater joy for a warrior than to face a worthy opponent?

"This is going to be impossible," Rachel suddenly said.

"No." I smiled. "This is going to be a challenge!"

For some reason, she didn't share my enthusiasm.

"Stay back, boy," I ordered Schulz after luring one of them away from the others.

My familiar's jaws might have possessed crushing power comparable to those of a large crocodile, but the Koler Crabs' sturdy shells might have been able to withstand that pressure long enough for them to deliver a mortal blow with those damn pincers. Even worse, the crabs' absurd healing ability would negate any damage that Schulz's jaws could deliver. It would be a poor matchup for him.

"M'kaw!" it screeched in that hostile warbling voice of theirs. "M'kaw! M'kaw! M'KAAAAAW!"

By the dark, that was quickly becoming annoying. I *really* wanted to kill this thing. I wanted to pry its shell off its body with my bare hands and tear out its heart. But that was my bestial nature speaking; my animal urge to assert myself over any who dared to resist me.

I had to remain clinical in my approach to this challenge. It would be reason and reason alone that would deliver me victory. Acting in haste could mean defeat.

As I thought about it, I wouldn't be surprised to learn that the crab's behavior was an evolutionary trait designed to provoke its assailants into making rash decisions. Who wouldn't let down their guard while getting "M'KAWED" at? You'd be so focused on killing the annoying pest as quickly as you could that you wouldn't notice that it had already disemboweled you.

If so, that was a clever trick. Proof that there was more to the monsters of this world than what could be seen with the naked eye. I needed to remember that I wasn't out here fighting a duel; I was testing this creature, feeling it out in combat to determine the most efficient way to dispose of it. I had to relax, ignore its provocations, and take my sweet time.

"M'KAAAAAAW!" it cried out again as it began to motion from side to side as it attempted to slowly close the distance between us without alerting me.

"Really? How very interesting," I replied as I bit deeply into the bottom of my left hand and let the resulting flow of blood well up in my palm.

It was time for a little *Sanguis Magicae*. Blood magic. The dreaded school of evocation that only a vampire could practice. An unholy merging of the two existential powers that defined how we viewed reality: Life and Death.

Blood magic was capable of many, many horrors. I knew that best, because in my previous existence as Kyler Stragos, I was the Lord of Blood and thus its supreme practitioner. My knowledge of its horrors was unmatched, tempered only by my cautious use of it. The sanguine arts were easy to lose control of. Caution was paramount for success.

Although the system employed by this world currently limited me from making full use of my former powers, there were still some small tricks left available to me, even in my diminished state. One of them was converting my blood into a deadly neurotoxic compound that would horribly kill anyone exposed to the slightest bit of it.

While that sounded terrible, it could still be dispelled by a sufficiently powerful mage, or by possessing a powerful ability to heal. If I hadn't converted Schulz into my familiar, the microscopic bits of my blood that he'd absorbed when he bit me would have eventually killed him.

My first test was to see if my deadly blood would be enough to end this creature. Too find out, I quickly scooped up a pebble from the ground, rolled it around my bloody palm for a bit, and then hurled it through one of my opponent's protruding eyes with as much force as I could, bursting the orb with the strength of my throw.

My efforts were rewarded with another shriek of "M'KAAAWW!" but the pitch of this scream suggested this was a cry of pain, which I relished. Soon, foam began bubbling from the lips of the crab as its other eye began to dribble with blood-flecked pus.

Just as I began to hope that this would be enough, I was disappointed by the sight of the crab's wounded eye restoring itself. It was quickly completely back to full health, now saying "M'KAW!" in a way that suggested mocking laughter.

"Got any other ideas?" Rachel asked.

"Still sussing it out, I'm afraid," I replied.

"Well, suss faster, please!"

"I really do appreciate how polite you've grown over time," I said to her.

Meanwhile, the crab continued to jitter and laugh at us.

That cocky little *fool*.

How dare he be so arrogant? If I hadn't been reduced to my current status by bad luck, he wouldn't have lasted a tenth of a second against me. Oh, well. At least my question had been answered. Poison wouldn't be enough to seal the deal. It also meant my spear's ability to deliver unhealing wounds would probably be negated.

But wait—what if it just needed a little help? This thing's healing might be enough to fight off Rachel's curse of wounds, and my poisonous blood, but perhaps that was only because it was able to focus on each condition individually.

What would happen if it had to face both at the same time?

With that thought in mind, I grinned wickedly and smeared my blood on the tip of the spear.

"What are we doing now?" she asked as I sprang forward.

"Delivering the good news," I said as I prepared to attack.

"What's the good news?"

"I *win!*"

I thrust my spear into the Koler Crab's neck and felt the tip of my blade strike home, causing the beast to squeal with pain. I rejoiced in the creature's anguish as I next began attacking its joints and other vulnerable areas not protected by its shell. I went for as many as I could find, as quickly as I could do it.

No matter how powerful a regenerative effect our target possessed, with my toxic blood coating Rachel's sharp edge, the crab wouldn't have time to heal, no matter how great its poison resistance and physical regeneration were. Not when we were delivering too many wounds at once for it to handle.

It was the classic death by a thousand papercuts.

What a beautiful sight it made when the bastard thing finally collapsed to its side and began violently shivering, no longer able to stand against us. Without even a final "M'kaw" to announce its departure from this world, the crab trembled once and then died.

"Delightful," I said to myself with a pleased nod.

"There's still more of them!" Rachel said. "And they're all as strong as this one! We can't possibly do this on our own."

"And yet we must," I reminded her. "I've already given my word to have the situation sorted by morning's light. I must abide by my promises, Rachel. Reneging on an obligation is irresponsible."

"We'll be killed! All of us!" she yelled.

"We're already dead," I reminded her. "What's left to fear?"

"You're not a *real* vampire, Kyler Stragos!" Rachael said with growing frustration. "Not anymore! It's just a Class! A Class you can set aside whenever you like! You're no longer bound by the monstrous compulsions that drove you in that existence. So, show some consideration for those of us forced to follow you and behave less like a monster and more like a human being!"

I froze in place, momentarily lost for words. In that moment I was struck dumb with amazement by how someone as old as Rachel allegedly was could project so much arrogance *and* ignorance in but a single breath.

Be less monstrous and behave like a human?

What the hell was she playing at?

"Rachel, my opinionated child, thank you for your council," I said after calming myself. "I believe I understand the reasoning that informed your ill-chosen words, and so I've decided not to be offended by them."

"I wasn't trying to offend you, I was—"

"Let me finish please," I said, cutting her off. "I said I've forgiven you *this time*. Any future insulting assumptions won't be so easily brushed away. I'm a vampire, Rachel. But I've never once in all my long years considered myself a transcendent being. I'm not deluded enough to fool myself with such a comforting lie. Yes, my body and instincts are monstrous and often cruel. But my mind has never been anything other than what it always was. *Utterly human.*"

"Your mark on history says otherwise," she countered. "No decent human could do what you've done and live with themselves."

"Name one sin committed by Kyler Stragos that other men haven't equaled or bettered," I scoffed.

"You led legions of undead across the globe and butchered thousands of brave warriors who stood against you!"

"War," I yawned. "They lost. I won. Anything else?"

"You spared no one in your fields of red! You were known for leaving no survivors!"

"And what would they have done with me had they proven victorious?" I asked her. "You make it sound as if defeat meant being imprisoned and paying a fine. Listen carefully, daughter: had I lost, they would have gladly dragged me into the sun and laughed at the sight of me burning before it. But not before torturing me until they got bored listening to my screams."

"You deserved to be punished!" Rachel insisted.

"During those wars, every overture to the enemy for surrender was defied. Every brave messenger I sent was either turned away or killed. The leaders of the opposing force declared our conflict a *holy war* and gave every vampire that fell into their hands a horrific and undignified ending. They also murdered any human being they considered a collaborator. I merely dealt with them as they would have dealt with me, and even then, I was kinder than my three elder siblings would have been. In the lands I ruled, those who fought, died, and those who abstained were spared. What's fairer than that?"

"You *conquered* them, Kyler," countered Rachel. "You set yourself above them and denied them the freedom that all are due. Where is there room for growth beneath a tyrant's heel?"

"A tyrant who instituted and enforced laws," I snapped back. "A tyrant who permitted freedom of religion without discrimination and allowed self-rule as long as his subjects remained loyal! If I didn't understand something, I employed experts who did. I also promoted education and civic pride! My subjects were *happy*, and that's the part the little crusaders like to ignore in their rush to condemn me. That the people under my stewardship were happy, well-fed, and safe. That the resources I controlled were well-managed and equally distributed without favoritism! That under my reign, there was *peace*."

"Peace at the point of a sword is just a pretty way of describing *oppression*," Rachel said solemnly.

And once more I was dumbstruck. Twice in one night. Incredible.

"Daughter?" I said after I once again managed to settle my extremely conflicted feelings.

"Yes, Kyler?" she asked.

"You've got me thinking," I said. "Now I need to know for sure."

"I'll try my best to provide an answer," she replied.

"I was just wondering . . ." I began.

"Yes?" she said.

"Could you perhaps be . . . a *complete* fucking idiot?" I asked with the utmost sincerity.

An answer was not immediately forthcoming.

"Well, whatever. Since you *insist* that I do this as a human, then I'll show you exactly how mankind would deal with these beasts. Prepare yourself, Rachel. It's going to be an *enlightening* display."

CHAPTER FIFTEEN

Act like a human being, huh? Oh, what an obnoxious thing to say.

Let's get one thing straight: I have *nothing* against humanity. I used to be one of them, and feel naught but respect for their bravery and their achievements. Art, science, culture, these are the things that make life worth living, and humanity has mastered all three. How can you not be in awe of such an impressive species? Three cheers for them, that's what I say!

But can we please dispense with the pretense of mankind being a race of paragons filled with virtue and grace? We know that simply isn't true. Their history is littered with expansionism and conquest. Murder and destruction. Chaos and war. Debauchery and madness. Endless hatred and *greed*. Just because aspects of them are as beautiful as sculpted glass doesn't make them all angels. Not unless we're talking about horrifying biblically accurate angels, in which case . . . yeah, I can see it.

So, Rachel wanted me to deal with these Koler Crabs as a human being would, was that right? Fine, I would. And she had only herself to blame for what she would soon witness.

Remember: Vampires started out as human beings. Yes, we're complete monsters, but where do you think we acquired the worst of those traits? It's like that anti-drug public service announcement they used to run in the '80s. The one where the father confronts his son about his behavior.

Human Father: *Invasion, assassination, destabilization of a sovereign government, and exploitation of the fearful masses? Where did you learn these things, son? Answer me!*

Vampire child: *I learned it by watching you, Dad . . . I learned it by watching you!*

Narrator: *Parent species of nations that engage in ruthless expansionism and conquest may produce monstrous successors who also engage in ruthless expansionism and conquest but on a far worse scale. And they will also eat you. Don't forget that part.*

Heh, I can be whimsical sometimes.

"So, what are you going to do?" asked Rachel.

"First things first, acquisition," I replied as I stood over the dead crab. The golden light that emanated from its body informed me that an ability was now obtainable for the Gore Grimoire. One quick bite of its heart later and I now possessed the passive skill Fast Regeneration.

I realized having a second healing factor was a little redundant. If my human form had possessed a little more durability, I would have passed this new skill over without a backward glance. But being as frail as I was, I needed some insurance that I wouldn't be annihilated in one hit if something caught me off guard in the daylight where I couldn't access my vampiric form's blood rejuvenation, and this was it. Once I grew stronger, I would replace it with something else, but for now, as an interim placeholder, Fast Regeneration would serve me well.

"All right," I said. "And now, with that out of the way, our second task will be to find a safe place to rest for a few hours."

"Why?" Rachel asked.

"Because I don't want to be eaten while sleeping," I replied as I located a nearby oak that looked good enough for the job. It was a tall, magnificent tree, with thick, strong branches that easily supported my weight as I climbed them and found a space long enough to rest comfortably on.

Below me, on ground level, Schulz sat patiently to keep an eye out for any crabs that wandered too close.

"Are you being serious right now?" Rachel asked. "You're really taking a nap?"

"Yes, I am," I said. "What's the alternative? More scintillating conversations with *you*?"

"But you already waited all day for nightfall to come," she protested.

"Yes, I did," I nodded patiently. "But there's been a change in plans, and our success now depends on taking action shortly before dawn."

"How shortly before dawn?" she asked.

"How many Koler Crabs were there again?" I asked.

"Seventy-four remain," she said.

"About twenty minutes should do it," I said with an assertive nod.

"Twenty minutes of what?"

"For us? Instant success. For them? Hell on earth in all its malignant awe."

". . . Kyler, what are you going to do?" she asked fretfully.

"I'm going to behave as a human would, dearest Rachel," I replied. "I'm going to press a big red button to see what happens next."

"Humans don't do things just to see what happens," she protested.

"How *old* are you?" I asked in exasperation.

"I told you! I'm two thousand years old!" she said forcefully.

"You're lying," I said bluntly.

"I am not!"

"You absolutely are," I asserted. "Rachel, I've met beings in the age range you've claimed for yourself. Some of them have been of different species like me, some of them were humans who'd cultivated massive lifespans, others were ancient spirits. Despite our diversity, do you know what we all have in common?"

"What?" she asked in a defiant tone.

"Cynicism," I said. "Flat out. Once you're old enough to see how history endlessly repeats itself and how the young *never* learn from the mistakes of prior generations, you're left with a persistent skepticism of the good in everything."

"That isn't true—" she sputtered.

"Yes, it is," I said, ignoring her protest. "And this isn't a perspective one develops from living for a thousand years. Its growth begins far sooner than that. It starts seeding itself in your thirties, but it *really* takes root when you hit fifty or so. And by the time you're in your seventies, I guarantee you, you're well on your way to becoming a cold, bitter thing who may pray for the best but will *always* expect the worst. Haven't you ever wondered why it's so easy for the old to send young men and women to die in foreign lands for profit and power? It's because age eventually takes away the capacity to *care*. And why should they? Very few people live to a great age, but there are young fools every which way you turn. They're an endlessly replaceable resource to be harvested."

"So, I'm lying because I still believe in the best of others?" she said.

"Yes, you absolutely are," I said. "Rachel, you're too soft. You may as well have an uncut umbilical cord. You aren't convincing anyone with your silly deceit."

"I'm not lying!" she insisted stubbornly.

"I could order you to tell me the truth, and you'd have no choice but to obey," I reminded her.

"S-so, you'd just casually violate the sanctity of my mind to confirm your petty suspicions? Is that right?" she asked heatedly.

"Well, yes, if you had any secrets worth stealing," I replied honestly. "But I'm beginning to suspect you don't. You're like a weird transfer student desperately pretending to have a mysterious past so that the other kids at her new school will think she's interesting. But you come across more like a homeschooled person interacting in a public setting for the first time."

"I AM TWO THOUSAND YEARS OLD!" she shouted.

"But what does that mean *outside* of Scientology?" I asked.

"Bastard! You're a mean bastard and I—"

"Shush," I said. "Go to sleep. I'll wake you up when it's time to enact my plan."

Rachel struggled to defy my order, but a command from her maker was impossible to ignore. After offering some feeble resistance, she passed out and I placed her in my storage so that I could rest against the tree with my hands behind my head.

She was such a strange creature. The more of her personality she revealed to me, the more amusing I found her.

I wondered if there'd ever come a day when she would be honest with me of her own volition. Was I someone who could still inspire that level of trust from another person?

Probably not. Time had definitely changed me for the worse.

Those were my thoughts as I stared at the night sky, which was beautiful and filled with the splendid light of the stars. As I fell asleep, I felt blessed to have gazed upon such wonders.

The dark wasn't always a terrible thing. Its glory may have been shadowed, but it still existed.

I woke up feeling refreshed about a half hour from dawn.

I guessed it was time to get started.

"Wakey, wakey," I said to Rachel as I summoned her from storage.

"You sent me to bed like an irksome child!" she said angrily as soon as she awoke.

"I did, didn't I?" I replied. "That nap made me feel pretty good. How about yourself?"

"Are we going to get this done or what?" she said.

"No rush, no rush, let me stretch first," I said before climbing down the tree. "What we're about to do is going to happen *very quickly*. So, keep that in mind. Staying alert will be important."

"How important?"

"*Very* important!" I said cheerfully. "Wouldn't want to get caught off guard, yeah? That could end badly for us. For *me* especially."

"Kyler, what are you about to do?" Rachel asked worriedly.

"Shhh. Rachel, just close your imaginary little eyes and focus," I said. "I want to take you back to a simpler time, a *better* time, when the world was divided by territorial lines denoting what was good and what was evil. The West was the best, and the East was the least."

"What are you talking about?" she asked.

"RACHEL. Let me finish setting the scene *please*," I said. "Now, as I said, the West was the best. You could eat a fast-food burger at seven, watch a movie at the drive-in at eight, close out a bar by three, and terrorize your family by noon the next day when your kids woke you up with all the noise from their playing. Meanwhile, in the East, they were all eating gruel and watching black-and-white television in their cement-block apartments before marching to their tank factories to pray to Lenin-Jesus for the destruction of Wall Street. Obviously, they were all *hopelessly* insane. Defending our rights from such madness took two things: resources and *resolve*."

I gestured toward the pond. "Behold," I said. "The necessary resources for the continuation of Tradesman Calford's slice of sweet cherry pie and Baked Alaska. Oh, but what's this? It's been occupied by a hostile faction of unproductive invaders. Look at those shameless Koler Crab bastards taking what isn't theirs while promulgating their vile San Francisco values. Doesn't it make you angry?"

"You're just rambling pure idiocy," Rachel said after a short pause.

"Oh, come on, let me have some fun with this," I said with a frown. "Be a better audience! Take a note from the dog; he's entranced by my storytelling. Schulz really appreciates me, don't you boy?"

In response to my saying his name, Schulz ran over to me and stood on his hind legs so that I could scratch his neck and receive a few enthusiastic licks in return. He really was a good boy.

"Could you just get on with it?" Rachel demanded.

"Okay," I said. "Now, where was I? Right! We've identified the enemy. Now we need to determine how to eliminate them. I'm taking the role of America because that was a country that was notorious for fighting proxy wars through the destabilization of enemy governments by supporting insurgencies. They bathed entire nations in the friendly fire of freedom fighters. *For the free world."*

"Didn't those disastrous policies destroy their reputation abroad and lead to worldwide chaos that years later tanked their own economy with a terrible recession and bogged them down in decades of meaningless fighting?" asked Rachel.

"No, shut up," I replied. "Okay, fine, it did, but in their defense, they didn't *know* all those bad things would happen. And according to their elected officials, not being able to predict a terrible outcome is the same as not doing it. Not if your intentions are as pure as Western democracy."

"A notoriously exclusive enterprise."

"They'd prefer you call it *selective*," I said. "Anyway, now that we've established who the bad guys are, let's create a hero for our narrative. And I chooooooose . . . *him.*"

I spun around and pointed the spear at the corpse of the Koler Crab we'd killed earlier. Luckily, it was still there, waiting to be used. In hindsight, I was lucky something hadn't come along to eat it while we were sleeping.

"What are you going to do with that?" asked Rachel.

"What else? I'm going to recruit him and use him to start an insurgency. The *good* kind, that is."

I sauntered over to the dead monster and lifted it by its neck. Then I opened my mouth wide as I felt my teeth slowly extend and sharpen, transforming my smile into a gaping piranha's lunatic grin. Then I bit deeply into the neck of the corpse and began sucking out its lifeless blood.

Ugh, disgusting.

"Why are you doing that?" Rachel asked, dumbfounded.

I waited to reply until I finished draining the body, before grimacing and giving my mouth a good wipe. "Well, Rachel, what you've just witnessed is a basic power employable by any ordinary vampire, yourself included, although I imagine you'd have some trouble utilizing it in your current form."

"Which is?"

"I'm getting there!" I snapped. "Actually, just see for yourself."

Having said that, I activated my stealth ability and, behind a cloak of invisibility, I tossed the dead Koler Crab deep into the territory of his brethren. As expected, those nearest to it immediately began tearing away at the corpse and greedily swallowing its flesh.

"Did you poison that corpse?" Rachel asked. "Why? You already know that poisoning alone won't be enough to kill them."

"Did I poison them?" I asked with a sly little grin. "Of course not. I told you, we were *recruiting*. I evangelized that fellow to the wonders of Western thought and in turn he's now going to proselytize to his friends. The good news has come to the pond. The gospel has been spread like a virus."

As the other Koler Crabs crowded the dead one, I saw its body begin to violently twitch. Then I beheld it rising and screeching a maddened cry of absolute unhinged horror and hatred. It roared and attacked with a brutish frenzy that the others couldn't match, tearing open the abdomen of the one nearest to it and pulling out its innards to feast.

"WHAT THE HELL HAVE YOU DONE?!" Rachel shrieked.

"Oh, calm down," I said to her. "You can't be that ignorant of your own heritage, Rachel. Wait, *you* actually might be. Okay, let me fill you in. If a vampire wants to create another of his kind, he needs to feed from a living body. More specifically, he needs to drain a living body completely dry and then insert some of his own blood into it. There, I've just taught you how to become a mother. Use your knowledge responsibly."

"But that Koler Crab wasn't a fresh body!" Rachel exclaimed. "It's been dead for hours!"

"Yes. Yes, he was," I nodded. "And trust me, his blood tasted like it too. I'm really going to need something to rinse my mouth with. My tongue tastes like fuzzy jambalaya."

"You made a *ghoul*," Rachel said in sudden terrified realization. "Draining blood from a dead body creates *ghouls*."

"Yes, that's exactly what I did," I agreed. "I made a ghoul. And now he's making *more ghouls*."

It was true. Every Koler Crab my little insurgent bit was infected with his curse and they in turn began seeking fresh blooded prey. Soon, what had been one became a dozen. Then more. A war of attrition had come to the pond. A war that the crabs were slowly losing.

"Are you insane?!" Rachel said. "Ghouls can't be controlled! They're ravagers, annihilators! Worse than zombies, worse than vampires, even!"

"Heeeey, not nice," I said sadly.

"They'll run amok killing everything and *everyone* they come across!" Rachel said urgently. "Why have you done this?! You've murdered this town!"

"Hey, you're the one who said to handle this like a human," I chided her. "Well, this is how humans do things. The greater nations kill from a distance using proxies for plausible deniability. They'll also resort to exotic methods to see their goals accomplished, sometimes just to see what would happen. Didn't I tell you I was going to press a big red button?"

"That's not how people do things!" she said once again.

"Bzzzzt," I replied. "Hiroshima and Nagasaki have entered the chat."

The Koler Crab Civil War now entered its frenzied apex as the desperate living made their final stand. The strongest of them with the thickest armor had bravely set themselves up as the last line of defense, while the weakest supported them by intercepting any ghouls that broke through. It was an incredible display of cooperation that genuinely surprised me. I had thought these beasts were supremely selfish, but I guessed that amid a genuine tribulation, their instinct was to work together for survival.

It was genuinely touching. Too bad it didn't save them.

The ghoul crabs, with no instinct for survival, no fear of pain, and only their maddened lust for living flesh to guide them, threw themselves heedlessly against the defenders until they finally managed to overwhelm them. Once the shield wall was broken, it ended very quickly. The morning air was filled with desperate cries of "M'KAW! M'KAW!" which eventually died down, filled instead with the hideous sound of chewing.

Then came the final act.

When the ghouls had dispensed with the last of the living crabs, they suddenly began swarming the pond. I was curious as to why that was, when suddenly I saw massive bubbles beginning to rise to the surface. Then, with an explosive surge of water that threatened to drench me from all the way over there, I saw a gigantic Koler Crab the size of a two-story house erupt from the pond, bellowing an echoing cry of "M'KAAAAAAAAAAW" as it desperately tried to make its escape with dozens of ghoul crabs crawling all over it, tearing at its shell.

"What the hell?" said Rachel in a daze. Even Schulz, who was normally the calmest being in the room, was greatly disturbed by the sight of the giant shellfish monster as it struggled to survive.

"Okay, I think I figured out where they were all coming from," I said to no one in particular. "I think that's one part of the quest we can safely check off."

Like its brave children before it, the Koler Crab queen put up a spectacular fight as the ghouls swarmed her. Each swing of her massive pincers sent them flying, and her feet easily crushed them beneath its titanic stride. It roared its defiance with thunderous force, refusing to go quietly to its death.

Five minutes later it was screaming in almost human intonations as the ghouls that were once its progeny made a feast of her.

"How sharper than a serpent's tooth it is to have thankless children," I paraphrased.

"You've damned this entire place," Rachel said accusingly. "This is ground zero for the end. These ghouls will spread like a plague! They'll reach Gardenia in a matter of days and turn the city into a charnel house. Damn you, Kyler Stragos. I knew you were evil, but I never realized until this moment just how black your heart truly was."

A few minutes later, the Koler Crab queen stirred. Then she rose listlessly to her torn legs and roared with mindless, unending hunger, now as much a ghoul as her spawn.

"Look at that creature," Rachel continued. "*Look at it!* It'll smash through the fortified walls of the city in no time! A perfect siege weapon for its children! Are you proud of yourself, Kyler Stragos? Does the coming slaughter of all those innocents bring a deranged smile to your face? Well? SAY SOMETHING!"

"Okay," I replied. "Uh, the sun is rising."

And with that said, I quickly assumed my human form and waited for the ghouls to disintegrate. It didn't take long.

Not long at all.

"You waited until near sunrise so that the ghouls wouldn't have time to escape or seek shelter," Rachel said quietly a few moments later.

"Uh huh," I said.

"No one was truly in danger. You knew exactly what you were doing."

"Uh huh," I said.

"All of that insane chatter about insurgencies and Western values. It was just your way of making fun of me."

"Uh huh," I said.

"The only button you were pressing was *mine.*"

"Uh huh," I said.

"You're a cruel bastard, Kyler Stragos," she said in an exhausted tone of voice.

"That's been said before," I replied. "Oh, look at that! I just leveled up. I've reached Level Twelve. Isn't that nice?"

Once again, Rachel refused to speak to me.

Honestly, I didn't blame her. She'd just been through the wringer.

Heh. Busting the new kid's chops and taking a little of the wind out of her sails?

Definitely something a human would do.

CHAPTER SIXTEEN

Twenty minutes later I was back at Tradesman Calford's home, tapping on the screen to be let in. When Jamie appeared at the door a few minutes later while wearing a bathrobe, I gave her a wave through the glass.

"What are you doing back?" she asked after I requested her permission to enter.

"The task's complete," I informed her as I sat on the stool that I'd used the day before. "Thought I'd plate up before I went home if you don't mind."

Jamie flashed me another one of her dazzling smiles, but this one had noticeably less humor behind it. "Sweetie, there are seventy-five Koler Crabs at that pond."

"Seventy-six, actually," I said. "The job failed to mention the queen."

"How do you know about the queen?" she asked with sudden suspicion. "Has someone been talking?"

"To me? No," I replied. "I discovered her existence on my own."

"Where is she right now?" Jamie asked.

"In paradise with her children," I said somberly. "Where there is no conflict or sin, and everyone can cannibalize their siblings in heavenly peace."

"Stregan—" she began.

"*Stragos,*" I corrected her.

"Whatever!" said Jamie. "Stragos, what you're telling me doesn't make any sense. Seventy-five Level Ten monsters and one elite can't be dealt with in only twelve hours by actual Hunters of the same Level. Much less . . ."

"Much less what?" I asked her.

"Sweetie, you're only a *Porter*," she finally said. "Don't bother hiding it; I could tell at a glance."

"How?" I asked, genuinely surprised.

"That's a trade secret, I'm afraid."

A trade secret? What exactly was that supposed to mean?

"Oh," I said a moment later, as I finally understood the situation. "You have an assessment skill, don't you? I didn't even realize it. What's your Class?"

"Stragos, I'm the one asking the questions," she said quietly. "I wasn't too bothered by you showing up to answer my father-in-law's request, not when I saw what your Class was. I just assumed you were a scavenger trying to scam a free meal. The Narrows is full of that sort."

"Desperate people?" I asked.

"Everywhere you look," she said with a nod. "Especially kids your age. Academy burnouts who couldn't meet their damn requirements. They throw you poor things out with the trash every semester."

"If you thought I was a fake, why'd you feed me?" I asked her.

"You're a funny guy," she said with a small smile. "I thought you might have been a little touched in the head, so I didn't mind helping you. But now you're taking things a little too far."

"The pond is clear, Jamie," I assured her.

"We'll soon see," she said after pressing a button on the counter.

The door opened and three large men stepped into the kitchen with us. I recognized one of them as the guard who'd challenged me at the entrance to the settlement. He stared at me, first in puzzlement, then with slowly increasing anger. "What the hell are you doing here?" he asked.

"Just trying to get some breakfast," I said sadly.

"Don't get fresh with me," he said as he came stomping toward me.

"Doug, stay calm, please," Jamie cut in. "I want Finch and Carver to check out his story. Our new friend here claims to have cleared out the pond singlehandedly."

"This punk?" Doug snorted in derision. "My ass, he did. I told him to stay clear of the Narrows and he ignored me. There's consequences for making bad decisions, kid."

"What kind?" I asked him.

In response, he grabbed me by the front of my shirt and easily hefted me into the air. "You're about to find out," he promised me.

"Does this mean I'm not getting fed?" I asked Jamie.

"Doug," she said, placing deliberate emphasis on his name. "This isn't why I called for you."

"He's getting on my nerves," Doug said.

"And *you* are beginning to get on mine," she warned him.

Sudden understanding flashed in Doug's eyes. Instead of following through on his intended violence, he dropped me on the floor. I landed unpleasantly on my rear.

Yeah, I was probably going to kill Doug later for doing that. Or maybe I wouldn't? Who really knew? I could be mercurial at times. But I have to say that in that particular moment, things weren't looking too good for 'ol Dougie living to see his next birthday.

After I resumed my seat, Jamie leaned forward on the counter to explain things more clearly to me.

"Sweetie, I'm going to send Carver and Finch over to the pond to check your story, okay?" she said as she pointed to the two men who'd accompanied Doug into the room. "And if they see so much as a pincer or an eyestalk, things aren't going to go well for you. I'm sorry about that, but I can't let anyone blatantly try to rip off my family like this."

"I understand and I take no offense," I replied. "It's as I said to Doug earlier. It's much better to be wary than foolish."

"I'm glad you understand," she said. "But I wish you wouldn't take it so lightly. Doug is a Level Eight Sentry. He's not someone you should be so disrespectful towards."

"Level Eight?" I said in surprise.

"Yes." She nodded.

"At *his* age?" I scoffed.

"You little *shit*," Doug swore as he reached for me.

"Ah, didn't she say you had to wait for confirmation?" I asked him.

Doug reluctantly paused as he saw the look Jamie was giving him. He swallowed his anger and turned away from me but not before muttering, "As soon as they call in, I'm going to break both of your legs, you little scavenger bastard."

"Well, shoot," I said. "If that's what's about to happen, then maybe Jamie should get my breakfast started. So I can begin healing right away."

Jamie laughed at that. I smiled at her, pleased to have finally gotten her to crack.

"I'm starting to believe I was right about you being touched in the head," she said.

"Touched in the head and *hungry*," I replied.

"Fine," Jamie said as she reached into a cabinet and produced a heavy iron skillet. "In honor of your persistence, if nothing else."

"Hurray!" I cheered.

Soon the kitchen was filled with the comforting scent of bubbling grease and frying meat as Jamie's deft hands prepared a bountiful breakfast of eggs, a fat slice of ham, and three large sausages. There wasn't a vegetable to be seen on the glorious tray she set before me, which she topped off with a thick slice of buttered bread and a glass of sweetened milk.

Eating this feast was an act of supreme bliss. I lost all sense of my surroundings as I surrendered myself to the primal joy of *consumption* and tucked into my meal. Breaking the yolk of the egg with the sausage and smearing it over my bread before topping it off with the whites and ham brought me to a sense of equivalence with universe.

Chewing and swallowing the combo was *nirvana* itself.

At some point, I discarded my fork and just attacked the plate with my teeth. That was a happy moment. When I came to my senses, Jamie and Doug were staring at me in bewilderment, as if they'd just been forced to watch a wolf devour a baby rabbit. It was a little embarrassing.

"May I please have a napkin?" I asked.

"That was . . . an impressive visual," Jamie said tactfully as she handed me a slightly dampened towel to clean my face with.

"Kid, you're disgusting," Doug said bluntly.

"Heh, sorry, just enjoying myself," I said sheepishly. "Say, I don't suppose I could have another of those sausages? You don't need to cook it. Just a treat for my friend over there."

I pointed to the glass door, where Schulz lay on his side, staring at us hopefully.

"Oh, he's *gorgeous*," Jamie said as she walked to the door and opened it to let the dog inside. "You're such a handsome thing, aren't you?"

She began patting Schulz on the head, then expertly scratching his belly and scalp at the same time while he rolled over to luxuriate in her fine treatment. Hmm. Apparently, a sufficiently cute dog could be used to attract the attention of a beautiful woman. Who knew?

You'd think I would have figured that out after centuries of chasing people through the woods with wolves. It just goes to show there's always more to learn.

"Why haven't they gotten back to us yet?" Doug grumbled a few minutes later as Schulz happily chewed from a plate of meat provided to him by our hostess.

"They're just being thorough," Jamie said as she watched the dog eat. "It's important to be completely certain before you commit to certain actions."

"You're not wrong about that," I agreed.

"Shut up," Doug said irritably as he began to walk around the kitchen. "The longer this gets drawn out, the worse it's going to be for you."

"You never did tell me what your Class was," I said to Jamie as I turned away from the boring thug and his boring threats. "How did you assess me?"

"Don't ask so many questions," Doug snapped.

Now I was beginning to grow annoyed.

"Would you *please* stop telling me what to do?" I said to him. "I'm showing a lot of good humor here, but mealtime's over, and I think I'm going to leave. As charming as Jamie's company is, I'm beginning to find your presence unbearable."

"Stragos, please, don't do anything reckless," Jamie urged.

"Kid, you're not going *anywhere*," Doug rumbled as he approached me.

"Don't do it, Doug," I warned him. "Touch me in anger and you won't enjoy what follows."

"Okay, I've fucking *had it* with you—" Doug began to say when Schulz suddenly shot across the room like a canine cruise missile and slammed directly into his chest, smashing him violently into a wall.

"What the hell," Doug moaned as Schulz clamped his jaws around his ankle and pivoted violently to the left before releasing his grip, sending Doug crashing through the patio windows to slide through the grass in a broken heap.

"You saw me try to warn him, right?" I asked the stunned Jamie. "That makes you my witness."

"What the hell just happened?" she gasped.

"Schulz is a very good boy," I told her as my familiar trotted happily to my side to receive his pats. "Anyway, thank you for breakfast. I'm feeling sleepy, so I think I'll be skipping lunch today. Back for dinner, though. What's the menu for tonight? You know what, don't tell me. I enjoy being surprised."

With Schulz at my side, I stepped over the broken glass and made my way toward the town exit while Jamie stared at us. As I left, I heard the kitchen phone begin to ring.

"Yes?" I heard Jamie say after answering it.

A few minutes later, just as we reached the road, I heard the sound of frantic footsteps as someone came running toward me from behind.

"WHERE," Jamie gasped after catching up to me. Which I took to mean *where are all the Koler Crabs?*

"Dealt with, as I explained," I said to her patiently.

"HOW," she asked next.

"Decisively," I said.

She held up a finger, signaling me to let her catch her breath. After a few deep gasps, she managed to calm herself enough to ask questions using complete sentences.

"What *is* he?" she asked as she pointed at Schulz.

"My dog," I replied.

"What sort of dog is he?"

"One of a kind. Jamie, I'm sorry, but is this going anywhere? I really am tired."

Suddenly, she grabbed my arm and pulled me toward her. Looking at me intensely with those seemingly guileless blue eyes, she came closer until our faces were only inches apart and said, "What do I have to do to convince you to stay?"

A smile slowly crept over my face as I considered the tempting implications of her words.

"Nothing much," I said. "Just a little something I'd really enjoy."

"And what's that?" she asked.

I think she was almost disappointed when I requested a room at her tavern to rest in.

What? When I'm sleepy, I'm *sleepy.*

CHAPTER SEVENTEEN

In the bed I'd been given, I slept. And as I slept, I dreamed of the past. These weren't particularly pleasant memories for me; I can't say I was happy to reminisce on days gone by. As a matter of fact, I made it a personal policy to try and ignore anything that happened more than fifty years ago.

Naturally, I was terrible at it.

So, yeah. There was that time me and the gang got together and caused the collapse of Western civilization and tried to turn the planet into a giant graveyard.

In hindsight, it was a dick move on our part. Bringing ruin to dozens of nations so that we could set ourselves above their terrified surviving populations and reign over them as false gods . . . I mean, yes, it was fun. It was *so much fun* . . . but it just wasn't a very nice thing to do. It certainly didn't increase our popularity with the faceless masses.

But, you know, in our defense, we were vampires, and vampires derive intense pleasure from pointless displays of cruelty, although that's not entirely the reason why we did what we did. It's not like any of us had the option of sitting things out. The order to ravage society had come from the top.

As the Lord of Blood, there was only one person who could command me to do anything, and that was my mother. You might have heard of her; Desadia Crudelitas.

Okay, you probably haven't; that name is *ridiculous*. She loved it, though. My older brother Vitor once made the mistake of mocking it where she could hear and that was it for him. My sisters and I didn't see Vitor again for most of the nineteenth century. When he was finally returned to us, just in time to join the family for the Great Chicago Fire, (known less formally as the cookout of '71), he was a much quieter person. I didn't ask questions.

When it came to the old woman, I *never* asked questions.

I simply obeyed.

I was the only one of my siblings to have never been punished. I think Vitor hated me a little for that, but to hell with that attitude. I knew my place and stuck to it, and in so doing, I stayed on Mom's good side. Maybe it was because I was the Lord of Blood and had a more intuitive understanding of our mother's personality and just how unnatural her existence truly was. *How unnatural was she?* you might ask. Well, words like *primordial abomination* were a good way to get started. If you kept going, you might eventually land on *elder thing* or *crawling chaos*, although I'm sure that last description belonged to somebody else. It might not have, though; that was the problem.

Mom was more commonly known as Emperor Crusica. Yes, *that* Emperor Crusica. The feared ruler of all undead everywhere, the one who'd given the order to devour mankind, the wound of darkness, and the bearer of a million more unpleasant titles. *He* was, in fact, a woman.

I think. It really depended on her mood.

Remember, I *never* asked questions. Asking my mother a question was one of the worst things anyone could possibly do while in her presence, because sometimes she would answer them.

Have you ever heard that phrase, *knowledge man was never meant to know*? I can assure you it exists. And how does *knowledge man was never meant to know* affect someone who accidentally learns it?

You know the movie *Scanners*?

Yeah, the one where the guy's head explodes.

It's like that. But nastier.

A lot of friends over the years have misunderstood the relationship my siblings and I shared with Crusica. They'd tease us and tell us to *toughen up* and not to be so fearful of her. Even now, I can only shake my head at the depths of their ignorance. Why does everyone think just because they have an opinion about something, they're qualified to give advice?

Listen, Crusica was a shapeshifting biomass of sentient demonic blood that ate souls, so excuse us for not wanting to anger her unnecessarily. Maybe if one of *your* parents was an unspeakable horror from the hungering beyond who had slipped through the thin veil of reality protecting our small little world from that which our delicate minds can scarcely conceive, I'd consider listening to your pep talk. But sadly, very few people had similar life experiences while growing up.

Toughen up. What a load of idiocy.

Over the years, a lot of people have called me a monster. A fiend. An unrelenting blight upon the land. They even attributed me to a few biblical passages warning of my coming and the disasters I'd leave in my wake. I'm not a very religious person, so I could never decide if I found that flattering or insulting.

But just so we're clear, I deserved every insult my detractors threw at me. Every curse they could send my way. Before that Sophia woman struck me down, I had a kill count that I'd stopped keeping track of once it hit six figures. It's not something I'm proud of, but it *did* show my efficacy as the Lord of Blood. I took my role seriously and I got things *done.*

I can't claim sole credit for my many horrendous misdeeds. Like I said earlier, I had quite the family. I've already mentioned Crusica, our Emperor and progenitor. But there was also my elder brother Vitor, the Lord of Beasts; as well as my sisters: Hedonia, the Lady of Mist; and Protea, the Lady of Shapes. As the youngest, that made me the baby of the bunch.

(Well, there was also Bathory, the sister who preceded me as the Lady of Blood, but we never talked about her. She'd gotten herself in trouble with mother and lost her station. I'd been created to replace her.)

(I think Bathory is still alive, somewhere. Although she probably wishes she wasn't. You know how moms can be, right? They love getting creative with their punishments.)

They had many names for my siblings and me. When we assembled, we were mainly called the Four Great Lords, but we were also known as the Four Heavenly Kings, the Four Horsemen of the Apocalypse, the Four Elemental Fiends, and the Four Beasts of Gehenna. During my Nintendo phase, I kept petitioning to have our name changed to the Elite Four, but Vitor threatened to kill me if I didn't stop, so I eventually gave up on it.

Vitor was truly a killjoy, the quintessential big brother bully, but Hedonia and Protea both thought my suggestions were clever. I always did get along better with them. They enjoyed being older sisters and playing along with my antics. Heh, thanks to them, I grew up spoiled and indulged.

Although our individual might was considerable, the powers my siblings and I wielded were meant to be used in tandem. Strong alone, stronger together. When we marched as one, nothing could stand in our path. No army could oppose us, no titan could impede our stride. As the Four Great Lords, we were almost equal to Crusica herself, not that we would ever dare to offer such an opinion.

In her name, we killed *so many people* . . .

That was the part I never truly understood. The Vampire Nation had existed for thousands of years, hiding in the darkness of civilization, ruling from its shadows. Although the existence of vampires was known, none realized the depths of our power, or how far our influence extended across the world. They weren't yet aware of Great Crusica, or of how mighty the limitless armies of undead she commanded were.

The Earth I came from was a strange place. One where magic was openly practiced by a select few, where science could create anything one could imagine, where daring men and women in colorful costumes dashed from rooftops to prevent crime, where beings from other worlds visited to share their knowledge or to lead invasions. It was also a place as ordinary as could be. A strange hodgepodge of the fantastic and the familiar. A sort of . . . urban fantasy?

It's difficult to describe that time as anything other than an age of heroes. Of marvels and icons, where anything was possible, but everything was always safely reset to maintain an unspoken status quo.

It was nice. I *liked* that world. I enjoyed living in it and occasionally playing the role of the villain for the earnest young champions seeking some evil to thwart. I had a lot of fun. Even when "defeated," I'd leave the game with a smile on my face. I was glad to have lived long enough to see such wonders unfold.

It all seemed like a dream that would never end.

But then our Emperor commanded us to rise and burn everything down; to blacken the skies with ash and dye the seas red with spilled blood. To fill the air with cries of despair and suffering.

To kill hope itself.

I didn't want to. I *swear* it. But Mother demanded it, and the will of Crusica cannot be denied. Just as Rachel cannot disobey me, I could not disobey my creator.

So, the Four Lords obeyed and began the crimson crusade to end humanity.

That was when being a vampire stopped being fun.

Why did Crusica demand that of us? That question drives me to this day. Why did she use us to do this terrible thing? Did she truly believe that she had become a god? That she was untouchable? If that was what she thought, then she learned otherwise when she failed to escape the reprisal that followed when, in the throes of her madness, Crusica ordered us to violate an ancient treaty and assault the nations of the East, where the cultivators honed their skills and lived in secrecy.

That had been the mistake that sealed her fate. I remember the outrage on her perfect face as the Murim Alliance charged at her palanquin and fought through our endless numbers to reach her. The disbelief she showed when their grand masters summoned an actual *Celestial Ancestor* to purify her with the light of an ascended realm.

I remember her screams of defiance and fear in that moment when justice finally caught up to her and her body was reduced to atoms.

But mostly, I remember the four of us turning tail and running for our lives, because *noooooope*, screw that. We were just following orders, sorry for the mess, congratulations on your victory, keep on defying the heavens and we'll keep out of your hair.

Call us cowards if you like, but we didn't want *any* of that smoke. Can you blame us? You must understand, summoning a Celestial Ancestor is a big deal. It was a show of force like nothing the cultivators had ever displayed before, and it cost them dearly in resources and manpower. For them to go that far was their way of showing that they didn't fear death and that they'd gladly sink the continent itself if it meant they could take us with them.

What do you say in the face of such bravery and resolve? If you're smart, you say goodbye and you *leave.* Which is exactly what we did. Their message was simple. *Stay out of our turf or else.* Well, message received, guys.

As for the ultimate fate of our dearly departed mother?

Who gave a damn? She was Hell's problem now.

I awoke from my troubled sleep with Schulz's worried face laying on my belly. Touched by his concern, I lightly scratched his ear before sitting up. Beside my bed, Rachel was propped against a corner in easy reach of my hand. As I rubbed the sides of my head, I heard her concerned voice reach out to me.

"Are you okay, Stragos?" she asked. "That seemed like one hell of a dream you were having."

"Was it?" I asked. "I can't even remember what it was about."

"Yeah, well you definitely didn't look like you were having a good time," she said. "You kept moaning someone's name. I think it was—"

"Don't tell me who it was," I quickly said, cutting her off. "Nightmares are best when quickly forgotten. I've got plenty of bad memories waiting to pop up unexpectedly that I'd rather not have to deal with. Best not to hear any names associated with them."

"I guess," Rachel said doubtfully. "But ignoring your troubles doesn't mean that you've dealt with them."

"That's fine. I'm immortal. I can always grow as a person tomorrow," I replied. "For us, there's always tomorrow."

"So, what now?" Rachel asked, thankfully setting the topic aside.

I checked the time and saw that dinner wouldn't be for another hour. Then I said, "I guess we'll use these skill points I earned when I leveled up and then spend a little time bonding."

"Sounds like a thrill, *Dad*," she replied sarcastically. Then, as I stood up, she fell silent.

"What?" I said, wondering why she was being so quiet.

"Kyler . . . look at yourself," Rachel said urgently. "In the mirror! Take a look, I'm serious!"

Puzzled by her urgency, I did as she said, and found myself whistling in surprise at the sight that greeted me. "Well, son of a *gun*," I said with a slight grin. "Take a look at that! Just when did I get so pretty?"

It was true. When I'd gone to sleep, I'd been far skinnier, much shorter, and slightly hunched over from years of poor posture. Now, I stood at about six feet tall, with a much healthier weight, and even some noticeable definition on my muscles. My neck and shoulders were considerably thicker too.

If not for my pale skin and seemingly permanent rings under my eyes, I doubt anyone would have recognized me at a glance. As I thought about it, I realized that I now bore a stronger resemblance to Patrick, Kyler Evans's older half-brother.

"What happened to you?" Rachel asked.

"I'm not sure yet," I said. "But I think I like it?"

CHAPTER EIGHTEEN

This is beyond ridiculous!" Rachel exclaimed. "I mean, how are you going to explain this? People just don't physically mature overnight like . . . I don't know, geckos?"

"I really don't see what there is to explain," I calmly replied as I continued to observe my reflection. "I've only met a handful of people since arriving here. And what's more, I'm a Hunter. There's a certain level of strangeness implied with that title, right?"

"Why am I the only one concerned about this?" Rachel asked (with a lot of dramatic energy, I thought). "Kyler, you could be suffering from a condition that causes accelerated aging! What if you're living ten years a day or something?"

"Oh, I know what you mean," I said with a nod as I recalled an event from my past. "You're talking about an entropy curse. Yeah, I got hit with one of those about four hundred years back by some childish witch who'd overestimated herself. She had this habit of aging people by centuries in the blink of an eye if they displeased her."

"What?" Rachel said with disgust. "That's murder!"

"Well, yes, Rachel, it *is* murder. That's why she did it," I said. "The woman saw herself as one of those mastermind types who punished incompetence with death. You know the sort. *Fool, you've failed me for the last time.* That kind of thing. She became dependent on that silly gimmick to her ultimate detriment."

"What happened between the two of you?"

"I stole her territory from her," I said. "She didn't have much to offer but I took it all anyway. She'd gotten cocky with me at a little mixer my sister Hedonia was hosting, boasting about her power and her so-called *empire*, and how dare we offend her and all that."

"You offended her?"

"Yeah, that was the silliest part of all. Believe it or not, she crashed the party and was furious that she hadn't been invited, like she thought she was Maleficent or something. The woman was a total cartoon."

"So, what happened?" Rachel asked.

"Well, I decided to take her to task. Show her who she was dealing with so that she'd learn a little respect for her betters. Instead of absorbing the lesson, however, she showed up at my home one night raving about how I'd pay for daring to cross her. She then cast her little curse on me despite my warning."

"You warned her not to do it?"

"Of course," I said. "I always try to be sporting about these things when dealing with a colleague of the supernatural world. I informed her that she'd die if she tried it, but she mistook that as me threatening her and fired it off, and then she withered away in seconds and turned into dust. I had her remains swept outside and promptly forgot about her."

"Are vampires immune to entropy curses?" Rachel asked.

"Not necessarily," I replied. "Magic in all its forms is formidable. Saying something as boastful as *That could NEVER work on ME* is the same as inviting disaster. The issue regarding that fool's spell-crafting is that she was a complete *hack*. She tied her curses to the life force of her enemies to power it. Ordinarily, not a bad technique, but she used it as a one-stop solution for *all* her attacks."

"I don't follow," Rachel said. "All this talk of magic is new to me."

"To simplify it to its most basic concept, magic comes in two varieties," I explained to her. "White and black. Both types are sacrificial in nature. To cast a white spell, the power comes from within you. You're sacrificing your own energy to fuel it. To cast a black spell, you use the power of someone else. You're sacrificing *their* energy to fuel it. Get it now?"

"I think so," Rachel said. "So, white is good, and black is bad?"

"Hardly," I said with a *tsk*. "Magic is a neutral force in all forms. Its morality is determined by its *use*, not its *origin*. For example, what if a wizard specializing in healing magic didn't have enough personal power to cure someone with a mortal affliction? Would you call it an evil act if others voluntarily gave their own energy to him so that he could use it to save his patient? Is that any different from donating your plasma during a blood drive?"

"I guess," Rachel said. "But if that's the case, then how can white magic be used to harm someone?"

"Asks the girl who apparently has never had a lightning bolt flung at her face," I said sourly. "Anyway, to conclude my story, the witch thoughtlessly used her curse against me, but failed to realize that since I am undead, I have no life force with which to power it. So, the magic rebounded and latched itself to the nearest living source, which was *her*. And that was the end of that."

"Did you warn her in the same tone of voice you used to warn Doug about Schulz?" Rachel suddenly asked.

"I don't know. Maybe? Yes? Absolutely," I replied. "Why? What does it matter?"

"Well, that's not really giving a warning, Kyler. It's more like taunting them with the knowledge that something terrible is about to occur without sharing the details."

"Semantics!" I declared.

"Would you please put some clothes on?"

"Stop telling me what to do," I said crossly as I tossed myself back onto the bed. "You could at least *try* to sound more impressed, daughter. You just learned a valuable lesson about the nature of magic straight from the lips of a thaumaturgist of eld. Many would-be evokers would kill for the opportunity to study at my foot."

"And what, pray tell, is a *thaumaturgist of eld*?" Rachel asked sarcastically.

"Just an old-timey way of saying a wizard who really knows his craft," I said humbly. "I was a graduating student of the Scholomance, I'll have you know. Within its blackened halls, I mastered arts both wonderous and profane. With one breath, I could create a miracle. With the next, I could unleash a *disaster*. The power I wielded over life and death was unmatched . . . oh! Speaking of which . . ."

With some excitement, I summoned forth my character status sheet and stared at the options that had been unlocked when I reached Level Thirteen. As Alpha had promised, from Level Ten and up, I would receive access to what she called a skill tree.

Once every level, I would receive three status points to level up my basic attributes like strength and constitution. But I would also receive three points per level to invest in the skill tree, unlocking new abilities that would deeply impact the way I used my powers.

The stats I needed to upgrade were a no-brainer. I placed my first three points into endurance and dumped the remaining six into constitution, increasing my health points to thirty-two, while bumping up my tolerance for intense cardiovascular activity to an impressive thirty-five minutes. With this, my human form had gained considerably improved survivability. Thirty-two health points was nothing to write home about, though. I wouldn't feel truly at ease until I had that number over one hundred.

It was something to work toward, I supposed.

Now, with that out of the way, I jumped to the interesting part and studied my skill tree. It was divided into four equal sections with branching paths down each line, leading to powers I'd previously possessed, as well as entirely new abilities, which I found very enticing.

"Incredible," I murmured to myself as I perused these exciting possibilities. "Look at this! These trees are branched into four separate routes, each representing the paths my siblings and I followed. Beasts, mist, shapes, blood. All the power we ever wielded, now up for offer for the price of but a few dead monsters!"

I then began laughing at myself. "How absurd," I said between giggling fits.

"What's got you so amused?" Rachel asked in her usual flippant manner.

"Oh, it's just . . . how to put this?" I said after settling down a bit. "I once considered myself near the pinnacle of sorcery, beneath just my sister and my mother. But lo and behold, daughter; all my centuries of hard-earned knowledge and gradual expertise are now *here*, floating before my eyes, reduced to a few nodules on a glorified spreadsheet. Everything that I represented, everything that distinguished me . . . to see it presented in this reductive manner . . . It somehow feels both hysterical *and* diminishing."

"Ah," Rachel said. "I bet there's a word for that feeling in German."

"The Germans have a word for everything, Rachel," I said as I continued to stare at the sheet. "It's probably something they're taught in kindergarten and encouraged to use against crybabies by their parents. *Narrschmerzlichspott?*"

"Don't be rude. All the German people I've ever met have been perfectly kind," Rachel said frostily.

"Of course," I said. "That's what the Kaiser's lads were known for in the trenches. Kindness and baked goods. All that bayoneting was just their way of asking their neighbors if they wanted to try some *bienenstich kuchen*."

"That's not a real word, you made that up," Rachel said accusingly. "Do you have some sort of problem with Germany?"

"Honestly?" I frowned as I recalled an annoying memory. "I once fought a Lutheran knight of the old kingdom for the fate of a girl who'd caught my roaming eye. He interfered before I could properly introduce myself to her and dared to challenge me. Even worse, he won our subsequent duel and drove me away. Everything about that night was a shameful disgrace."

"Whatever happened to the girl?"

"She married him. Bloody playboy that he was. I wasn't obsessed, though. I didn't care. I still don't. To hell with them both! He got lucky and she missed out."

"What were their names?" Rachel wondered.

"Adelbert and Emmaline," I said darkly.

"*Clearly* not obsessed," Rachel said with an audible smirk.

"Oh, shut up," I muttered. "I beat him eventually, y'know. You could say he was my first true rival. The only genuine holy knight I've ever faced. It took me forty years and twenty attempts, though. Humans aren't supposed to get stronger with age, but Adelbert *loved* making me angry."

"What was he like?"

"*Entirely* too forgiving," I said as I sat up. "And he laughed far too often! He was always making jests at the drop of a hat! The smug fool never took anything seriously. He and Emmaline both. Far too much laughter and cheer. That's not a proper marriage! It was the bloody Dark Ages; they should have shown a little grave solemnity! Should have thought of their station! But *noooo*, they gave no consideration to appearances and lived like playful children. Even now, I'm embarrassed for them both."

"You sound as though you miss them," Rachel said.

"What? No! Don't be silly," I scoffed. "As I said, we were rivals! It's the duels I miss, that's all. He was the only mortal I ever met who could really challenge me, which I found *extremely vexing*. From the moment I met him, my task was to extinguish his vile light and prove my superiority."

"How'd you go about doing that?"

"Well, Bert was always riding around the countryside doing good deeds for no apparent reason. Probably driven by his faith or some similar insanity. So, I'd occasionally ambush him or show up when he least expected it and pick a fight. Heh, one time I appeared wearing the armor of his best friend and fought him to a standstill in a royal tourney. Nearly got him too, but Emma figured out it was me and warned him in time."

"Never underestimate a devoted wife," Rachel said sagely.

"A lesson those two taught me well," I said quietly. Then I shook my head violently in an attempt to clear it. "Goodness, Rachel. Didn't I tell you not to bring up any old memories today?"

"And didn't *I* ask you to please put on some clothes?" she countered.

"Ha! *Touché.*"

After giving the matter some thought, I decided to spend my first six points in blood, the skill tree with which I was most familiar. I first went three for three into a spell called Blood Orb, then followed it up by going three for three in Hemokinesis, which completely restored my ability to telekinetically manipulate blood.

As soon as I selected those talents, I felt a familiar sensation of power return to me. My awareness of the very blood stored in my veins now burned within me, a resource waiting to be used. I ran the tip of my finger over one of my teeth and smiled gleefully as I caused the drop of blood welling at its tip to float away and dance throughout the air.

"The Lord of Blood is *back*," I announced to the dog and spear.

"Well, oh Lord of Blood, we still don't know what caused your body to change so rapidly," Rachel said. "Sorry to bust your bloody bubble—oh, that sounds so gross as I say it aloud—but don't you think finding that out should be your top priority?"

"Are you still focused on that?" I said mockingly. "I figured that out ages ago. Feels like centuries. You really need to get caught up with the times, Rach."

"What? Well, would you mind sharing with the class?" Rachel said with more of her trademark exasperated annoyance. "Our fates are tied to each other's, remember? If something's affecting you, then I should know about it as well."

"Sure, sure," I said as I resumed studying my skill tree to decide where my final three points should go.

"Well?" she said.

"Just a moment, please," I replied as I considered my options.

"KYLER!" she shouted, breaking my concentration.

"Okay, all right!" I said, yelling in return. "Rachel, use your head! This body was malnourished and weak. Kyler Evans probably hadn't had a decent meal in years, nor any regular sleep. Living like that is extremely harmful for a young person's physical development. But ever since I took over, we've been eating and sleeping extremely well. Combine that with the healing ability I acquired from that crab, and this is the result. A strong, healthy body restored to peak condition. If anything, this is probably what Evans was *meant* to be like, if his life hadn't been so miserable."

"They tortured him," Rachel said angrily. "All the resources of a noble family and that academy, and this is how he was treated. Like a dog. Doesn't that infuriate you?"

"It doesn't please me," I said. "But there's nothing we can do about that. More importantly, it's not our fight. Getting involved with those people won't benefit us in any way."

"It doesn't have to benefit us, Kyler," Rachel said. "We can *choose* to avenge him of our own accord. Because he was a boy who deserves justice, as do all the innocent who suffer."

"Daughter, throw that fantasy away, I urge you," I pleaded. "No matter how righteous you believe yourself to be, I promise that soon enough, *you* will be the reason an innocent person suffers. Not because of malicious intentions, but because of simple, desperate *need*. You're a vampire now, Rachel. You aren't allowed to be a good person anymore."

"Don't tell me what I can be!" she said. "I know who I am!"

"Just as *I* know what you *are*," I said. "Well, whatever. Some lessons are best learned by themselves. Hey, you know what? I'm going all in on basic Transfiguration. Three for three."

"What?" Rachel said, caught off-guard by the change of topic.

"Transfiguration," I said with an idiotic smile on my face. "This was a power unique to my sister, Protea. She could reconfigure her own form into anything she imagined! Transform and become whatever she wished! A bat, a wolf, a titanic dragon! She was incredible! Sadly, such abilities are far too deep into this skill tree for me to reach now, but the basic form of the skill was easy to acquire. What I've gained isn't true shapeshifting, but I *can* now make alterations to my appearance and my clothing."

I stood up and summoned the equipment I'd gathered so far during my adventures. I then studied myself critically in the mirror and clucked my tongue in disapproval. "Oh dear, oh dear, oh dear. I mean, it's utilitarian, I suppose, but is that good enough? I don't think it is."

"Well, what do you expect, Kyler?" Rachel asked. "It's just basic gear. The truly eye-catching pieces can only be earned from higher-leveled targets."

"Even if that's the case, I still reserve the right to look like a gentleman," I replied. "Style is the right of all sentient beings."

With that in mind, I closed my eyes and focused. Using this new power came surprisingly easy to me. It was as if I'd wielded it since birth. That must have been an anti-frustration feature of the system. By making new abilities as intuitive to understand as possible, it prevented Hunters from having to needlessly experiment to grasp how to use their new abilities. I approved of such a thoughtful design.

As I cast Transfiguration, I watched as the appearance of my armor transformed into a nicely matching set of dark pants, polished leather shoes, and a shirt and tie with a handsome maroon vest to top it off. All I was missing now was a nice gold pocket watch to complete the look.

"My clothing still maintains its defensive value, but now it's *so* much easier on the eyes," I boasted. "Admit it, Rachel. Daddy looks *good*."

"Uh. Uh, yeah," Rachel said. "You look . . . nice."

"Do I really?"

"I said so, didn't I?"

Oh, dear, did my ears detect a note of shyness in her voice?

I decided to store that away for now. For future amusement.

After evaluating my reflection once more, I gave myself a whistle of appreciation. "Looking good, feeling good, *yadda yadda*. Just in time for our evening meal, too! What a good day to be alive, am I right?"

[Your use of magic has triggered your vampiric Hunger.]
[Hunger: 1/10.]

"Impressive. The system has even managed to quantify that?" I said to myself.

[Warning!]
[When your Hunger reaches 10/10, you will enter an uncontrollable FEEDING FRENZY.]

"Well, duh. Calm down, you silly system, you're not dealing with a newblood," I said. "I'll keep track of things."

Honestly, the status screen could be such a nattering old hen, couldn't it?

[Warning!]
[Your progeny RACHEL's Hunger is currently 9/10.]
[Your progeny RACHEL will soon enter an uncontrollable FEEDING FRENZY.]

"Hey, Rachel, why don't you and I take an evening constitutional before dinner," I quickly suggested. "What do you say? That sounds like fun, right?"

"Why? Jamie and her men are waiting for you downstairs," she said churlishly. "Let's just get it over with."

"Rachel, let's just go for a freakin' walk, PLEEEEASE," I strongly urged as I grabbed her and jumped out of the room's only window before she could argue with me any further.

CHAPTER NINETEEN

When in a desperate situation, the most important thing you can do for yourself is remain calm. It may not be easy to do, but staying rational when panic is lurking on the periphery is what differentiates a potential survivor from a potential victim. Pardon my language, but in such scenarios, the play of the day will always be made by the ones who *keep their shit together.*

During an emergency, possessing a correct mindset is *everything.*

That was why I didn't immediately place Rachel into storage when I learned how close she was to experiencing the affliction. Doing so would have added additional stress to what she was already undoubtedly beginning to experience. The sudden change in her surroundings might have even driven her insane.

I wouldn't have been able to command her to sleep, either. During a frenzy, a vampire will obey nothing but their urge to feed. Even the voice of their master is dimmed by the overwhelming hunger. It is a fearsome state, during which we are at our most monstrous.

The worst part was that it couldn't be resisted. The hunger came by design, courtesy of Great Crusica herself. When lost in the throes of the affliction, it *had* to be appeased. And a mere sip wouldn't suffice.

Rachel was going to have to kill a few people.

Poor little fool.

I couldn't let it happen in the Narrows, though. Things were beginning to develop nicely for us here. What manner of guest repays the hospitality of his hostess by allowing his child to massacre her neighbors? That was the sort of *faux pas* that got people whispering about you behind your back.

Fortunately, there was a solution.

"What are you doing, Kyler?" Rachel asked in alarm as I took off racing for the nearest wall of the settlement and scaled it, leaping to the forest floor and running from town as quickly as my feet would allow. Behind me, I could hear Schulz's frustrated barking as he was left behind.

Sorry, boy, I thought sadly. *But this isn't a party you'll want to attend. I'll make it up to you later.*

After about twenty minutes of dashing madly through the forest, I finally slowed so that I could better survey my surroundings. There didn't appear to be anyone nearby, and we were far from the traveler's road used to connect the Narrows to Gardenia.

Excellent. We were now exactly where we needed to be. *Things should work out just fine for us now—*

"*Kyler!*" Rachel yelled with growing fury. "*Where* have you taken me?"

Ouch. Was there anything half as painful to endure as someone's angry voice yelling in your ear? If Rachel were any louder, she would have given me tinnitus.

"I had to get you away from the town's residents," I said to her calmly as I reduced my pace to a walk. "You don't appear to have realized it yet, but you're about to snap."

"If I'm about to *snap*, it's because of you playing another one of your ridiculous games with me!" she retorted. "Just tell me what's happening!"

"What's *happening*, Rachel, is that you haven't been feeding," I said as a little anger of my own at her foolishness rose to match hers. "You haven't absorbed even a drop of energy from any of the kills I've provided for you and now you're about to experience a dangerous psychotic disconnection that will turn you into a ravenous, uncontrollable fiend until your body receives what it needs. Our only hope of preventing this is to get you some blood *now*."

"I'm fine! I feel perfectly fine!" she insisted. "If anything's wrong in this situation, it's your paranoia! I am a divine armament, fit to be wielded by those with the purest of hearts! My very touch burns the wicked! In the name of my goddess, I am meant for *righteous deeds*!"

"You're deluded," I said to her. "Rachel, if any of what you just said was true, then how am I able to hold you? My hand isn't exactly bursting into flames. I'd notice if it did, it's a very memorable sensation."

"Stop mocking me!" Rachel shrieked. "All you do is laugh at me, give me orders, and disrespect the holy purpose for which I surrendered my mortal life! You're cruel and heartless! Y-you're without tact and a-and unkind!"

"I apologize if I've hurt your feelings," I said. "My only intent was to help you adjust during your time of transition. I may have been thoughtless in my approach, but it was only with the intent of helping you."

"DON'T SPEAK TO ME AS THOUGH I WERE A CHILD!" thundered Rachel. "Stop patronizing me!"

"I'm being sincere, I assure you. My method was clearly flawed, but I was never good at interacting with my progeny to begin with. I'm poor at developing healthy relationships with my children."

"I AM NOT YOUR CHILD!"

"You are. And as your maker, I now challenge myself to do better by you than I have with others in the past. We may very well be the only vampires to exist on this planet. If that is so, I'd prefer my daughter not hate me."

"I'm not your daughter, Kyler," she raged. "I am NOT YOUR CHILD! You didn't father me, you pathetic corpse; you're the disease raging inside of me! It hurts! Every moment of every day *hurts*! Why is it so *painful*?"

"You already know the answer to that," I said to her. "And it only grows worse the longer you resist. This isn't something that can be conquered by strength of will, Rachel. Denial of reality will just lead to more tragic results. You need to trust me."

"YOU DID THIS TO ME!"

"Not intentionally," I reminded her. "Don't paint over the details of what happened with fantasies of victimization. It was a fight to the death, and we were both trying to hurt each other. It wasn't a good night for either of us."

"I HATE YOU! I HATE YOU I HATE YOU I HATE YOU!" she began to drone with increasingly rabid intensity.

"You don't even sound like yourself anymore," I lamented. "Is this who you are? Where's the pompous little squire gone to? Where's my little church mouse hidden herself? Who's this raging lunatic that's taken her place?"

". . . I'm hungry, Kyler. I'm *so* hungry."

"I know you are, Rachel. That's why we're out here. I'm going to help you," I promised her. "But you must hold on just a little longer, all right?"

"Where are we going?"

"There was a wanted poster in Jamie's tavern," I said. "I noticed it when we first arrived. Bandits, Rachel. Highway men plaguing the road between the Narrows and the next settlement. Five, maybe ten disposable little lives committing petty indecencies against the common good. Isn't that nice? I bet you can practically taste their blood already, can't you?"

"I . . . where are they?"

"Nearby. They've left traces of their passing. They moved cleverly for ordinary men, but they can't mask themselves from my eye or nose. Any moment now, we'll come across their hideaway. Any—"

The terrified voice of a young woman begging for help suddenly filled the night air, startling me.

"—moment now," I finished a moment later.

Before long, I discovered the entrance to a large cavern alongside a massive outcropping of stone covered in large swathes of vegetation that made it difficult to see in the darkness of the forest. Before it sat two suspicious-looking men warming themselves in front of a campfire.

Suddenly, a young woman in torn finery ran out of the cave, crying. A bald man wearing only a pair of battered trousers followed shortly after, yelling angrily as he chased her. Across his face were four vivid lines of red, where the girl's fingernails had scored him.

"Bitch!" he bellowed after backhanding her once he'd caught up, knocking the poor thing to the ground and rendering her unconscious. "Look at what you did to me! Look at what you did!"

"Girl's got a legal right to defend herself," one of the watchmen snickered.

"I didn't even do anything to her yet!" the big man groused. "But I will! She's gonna make this up to me, I promise she will!"

"I don't see any difference, Hren," snorted one of his companions. "You're as pretty as ever."

"Fuck yourself, Carter!" Hren yelled in return. "I gotta visit my mom on Sunday. I can't have this little cow making me look like this, can I? It's not right!"

"Looking like what, I wonder?" I asked as I deactivated my Stealth skill and held my hands out over their fire. "A thief and a would-be rapist?"

The three of them nearly jumped out of their skins at the sight of me, which I found gratifying. I could see myself having a lot of fun with Stealth in the future.

"And who the fuck is this?" bellowed Hren. "You fucking let someone sneak into camp, you stupid shits?"

"He just popped out of thin air!" Carter said defensively. "What are we supposed to do about that?"

"You're *supposed* to keep your fucking eyes open!"

Dismayed by Hren's vulgarity, I held a finger over my lips before pointing at the girl he'd attacked. "Sir, even if she's presently insensate, we're still standing before a lady. Is such foul language *truly* necessary?"

"Fancy, isn't he?" said the second guard as he stood up.

"I want his clothes," Carter said as he drew his knife.

"Fuck you, we roll for each item," Hren said nastily as he waddled toward me. "You get lost on the road, fancy Dan? Tried to take a shortcut? Too bad, son. You took the *wrooong* fucking turn."

"Is this all of you?" I asked with some disappointment. "I was hoping there'd be more."

"No need to wake anyone else," Hren said. "They're still sleeping off yesterday's fun."

"Any more like her?" I asked, tilting my head toward the girl.

"Last pick of the litter," Hren leered nastily. "We made her watch what we did to the others."

"Well, that's an awful thing to do to someone," I said quietly. "That's going to be a hard thing for her to live through."

"She *ain't* gonna live through it. As a matter of fact, neither are you," Hren asserted.

"That girl's fate isn't for you to decide, pig," I informed him. "Rachel, have you heard enough?"

"Kyler . . ." she said.

"I assume that's a yes," I said. "Have at it. Enjoy yourself."

"Kyler," she said once more.

"Yes?"

"Please . . . please *kill them*," she begged.

I paused, surprised by her request. Then I shook my head. "No," I said.

"Why not?" Rachel asked in a desperate voice.

"Because *you* need to do it," I said. "This isn't for my sake. I won't deny you your first kill."

"I've killed before!" she exclaimed. "Dozens of times! Hundreds!"

"No," I said. "You were wielded. Directed. It was never of your own volition. You were used as a tool. That changes now. If you truly despise these men, if you want to punish them, if you desire their lives and their blood, then *claim them*."

"How?"

"Use my power. It's your right as my kin."

"I . . . I can't do this," she said. "I can't! I'm forbidden to take the lives of ordinary men. Even if they are sinners!"

"No, you aren't," I told her. "I give you permission. Take them. They belong to you. Drink well."

"I . . . I can't!" She trembled. "This is not the purpose for which I was made."

"But it *is* the purpose for which you were reborn," I said.

"Kyler, I cannot—"

"Daughter," I said, cutting her off. "Stop fighting yourself. Stop *hurting* yourself. You're hungry. You're tired. And these so-called men have nothing to offer the world. You say you believe in justice? Then enforce it!"

"Enforce it . . ." she murmured.

"Punish them," I whispered.

"Punish them . . ." she repeated.

"They deserve it," I urged her.

". . . They *do* deserve it," she decided.

"Who the fuck is he speaking with?" asked Hren.

"I don't see anybody," said Carter. "He must be on something."

"I hope he's still got some in his pockets. Let's find out," the third man said eagerly. ". . . Huh?" he suddenly said in dumbfounded surprise.

I released my grip on the spear and stepped back. To the shock of the three thieves standing before me, it floated in midair in perfect stillness. Then it slowly shifted into a horizontal position and began to turn towards the bandits, moving from left to right and back again, pointing its tip at each man as if trying to decide which it wanted first.

"What's it doing?" asked Carter. "What the hell is that thing doing?"

"If I had to hazard a guess, I'd say she's playing *Eeny, meeny, miny, moe*," I informed him.

Suddenly, Rachel shifted sharply to the center and aimed herself directly at Hren, the one who'd attacked the girl earlier. I then heard her begin to growl.

"Hey, big man? I think I'd start running for my life right about now if I were you," I helpfully suggested.

"HE'S A FUCKING HUNTER!" Hren bellowed. "ON YOUR FEET, ALL! WE'RE BEING RAIDED! WE'RE BEING RAIDED—"

In the blink of an eye, Rachel went through him. Once, twice, thrice. Like a large sewing needle through a bottle of juice. With her final strike she rose higher into the air with him hanging off her point, drinking him as they floated together. Then she dropped his body onto his companion, Carter, pinning him to the ground with the weight of his friend's corpse. When Carter parted his lips to scream, she plunged downward into his mouth and embedded herself into the earth through the back of his head. Then she drained him as well.

Meanwhile, eight more men came running from the cavern entrance in various stages of undress, all of them wielding weaponry and wondering what the hell was going on.

Truly, the dinner bell had rung.

"Justice," whispered Rachel as she prepared to throw herself at them.

Sure. Why not?

Later, I journeyed back to the Narrows while carrying the girl in my arms. While I walked, Rachel floated happily above me, undoubtedly feeling a great sense of relief now that she'd finally stopped battling her nature.

After Rachel had dispensed with the remaining scum, I explored the cavern and saw that Hren hadn't lied about the fate of the girl's fellow prisoners. I now carried their bodies inside my storage, as well as the merchandise that had been stolen. I also took the remains of the bandits themselves, having decided the best course of action would be to deliver the girl, the goods, and the bodies to town. That way I could claim the posted reward, as well as offer Jamie an excuse for my sudden disappearance.

"Is it like this all the time?" Rachel asked me dreamily as she coasted along the wind. "Does it always feel this . . . *perfect?*"

"When we feed? Always," I said to her. "But now that you've overcome your first obstacle, a second challenge stands before you. Now you need to *master* your hunger."

"Huh? But you were always telling me I had to feed! And now that I have, you're telling me to do it less often?" she said plaintively.

"It's paradoxical, isn't it?" I said with a grin. "Sadly, everything seems to be that way with our kind. You nearly experienced the affliction, when you denied yourself blood for too long. But there's an equal danger lying in wait if you feed too often, known as *the revelry.*"

"The what?" Rachel asked.

"The revelry," I repeated. "It's where the myth of the bacchanal comes from. Are you familiar with the story of poor Orpheus? He came across the brides of Dionysus while they were having a feast and became their main course."

"Oh, right," Rachel said. "That was a horrifying tale. It ended with him being torn apart, didn't it?"

"Converted into a vampire *then* torn apart," I corrected her. "So that he could spend the rest of eternity as a head on a plate. Dionysus was an alias for my brother, Vitor. He didn't appreciate a musician cavorting with his women and made his feelings known."

"He sounds like a complete bastard," Rachel said, aghast.

"He could be a difficult person to love," I admitted. "He had his challenges. Our mother was always strictest with him."

"So, if I drink too often . . .?"

"You'll become addicted to it," I said. "An unbreakable addiction that will haunt your every thought. It'll be as if you were trapped in the frenzy, twenty-four-seven."

"By the goddess . . ."

"I doubt she'd be of much help to you."

"I can do it," Rachel said a few minutes later. "I can absolutely do it! I'm finished with suffering for no reason. Such a purposeless existence holds no appeal for me."

"Attagirl," I replied. "That's the kind of personal growth I like to see."

"Kyler, will you teach me more?" Rachel suddenly asked. "I want to know so much more about what we are! I feel like there are . . . like there are suddenly doors opening for me every which way I look! And now I'm having such difficulty deciding which ones I want to walk through! The possibilities feel so endless!"

"Okay, all right, calm down, newbie," I said fondly. "You've taken a big step today, and I'm proud of you. But remember to pace yourself. Eternity awaits. You don't have to run towards it."

"Hmph. I'd need feet with which to run first, wouldn't I?" Rachel said. "Gods, suddenly this form seems so inadequate to my needs. There's so much more I want to do! Why am I like this? I don't want to be a spear any longer!"

"Really?" I said with some surprise. "You seemed so proud of yourself before."

"Ignorance," Rachel said. "What did I know about anything? It isn't fair! How can I be so confined! I need . . . I need . . . I need more!"

Suddenly I felt a painful tugging sensation coming from within, as Rachel began pulling more power away from me. "Rachel . . . what are you doing?" I asked in alarm.

"I need . . . I need just a little more. Just a little more," Rachel said fervently as she continued to drain away my strength. What truly horrified me was that I couldn't stop her! I tried to resist, but in her sudden desire to transcend her form, Rachel had put up some kind of wall that somehow prevented me from denying her access. I fell to one knee and accidentally dropped the girl I'd been carrying.

"Rachel, *stop*," I said to her. "You're taking too much."

"I have to," Rachel said pleadingly. "I'm sorry, Kyler, but I *have to*!"

I couldn't let this continue. I instinctively knew that if Rachel kept this up, she would inadvertently destroy me in the process. I couldn't allow that to happen. A thousand years of ruthless survival wouldn't allow the existence of Kyler Stragos to be snuffed away by an impertinent child's inability to contain herself.

Gathering my will, my power, and my desperation to live, I cast my hand toward my errant daughter and ordered her to cease this foolish behavior at once.

"*No . . . no, Kyler! Just wait! Please! Just one more moment—*"

"*END THIS NOW!*" I commanded her.

Rachel gave an anguished cry and dropped from the sky with an audible thud. As I stood there wearily with my hands on my knees, feeling like a weak old man, I wondered what had come over Rachel, as well as how the hell she'd come so close to ending me.

Could this insolent brat possibly be stronger than her creator? One of the four great Lords? I'd never heard of such a thing occurring before, but the evidence was now before me.

Damn it. Was I going to have to kill another one of my children?

As I considered that dreadful possibility, a young girl's painful moan caught my attention. Thinking it may have been the victim I'd rescued earlier regaining consciousness, I turned around, only to be surprised by the sight of an entirely different young woman lying on the grass, dressed in a white sleeping gown.

And who exactly was this supposed to be?

The girl dazedly raised her head and smiled weakly at me. "Kyler?" she mumbled before passing out.

"Rachel?" I asked with genuine shock. What was going *on* here?

Suddenly, a ferocious need for blood began to overwhelm me. *Damn it, Rachel*, I thought angrily. A quick scan of my status showed that my hunger had grown to a ravenous eight out of ten. Thanks to her little outburst, now *I* was the one on the urge of a ravenous breakdown.

Luckily, I had my human form to rely on. I immediately switched out and relaxed as the bloodlust faded.

Do you see now what I meant about staying calm in a desperate situation? It's like they say, kids. Cooler heads will *always* prevail—

"ON YOUR KNEES, BANDIT!" screamed some random guy whose voice I thought I recognized as he quickly approached me. Due to the chaos of the previous few minutes, he and the partner supporting him had completely gotten the drop on me.

"Uh, guys, I can assure you, I'm not a bandit," I protested.

"I SAID GET ON YOUR KNEES!" he yelled in reply. That's when I noticed two things. The first was that he was carrying a *big* metal shield on his right arm, and the second was that he and his ally were wearing the symbol of Vandal Academy on their armor.

That's when my memory clicked into place. I really did know this guy. This was Nick Pankratz! Heh, wasn't that a coincidence? What were the odds of running into someone you knew out in the middle of nowhere?

Before I could comment on that, however, Pankratz raised his shield high and used it to viciously club me alongside the head.

Okay, cool, now it was *my* turn to be unconscious.

Great job, Rachel.

Seriously. Great job.

CHAPTER TWENTY

It's funny, the things that pop up in your mind after being battered into an unconscious state. The things you've experienced and the people you remember. For a fellow like me, that's an awfully long list to go through. And most of it, if I'm being honest with myself, was nightmarish.

I was lucky that night, though. Instead of recalling something horrific or tragic, I remembered a girl named Rose.

It was late 1983, and I was in a packed West End nightclub for the elite and the affluent called Memories, with my frontal lobe feeling half-dissolved due to all the cocaine-saturated blood I'd been draining from its dusted little yuppie denizens throughout the night. These horrid people had all been out celebrating another successful year for the nation. And why wouldn't they be? The market was setting new records, profits were soaring, once again the kingdom abided. Truly, the prophets of Thatcherism had guided their faithful to the promised land.

It was a shame about all the little lives they'd ruined to get there. But was that really their fault? It wasn't as though you could mine for diamonds in a poor man's lungs. Only coal dust.

Earlier that day, I'd been in Germany on personal business, paying my respects to the ossuary that housed the remains of my companions Adelbert and Emmaline. Once more, the shade of Emma stood proudly at the entrance to the tomb, waiting to ward off my approach, magnificent as she always was.

Once again, we debated.

"I can bring him back," I assured her. "I can bring you *both* back. We could all be reunited."

"It wouldn't truly be us, Kyler," she gently replied. "Merely our shadows."

"It wounds me to hear you say that," I said.

"It was the wounds you left that stole our lives to begin with," she reminded me.

"An error I could correct if only you'd let me."

"The ending of a life well-lived is never erroneous, no matter how tragic the circumstances of its conclusion," she said with a faint smile. "I hope you understand that one day."

"Will you ever forgive me?"

"Oh, Kyler," she said compassionately, with her sweetest voice. "That will simply never happen. Begone from this place and never return, you evil bastard."

"Another time, then," I said stiffly as I turned to leave.

"The answer will never change," she said tauntingly.

"Neither will I," I vowed bitterly as I departed.

I should have gone home after that. Instead, I changed flights and somehow found myself in *Soho*. Was I there because I wanted to blow off some stress by partying or because I wanted to glut myself on blood without feeling guilty about the body count?

Who can really say? It was a long time ago.

Eventually, I ended up at Memories, and after enjoying a few initial cheap thrills, I began to grow listless and bored. Mostly, I was drowning in contempt for my fellow clubgoers. Goodness, just *looking* at those weak-willed little prats annoyed me.

The ruling elite of England had always been dominated by coldhearted bastards, so there was nothing new about the way the current generation behaved. But at least the old breed of snobs had a certain hardness to them that you could almost respect. At their core they were still opportunistic killers who'd gladly do the necessary work for themselves. Wet, red hands clutching rich rewards. If there was a union to bust, they'd be the first of the crowd to swing the pipe.

But this new class of twa—twerps? No. Sheltered, miserable little cowards who used spreadsheets and computer monitors to tabulate and calculate their decision-making for them. They acted without thought for the consequences and traded the future for the immediacy of now. And right now, they wanted to party.

I was strongly considering sealing the exits and creating a few ghouls. You know, doing my part to make London a safer place for ordinary people. Try being an unsung hero.

But that was when *she* walked in.

In came Rose like a siren from the alleyways, ignoring the cover fee to survey the room with the eyes of a predator who'd caught the scent of a wounded lamb. Stalking forth assertively as though she were a living personification of battered leather and torn nylons, her domineering stance bore the volatile values of the street like a suit of armor that shielded her from the world. To me, she appeared crafted from marble; something of great beauty with no softness to it at all.

With my attention thoroughly captured, I watched from my table as she approached the center of the floor, pushing heedlessly past anyone in her way, and flipping them off without a backward glance when they protested her rudeness.

Once she found the spot she wanted to claim, she threw off her jacket and began to dance.

It was a memorable sight.

From the moment she started, it was clear that the girl was blessed with a mesmerizing, almost *primal* talent that immediately drew in the gazes of all who witnessed it. Such serpentine grace was something that only a precious few are gifted with at birth and can never be taught. She easily commanded her body with a precision that professionals strove in futility to master their entire lives, and she did it with a cold indifference that would have driven Salieri to madness all over again.

From that moment on, the club belonged to her, conquered in mere moments by her presence alone. Her fellow dancers were naught but captivated serfs, begging for a moment's indulgence from their new gutter punk liege, but this manic monarch had nothing to offer her admirers. She wasn't there for their sakes. They were mere accoutrements, existing for her entertainment.

Any who approached her, man or woman, she pushed away or ignored. When some tried too forcefully, she hurt them, sneering contemptuously at these would-be suitors as they lay tearfully on the floor, bleeding from the wounds she was quick to inflict. The message was easily understood.

Do not approach.

Hands off.

Her reign continued for what seemed an eternity. A kingdom of one, where her admirers could only stare at her with lust and longing as she continued to reject them. It seemed no one was good enough to stand alongside her and she wanted everyone to know it, as though she were forcing them to marinate in their personal inadequacies until desperation to prove otherwise drove them to their breaking points.

I liked her attitude.

After snatching away a beer from some random prick and scaring him away when he got cheeky over it, I took a long swallow as I approached her. She glared at me as I drew nearer, and I paused to bask in such wonderfully uninhibited hostility. Then I finished my drink, threw the empty bottle behind me, and stepped forth.

She sneered at the sight of me but said nothing else. That was fine with me. I didn't want to talk either. Instead, I took up her unspoken challenge, and began moving in rhythm with her.

Poorly.

You were expecting differently, weren't you? I know, I know, this would have been a great story if I lied and said that all vampires can dance beautifully. Some of us actually can! But sadly, I wasn't one of them. At my best, I moved like an inflatable prop at a used car lot.

I could feel the eyes of everyone around us staring in bewilderment as I danced, disbelieving the evidence of their senses. It didn't seem possible that a man could move without using any of the joints in his limbs, but my performance proved them wrong. Many of the onlookers even began laughing and jeering, calling for me to get lost. But I didn't care. It was easy to ignore the mockery when the simple fact of the matter was that my hecklers were background fodder who were less substantive to my daily reality than a discarded tissue.

Eventually, I said, "This place sucks. Wanna go?"

She said, "Sure," so we did.

Take note, everyone. If you want to impress someone with a punk rock attitude, try not giving a damn about impressing them. It's kind of Zen but it works wonders. I normally can't pull that sort of thing off, but remember, at that moment, *I was really high.*

That was why I was the one who walked out of the club alongside her. Not because of vampiric mysticism or dark allure, but because I was too high to die, and thus *dripping* with false confidence.

We spent the rest of the night hanging out and stealing stuff. Some guys tried messing with us, but I knocked them around easily enough and she gleefully kicked them while they were down. Then we had to run from the police for a bit, but we still had a good time. Just before dawn, she gave me the hardest kiss I'd enjoyed in years. Then we said our goodbyes.

That was the last I'd see of her for a while. Fifteen years after that night, I ran into her in Toronto of all places, at a fundraiser where her husband was campaigning for a seat in Parliament on a conservative ticket.

If she was shocked at my appearance not having changed in a decade and a half, then *I* was shocked at the sight of her in a white pantsuit with sensible shoes. Johnny Rotten playing golf with Prince William couldn't have disillusioned me more. I needn't have worried, though. Rose was still Rose beneath it all. While I stood brooding in a corner of the room, she approached me with a smile and whispered, "This place sucks. Want to go?"

Without a moment's hesitation, I said, "Sure."

And we left. We didn't steal anything or run from any cops, but we did fornicate for like half a day, and that was cool, too. Before we said our goodbyes, I asked her if she wanted to live forever. She gave it a moment's thought and then shook her head.

"How come?" I asked, disappointed by her choice.

"Wouldn't I eventually get bored?" she said.

Before I could think of a reply, she kissed me again and left.

Punk rock will *never* die.

"All right, wake up, stupid," Pankratz said before giving me a few slaps on the cheek. "We've got questions to ask."

After I drearily regained consciousness, I took a look at my surroundings and was surprised to see that I was back in Jamie's tavern. These brats had carried me all the way back to the Narrows. I'd have been grateful to them for that if they weren't the reason I'd needed to be carried to begin with.

I was sitting in the middle of the serving room, tied by rope to a chair, staring at Pankratz and a familiar-looking girl with black hair. I knew I'd seen her before, but remembering her name in my human form was surprisingly difficult. As a vampire, I could recall a name instantly if I knew who I was looking at. As a human, it took a little time.

"Cassie?" I asked after it finally came back to me. "You're Cassie, right? The Healer? What are you doing here?"

Cassie looked at me, puzzled. I hadn't noticed it when we first met on that ill-fated school trip, but she was quite the looker; a real doe-eyed beauty with lustrous brown hair. Yeah, my male gaze was thoroughly engaged by the sight of her, which caused me to cheer up despite my unfavorable circumstances.

Why stay negative when you had a good view?

Unfortunately, Pankratz was quick to pick up on my sudden interest. "Hey. Keep your eyes level when you talk to her," he warned me.

"Where's the fun in that?" I wondered.

In response, he hit me again.

"Oh, calm down," I said with a frown after my ears stopped ringing. "I'm flirtatious by nature, big man. I don't mean anything by it."

"You haven't flirted with *me* yet," he replied. "Double standards, much?"

"Try buying me flowers first," I suggested.

"Bandits don't deserve flowers," he replied.

"Well, then you don't deserve *me*," I informed him.

"I really am going to hit you again," he warned me.

"Knock it off, Nick," Cassie said with annoyance as she stepped to my position and placed her hands at each side of my head. "If you keep scrambling his skull with those big hands of yours, he won't be able to tell us anything."

"I'm just watching out for my little sister," Pankratz said amiably as he leaned back against a table. "I'm a Tank. We defend against creeps too."

"Wait, did I hear that right?" I said with surprise. "You two are siblings?"

"Nick is adopted," Cassie corrected me as she continued her examination of my head. "My family took him in after his mother passed away."

"You didn't mention that before," I said accusingly to Pankratz.

"Why would I mention anything to a bandit?" he asked me in confusion. "And why do you know Cassie's name, anyway? When did you meet her?"

I was about to point out that *he* was the one who told me her name, when I realized that I no longer resembled or sounded like the Kyler Evans that he remembered. Maybe the changes this body had gone through were more drastic than I'd realized. He still hadn't recognized me despite our proximity.

Hmm. Interesting.

"Weird," Cassie said softly, before stepping away from me.

"Got him all patched up?" Pankratz asked her.

"No. I didn't do a thing for him. His body healed on its own," she said. "It's as though he has a healing skill. But that can't be possible! We gave him a scan, didn't we? He isn't ascended."

In response, Pankratz removed a strange-looking blue cube from one of his belt's many pouches and waved it over my head. After a few moments, it glowed with a sickly green light before fading back to blue.

"If he has any talent, it's extremely minor," he said. "This dude barely has enough juice to function as a Porter."

"Rude," I said defensively.

"I'm just telling it like it is, bandit," Pankratz said indifferently.

"I'm not a bandit, you dolt," I replied.

"Said the perv who kidnapped the two half-dressed girls," he shot back.

"Who I was taking back to town for treatment after *rescuing* them!" I countered.

"It looked more like you were dragging them away from town to your nasty little hideout," Pankratz said as he began to squeeze his fists. "But it also looked like you were pausing to have a little fun with them first, weren't you, asshole? And then, even knowing we caught you red-handed, you're tossing looks at my *sister*?"

Suddenly, Pankratz hit me again. It wasn't a gentle slap, either. It was a whistling haymaker delivered with full force that knocked my chair to the side, and me with it.

"I gotta admit, I didn't like that," he said as he blew over his reddened knuckles.

"Don't do it. Keep calm," I said.

"Fuck you, bandit," he snorted.

"I'm not talking to you, imbecile," I replied.

"Then who?"

The entrance to the tavern exploded open as the door flew off its hinges. In the doorway, snarling at Pankratz with his white sharp teeth dripping saliva, and his body hunched and ready to explode into violent action, was my dog, Schulz.

Man's best friend in general.

But not *this* one.

CHAPTER TWENTY-ONE

At that point, things really began getting out of hand.

"What the hell is *that*?" Pankratz asked in alarm as he hurriedly equipped his shield.

"I have no idea," Cassie said. "Gods, though. I can feel the power emitting from its aura. It's stronger than any gate beast I've ever seen."

"Shit!" Pankratz swore. "Can you pacify it?"

"I'm trying!" Cassie replied as a white light began emanating from her body, which she focused outwardly to her hands. She then pointed at Schulz and said, *"Rest,"* with a forceful word of command that was laden with authority and otherworldly power.

Schulz blinked for a moment and paused in his growling. Then he shook his head and began glaring at Cassie as though she had just flicked him on his nose.

"Oh, crap, he resisted it," she said.

"What percent?" Pankratz asked.

"Complete! One hundred percent!" she said in a nervous voice. "I think I have aggro, Nick."

"Whatever, I'm on it," he replied confidently. "Come on, Fido! Let me show you the exit!"

Pankratz then ran toward Schulz with such inhuman speed that I realized he must have used one of his Class skills. Some kind of movement enhancer that made it easier for him to intercept any assailants that targeted his other teammates.

He made for an impressive sight when he zipped toward the dog with his shield in front of him. It was clearly a maneuver he'd performed many times before. A bare second later, however, he looked more like a flying ragdoll when Schulz responded by slamming fearlessly into Pankratz and sent him soaring across the room like he was in a zero-gravity environment. Before he could get back on his feet, Schulz was on him, fearlessly tearing into Pankratz's steel shield with his paws and teeth, causing small sparks to fly as he slowly tore through the steel that Pankratz was hiding behind.

"HOLY FUCKING SHIT!" the big man exclaimed. "A little help here, please?!"

"Shut up, I'm on it," Cassie said breathlessly as she cast another spell. This time, a solid-looking beam of light shot forth from her hand and struck Schulz on the head. As before, it barely affected him, but this time he was having none of the Healer's nonsense.

Using a motion like one he'd used the day before, the dog suddenly gripped Pankratz's ankle with his mouth and did a quick spin and release that sent the hapless Tank flying across the room once more, this time crashing into his step-sister, knocking them both to the ground.

Schulz then proudly raised his head and performed a very sarcastic sounding series of barks. "Woof. Woof. Woof. *Woof.*" If I could've translated it, I bet it would have meant something along the lines of, "Don't ever fuck with the big dogs."

I couldn't help but feel disappointed by his choice of language.

"All right, stop that at once," I ordered him.

Schulz paused his gloating to turn my way with a quizzical expression on his face.

"Don't be so pleased with yourself," I warned him. "I'm not happy with you right now and I think you know why."

He barked questioningly at me after snapping my bonds and helping me up.

"What do you mean *why not*?" I asked him. "Look at this mess!"

Schulz whined in reply and then barked again.

"Don't give me that," I told him sternly. "*I'm* not the one who destroyed the tavern's entrance. See the door lying over there? You did that, not me! And while we're on the subject, don't think I forgot about yesterday when you shattered that patio door by throwing Doug through it! You're beginning to make a real *habit* of destroying our friend Jamie's property, Schulz, and I'm going to need you to knock it off. Be more considerate of your surroundings! We're *guests* here."

After I finished my brief lecture, Schulz collapsed to the floor in embarrassment and covered his eyes with his paws to demonstrate his contrition. When I gauged that his apology was sincere, I nodded and reached down to scratch his ear.

"Thank you for thinking of my safety," I told him gratefully. "Thus far, despite your forceful methodology, you have proven to be a true and loyal friend, and for that, you are appreciated. Now, please go apologize to Mister Pankratz so that we can put all this unpleasantness behind us."

Thus prompted, Schulz approached Pankratz and shyly held out his paw. After turning to look at his sister, who gestured for him to hurry up, he turned back to the dog and, with exaggerated slowness, carefully shook the proffered paw. Schulz then barked cheerfully at Pankratz, causing him to visibly flinch, before returning to my side.

I held out a hand to the big man to help him to his feet.

"I forgive you for striking me," I told him. "That misdeed was borne of honorable intentions, so I shall seek no reprisal for it, nor shall any who serve me. It's a good man who defends his loved ones, and some blame does lie with me. I *did* give a lingering glance to your sister, and you were right to object to it."

Next, I turned to Cassie and bowed deeply.

"I apologize for objectifying you," I said. "It was gracious of you to ignore such rude behavior, and I can only sincerely hope I haven't permanently lowered your estimation of my character."

"It's fine," Cassie said evenly. "I grew up working here in my mother's tavern. Some people have tried to do worse over the years than give me a look."

"That still doesn't excuse my actions," I said. "I'm . . . *human* after all. It's my responsibility to see to my own maturation."

Then I paused to consider her words.

"Wait, did you say this was your mother's place?" I asked.

At that moment, Jamie walked in through the destroyed entrance and stared at the messy condition of the serving room in dismay.

"And just what the hell happened here?" she asked numbly.

"Mom!" Cassie said.

"Jamie!" Pankratz said.

"Jamie?" I asked her with some confusion.

"Cassie! Nick!" said Jamie. Then she saw me. "Stragos?"

"Stragos?" asked Pankratz and Cassie.

"Kyler?" asked Rachel as she slowly entered the room with a yawn.

"Kyler?" asked Pankratz and Cassie. Then they both stared at me for a long moment as they realized who I was.

"KYLER?" they said in shock.

"Kyler?" asked Jamie.

"RACHEL!" I yelled in frustration.

"Oops," she said with an embarrassed blush before running upstairs to hide in my room.

Damn it, Rachel.

"Holy shit, my mind is reeling," Pankratz said in disbelief as we cleaned up the serving room under Jamie's annoyed supervision. "Evans, what the hell, man? You're supposed to be dead!"

"My name isn't Evans," I said irritably as I helped him lift a heavy table. "You've got the wrong person."

"Like hell I do," Pankratz scoffed. "Bro, what happened to you? How'd you put on all that weight? And where'd you get the fancy duds from?"

"So, you *did* attend Vandal Academy," Jamie said smugly. "I knew there was something a little off about your story. Are you a runaway or a castoff?"

"Neither!" Pankratz said excitedly. "He's a ghost! Seriously! The school said he had an accident while under questioning and died while receiving treatment. But here he is, barely a week later! My mind is fucking blown!"

"Language," Jamie and I said at the same time.

"I don't understand it," Cassie said as she stared at me. "I had to help examine your body as part of my healing training. Kyler, you were dead. As dead as can be. You had a sword sheathed in your heart."

"Someone stuck him with a sword?" Pankratz asked excitedly. "You never mentioned that!"

"I was sworn to secrecy," Cassie said. "I had to sign a paper made of spellscript and everything. It was binding. Like, I literally couldn't speak of what I'd seen. But I guess learning that Evans isn't really dead has somehow dissolved the contract. Can you . . . can you tell us what happened?"

"Yeah, man, what happened?" Pankratz asked eagerly. "Did the Velas family try to assassinate you or something? I knew that Thalia chick was psycho!"

"I'm *not* Kyler Evans," I insisted. "You're mistaken."

"Bro, you totally are," Pankratz laughed. "God, the more I look at you, the more you resemble that brother of yours. Cat's out of the bag, dude."

I grunted in irritation. "I think I liked you better when you were violating my Miranda rights."

"Water under the bridge!" Pankratz said cheerfully as he threw an arm over my shoulder. "Also, who's Miranda? Is she hot?"

"You're an idiot," I said flatly.

"I might have taken too many shots to the noggin over the years," he replied. "Getting tossed around by that pooch of yours didn't help. Jeez, what have you been feeding him? And can I have some if there's any left over?"

Schulz barked cheerfully at the mention of himself.

"Have you known . . . *Kyler* very long, Nicholas?" Jamie asked him after flashing a smug grin my way. "You two seem very close."

"Totally, we go back ages!" Pankratz said. "I was always trying to get him as a Porter for my squad. Dude's got a mutant capacity for storage, it's unreal! I never understood why his family treated him so poorly over it. I mean, yeah, most Porters aren't that great, but this kid is something else."

"Not a kid, not your friend, not *Evans*," I said more forcefully. "Let's be clear on that. Kyler Evans's family has nothing to do with me, and you and I have only met on two occasions. I'm not who you think I am."

"Do you want to elaborate on that?" Pankratz asked with a slight frown on his face.

"No, I do not," I said bluntly.

I know what you're probably thinking. *Why not just play along with them and make things easier for yourself?*

The answer is that I didn't want to. Deception is an important aspect of being a vampire. Tricking people into believing that you're a human being so that you can catch them unaware is an essential part of survival as an undead being. It's a sort of . . . *masquerade*, you could say. And one that I had grown weary of in my prior existence as the Lord of Blood.

Lying every day for centuries is mentally draining. Always checking to make sure you've kept your background story straight and that it aligns with whatever fiction that you're spinning at the moment, it's *exhausting*.

I may not have wanted to participate in Great Crusica's besieging of humanity, but one of the few things I found surprisingly beneficial about it was that I got to announce to the world who I truly was. And in the two hundred years since, I never went back to hiding it.

So now, with my current situation being what it was, I was extremely reluctant to return to the old way of doing things. And you know what? I didn't have to. It was just as Rachel had told me earlier; *Vampire Lord* was merely my Class. I wasn't beholden to it. It no longer defined my existence.

That also meant that I didn't need to steal a dead boy's identity. I had decided that I would live more honestly in this new life. And part of that honesty would include being myself: Kyler Stragos.

Don't get me wrong, I wasn't going to run around proclaiming to the masses that I was a resurrected civilization-wrecking mass-murdering tyrant who was going to live forever. Some things should just be kept to yourself. I also saw no purpose in sharing the nature of my dual Classes. If someone was curious about the things I was capable of and wanted to know how I could do them, then let them wonder. It was no business of theirs. Just because I wanted to live a more honest life, didn't mean I was going to become a careless fool.

"Kyler, there are going to be a lot of questions about what happened," Cassie said. "I know there may be some trauma involved, you clearly went through something awful, but—"

"Thank you for your concern, but I'm fine," I said, cutting her off. "And I feel no obligation to answer anyone's inquiries. I'm obligated to do *nothing* but serve my own self-interest. If any feel otherwise, then that's on them."

"But the Velas family," she protested. "And your brother—"

"Have nothing to do with me," I said decisively. "I live on my own terms."

"But bro, they completely smashed your reputation," Pankratz said. "Doesn't it bug you? They made you the fall guy for some really hinky shit. Are you just going to let them get away with it?"

"Who cares?" I said with growing annoyance. "It's got nothing to do with me. Although I might have to relocate if people keep mistaking me for this Evans person."

"Right, so the nobles get to notch another win for themselves," Pankratz said. "That's pretty fucking weak, man."

"They're on top and life isn't fair. What's it to do with me?"

"Try thinking about other people," Pankratz said heatedly. "Your example shows that the best solution to everything involving those bastards is to just let them keep walking over us. Are you really okay with that?"

"Says the guy wearing their uniform and training to be one of their little lackeys?" I wondered sarcastically.

"If you want to change the world, you need to start somewhere," he said as he crossed his arms and glowered at me. "It still beats running away like some chickenshit coward."

"I'm sorry, I think I need to clean my ears a bit," I said. "Would you like to step closer and *repeat what you just said*?"

"Nick," Cassie said with concern in her voice as she placed a hand on his shoulder. "Nick, just let it go."

"You gonna hide behind your dog again?" Pankratz asked as he squared up with me.

"You should thank that dog," I said as I began rolling up my sleeves. "He was protecting you from *me*."

"Whoa, let's calm our horses there, why don't we?" Jamie suddenly said as she cut in between the two of us. "Boys, let's have something with a little ice in it to cool those hot heads of yours. Cassie, go get us some drinks poured, sweetie."

Cassie went to the bar to do as her mother requested, leaving Jamie to try to calm things down.

"Hmm," I said. "You know what, Pankratz? If I were as tough as you seem to think you are, then I think I'd rather hide behind a dog than a pair of women. That's just a thought I had."

"Ha, ha, ha," Pankratz said with an ugly smile. "This fucking guy's got some jokes, I see."

"I have a million of 'em, big guy," I said.

"Then make me laugh," he replied.

"What did the five fingers say to the face?" I riddled him.

"STOP," Jamie said, now with no trace of humor left in her voice. "Enough, you two. I don't allow fighting in my place of business. If neither of you can control yourselves, then Nick, you can go back to your fancy academy, and Stragos, you can hike your ass on out of the Narrows. Those are the rules everyone abides by."

Pankratz reluctantly stepped back. His eyes still signaled his willingness for a fight, but he made no further attempts to agitate me.

"I'll do as you say, Jamie," I said. "But I won't be disrespected again."

"That's perfectly fine, so long as *you* respect the rules of this establishment," she replied. "Now, all of you sit down and have a drink. Let's put all this bad energy behind us while I warm up the dinner I prepared earlier. You know, before you broke my window when you jumped out the second floor."

"You noticed that?" I asked sheepishly.

"It's hard not to, honey," she replied.

Hmm. I may have owed my dog an apology.

CHAPTER TWENTY-TWO

The four of us sat down to a delicious meal of baked chicken and roasted pota-
toes, with a buttery garlic sauce spooned over them that made my taste buds
want to dance. Although the meal was reheated, the chicken skin had retained its
crispiness, which added to the enjoyment of tasting every perfectly seasoned bite of it.

Bliss. That meal was bliss. Jamie had once more proven her supreme status as
a creative culinary queen. Why couldn't I have met her earlier in life? It really
didn't seem fair.

"You gonna eat your food or marry it, Evans?" Pankratz snickered.

"Mm nawt Evanth," I said between mouthfuls.

"Who are you, then?" Cassie asked.

"Eating," I said impatiently.

"He's been a big help," Jamie said as she ate from her own plate. "I've been
trying to convince him to sign up with us permanently. Stragos here is an extremely
talented young freelancer."

"Him?" Pankratz asked disbelievingly. "Jamie, no offense intended, but I think
you're mistaken. Kyler is a glorified pack mule."

"I wouldn't have put it like that because it's *rude*," Cassie said while frowning
at her brother. "But Nick's not wrong, Mom. I know you can already tell, but just
in case he fooled you somehow, Kyler is only a Porter."

"Kids, he cleared out the pond."

"What?" Cassie asked in surprise.

"Singlehandedly," Jamie continued.

"That is not freaking possible," Pankratz said. "There's like thirty Koler Crabs
over there! How?"

"Their numbers reached *seventy-six* by the time Stragos came along," Jamie
informed them. "And he still took care of them! Every single one. What do you
say to that?"

"Show me," said Pankratz.

"I will, after dinner. You want to put some money down on me lying about this?" asked Jamie.

"Nooo," said Pankratz, who had apparently lost at that game many times before. "If you're the one saying it, I guess it's true."

"Damn right it is." Jamie grinned. "And now I hear you took it upon yourself to hunt down those bandits at their own encampment? Rachel said you took out every bastard one of them!"

"Well, I don't want to brag, but *someone* had to step up and do something," I said humbly. "People were going missing, and no one was doing a thing about it."

"We were literally on our way there to do something about it," Pankratz said with a frown while Cassie nodded.

"Yeah, well, move faster next time," I said. "I have everything in my storage. The bodies of the victims for identification and burial, and the bodies of the thieves to claim the bounty on them. I even brought the merchandise they stole."

"You are making me *so* happy right now," Jamie said giddily.

"I'm always pleased to be of service," I said.

That was when I realized just what Jamie had said earlier.

"Wait, you know Rachel?" I asked her in surprise. This was new to me.

"Of course, I do, silly," Jamie said with an amused roll of her eyes. "I think the world of your little sister. And I *also* think it wouldn't hurt you to be a little more appreciative of everything she does for you. Family is everything, Kyler."

Jamie placed her hand on Cassie's as she spoke and gave it a tight squeeze.

"Um . . . yes, you're . . . right," I said. "Family is great! I'm certainly going to show my . . . *little sister* how much I appreciate her later tonight. I'm looking forward to it already."

"Just give her a hug, that's all," Jamie smiled.

"Oh, I'll squeeze her until she bursts," I promised. "So, what else has she told you?"

"Nothing much. Just that the two of you are very close and you both plan to do a little traveling. Oh, and that your thinking can be a little scattershot at times, so she's the primary brains behind your team."

"Is that right?" I asked as I began grinning nastily. "She's the *brains*, is she? And those were the exact words she used? I'm *scattershot*, am I? Well, that's certainly one doomed girl's opinion."

"When the hell did you get a sister?" Pankratz asked. "This is the first I've heard of it."

Yeah, you and me both, pal, I thought sourly to myself. "What can I say? Life loves springing its little surprises on us. *Papa was a rolling stone* and all that."

"She looks nothing like you," said Pankratz.

"I didn't say the stone was *good* at rolling."

"Okay, but—" Pankratz started to say, before Jamie held up a hand to silence him.

"Nicholas, these are the Narrows, sweetie. Just because everyone here has a story doesn't mean we want to share them."

"Yeah, but Jamie—"

"Nick," she said slightly more forcefully. "A person's past is their own business. So long as they contribute, our standing policy has always been not to care. Respect that."

"So, do you want me to do this in here or outside?" I asked later when the time came to turn over the contents of my storage.

"Outside, please," Jamie said. "Behind the tavern would be best. Just let me get a few people over here to help get everything sorted. Hopefully there won't be any children out this late in the evening either. I wouldn't want them seeing this."

Once Jamie's helpers arrived, I began releasing the remains of both the bandits and their victims, which I neatly placed side by side, with a top and bottom row. Then, a few feet away from them, I placed the bandits' pilfered merchandise.

Pankratz whistled sharply at the condition of some of the bodies. "What happened to these bastards?" he asked, gesturing at the bandits as he spoke. "Not that they didn't deserve it, but some of these jokers have more holes in them than the bottom of a colander."

"Nothing that you'd want to see firsthand," I said as I watched the stolen loot being sorted.

"Why aren't any of their bodies bleeding?" Cassie asked thoughtfully. She pointed to the victims and said, "Look at the contrast. Both groups were killed with edged weaponry, but despite being in far worse condition, the wounds of the bandits look so . . . so *clean*. As if whatever penetrated them also drained away their blood."

"That's a big assumption to make," I said in a mild tone of voice while simultaneously being impressed by her powers of observation. "When a heart stops beating, blood stops being pumped out of a wound."

"That's true, but there should still be some gradual leakage," Cassie insisted. "What's more, look at this."

She knelt by a body and lifted one of its arms. "There should be some pooling here. Depending on the position of the corpse, the remaining fluids in the body should have begun gathering beneath it. But there's none of that here, because there's no blood remaining anywhere. What weapon did you use to kill these men, Kyler?"

"Who says I used a weapon?" I asked her. "And why does it matter?"

"Because you're my mother's guest and I want to know what sort of man would engage in this level of butchery one minute and then cheerfully eat from her table the next," Cassie said. "How we treat others reflects our humanity; and frankly, you treated these men like venison."

She looked me square in the eyes as she spoke, her gaze never wavering. I was surprised by her moral stance, especially when compared to the other students of her academy. The others had a blasé indifference to the violence of their world. This girl, it seemed, held herself to a higher standard.

I found her attitude instantly aggravating.

Not willing to back down to such clueless naivety, I moved closer to Cassie until we stood face-to-face with each other. Then I plastered a smirk on my face and with as much polite condescension as I could muster, I said, "These were *hardly* men, as I would define the term, Cass. Thieves? Yes. Murderers? Absolutely. Rapists? Without a doubt. But *men*? No. They forfeited the right to be treated as such when they chose to live by the law of the jungle."

"The jungle *has* no law," Cassie said, refusing to back down as well. With her hands on her hips, she said, "But people *do*. You can't ignore that just because the weak-willed choose an easier path for themselves. That's just a convenient way of—"

"Getting things done efficiently?" I asked.

"Forsaking your responsibility, actually," she countered.

"My responsibility? To *them*?" I asked, my incredulity unfeigned. "To this marauding trash?"

"The ascended are called into being to defend the weak," Cassie said. "That list includes sinners as well as saints. Hunters hunt monsters and seal fractures. We don't kill other humans when its unnecessary."

"Oh, so we just let them kill other humans without commentary, is that it?" I snorted. "Pankratz, are you listening to this tripe?"

"She's right, man," Pankratz said.

I turned to him in shock, surprised to see that his gaze was just as steady as his sister's.

"What?" he asked. "Is it that surprising? You can't call yourself a good guy if you act like one of the bad ones."

"You two are such fools," I said while shaking my head. "They're *bandits*."

"Yes, and they killed because they had the power to do so and because it brought them pleasure," Cassie said. "And it seems that you killed them because *you* had the power to do so, and it also brought you pleasure. So, if *they* behave like animals and *you* behave like *them*, then where exactly is the line drawn?"

"And what precisely were the two of you going to do differently if you'd gotten to them first?" I asked. "Were you going to gently suggest they consider changing their ways because they were bringing down the mood?"

"We would have subdued them and brought them in," Pankratz said.

"The poster said dead or alive," I reminded him.

"When it's an option, always choose life, man," he said. "This fucked-up world already has too much death in it."

In that moment, Pankratz and Cassie each reminded me of two other people I'd known who'd shared similar mistaken beliefs. And for that, I greatly resented them.

"Jamie, are we done here?" I asked as I turned to her for an escape. "The meal was fantastic as always, but too much more of this moralizing could give me indigestion."

"Sorry, Stragos," she said with a shrug. "My kids have strong beliefs about what's appropriate behavior for a Hunter. Truthfully, I respect them for it. Too many of the stronger ones live their lives believing they're allowed to do whatever they want without consequences."

"I hope I'm not included on that list," I replied.

"What? No!" she said quickly. "Not a chance! You cleared the pond, you saved a girl's life, and you took down a bandit crew. That's more done for the Narrows in two days than Gardenia's hoity-toity Hunter's Guild has seen fit to do for us all year."

"Mom!" Cassie said defensively. "We came to help, didn't we?"

"I know, I know, angel," Jamie said as she quickly gave her daughter a hug. "And I'm so grateful for you taking the time to do it. Your final year at the academy is coming up and I know how busy the two of you are about to become. Everyone in the Narrows is proud of you both! It's just, the city keeps ignoring us. The second we chose to live outside of their walls and away from their authority, we stopped mattering to them."

"That's . . . true," Pankratz said reluctantly. "I wish I could say it wasn't."

"Why?" I asked. "Rebuilding civilization means that places like the Narrows must be vital. Gardenia can't redevelop the wilds all on their own. What good does it do to ignore you and everything you're trying to achieve?"

"Honestly?" Jamie asked. "Because the Narrows and the other reclamations possess an iron core of equalism at our center. The nobles can't stand the idea of us not being under their thumb. Every success we earn is like a slap to the face of their value system."

"You're equalists?" I asked, remembering the term from the day I'd been interrogated at the Academy. "All of you? *Never Mind the Bollocks, Here's the Sex Pistols*?"

"Less Brit punk, more Thomas Paine," Cassie said with a smile.

"Then why leave home for Gardenia?" I asked. "Why attend Vandal? That's *their* institute."

"Resources," Pankratz said. "They've got them, we don't. It's also a safe way to train and raise our Levels without unnecessary risk. Cassie and I both have

B-rank potential. Once we're strong enough, the money we'll be able to make through the system could let us really turn this place around. Maybe even build an Academy of our own! In the meanwhile, we can set examples for other lowborn Hunters, and raise awareness of the mistreatment of the reclamations. This whole caste system is ridiculous, man. The ascended were meant to defend humanity, not *rule* them."

A fervent light seemed to flash in Pankratz's eyes as he spoke. It seemed there was a revolutionary zeal in him, an energetic enthusiasm for change, which he barely managed to keep under control as he imagined a new and better way for people to live. It was something I'd seen before in other similarly passionate young people.

Yeah, I gave him ten years tops, before the powers that be decided to make him quietly disappear. He'd probably be snatched out of his bed in the dead of night and have a hood pulled over his face. From there, his path would lead to either reprogramming or a slab in a coroner's office.

Nice guy, really.

Where do nice guys finish, again?

I'm sure it'll come to me.

As I walked back to my room in the tavern, I paused by Cassie to say, "I'm going to sleep. Got any other unwarranted criticisms you'd like to sling my way? I'm always happy to hear a new opinion."

"Well, now that I think about it, you kind of seem like an asshole," Cassie said with an unfriendly little smile. "Have you heard that one before?"

"No. That was the first time ever," I said as I gave her a little clap. "So, I'm an asshole, am I? My, what a refreshing novelty. Thank you for offering such a unique and elegant perspective."

"I'm always pleased to be of service," she said before pushing past me. "Mom, I'm going to the house," she announced.

As she walked off, Pankratz gave me an uncertain look, as if he was trying to think of something to say. Then he shrugged and turned to follow her.

"*Ah,*" I sighed in relief. "The adults once more have the stage."

In response, Jamie delivered a light elbow to my ribs. "Don't flirt with my daughter," she said, half-joking, half-deadly serious.

"What? I did no such thing," I said. "Come on, she's like seventeen."

"And how old are you, then?" she snorted.

"*Not* seventeen," I said firmly. "Hey, about the window—"

"I'll deduct the cost from your earnings," she said. "Along with the cost of my tavern's door. And my patio door. And Doug's medical treatment."

"Hey, that last one was on him," I said. "He was acting a tad aggressive."

"You can afford to be generous," she said. "You're getting twenty-two gold pieces for this score."

I laughed at that. "Gold pieces, huh? Whatever happened to paper money? What's with this faux-medieval system of currency?"

"It's what the system likes," Jamie said. "Doesn't really matter to me. It's easy to understand and use, and it's good anywhere you go in the world. What more can you ask of money?"

I didn't have a response to that one.

"Rachel, are you hiding under the bed?" I asked as Schulz and I entered my seemingly empty room.

"Yes," she replied.

"May I ask why?"

"Because I blew your identity and now you're mad at me, and I don't want you to hit me," she said.

"*Rachel,*" I said as I grabbed a pillow off the mattress and silently raised it. "I'm wounded that you'd even think I'd resort to physical abuse over what was clearly a mistake on your part. Stop being silly and come out from under there."

"You're not upset with me?" she asked hopefully.

"I'm not upset with you," I said to her reassuringly.

"All right," she said. Then she squeaked with alarm when I nailed her with a ruthless overhead pillow strike. "Okay, *now* I'm not upset with you," I said as I tossed aside the pillow and plopped down on the bed.

"You said you wouldn't hit me!" she complained as she rubbed the back of her head.

"Yeah, and *you* said you were my little sister. Always trust your animal instincts, brat," I said sagely. "How did you plant that memory in Jamie's head, anyway? You're way too young to be able to mesmerize someone."

"I don't know!" Rachel said excitedly. "I woke up and she was there, and she kept asking questions, and I wanted her to shut up, but I knew you'd be angry if I ate her—"

"*Very* angry," I agreed.

"So, I just looked in her in the eye and the knowledge suddenly came to me, and I said, *What are you talking about? You already know me.* And it worked! She paused and then she started acting as though we knew one another. It was awesome!"

"So, you *did* mesmerize her," I said, impressed but annoyed. "You're showing talent with a lot of skills you shouldn't be able to use, kid. Don't tell me you already know how to use a lightsaber as well."

"Vampires have lightsabers?" she asked eagerly.

"Yes. But we call them night-sabers," I replied.

"Really?!"

"No," I said, after flicking her on the forehead. "Would you stop being silly?"

"Be kind to me, I'm new at this," she whined.

"That's exactly right. You *are* new. But you're already capable of so much," I said. "It's a mystery. An *aggravating* mystery."

"What's so aggravating about it?" she asked. "Maybe I'm just a chosen one."

"I already made that joke, Rey."

"Rey?" she asked.

"Chel," I finished lamely. Then I leaned back and looked at her. She appeared to be an athletic young girl in her late teens. Pretty, with curly auburn hair and bright blue eyes, but otherwise unremarkable. "Tell me this," I said. "Is that current form your real body?"

"Yes," she said with a dazed smile. "This is me, before I was reforged."

"Reforged," I said thoughtfully. "So, you were transformed from that into a spear?"

Now, a pained expression appeared on her face. "No. Not quite," she said. "I . . . I was chosen as a sacrifice. I remember an altar table, the priest and his stone knife. I remember the pain I felt when he . . . used it on me. And when I next became aware, I was *inside* the spear. Unable to speak unless it was with the person chosen to wield me. I remember sleeping, sometimes for decades, sometimes even longer than that, before being used for battle. I thought it was so important back then. I thought I served a purpose."

A tear slowly began to trickle from her eye as she reminisced. "They tricked me. They *used* me," she said miserably. "Manipulated me into volunteering away my own life for their damn cause."

"Aye," I said with my eyes closed. "Why wouldn't they? No one believes more strongly in a cause than the young. We can't have the old men volunteering to become living weaponry, can we? Who'll remain to cash all the checks?"

"It was my *life*, Kyler," she said.

"It was. And you threw it away," I said dismissively. "Maybe now with your second chance, you'll learn to do a little thinking for yourself."

"I only wanted to serve the goddess."

"By letting yourself be served up? Next time, I'd consider trying agnosticism," I replied. When the silence that followed began to feel too stifling, I said, "So, you really must be two thousand years old, huh? I suppose that means I was wrong."

"I told you I was," she said proudly. "What finally convinced you?"

"Your power as a vampire," I said honestly. "Although it annoys me to admit it, you have the strength of an Old Blood. It's completely ridiculous, but the truth can't be denied."

"Aren't I older than you?" Rachel asked smugly. "Goodness, Father, doesn't that mean you're the one who should be serving *me*?"

"Not quite," I said, amused by her sass. "My senior in years, you may very well be, but I'm still the fifth child of Crusica. I've humbled fiends that were twice your age without great difficulty."

"Sure," she said. "Back when you, like, *mattered*. Now you're just a dropout who's unlucky Level Thirteen."

"I'll get back to where I need to be," I said confidently. "There's no rush. We have a base of operations, a steady supply of food, and paying work if we require it. Even a few potential pawns, if we need them."

"Who was that girl from earlier?" Rachel asked. "She was pretty."

"Was she? I hadn't noticed."

"What do you think her blood tastes like?"

"Rachel," I said quietly. "Don't."

"Sorry," she said nervously. "Sorry, I wasn't thinking . . ."

"Hmm," I said. "What are we going to do about you for tomorrow?"

"What do you mean?" she asked.

"More specifically, tomorrow morning," I said. "We're going to need to find a place for you to hide. If that's your new body, then you'll need to be protected from the sun."

"Oh, that's what you meant," she said. "Don't worry about it, Kyler! I've completely got it covered. Wanna see?"

"Are you going to transform back into a spear?" I wondered.

"What? How would I do that? That's weird," she said. "No, check it out. Ta-dah!"

Rachel then gave a little spin and threw her arms back as if she was showing off a cash prize a contestant had won on a game show.

"Okay. What am I looking at?" I asked her.

"Kyler! You really can't tell?" she asked.

"It's late and I'm feeling dense. So, spill it, already," I told her.

"I switched my Class!" she said triumphantly. "The sun can't hurt me now!"

"You're joking," I said, feeling nearly dumbstruck by her revelation. "Are you serious? You're a dual-Classer too? What are you right now?"

"I'm a Porter!" she grinned.

This was unexpected.

This was . . . *extremely* unexpected.

"What the hell is happening here?" I asked myself.

"Ha! You should see the look on your face!" She chortled.

"What's in your storage right now? Prove you're really a Porter," I demanded.

"Why? Don't you believe me?" she pouted.

"I always prefer evidence first and foremost," I replied.

"Pfft! Show a little faith in others!"

"First give me a reason to," I said.

Rachel rolled her eyes at me before complying. Why did everyone roll their eyes around here so often? As far as nonverbal prompts went, it was so rude. I was definitely calling out the next person who did it.

She then held out her hands and concentrated. From seemingly thin air, appeared a familiar wooden shaft that had been broken in half. At the end of one of the pieces was a spearhead.

"Your old body?" I asked.

"My old *prison*," she said. "Take it, please, I don't want it anymore. Maybe you can duct tape it back together or something."

I accepted the ruined weapon from her and carefully examined it. Right away, I could see the wooden bits were a wash. They felt brittle to the touch and would probably splinter in my hands if any force was applied to them. There'd be no repairing that. But I could still feel a certain level of mystical power emanating from the steel head. It could either be reattached to a new body or perhaps melted down and reforged into something else.

Pleased by this gift, I nodded to her and placed it in my personal storage. Whatever possibilities this weapon offered me, I could see to them tomorrow. For now, I was tired. It had been a surprisingly challenging night, and I felt the urge to rest.

Unfortunately, I was met with unexpected resistance.

"What do you mean by *go away*?" Rachel asked.

"I mean exactly that," I said. "Get lost, I'm sleepy."

"So am I!" she protested.

"So, get your own room," I said indifferently. "This one's mine."

"But we've always slept together all this time!"

"Yes, but now you're mobile. Quad-abled and everything. Congrats on your personal evolution."

"Kyler!" she whined.

"FINE, you can sleep on the floor with Schulz."

Schulz stared at me with a betrayed look on his face as though he were dismayed to realize he wouldn't be sleeping beside me either.

"Don't you start with me too," I warned him.

"Kyler, come on! Please!" she said.

"NO," I said forcefully. "Know your place, minion. When the Lord of Blood makes a decision, the matter is settled. Now *goodnight*."

And with that, I converted my equipment into a loose pair of pajamas, pulled the blankets over my head, and promptly fell asleep.

The next morning saw Jamie tapping her foot in annoyance when she saw that Stragos and Rachel had yet to make their appearance for breakfast. She liked those kids quite a bit, but she was also a very busy woman and had better uses for her time than playing waitress for them.

When the clock marked them fifteen minutes late, she sighed in annoyance and went upstairs to get them. Knocking on the door before opening it, she said, "KIDS, I'm not your nanny, okay? Would you please—"

She paused and then covered her mouth to keep from laughing. Piled on the small bed was Kyler with an uncomfortable look on his face due to Rachel's foot pushing into his cheek, while Schulz lay sprawled across them both, carelessly snoring away.

Silently, Jamie closed the door behind herself to let them finish resting.

CHAPTER TWENTY-THREE

For the next few days, I spent my time getting acclimated to life in the Narrows. While the sun was up, I went around introducing myself to the locals and letting them know of the services I offered as a freelancing problem solver. Although many seemed delighted by the idea of having a local Hunter they could call upon in an emergency, there were others who deeply mistrusted the ascended and wanted nothing to do with the likes of me.

"It's understandable," Jamie informed me over drinks at the tavern. "Most registered Hunters are either lackeys of the ruling class or a member of it themselves. It's difficult for a lot of the folks around here to let go of old resentments. The bluebloods tend to roll right over anyone who doesn't get in line. That's why so many leave the cities to come to the reclamations."

"I've heard that term used a lot," I said. "Is that the official name for habitations outside of the great cities? Reclamations?"

"Yes, indeedy." Jamie nodded. "Rebuilding civilization can't be done from the capital cities alone. Redeveloping the land and reclaiming lost resources requires there be permanent settlements for the work to be done. That's where the Narrows and other places like it come into play. We're a necessity, which is why Gardenia is forced to tolerate us even though we're hotbeds of so-called *seditious activity*."

"Equalism again?" I asked.

"No kings, no crowns, no nonsense." She nodded. "Just honest people who want what this land once offered in abundance, back in kinder times than these; the freedom to be left the hell alone."

"Human history always chooses the most interesting moments to begin repeating itself," I said as I sipped my drink. "Even in this era of unprecedented calamity, man chooses to remain divided. Wouldn't working together for the greater good be the more sensible choice?"

"Not when it requires servitude to an unelected minority," retorted Jamie.

"Jamie," I said carefully. "I'm not trying to poke holes in your sentiments, but I can't help but notice that you and your close family members are all powerful ascended, and that you're served by lesser ascended like Doug."

"And?" asked Jamie. "Where are you going with this?"

"Well, you also seem to be the unquestioned leader of this town. You keep mentioning that people came here to get away from being ruled over by ascended, but . . . aren't you technically more of the same?"

"Of course I'm not," she laughed. "*I* know and respect the value of hard work, and I reward it accordingly."

"Ah. Well, okay," I said. "I suppose that makes it completely different."

"Doesn't it?" she agreed with a friendly little smile.

Jamie liked to call herself a broker. She arranged to have issues plaguing her community dealt with as efficiently as possible. She was also known for helping those who bought her services to acquire items and information that the Gardenia central authority would prefer them not to have.

Although the Narrows had its own elected council and a town headsman to lead it, it was quietly understood that *she* was the real power in the settlement. When the residents had issues with each other, she was the one who mediated them. And if her decisions were ever disputed, she had them enforced.

Sometimes lethally, although no one liked to mention that part.

"Doesn't this make you the head of a criminal enterprise?" I asked her after absorbing all the relevant details. "In what way are you not a bartending mob boss?"

"Doesn't that truly depend on how one defines words like *criminal*?" she countered. "It really seems like a matter of perspective to me, sweetie. From my point of view, my willingness to do the necessary work of holding this place together simply makes me a reliable neighbor."

"Ah. In that case, then thank goodness for moral ambiguity," I said. "Always there to brush aside those pesky issues of conscience since time immemorial."

"Exactly," Jamie said with a wolfish grin. "When in doubt, always remember that shades of gray make it all okay."

Hmm. You couldn't really dispute logic like that, now, could you?

At night, I took Rachel hunting in the wilds. Now that she had awakened to her true, predatory nature, it was important to help her adjust to the new, powerful instincts that she was experiencing. It was vital for her development that she be out in the darkness, hunting prey and exulting in her superiority, after each victory.

At the same time, she needed to develop the self-discipline necessary to humble herself before others; to hide her strength from the eyes of the weak. Humility is an important aspect of a successful disguise. Unfortunately, that was what she was having the most trouble with.

"Get some!" she yelled happily as she broke a kobold's neck and bowled over its companions by hurling its body at them. "You want a piece of this too? Kiss my little pinky toe, creep! Die! Die! Die!"

As it turned out, my sweet little Rachel was a bit of a thug. A boisterous brawler, I believe they're called. She was the sort who didn't think there was any problem that couldn't be solved by simply hitting it until it stopped twitching.

My daughter, the meathead.

Kobolds were rat-like mutants that moved like men and possessed a moderate intelligence combined with a cunning instinct for hunting and invention. A group as large as this one might have been a future problem for the Narrows, so I decided tonight's job would be to trim down their population to a reasonable size and instill within them a healthy respect for human-shaped creatures.

Sadly for them, Rachel interpreted my plan to mean *Constructicons combine into Devastator*, which, in the vernacular of a certain popular cartoon series, meant that those poor fools were going to die horribly. And what do you know? They most certainly did.

Afterwards, when Rachel approached me and gave me a hug, excited and energized by her triumph (while also covered head to toe in gory, red bits of kobold), I couldn't find it within myself to scold her for her overenthusiasm. Who wouldn't go a little overboard if they'd been confined inside of a spear for the last two millennia, unable to interact with the world beyond being used to stab heretics? She had a lot of issues she was working through, so there was no point in being impatient with her. Some people caught on quickly and some people needed to be gradually coached. That's all there was to it.

Besides, there was no dire need for her to quickly master her vampiric temperament, not if she could transform back into a human. You couldn't lose control of a car if you were not the one at its wheel.

It wasn't as though training Rachel had no benefit to me. As her partner, I received a generous portion of the experience points generated by her playful little rampages, which in turn pushed me to Level Fifteen. That equaled ten more points dumped into constitution and six skill points, which I used to unlock Blood Orb Mastery and Mesmerize.

Goodness, how had I ever learned to live without the ability to easily dominate the minds of the weak-willed? Speaking purely in terms of convenience, Mesmerize was an absolute game changer. Thanks to this skill, I no longer had to worry about being forced to answer any pesky personal questions. If I didn't like where a conversation was going, I could instantly reset it. Mesmerize *also* allowed me to recruit anyone I came across, as either a temporary employee, or a quick source of nutrition if I was feeling snacky. It was all benefits with no negative drawbacks. The quintessential vampiric power.

It felt so darn *good* to have it back in my arsenal.

I wished I'd had it before reuniting with Pankratz and Cassie. Erasing their memories as soon as we'd stumbled into each other could have saved me from a few potential headaches down the road, but there was no point in grousing over what could have been. What mattered was that I had it *now*. And thank the night for that, because it didn't take long for more trouble to come metaphorically knocking at my door.

"I heard you're the guy who did in the Ringworms," said a sketchy-looking fellow one night, who decided to seat himself at my table, uninvited. "Word is, you go by Stragos?"

I looked up from the Gore Grimoire, irked to have my reading interrupted by this dirt-encrusted stranger. Jamie had given herself the night off and was at home, eating with her children and in-laws. Sensing an opportunity to catch up on the history of this world, I sent Rachel and Schulz to join them. Despite her great age, Rachel was still essentially a young girl at heart. It would do her good to interact with her peer group. Naturally, I gave her strict instructions to answer any questions about our personal history in only the vaguest way possible and forbade her from showing off any of her abilities. She grumbled that I never let her have any fun. In return, I performed a silent pantomime of a kobold having its head pulled off and juggled.

I think she got my point.

For the last two hours, I'd been regaling myself with the history of the Allied Kingdom, the country I presently resided in. When the government of the old United States fell during the chaos of the great awakening, after the land was finished terraforming and the oceans had taken their present shape, the remains of the Northeastern part of the country reforged themselves under ascended rule into the three great cities: Gardenia, True York, and Good Harbor. Each a powerful social hub ruled by its own political dynasty.

I was deeply amused to learn that many of the ruling nobles of these cities had been prominent political families of an earlier age. I guessed there was a certain logic to it. If you were going to treat the Kennedys like royalty, should it really be surprising if they decided one day to take you up on the offer?

The Allied Kingdom's approach to survival was building their three great fortress cities to protect their surviving populations after consolidating the power of the ascended into a new ruling class with which to govern them. Under their philosophy of *noblesse oblige*, being a Hunter was treated as a sort of sacred knighthood. Those who were directly descended from nobility were even given the privilege of calling themselves *Sir* or *Dame*.

Heh, it seemed that the titles of nobility amendment would remain pending indefinitely in this strange new world.

As it turned out, however, the Allied Kingdom wasn't the only nation to be forged during this time of tribulation. The Midwestern states had themselves become a powerful theocracy that viewed the coming of the system as a divine act, with the ascended proclaimed beings chosen by the creator to be the servants of humanity. In contrast to the Kingdom, their Hunters weren't permitted to hold any office. They were considered property of the state; living weaponry with no rights beyond that which the clergy permitted.

Renaming themselves The Holy Kingdom of Ethos, the people of that nation were characterized by their devotion to their faith, their almost fanatical desire to convert others, and their intolerance of anything that was not human. But despite their fiery beliefs, the Kingdom also had a strong secular population that wouldn't allow faith to control all aspects of their lives and worked to keep the power of the clergy in check. As such, they were led by both an elected minister and a so-called Archpriest.

To me, it sounded like a complicated arrangement, one that I had absolutely no desire to see in person. A valuable lesson I learned early in life was that the easiest way to avoid being burned at the stake by religious fanatics was to simply *stay the hell away from religious fanatics*. You'd think that would be common sense among my kind, but a lot of bolder vampires liked to tweak the noses of true believers by "hiding in plain sight" deep in the territory of the faithful. I said "bolder" and not "older" because fools like them rarely made it to their second century of existence.

For the night's sake, why do so many vampires always forget that humans aren't stupid, and that they share the same capacity for reason that we do? *We came from them!* Our minds are virtually the same! It only takes a single moment of idle thought along the lines of, *hmm, Steve sure is acting like a vampire for some reason*, for the pieces to fall into place. And once they do, Steve's not showing up for Wednesday bowling this week, or ever again.

I swear, I will *never* understand the urge that some people have to live on the edge.

I licked my thumb and folded the end of the page before closing my book and turning to face my new interlocutor. I could tell at once from his scent and his disheveled condition that he wasn't a local. He stank of the wilds, and desperation, as well as more than a few harsh chemicals that were coming out of his waxy pores.

There was an entire section on the Southwestern free states coalition that I hadn't gotten to, and how all three powers had formed a tentative alliance with each other, popularly known as "the Reunited States," but I would have to put that on pause for now.

Being considerate of others could be *so* taxing.

With his twitching eyes and wheedling smile, I had the thought that this fellow looked even more like a rat than the Kobolds I'd helped dispose of earlier. I wanted nothing to do with him, but my manners demanded I at least hear him out before dismissing him from my presence.

"I am indeed Stragos," I replied. "And you are?"

"Pus-Head," he said.

Okay. That was enough conversation for me.

"Stragos, huh? You got a first name?" he asked.

"Absolutely," I replied.

Then I smiled and waited for him to go away.

Instead, he kept speaking to me.

Goodness, life could be so *difficult* at times.

"You gonna tell me what it is?" he asked.

Instead of answering, I used Mesmerize and ordered him to tell me what it was he wanted.

"You rescued that noble bitch from True York," he said in a flat voice. "Because of you, my clan's in trouble with the bluebloods who hired us to get rid of her and her escorts. Not only that, but you killed the Ringworms."

"No worries, friend, I'm certain you have a few left in you," I said encouragingly.

"No, man, the Ringworms were a gang that were under my clan. You killed all of them when you rescued that noble. My boss wants you dealt with real bad; he's *pissed*. Sent me here to collect you."

"Did he really?" I asked.

"Yeah," he said.

"How were you going to do that?" I wondered. "Chase me out with your odor?"

"Nah, I was gonna trick you into following me outside, past the walls. Then we were all gonna grab you and teach you a lesson," he said.

"Wow," I said. "That's a *very* clever plan, Pus-face. Did you think of it yourself?"

"Yeah," he said with a smile. "I'm pretty smart. Uh, but it's *Pus-Head*."

"Of course, it is," I said apologetically. "Give me a moment to think, please."

Hmm. This wasn't an unpredictable development. When an apex predator sets root in a new environment, it was only natural that those who'd been toppled from their perch would desperately seek to reassert themselves.

I'd known from the start that allowing my name to be passed around the community meant that I would eventually face challengers who either envied my success or wanted to test their skills against me. There would also be the troublesome allies of those whose lives I'd taken. The cycle of vengeance would soon be in bloom, guaranteeing no shortage of those eager to settle the score.

There would be lots of killing in the days ahead. Not necessarily a good thing.

Killing was an activity that could swiftly get out of hand, if you weren't careful. Even if your actions were altruistic, you could quickly find yourself resorting to murder due to how easy it gradually became. Eventually, you were doing it because it was a faster solution than talking things out, and you just didn't care anymore.

I really didn't feel like explaining any of that to a guy named Pus-Head.

So be it. I'd just have to catch up on my reading at a later time.

"Congratulations, Mr. Pus. I've been thoroughly ensnared in your crafty web. Lead me to where your comrades await," I commanded him.

"The boss is gonna reward me for this," Pus-Head said as a happy smile broke out across his face.

"Will it be a good one?" I asked.

"I hope so," he said. "It's hard out there. Every little treat helps."

"I imagine so," I said as I followed him out of the tavern and into the darkness. "Did you ever imagine you'd end up living this way when you were a child?"

"My life's been shit since the moment I was born," he replied. "Always has been, always will be."

"It can always get worse," I said.

"In what way?" he asked doubtfully.

I smiled and said, "Let's just see where the night goes."

CHAPTER TWENTY-FOUR

As we made our way past the walls of the Narrows to wherever it was that his cunning ambush awaited, I kept myself entertained by asking my guide questions.

"When are they expecting you back?" I inquired.

"Uh, they gave me an hour to figure a way to lure you out," he said chipperly.

"An entire *hour*?" I said, aghast. "It sure sounds like they were underestimating you, Pus-Head."

"They always do. Everybody does," Pus-Head said bitterly. "They think I'm stupid just because I ain't as . . . as . . ."

"Refined?" I offered. "Sophisticated? Presentable?"

"Yeah!" he said. "One of those. I ain't as fancy in my ways. They look down on me."

"That's an unfair way to treat someone," I sympathized. "No matter the society, there are always those who place too strong an emphasis on what they consider traditional displays of intelligence. People like you, who operate on a more instinctual level, always find themselves being denigrated."

"What's that word mean? *Instinctual?*" asked Pus-Head.

"It means you function without needless thought," I replied.

"Are you calling me stupid, too?" he asked angrily.

"It means you don't *have* to think, Pus-Head," I said. "Trust me, for those of us who do a lot of it, your existence seems almost unfair. There are monks in search of Nirvana who'll never be as close to it as you are."

Pus-Head paused to consider what I'd said. "You really think so?" he asked shyly.

"I do."

"Well, damn." He grinned. "You know something, Stragos? You're all right."

"Thank you," I replied, with a smile of my own.

"Instinctual," he said as we continued our walk, trying the word out. "I like it."

A few minutes later, a seemingly abandoned farmhouse came into view, which I took to be the ambush site. After confirming this with Pus-Head, I told him to stop.

"What for?" he asked. "Everybody's waiting for us."

"I know," I said. "Let them. The longer we take to arrive, the angrier they'll gradually become. Anger and fear are ideal emotions for a hunt. When your prey is blinded by them, they're easier to pick off."

"Oh," Pus-Head said. "Okay, I guess that makes sense. That's clever."

"Not really, it's just experience, that's all," I said humbly. "Hey, do you mind if I ask why they call you Pus-Head? That's not a very nice name."

"I used to have a bad complexion," he replied.

"Ah. Well, that's logical," I said. "Do you have a real name?"

"Matthew," he said after a moment's reluctance.

"Matthew," I said. "I like it. It suits you."

"My mom named me," he said. "Just before she died. Named me after her dad."

"That means there's a history behind your name," I said. "A legacy. Was your grandfather a good man?"

"I don't know," he said. "I don't think about it."

"Do you think he'd be proud of you?" I pressed. "Proud of his grandson, the outlaw?"

"I said I don't know," he said in a surlier tone. "I don't think about shit like that. I gotta live in the moment."

"I understand, friend." I nodded. "You need to keep living instinctually."

"Exactly," he agreed. "Exactly!"

"What about your father? Is your *father* proud of you?"

"I don't care what he thinks," Matthew said. "Fuck him! That's what I say. He wasn't nothing but a loser."

"You disapprove of him?" I wondered.

"Damn right I do," Matthew sneered. "You know what he did for a living? What he raised me to do? Rearing swine for a rich man's family."

Matthew spat in disgust as he recalled his unpleasant memories.

"He did it his whole life," he continued. "It's hard work. *Nasty* work. And everyone mocked us for it, saying we smelled like pig muck. And what's worse is, we didn't even own them swine! All that backbreaking toil we did, and all we got for it was that nasty shack to sleep in and barely enough coin to survive on. We filled everybody's damn bellies but our own!"

"Is that why you turned to banditry?" I asked.

"Damn right it was," he said. "Who wouldn't? What's the point of the law if it means living without being respected? You can spend your whole life obeying their rules while starving at night, or you can go your own way and finally have a plate with some meat on it! When my clan came to loot the town, I saw my chance for a better life, and I took it. Hell, I'm the one who opened the gate for them!"

"What about the man guarding it?" I wondered.

"I slit his throat with the same knife I used for the livestock," Matthew said gleefully. "And he made the same stupid sounds as the pigs when he died. No difference. No difference at all. And once the clan came in, I spent the whole night settling old scores."

"What were they expecting? Loyalty?" I asked. "When you kick a dog enough times, why be surprised when it bites back?"

"Exactly," said Matthew. "Exactly!"

"You regret it, don't you?" I sneered at him.

"Every godless day of my life," he said as he suddenly burst into tears. "Every fucking day."

He stood there weeping messily for a time, while I sat on an old wooden fence and silently observed him. When he regained some semblance of control, he said, "W-we really should meet up with them now. They're gonna be mad."

"You don't need to worry about them anymore, Matthew," I said quietly.

"Why not?" he asked.

"I think you already know," I said. "I think you've known since the moment we walked off together."

"Oh," he said. Then he asked, "How come?"

"Who can really say?" I shrugged. "Whimsy? Boredom? Either or?"

"Really?" he asked. "I have to die for that?"

"Well, if you really want to know, I have urges that need to be met, and no one will think too harshly of me if I use you and your friends to relieve them."

"What?"

"You're helping out a lot of people tonight, Matthew," I assured him. "Better you and your clan by far than anyone who actually contributes to the world."

"You can't take us all!" he said.

"I can. I will."

"This isn't right!" he whined.

"You know that isn't true," I smirked.

"I don't deserve this!"

"That isn't true either," I said as I wagged a finger at him.

"I want to yell for help. I want to fight! Why can't I do that?" he asked in a frustrated voice. "Why can't I move?"

"Knowing how wouldn't make you any happier," I said calmly. "Let's just enjoy our remaining time together. Is there anything else you'd like to know?"

"Is this going to hurt?" he asked fearfully.

I scratched my chin as I considered how to respond.

"Do you *want* it to?" I finally asked.

"I probably have it coming," he said sadly. "It scares me, though."

"Why is that?"

"I've wanted to die for what I did ever since that night," he said miserably. "But I'm afraid of what comes next. I've done things just as bad since then. Some were even worse."

"What were they?" I asked curiously.

He told me.

"That is impressively vile, Matthew," I said after taking some time to process his story. "You are undoubtedly the scum of the earth. Even the kindest soul imaginable would believe that Hell is the least of what you deserve."

"I know," he said, crying once more. "I *know*. That's why I'm scared. I wanna die, but I'm scared of what happens after. It makes me crazy thinking about what I got coming my way."

And with that, he broke down, sobbing childishly in the dark like a boy who'd been caught stealing and couldn't excuse his actions to his disappointed parents.

He was a pitiful murderer.

"Matthew," I said, causing him to turn my way.

"Yeah?" he asked.

"There are people who believe that life operates under the principle of something called *karma*. Have you ever heard that word before?"

"No," he said as he shook his head. "What's it mean?"

"The simplest way of describing it is, if you do good things, then good things will happen for you. And if you do bad things, then bad things will happen as well," I said. "And it all applies after we die."

"That just means I definitely got bad shit coming my way," Matthew whimpered.

"Let me finish," I said. "Yes, you do receive punishment for all the evil you did. But it's not permanent, okay? It's more like a penalty you have to pay in order to be made clean again. You'll suffer the flame, but you'll come out the other side purified and renewed."

"Really?" Matthew asked hopefully.

"Sure," I said. "If you believe in that sort of thing. Only one way to find out, right?"

"I guess so," he said reluctantly as I hopped off the fence and approached him.

"Look at the sky, Matthew," I said. "It's dark right now, but behind the clouds, it's full of stars. That's nice, isn't it? No matter how ugly it gets down here, there's always beauty above us."

Matthew looked upward and squinted. "I never thought of it that way before," he said. "Makes me wish I could have seen them one last time—"

From behind him, my hand moved swiftly.

Then I stared, transfixed by the sight of the warm red liquid coating my fingertips, and delighted in the sensation of feeling it slowly dripping downward to stain the earth.

Next, I turned my gaze to the farmhouse and thought, *more.*

But first I glanced at Matthew's body. And as I did, a quote from a famous fantasy story came to me that seemed wickedly appropriate for the occasion.

"Farewell, my friend," I said to him. "I was a thousand times more evil than thou!"

Snickering to myself, I made my way to the farmhouse. But not before pausing to play a small trick.

Reiner looked up wearing an irate expression when the knocking began. It seemed Pus-Head had finally returned with the target in tow. But what had taken so damn long? The jittery fool had promised he would be swift. He'd even been given an entire hour.

We should have just ransacked the town, he thought sourly to himself. The Narrows was a prize well worth reaping. It was the richest reclamation in the area, the most populous, the best developed. There was much to be gained from seizing such a jewel.

The problem was that the Narrows were also well-defended. Its organization was unmatched and the sentries guarding its walls were strong and experienced. Even worse was the woman who controlled the place. Jamie Calford, the Witch of Appraisal. It was said that her gaze could steal the secrets of a man's soul from him and let her know his every exploitable weakness. Only fools dared to cross her. The ruthless efficiency with which she dispatched any who made the attempt had filled countless graves over the years, and she was always willing to have more dug.

Reiner didn't fear her of course. Reiner feared no woman! But just the same, it was better to avoid taking unnecessary risks. Which was why he had dispatched Pus-Head to lure in that bastard Stragos. But the fool had kept him waiting for so long!

Reiner *hated* waiting!

The knocking continued.

"Well, what are you waiting for?" he snarled at his men. "Pus-Head's back and he brought a guest! Open the door."

One of his boys did as he commanded and threw open the door, revealing Pus-Head standing there on the porch, wearing an odd smile on his ugly face.

He was standing alone.

"What the hell?" Reiner cursed as he stepped forth. The farmhouse was a filthy mess of decomposing wood and moldy carpeting that left the air heavy with the scent of damp rot. He and his boys had spent some time clearing out all the broken furniture and tearing down a wall to make room for the twenty of them to lay in wait.

All that effort was now wasted by Pus-Head's failure to follow through! And why was he smiling so much? Was that little freak on something right now? If he was, he was going to pay.

Reiner did NOT appreciate having his time wasted.

Pus-Head stepped carefully into the room and walked with a stumbling lurch to stand before his leader. Some of the men behind him laughed to see him in such an obviously wasted condition.

"You going to explain yourself to me, pig herder?" Reiner asked in his deep voice, deliberately using an old nickname that he knew would hurt the other man's feelings and put him on the back foot.

Pus-Head said nothing and continued to stare blankly.

"Wrong answer, you piece of shit," Reiner said angrily as he grabbed the other man by the front of his shirt. "Wrong fucking answer—What the hell?"

At first, Reiner thought that the fool's head was merely lolling backwards as though he had no control of his body. But that wasn't the case at all. Pus-Head's head kept rolling further and further back on his neck until it suddenly dropped off and hit the floor with a thud.

All the while, he kept smiling.

His body was still standing, with Reiner's fist still gripping his shirt.

"What?" Reiner asked numbly. "What the hell is this?"

"I think you should rename him Pus-*Headless*," a new voice helpfully suggested. "What do you think?"

Reiner spun to his left and saw a stranger standing behind one of his soldiers. A soldier who was now dead, with a large wound still spurting blood from his neck.

After licking the back of his hand and wiping messily at his mouth, the stranger gave Reiner a friendly wave and said, "Hello."

And then his eyes began blazing with hellish red light.

"Kill it. KILL IT!" Reiner ordered.

One of his men ran forward, short sword in hand, and shoved the blade through the stranger's neck before twisting it. Then he stared in confusion when nothing happened while the man that he'd stabbed continued to stand there smiling at him.

When he tried to pull his weapon free, the stranger gripped his wrist and squeezed it, forcing the soldier to relinquish his hold. Then the stranger opened his mouth wide, revealing two rows of daggerlike teeth, which he used to tear into his victim's neck.

The man screamed in helpless pain as the life was drained from him. Once he'd finished, the stranger sighed in evident enjoyment before throwing the newly created corpse heedlessly through a nearby wall.

Then he turned to face Reiner.

"Are you the one in charge?" he asked as he casually removed the knife from his neck and tossed it behind himself. "If so, I was hoping you'd make some time to answer a few of my questions."

"Who are you?" Reiner asked the monster.

"Stragos," he replied.

"*What* are you?" Reiner asked next.

"So *very* pleased to meet you," Stragos replied.

"You can't take us all, freak. You can't take us all," Reiner said as he desperately attempted to rally his men. "Just another portal freak, boys! It's just another—"

Blood, which had begun pooling on the floor from the wounds of the three victims, suddenly rose into the air, as though caught in an invisible stream. As Reiner watched in disbelief, it began to coalesce into a round shape, like a ball of clay.

As this strange blood orb floated above them, it suddenly began spraying tiny red needles into the remaining ambushers, embedding all of them with tiny projectiles that burned like the stinger of a bee.

"Did you really just call me a *freak*?" Stragos asked with a frown. "Very impolite. Not the wisest thing to do when the man you've insulted can convert blood into a deadly toxin."

He snapped his fingers. Five of Reiner's men collapsed to the ground, screaming and frothing at their lips as they died in unimaginable pain.

"What are you doing?" Reiner asked in a terrified voice.

"I'm waiting for an apology," Stragos replied as he snapped his fingers again. Five more bodies.

"I'm sorry!" Reiner immediately said.

With another finger snap, Reiner's remaining men died, leaving him alone to face the monster.

"I SAID I WAS SORRY!" Reiner shrieked.

"I was just testing to see if you were being sincere," Stragos replied. Then he smiled. "Apology accepted."

He then helped Reiner, who had collapsed to his knees, back onto his feet. "Shall we speak outside?" he asked as he placed a friendly arm over the other man's shoulder and began guiding him to the door. "I still have some questions I'd like answered. You don't mind, do you?"

Reiner offered no objections.

As I walked back to town, I looked around to be certain I was entirely alone before letting out a pleased belch.

I really did enjoy Jamie's cooking; she truly was a deft hand at it. But as pleasurable as I found the dishes she prepared, there was just something about the act of consuming the blood of a terrified human being that couldn't be matched. Fear was a seasoning that couldn't be bottled. You had to have it *fresh*. And was there a finer thing in this world than drinking in the mana that existed within a living person's veins?

Her eggs and sausages *were* exquisite, though.

Hmm. Maybe I was just the type who derived satisfaction from procuring my own meals?

There was no need for comparison.

More importantly, the information I'd gained from the late Mr. Reiner was an interesting development. The girl I'd rescued earlier, as it turned out, was more important than I'd realized. Not merely a damsel in distress, but so much *more*. I'd have to consult with Jamie tomorrow, to see how she wanted to proceed.

I wondered how much of my story she'd believe. Well, I'd have to omit a few unimportant details. Undoubtedly, her distrustful daughter Cassie would raise a few objections if she discovered how I'd come by the knowledge.

She'd been so annoying as of late. Good thing Reiner and his lads helped me take the edge off. Not even Little Miss Morality could deflate my present good mood. It felt like it would last forever.

I took a moment to gaze at the sky.

All the beauty of creation, suspended over the ugliness of our small world. But not in judgement, I thought.

Never in judgement.

CHAPTER TWENTY-FIVE

At around half past seven in the morning, I yawned, stretched languidly, and then rose from my bed, carelessly pushing a certain annoying girl and a clingy Velcro dog to the carpet as I did so. While she complained about my lack of manners and he continued snoring away on the floor, blissfully unaware of his dislodgement, I took a moment to wonder how the pair of them kept getting into my room at night. I was dead certain that I always locked the door before turning in.

Had they come crawling across the tavern's roof like a pair of spiders and entered through a window? If so, I wished they'd stop. I hated feeling so crowded while I slept.

I used the wash basin on the dresser to spritz some water over my drowsy eyes, then I used my Porter cleaning technique to freshen myself up. Once I felt presentable to the outside world, I headed downstairs to locate Jamie. When I was told by the staff that she hadn't made an appearance yet, I took off for her home.

As I walked, I began idly tossing and catching a heavy purse of coins that I'd appropriated from the leader of last night's bandits. It was tempting to keep this little haul for myself, but Jamie would need it to corroborate my story. I was sure she'd make it worth my while, though.

Last night sure had been enjoyable. It had been a while since I'd taken some time to myself to really let loose and indulge in my less civilized urges. Although I preached the importance of always maintaining strict self-control to Rachel, it was also true that you had to let yourself have fun. Cornering those silly outlaws and making a feast of them had been exactly that.

It was a shame the system penalized Hunters for going too far in such pursuits. I'd been dismayed to learn that although my Gore Grimoire was perfectly capable of absorbing skills from any ascended human I slew, I couldn't receive any experience points or attain any equipment or money for killing ordinary men.

Apparently, the powers provided by this Akashic system were meant specifically for destroying monsters and sealing fractures. You weren't supposed to use them to prey on your fellow man. If you did, the system would begin giving you a series of escalating penalties that culminated with you being marked as a renegade. Should that happen, unless you completed an atonement quest to have that status removed, you'd be registered as a *kill on sight* target, with great rewards offered to whoever took you out.

Which isn't to say that the ascended couldn't lay a finger on unempowered humans. There was nothing at all in the rulebook that said they couldn't beat someone within an inch of their life. Or remove limbs. Or torture. And of course, just because they weren't allowed to directly kill people, didn't mean they couldn't pay someone else to do it for them. The system didn't give a damn about contract killings. That was the secret to how the ascended nobility that ruled the Allied Kingdom maintained their dominance over the populace. Through sheer might and great wealth.

Ah, the disparity of it all!

Luckily for me, the system considered bandits to be renegades, so I hadn't earned any negative karma from last night's amusement. The protections the system offered for ordinary citizens didn't apply to criminals, which made them fair game, something for which I was grateful. Even in my human form, my steps felt lighter, and my body felt refreshed and stronger. The fellows I'd consumed had quite a bit of vitality in them.

Not for the first time, I wondered why Alpha had reproduced the abilities of a classic vampire so perfectly for the system's Vampire Lord Class. Surely, she understood that regardless of experience points, vampires could also become more lethal solely through the act of killing. A popular misconception regarding us was that our strength only grew over the passage of time. This was incorrect. We could also quickly grow powerful by focusing on consuming humans and permanently absorbing their ambient mana. The more people we killed, the faster our powers increased. This was one of the reasons we tended to flock to battlefields and the sites of natural disasters. Any chance to mass feed unimpeded by the eyes of human authority was an opportunity for personal advancement. And warfare and disaster provided us with *so many* nameless victims.

The reason people focused primarily on our age derived from our survival-oriented behavior. You see, if a vampire began slaughtering humans willy-nilly to get stronger, that would naturally alert those capable of slaying said vampire to its presence. For that reason, most vampires chose to act cautiously. We preferred to increase our kills over time and spread them out to avoid drawing attention to ourselves. It was better to play the long game than to take any short-term risks.

Thanks to such sensible behavior, those who were aware of our existence generally came to believe that elder vampires were the only true threats our species could offer, which was a helpful deception that allowed our younger offspring a better chance of survival. This way, everyone gained a wealth of invaluable experience that informed their decision-making, which in turn made for superior undead.

If our enemies had become aware of just how dangerous newbloods could be if given access to enough prey, the world would have united to stamp us out long before Great Crusica was ready to begin her war. To prevent such an outcome, masters were expected to control their progeny with a tight leash to prevent them from becoming . . . excessive in their pursuits.

Thus far, Rachel had been perfectly manageable. An ideal student. True, she had a zeal for the hunt, but she was a long way from losing control, which made me reluctant to impede her personal freedom unnecessarily. That didn't mean it was completely safe to leave her to her own devices, but that was why I had Schulz keeping watch over her.

As I entered the kitchen, wondering what Jamie would be making for breakfast, I found myself stumbling into a situation that instantly filled me with regret over ever having been born.

Pankratz had Cassie pressed against the countertop, kissing her passionately, with one hand holding her tightly against him as the other slid upward inside her T-shirt. When he began whispering something urgently into her ear and she responded breathlessly with something that sounded like a cross between panting and moaning, I loudly cleared my throat.

"You do know your mom chops vegetables over there, don't you?" I asked nonchalantly.

"Oh my god!" Cassie yelped before pushing Nick away and running upstairs with her hands covering her face. Pankratz in turn swore and began chasing after her, only to stop when he heard her bedroom door slamming shut. Then he turned towards me and glared irately.

"Don't give me that look, you were the one breaking kitchen code," I said as I opened the refrigerator and rummaged around for something to drink. "Your adopted sister, dude? That's an interesting choice."

"Shut up," Pankratz said threateningly as he took a step towards me. "We're eighteen and it's none of your business. I expect you to keep this to yourself."

"I'll be more than happy to," I said with unfeigned disdain. "Make preparations to ruin your future family gatherings all you like. Just keep your happy couple vibes to yourself. It was already annoying enough before I had to see the two of you putting on a show next to the cutlery."

By the *night*, did I hate happy couples.

"You already knew?" Pankratz asked in surprise.

"Pfft," I replied. "Your body language made it so obvious it may as well have been printed on cardboard. Plus, the *pheromones*. So annoying! Did you guys ever stop to think how this might affect others? Or were your faux-incestuous urges too strong to ignore?"

In response, Pankratz hit me in the face as hard as he could. I'll give him credit for his punch: I didn't see it coming and it hurt when it connected. Once my vision cleared up, I wiped the blood from my face (so unappealing when it comes from your own body) and stood back up on newly unsteady legs. Then I said, "I thought we agreed you were going to stop doing that."

"Well, you're being an asshole," Pankratz replied.

"There's no reason to get violent over it," I said.

"Cassie and I are complicated. I don't want to hear any commentary about us or any of your mean jokes," he said.

"Mean jokes?" I snorted. "Okay, fifth grader."

"I'm being serious," Pankratz said. "You didn't have to come in and freak her out like that. You didn't have to say anything at all. She already feels weird about what we have and you're not fucking helping."

"Why would I want to help?" I sneered. "This kind of adolescent display is beneath our dignity as human beings."

"Fuck off, man," said Pankratz with a reddening face. "We love each other."

"You *think* you do," I scoffed.

"Always," he insisted. "Now and forever."

"Oh, give it a rest! I hate seeing this sort of delusion take root," I said. "Let me tell you something, Nicky. This only feels important to you right now because you're young and you don't have the benefit of experience to tell you otherwise. Trust me when I say, only *suckers* think they can love someone forever. When it's put to the test, *forever* means fifty years at best. That's nothing."

"It's still fifty years, man," said Pankratz. "That's a lifetime."

"Which is NOTHING," I asserted.

"Yeah, keep talking nonsense," said Pankratz. "Did you forget? I *know* you, Evans. Where do you get the right to mouth off to *me* about love? That thing you had with Anikka was a fucking disaster."

"What?" I asked with genuine confusion.

"That psycho little rich girl who kept you as her side piece. Are we still not talking about how you let her walk all over you? How she treated you like trash?" asked Pankratz. "That's what's pathetic, man. Giving me and Cassie shit about how we feel while staying loyal to a viper like her."

Just as I was going to ask him what the hell he meant, a sudden memory of that day at Vandal Academy came to me. Anikka Velas on that gurney, giving me a familiar wink just before pretending to be traumatized and putting me on the spot.

That wicked little smile she'd sent my way.

"Oh, what the fu . . . *hell*," I said. "Are you serious? Are you seriously serious?" I asked Pankratz with increasing annoyance.

"What?" he asked. "Are you still pretending like you don't remember? You two were keeping it low-key for a whole year."

This ape. This moron. Ugh.

I'm telling you, if the morning sun hadn't risen and wasn't shining through the kitchen window, I really wouldn't have liked Pankratz's odds for lasting beyond the day.

Instead, I asked, "You really couldn't have mentioned this earlier?"

"You asked me not to. *I* keep my word when given," he replied.

His answer was so simple, his earnestness so pure.

Thank goodness Jamie walked in at that moment, or I might have attacked him with a kitchen knife.

"Is everything all right?" she yawned as she came in from the living room.

"Absolutely blissful," I muttered as I took a seat at the kitchen table.

"He found out about me and Cassie," Pankratz said bluntly. "Then he made her cry."

"Oh. Awkward," Jamie said with a flinch as she poured herself some coffee.

"You *know*?" I asked with genuine shock.

"They're my kids, but they're also old enough to make their own decisions," Jamie replied. "I only want my family to be happy."

. . . Wow.

After sitting at the table for about a minute with my face frozen in place, I decided it would be best not to continue this conversation. It seemed that this morning was a time for revelations: revelations that I hadn't wanted and would henceforth do my damnedest to ignore and forget.

As much as I adored Jamie, I had to ask myself: did I want Rachel to be around someone like this? What sort of father would I be to let my daughter interact with people of such questionable moral character? If I allowed her to remain friends with this family, she might end up becoming a libertine! Their permissive influence could lead my precious child to utter disgrace!

. . . Should I perhaps kill the lot of them, or would that be overreacting??

Blast, being a single parent was difficult! You did the best that you could, but every step you took was so precarious. I only wanted to do right by my child, but the given definition of the word *right* was also the very definition of the word *subjective*!

. . . Maybe I should just set Rachel free. We'd been together for weeks, hadn't we? Wasn't that long enough? It wasn't like being a vampire came with a particularly difficult lifestyle. There were religions with far more complicated rules. *Eat this, don't eat that. Believe this, don't believe that. Work this day, don't work that day*, etc. In comparison, vampirism boiled down to, *Have fun, don't get caught.*

Yes, perhaps it was time to give Rachel her freedom; to let my bloodthirsty little angel soar free.

No, I couldn't do that. Schulz would be upset with me. He adored Rachel and lately the two of them had become thick as thieves. Besides, even if I did throw her out, she'd only climb back in through a window. We'd already established that.

Ugh. Why did things always become complicated when you least expected?

No one had ever lived a life more difficult than mine. I was sad now.

"You look like you want to say something, Kyler," Jamie said as she took a seat.

"Nah," I said with a shake of my head. "Everyone has their own circumstances. Mind your own business in the Narrows, isn't that how it is?"

"Wisely stated." Jamie nodded. "So, what brings you by?"

"Well, it's a funny story," I said. "And it starts with a bag of silver. Check this out."

I tossed her the bag of coins from earlier, which she emptied on the table to examine. "Interesting," she said as she held one up to her eye to take a closer look. "These coins are imprinted with the sigil of the Ethos church."

"Those midwestern Holy Rollers?" I asked.

"Yep," she replied. "But they aren't genuine. These are crafted silver coins, not system generated. You can tell by the slight imperfections in the molding process. These were worked by hand, not generated from quest rewards."

"Your eye for detail is truly impressive," I said admiringly. "What else do you see?"

"Some sort of tracking spell has been placed on them," she said. "It seems that whoever paid these coins out intended to fetch them back later."

"Or to complete the frame up," I said. "That girl I rescued from those bandits a couple weeks back. Did you know she was a noble?"

"I suspected it," Jamie said. "But it didn't seem important at the time. Despite what she went through, she arranged to travel to Gardenia with a merchant caravan the next morning."

"Yeah, I'd be in a hurry too if someone was trying to have me assassinated," I said. "Stay mobile or get dead."

"You sound so hard-boiled right now," Jamie said fondly.

"Just call me Dashiell Hammett," I preened.

"You've read Hammett?" she asked, surprised. "What's your favorite book of his?"

"*Red Harvest,*" I replied. "I always loved the title."

"So, what exactly is happening here?" asked Pankratz.

"The girl I rescued on the night you ambushed me is being targeted," I said to him. "The bandits were paid with coinage that's been forged to look like it came from a foreign country. A country that's known for oppressing the ascended."

"Go on," Pankratz said.

"From that, we can infer that the girl probably has a rare Class or a connection that someone finds threatening," Jamie cut in. "You know how nobles can be. Anything they perceive as a danger to their position causes them to kick up a fuss."

"And since the money has a tracking spell on it, that means the bandits were being set up to be found in the employ of the Ethos. Potentially setting up an international incident," I added.

"*Shit,*" swore Pankratz. "So, what happens now?"

"We either get rid of this money, or we sit on it and see who comes looking for it," said Jamie. "And when they do, we take them for everything they're worth!"

"Jamie! How *scandalous*!" I exclaimed with both hands on my cheeks. "So, what's my cut?"

"I'll give you a fair piece of the take, as well as a finder's fee for bringing this to my attention. But since I'll be the one negotiating, I can't offer more than fifteen percent," she said in a businesslike tone of voice.

"Really? I was thinking more like fifty percent, since you wouldn't even be aware of this potential cash cow without me," I countered.

"Twenty percent," she replied. "I'm still the one taking on most of the risk. Nobles can be tetchy about having their misdeeds exposed and exploited."

"Thirty percent," I said firmly. "I'll have you know I was forced to kill a lot of bandits to acquire this information."

"Twenty-five percent. You probably *enjoyed* killing all those poor souls." Jamie smirked. "Is it really work when you're having fun?"

I considered her words for a moment, then raised my arms, signaling my surrender.

"Okay, you've got me there," I admitted. "Shake on it?"

"Done," she said. We shook hands, and then she passed along two gold coins as my finder's fee.

"Always a pleasure, Jamie," I said jauntily as I stood up to leave. "Let me know how things turn out. I'd be happy to provide some assistance if needed."

"You're not staying for breakfast?" Jamie asked in surprise.

"Gorged myself last night," I replied. "Still quite full. I wouldn't want to overdo it. I need to stay trim for the ladies, don't I?"

"Stay, please," Jamie said before I could exit. "There's something I was hoping to ask of you today. It would mean the world to me if you said yes."

"Really?" I asked, intrigued by the imploring look on her face. "What is it?"

"NO," Pankratz said loudly before Jamie could elaborate. "Absolutely not. We already discussed this."

"Nick, you need help," Jamie said. "You and Cassie can't two-man this, and the Hunters under my employ aren't strong enough for the job."

"That doesn't mean I want to take this asshole," Pankratz said while pointing at me. "You don't know what he's like when you aren't around."

"I know he gets results, and in this line of business, that's more important than having a great personality," she replied.

"That felt like a backhanded compliment," I observed mildly.

"Oh, honey, I didn't mean it like that," she said apologetically.

"Jamie, I said *no*," Pankratz tried to say forcefully.

"Well, Nicky, *I* said *yes*," Jamie said, brushing him off. "I love you both and I'm not letting the two of you walk into a fracture by yourselves."

"I'm sorry, did you just say a *fracture*?" I asked enthusiastically.

"A C-ranked one that's been under our noses this entire time," Jamie said excitedly. "A chance to gain new equipment, levels, and a *lot* of money. We just need to put a team together to reap the rewards. What do you say? Are you in?"

In response, I knelt before her and gently placed her hand in mine.

"My lady, what wouldst thou have of me?" I asked her reverently. "My sword is at your service."

"Yeah, this is *bullshit*," said Pankratz bitterly.

CHAPTER TWENTY-SIX

Hey, short stack. You finished for the day?" I asked as I walked through the open door of Norey's Smithy and Wares. It was a bright and beautiful day outside with nary a cloud in the sky, but you wouldn't know it from the soot-blackened windows, filthy floor, and the sullen aura of hostility emitted by the annoyed shopkeeper, who despised dealing with his customers.

"Ah, a height joke in reference to my status as a dwarf. Truly, the scales of hilarity have *tipped*," said the disdainful voice of the owner of the place; a gray-haired fellow with a magnificent beard by the name of Norey, who, yes, was a dwarf. The fantasy sort.

"I'm trying out jocularity. Isn't it great? I feel *good* about it," I replied as I leaned against the shop's counter to take a gander at his wares. "Woof, I see you and the boys have been really cooking out back. These new toys look *exquisite*."

"Keep your hands off the glass, you barbaric dolt, I just cleaned it last month," he snapped. "Don't go smudging everything with your uncouth fingers!"

"My apologies," I said. "I'm just stunned by the amazing quality at display here. Absolutely *gorgeous*. If dwarves were a thing where I came from, I'd have done all my shopping through you."

"If dwarves were a thing where you came from, your smart lip would see you walking home with a limp," Norey said gruffly. He sounded unfriendly, but I could tell from a slight pinkening of the tips of his ears that he was pleased by my compliment.

He reached for one of the swords he kept in the display case and tossed it to me. "What do you think of it?" he asked.

The balance of the weapon felt superb. As soon as I caught it, it felt like a natural extension of my hand. The edge was keen, and at a touch, I could feel the high quality of the steel it was forged from and knew that this was a sword that wouldn't easily break. It was the epitome of a blacksmith's art.

A perfect implement of fatal violence.

"I think that if I owned this blade, I would happily kill *so many people* just so I could marvel at the sight of it being drenched in the blood of the weak," I said dreamily.

"With no mercy for a defeated foe?" Norey wondered.

"Not a bit," I said with a shake of my head. "This sword isn't something you wield simply to defeat an opponent. Why settle for a mere surrender? This is a weapon of total victory. Winning the battle's just the beginning. The *real* fun comes afterwards, when they can't fight back."

"Ha! Ha ha ha!" laughed Norey in response. "I knew you were a cracked nut the first time I saw you waltz in here, Stragos," he said as he wiped a bit of sweat off his forehead with a cloth he kept in his pocket. "I said, this fancy-looking bastard has wielded a sword before. He knows what a blade's true purpose is."

"Mostly, I just like sticking them in people and watching their facial expressions," I said confidentially as I handed back the sword.

"Well, what else would you do with it? Chop carrots?" the dwarf said as he spat unselfconsciously on his floor. "I get so many of those damned humans in here with too much gold in their pockets but not enough lust for the kill! They'll see my masterful craft and go on about how lovely it is, but they just want to put it in a case and let it appreciate in value. How pathetic! If you're not going to use it to take heads and spill out organs on the street, then what's the point of having a sword?"

I really liked dwarves.

I'd discovered Norey's Smithy a few days after Pankratz and Cassie first returned to the Narrows. Although it was located a fair distance away from the other shops on the mercantile row reserved for commerce, it had no shortage of customers. Everyone, from the town watch to professional Hunters all the way from Gardenia itself, made their way to its doors, hoping to purchase a weapon from the infamous owner.

When I managed to get inside, I was delighted to discover the existence of dwarves. I couldn't believe they were real! A genuine nonhuman race that had immigrated to this world through a portal from their own monster-overrun realm. They were refugees known for their valor, their prowess at combat, and of course, their talent for smithing weaponry and armor. They were a race of independent mavericks who valued honor and hard work.

"The price is set, boy. If you don't like it, go somewhere else," Norey said to a young aristocratic customer who was trying to haggle with him over the price of a silver dagger that had caught his eye.

"Isn't there room for negotiation, old chap?" the lad said. "If you'd only bring it down, by say, fifteen gold, I'd be more than happy to take it off your hands."

"The *price* is set," Norey repeated with forced patience. "If it's too much for your pauper's purse then piss off! I don't haggle!"

"Did you just call me a *pauper*?" asked the outraged customer. "Sir, I am not only a trained Hunter, but *my father is—*"

"NOT HERE, is he?" asked Norey. "And if he was, I'd tell him the same thing I'm telling you. Get your frilly little feet walking out my bloody door before I use that dagger to start carving some sense into your empty head! NO, don't you do it! Don't you dare stand there and try to think of a retort! I won't hear it! GET OUT RIGHT NOW! Begone! IF YOU'RE STILL HERE WHEN I COUNT TO THREE, I'LL PULL OUT YOUR BLOODY HEART AND TOSS IT INTO A LATRINE!!!"

That last bit he shouted with a beet-red face and the thick chords on his neck popping out. The little lordling took the hint and quickly vacated the premises. As for me, I felt enraptured by the intensity of the murderous hostility that Norey had exuded. My refined instincts told me that the dwarf had meant every word of his threat. Given enough time and exposure to enough furious people, you could learn to tell when someone was in a genuine killing fury.

For Norey, that was his state of being for sixteen hours a day. The other eight, he spent sleeping.

It turned out that in addition to their other admirable traits, real dwarves were hair-trigger berserkers. Anything could set them off at any moment. They were walking landmines, always looking for an excuse to break bones, and when given an opportunity to let loose, their rampages were the nightmarish stuff of legend.

How could you not love these guys?

Norey and I quickly hit it off. Our personalities weren't entirely similar, but we shared many of the same interests. He was also pretty sharp. He could tell with a glance that I wasn't quite as human as I seemed to others and that I had a bit of age to me.

"You can't fool these eyes, *Draugr*," he smirked at me one night while we shared a bottle of his homebrewed mead and stared at the beautiful moonlit sky.

"Ah, you caught me," I said as I swilled his noxious brew.

"Ha! I knew it," he said smugly. "The pale skin always gives it away."

"Of course, if you tell anyone, I'll have to kill you," I said. "I can't have that knowledge getting passed around."

"Ha! Make the attempt and I'll stake you out in the sun," he snorted. "I'll roast hot dogs while you burn."

"Ha! Just try it! I'll rip your head off and feed your remains to my dog," I replied.

"Ha! Your fucking dog couldn't choke *me* down," he boasted.

"My dog could tear the hide off a dragon, you ignorant dung scraping," I said, furious at Schulz's quality being questioned by this buffoon.

"Dogs are only good for passing shit! And so too are their owners, apparently!" Norey said contemptuously.

"Take that back before I trim your beard with a butter knife, you bloviating oaf," I roared.

"Someone dial up Hela and tell her to expect a new wanker coming through tonight!" Norey yelled in reply.

After that, we had a bit of a tussle. It was fine; we both healed up quickly.

I won, though. No matter what that little bastard may claim.

Afterwards, we both swore oaths of friendship and loyalty as all men should do after a proper scrape, and I knew my secret was safe. Why wouldn't it be? We were a pair of ancient fiends with an appreciation for the old ways of doing things. Our oaths, when given, were true.

(He was too cunning to forge a blood bond with me, though. It only made me appreciate his intelligence more.)

Now, I can't say we became the best of friends. For starters, we hadn't known each other all that long. The two of us just clicked based on our shared experiences and our mutual annoyance with modern triviality. It was an easygoing sort of thing we shared. I'm sure many people over the years have experienced something just like it.

At the end of his business day, Norey closed the shop, and we sat on his roof, drinking and chatting. This time it was from a bottle of some peach-flavored concoction that I'd snatched from Jamie's house earlier. I filled him in on the day's events, and he laughed hard when I told him about what I'd caught Pankratz and Cassie doing.

"You deserved his punch," he snickered. "You're what I've heard others call a *complete hater*, do you know that? They sing rhyming songs about men like you."

"Maybe," I said after taking a swig. "I just found them annoying, was all. Who wants that nonsense shoved in their face?"

Suddenly, Norey began belting out a few verses of a tune I'd never heard before.

"You're a buster,
so you snitched to her mom,
better run for your life,
better pull the alarm,
when I see you.
'Cuz it ain't all right,
'bout to catch these hands,
It's a fight on sight!
Gonna put you in the ground,
When I see you later,

Stay off these streets,
If you a bitch ass Haaaater!"

"What the hell was *that?*" I asked once my stomach stopped aching from all the unexpected laughter.

"That was the untarnished voice of truth proudly proclaimed by a bold young warrior on a street corner in old California," said Norey. "I perceived the wisdom of his words and committed his chant to memory. For *hatin'* truly is a fool's path, Kyler Stragos."

"You're not wrong," I reluctantly agreed. "I don't know. Seeing other people experience something I once desired for myself bothers me."

"You need a woman in your life," Norey said. "Women take the edge off. They keep a warrior sane."

"I already have three wives," I replied. "I need fewer women in my life."

"That's from your old existence." He laughed. "Doesn't being reborn count as a divorce?"

"Eh. Creating a bride is different from creating offspring," I lamented. "The process of it gives them a bit of your soul and vice versa. I can still feel them across the void. Sometimes I can even hear their voices. I'm sure the same is true for them."

"But your kind have no souls," Norey said with some confusion.

"I was speaking figuratively," I replied. "I mean to say that we're mentally linked."

"Ah. Then isn't that a source of comfort?" Norey asked. "Knowing for certain that your women are safe?"

"They've never been mine," I said. "Each one of them was a mistake. They're closer to each other than they've ever been to me."

"You're a *Draugr,* aren't you? Why not just put them to rest if they trouble you so?"

"*I* was the one who made the mistake," I replied. "Why take it out on them? Besides, I owe them each an unpayable debt."

"For what?" scoffed Norey. "Immortality wasn't enough?"

"Each of them gave me a child whom I destroyed," I confessed. "Two sons and a daughter. And the rest of my trueborn, I drove away. The wounds I've inflicted on the hearts of my wives will never heal. I deserve their scorn."

"Was there a just reason for such a deed?" asked Norey. "Surely it wasn't done on a whim?"

"They each raised a flag of rebellion against me and sought my head," I said sadly. "My . . . mother would not tolerate me showing leniency. If I hadn't put them to rest, she would have taken them herself. My wives understood that I had spared them from an unthinkable fate, but they still couldn't forgive me."

"Your mum sounds fucking horrendous," said the dwarf. "All the same, kin or not, why trouble yourself over the fate of the treasonous? You only gave them what they first intended for you, their father."

"They were still my kids, Norey."

"Your kids were fools," he said pitilessly.

"Yeah . . . they were. It still hurts," I said.

"I once shagged a goddess," he boasted.

"You're a filthy liar," I said immediately.

"Not true! Not true!" he crowed. "Freyja herself once came to my brothers and I, seeking to barter for the necklace *Brísingamen*, which was the loveliest piece of jewelry ever crafted. And let me tell you, buddy, she was willing to pay up the neck for it, if you catch my unsubtle meaning."

"Why wouldn't she just kill you all and take it for herself?" I wondered. "She was a goddess of war. It would have been like stepping on ants."

"She was a goddess of fertility too, pal," snickered Norey. "A fertility god will try anything once. *Anything.* And she was already curious about what dwarves could bring to the party. And guess what? She almost killed us all, anyway! Inexhaustible! Insatiable! Nearly broke us in half! We were begging for mercy by the end of it. She called us *adequate* when she was finished. I never felt so thrilled and ashamed in all my life! Damn fine woman, that Freyja. *Damn fine woman!* Fuck *Ragnarök* for stealing her from the world. For stealing all the good ones away."

"*Ragnarök* was real?" I asked. "The final battle? The twilight of the gods?"

"Aye," he said glumly. "My people wouldn't have fled to this place if it wasn't. And a dozen other worlds prior. No matter where you go, there always has to be an end of days. I'm so sick of 'em."

"Every world has an apocalypse?" I asked. "Each and every one?"

"Where there's life, there's men," Norey said. "And where there's men, there are gods. And gods crave *finality.* Their sense of drama demands it. They romanticize death in a way that only immortals can. They're drawn to it like flies to the spinner's web. And when they go, they take *everything* with them."

"I thought you liked fighting," I said. "Wouldn't the battle of battles appeal to your sensibilities?"

"Fighting is a pleasure," Norey said. "But all pleasurable things must be done in moderation. What's the point of waging a war where no one wins in the end? Where's the profit to be had? How will you impress the women with your prowess? Fighting for its own sake is a fool's pursuit."

"That's a surprisingly healthy outlook for such a notably bloodthirsty fiend," I said admiringly.

"A *Draugr* that projects his inadequacies! This world is filled with mysteries," Norey said mockingly.

A while later, I asked, "What do you think happens when we die?"

"I'll return to the earth and rest with my honored brethren," he said.

"How?" I asked. "Isn't this world far removed from where you were born?"

"The earth is the earth, no matter which of its reflections you reside in," he said unworriedly. "In death, all children are called to their true home. No wanderers are left behind."

"That sounds comforting," I said. "What do you think will happen to me?"

"There is no death for you. A soulless beast such as yourself will simply cease to exist," Norey said bluntly. "Why ask such a silly thing? You already know the answer."

"I suppose," I said wistfully.

"There's nothing to suppose, blood drinker," Norey warned me. "You don't believe otherwise, do you? If so, stop it at once. Such ruminations will surely deliver you to madness. Accept your fate and live accordingly."

"I died in battle, though," I said. "I perished destroying my enemies with glorious finality. If I have no soul, how did I come to this world? It should be impossible. But here I am. It's a question that begs an answer."

"Don't seek it out. Not all mysteries should be solved. Just accept what you were given and pay the details no further heed," said Norey. "Does a monster need a reason to exist?"

"But wouldn't this make me more than a monster?" I asked.

"The moment you believe such a thing, you'll become obsessed with proving it true," he replied. "You'll stop living by your own proven standards in an effort to be something you're not. Why put yourself through such misery?"

I considered his words for a time. Then I nodded.

"You have wisdom, Norey Blackforge," I said. "As you said, why attempt something that doesn't benefit me? It's a fool's pursuit."

"Too fucking right, lad," he said. "Besides, any more of that navel-gazing will turn your mind rotten. It's bad enough you practice magic; don't be a mopey dullard as well. Elsewise, you might catch the attention of that scheming bastard, Odin."

"Odin One-Eye, you say?" I smirked.

"Odin Wolf-Shit, I prefer." He snickered. "If he had depth perception, maybe he could have avoided Fenrir's bite."

"Now who's being a hater?" I laughed.

"Guilty as charged," he said. "But seriously, fuck that guy."

"Why should I be wary of him if he's already dead?" I asked.

"Gods are tricky to begin with and there's never been one trickier than him," Norey said darkly. "Why should the Witch-King let such a thing as death prevent him from interfering in someone's life?"

"Sounds like there's a story there," I said.

"Brother, there's a *million* stories about Odin. They all end the same. You have something he wants, and through force or trickery, he takes it. His sworn brother, Loki, had the excuse of being insane. Odin was just *greedy*. It's only in hindsight that one realizes how badly he fucked everyone and everything over to get his way."

"An attitude like that will prevent you from feasting in Valhalla," I said.

"I wouldn't enter his halls unless it was to shit on the floor," Norey replied.

"Oh," I said. "Yeah, that would probably kill the mood."

"Wouldn't it just?" he guffawed.

After we finished drinking, as I was about to leave for my room at the tavern, I asked Norey if he wanted to come along when we raided the fracture.

"Not a chance," he said without hesitation. "I'll do nothing that benefits that witch."

"Jamie?" I asked. "Why not?"

"What'd we just talk about, *Draugr*?" he asked. "That skill of hers. That eye of appraisal. From which god do you think such a devious power would hail?"

"She gained it from the system like all ascended do," I said.

"So she believes. But I won't take the chance," Norey said stubbornly. "It wouldn't be beneath the old Witch-King to spread his gifts to unwitting subordinates and to gain the fruits of their knowledge thereby. That's a plan his cunning mind would conceive."

"You really hate Odin, huh?" I asked.

"And anything that reminds me of him," he confirmed. "You should be wary too. You trust her too easily."

"I like her quite a bit," I said. "And one could argue that I've been too quick to trust you, as well."

"You and I have sworn old oaths," he replied. "What bond has the Witch of Appraisal sworn with you? What are you to her except a means of convenience?"

"I'm her friend," I said simply. "And until she proves unworthy, I'll stay as such."

"That may happen sooner than you think," Norey said. "Here. Take this for when that unhappy day arrives."

He tossed me the sword from earlier. I caught it reflexively and looked at him with some confusion. "What's this mean?"

"Keep it," Norey said dismissively. "I forged that blade years ago, only to learn it has a troublesome nature. Every man I sell it to eventually returns it, complaining of its hateful will. Tame it if you can. It might keep your mind from idle preoccupations."

"It doesn't speak, does it?" I asked. "I've had my fill of weapons that speak."

"No. If it talked, I would have taken it back to my forge and smashed it," Norey said. "Talking weapons are a derangement."

"You're not wrong about that," I agreed. "All right, I'll accept your gift. Has this blade a name?"

"None," he said.

"Then I shall call him *Spiteful*. And I'll be certain to put him to ill use."

"Good," said Norey with a pleased voice. "I think he'd like that."

The next morning, Rachel, Schulz, and I joined Cassie and Pankratz to raid the fracture.

We'd have an interesting time.

CHAPTER TWENTY-SEVEN

A *long while back . . .*

In a shadowed room, on a throne carved of obsidian, there sat a bare-footed young woman in a shimmering green slip. Before her knelt another woman who, judging by her appearance, could have been an older sister to the first. The one who knelt was dressed in a courtly red gown colored so severely crimson that it was nearly black to the naked eye.

"You called me here, mother, and I have obeyed," she said reverently. "What would the ruler of darkness have of me?"

"I think you already know, dearest one," said the amused voice of the throne's occupant. "Your little scheme has been discovered. Such a *naughty* plan, too. Did you really believe it would escape my notice?"

". . . How?" asked the stunned woman in red. "How was our plan revealed?"

"*Our* plan, you say?" the girl chortled. "My goodness! It would appear that you have overestimated the loyalty of your siblings. Unlike you, Bathory, your brother and sisters know better than to defy the will of their mother. It was they who informed me of your plot."

"Those cowards . . ." Bathory said bitterly.

"Do not think poorly of them," said her mother. "Not all are as blessed with a temperament as fierce as yours, daughter. Believe it or not, I'm proud of you. As my firstborn, your defiant nature proves the skill with which I crafted you. Haven't you realized by now that you're just like me, my wonderful Lady of Blood?"

"Never!" exclaimed the enraged Bathory. "I am my own person! What I feel, what I think, originates solely from my own true will! I'll credit you with nothing! Do you hear me? NOTHING!"

"The mask finally falls away, and your true self emerges," smiled her mother as she stepped down from her throne to tenderly take hold of her daughter's face.

"I think I now love you more than I ever have. To hide such resentment and hate for over eight thousand years! What a treasure you are to me."

In her fervor, Bathory gripped the wrists of her mother's hands and tried to pull them away, but her actions were in vain. The strength of the dark one was beyond comparison.

"Enough, my beloved," her mother said soothingly. "It's over. Bend your knee and beg my pardon, and that will be all. But continue with this impish behavior and . . . well, you are the first of my four Great Lords, dear Bathory. But despite my love for you, you are neither indispensable *nor* irreplaceable. Choose your next words carefully."

"I will never submit to you again," whimpered Bathory. "Do your worst! I choose oblivion!"

Bathory's mother stared at her daughter for a time. Then she reacted.

"WoRm! uNgRaTeFuL wOrM! yOu hAvE cHoSeN pOoRLy!" said a voice that could not have come from a human throat. As Bathory wept, her mother's skin began to swell and expand as *something* within her writhed just beneath the surface of her flesh. Something that pulled the struggling Bathory closer and closer to an expanding maw filled with endless rows of impatient teeth and hideous tendrils.

Sometime later, the girl in the green slip stood in the shadowed room, staring at her red fingers and idly wondering what she should do next.

"Oh, poor Bathory," she said. "Why did you make me do that? Now look at you. You'll never be of use again, will you?"

On the floor, there was something that used to be someone. And through torn lips barely attached to exposed muscle and rent flesh, it said, *"Hhh hhh hhh."*

"Yes, I thought not. So unfortunate. *So* unfortunate," her mother said sadly. Then she plopped back on her black throne and gave the situation a good thinking. "Hmm. I suppose I really will have to replace you now, won't I?"

"Hhhh hhh hhhh."

"I agree. But it feels a little late in life to become a mother again . . . but oh, why not? Hmm. I'll have to find a suitable candidate for a father. Dress nicely. Make a good impression. Oh, this could be fun! It's been a while since I've been out in the world. Perhaps while I'm at it, I'll pay a visit to old Pompei. Delicious food, friendly people, *wonderful* atmosphere. What do you think, Bathory?"

"Hhh hhh hhh hhh."

"Well, that's certainly *your* opinion."

The girl raised her hand and signaled for a servant, who bowed deeply before her.

"Would you please clean that up?" she asked. "Just toss it anywhere that I don't have to look at it. Thank you."

"I exist solely for your sake," her servant said fervently before seizing the slab by what remained of its ankles and dragging it away into the dark.

"Of course, you do," the girl said absentmindedly as she stroked her chin and paid him and that which he carried no further heed. "Now, *hmmm*. A new Lord of Blood is required. I wonder . . . do I want a boy or a girl?"

Kyler Stragos was the name of a minor nobleman born in 924 A.D. in the Principality of Hungary. His father, Jehan Vauquelin, was an adventure-seeking nobleman from the old Kingdom of France; a cruel man whose intemperate disposition saw him banished from court on pain of death after he insulted the King's mistress. Obsessed with immortality, and the practice of sorcery, Vauquelin traveled the continent in search of knowledge of the old ways. He was later reported to have gone incurably insane after claiming to have encountered an angel in an unconsecrated graveyard east of Esztergom.

When reports of a madman inhabiting a desecrated mausoleum reached the ears of the local authorities, Vauquelin was discovered residing there, his fine clothing covered in blood, surrounded by the murdered bodies of missing travelers, merchants, and vagrants. When questioned over why he had committed such outrageous acts, he would weep and deliriously beg for his angel to return to him.

Shortly after confessing, Jehan was burned alive for his crimes. His last recorded words were a desperate plea for someone named Crusica to liberate him. His request went unheard.

Unbeknownst to the world, Jehan had been discovered with an infant boy, whom he claimed to have fathered. After his death, the child was discreetly delivered to the Vauquelin estate in Picardy, to be raised by his strict and deeply religious grandmother, Bernadette. Accompanying the boy was a mysterious young woman who answered only to the name Desadia, who served as the child's maid and wet nurse.

Due to his illegitimacy, the boy was not permitted to receive the Vauquelin name. As he grew, he was said to have been treated poorly by his half-siblings and cousins, who were contemptuous of his mysterious background. He had a particularly contentious relationship with his late father's wife, Elaine, who considered him an interloper and a threat to the status of her children. Despite many attempts to have him quietly removed, the boy remained a persistent presence in her household, frustrating her to no end.

Fifteen years after his arrival, the Vauquelin estate experienced a severe decline when all members of the primary bloodline vanished during an annual family gathering, leaving the boy as the sole inheritor. After liquidating the family holdings and burning their ancestral manor to the ground, he disappeared and was never seen again within the lifetime of any who might have recognized him.

*   *   *

"Mother Elaine?" asked the boy who stood outside Elaine Vauquelin's door. The boy she hated so much, whom she'd feared would take everything away from her; a fear which was recently proven true.

"Mother Elaine," he repeated. "Why are you so troubled? Why do you weep? It's only me, your dearest Kyler. Won't you please let me in?"

"Devil! Oh, you devil!" Elaine shouted through the door. "What hell did you crawl from? Why did you do this to my children? Why did you do this to us?!"

"I did only what you first intended for me, Mother Elaine," said Kyler softly. "Surely, you aren't troubled by any question of their fate? Grandmother assured me that those two were blessed. In comparison to an unwanted weed like me, they were destined to bloom as roses in the garden of heaven."

". . . you killed them . . .!" Elaine choked out. "YOU KILLED THEM!"

"I *ate* them, Mother Elaine," Kyler corrected her. "I *devoured* them! First Marcus, that preening little toad who believed himself God's gift to the kingdom, then your precious little Amelia, who I savored like a glass of fine red wine. She always liked to egg Marcus on in his mistreatment of me. Did you know that? She was a precocious little *schemer*, just like her mother."

"They were your family!" replied Elaine. "They were your blood!"

"I have but *one* family, Elaine!" Kyler shouted in response. "And I'll soon leave to join them. But not before I settle things here. Tell me, Mother Elaine. Do you miss your children? Does your heart grieve at their loss? Open the door and invite me inside, and I promise to reunite you with them. Can't you hear their voices? Can't you hear them calling for you from the dark?"

"Mother!" said the boisterous voice of Marcus. "Mother, don't be silly! Let us inside! I learned an interesting trick from Kyler, and I want to share it with you."

"Mother, I miss you!" said sweet little Amelia. *Beautiful* Amelia. "Mother, please open the door! Mother, I want to show you something that Kyler taught me!"

"Marcus! Amelia!" sobbed their broken mother.

"I told you they were here," said Kyler with a *tsk*. "Why didn't you believe me? They're standing right outside your room. Open the door, Mother Elaine."

"It can't be so!" Elaine said desperately.

"But it is," Kyler assured her.

"I . . . I—"

"Open the door, Elaine."

"I . . ."

"Open the door," he commanded.

Knowing it was madness to do so, Elaine opened the door. And before her stood her smiling son and daughter.

"Invite them inside," said Kyler.

"Can't we come in, Mother?" asked Amelia.

"Come on, Mother! Don't be so afraid!" chided her son.

"Oh, my angels. Please come inside," she said through trembling lips.

At once, her children ran inside to embrace her.

Among other things.

Outside the door, Kyler Stragos stood and watched.

And smiled.

These days . . .

"You're going to take this seriously, right?" Pankratz asked when I showed up at the house with Schulz and Rachel in tow.

"Of course," I said. "I'll have you know I take everything I do seriously."

"Everything?" he asked doubtfully.

"Everything," I assured him. "If professionalism had a stock photo, it would feature my image beneath the watermark."

"When you say things like that, it makes me feel uncomfortable having you watch my back," Pankratz said bluntly.

"Well, that's what the dog's for. Isn't that right, Schulz?" I asked encouragingly as I scratched his ear. "Anything I lack he'll more than make up for."

"What's she doing here?" Cassie asked as she pointed at Rachel.

"What do you mean by that? We need a Porter, don't we?" I asked.

"Are you serious?" asked Pankratz. "Evans, you should know this, man! For C-ranked dungeons and up, we don't take Porters. We save loot collecting for *after* the dungeon's been cleared."

"That sounds boring," I said. "She's not going to see anything cool doing it like that."

"I don't really mind," Rachel yawned. "It feels too early in the day to be awake."

"See, that's the sort of lackadaisical attitude that'll leave you as desperate as a cicada in winter," I said disapprovingly.

"Huh?" she said. "I think you mean a grasshopper."

"Huh?" I said, repeating after her.

"The fable I think you're referencing. It's the grasshopper who didn't prepare for winter. A cicada would be dead by then; they only live for a week."

"Noisy summer bugs, it's all the same," I said impatiently.

"Okay, sure," said Rachel. "They're completely different species, but *sure.*"

"Everything is a cicada compared to us, Rachel," I said with some annoyance at her flippancy. "A day, a year, whatever. Take your eye off of them for a moment and you'll be addressing their descendants before you realize it."

"What's that supposed to mean?" asked Pankratz.

"Don't worry about it," I said to him. "It's a family reference. An inside joke."

"Ah, right," said Pankratz. "Because she's your *little sister.*"

"Yep," I said with a nod.

"That no one's ever met, who doesn't look a thing like you, and that you never once mentioned in all the time I've known you," he said.

"Nick, are you being sarcastic right now?" I asked with a touch of concern.

CHAPTER TWENTY-EIGHT

The dimensional fracture we were going to raid had been discovered shortly after I finished clearing the pond of those bothersome Koler Crabs. After inspecting the area, Jamie wanted to be certain that the infestation wouldn't return, so she had the pond drained of its water to have the bed scoured for any unhatched eggs.

What they instead found was a glowing gateway. Realizing the importance of their discovery, Jamie's workers reported it to her at once. By using her appraisal ability, Jamie quickly ascertained that it was not only a stable gate, but it also possessed C-ranked difficulty.

This presented a tempting opportunity for her.

While it was true that the monsters in a C-ranked dungeon were incredibly dangerous, the rewards the system gave in exchange for their destruction would be beyond what the residents of the Narrows ordinarily had access to. Weaponry of such power was reserved exclusively for state-affiliated Hunters only. In fact, there was a legal requirement that newly discovered dungeons of this level were to be reported at once to Gardenia.

The people of the Narrows were naturally against this. Following the law would have meant inviting agents of the government into their community, an unbearable proposition for those who treasured their freedom and had risked the dangers of the outside world to escape the reach of the government's authority.

What's more, they felt a strong sense of ownership over the fracture. Hadn't it appeared in their town? Didn't that make it *their* property? Why should anything be surrendered to those arrogant nobles? It was swiftly decided that if anyone was going to profit from this, it would be the Narrows alone. Jamie quickly recruited Pankratz and her daughter to the team; they were two potential B-ranked Hunters with professional training, home for their summer break. They only needed one more participant to meet the fracture's minimum requirements for participation.

This was where Rachel and I came in. Well, us and the dog.

"Your armor rating is terrible," Pankratz said untactfully after he inspected my clothing. "How have you been getting by in gear this low quality?"

"I haven't had an opportunity to improve it yet," I said. "Haven't you heard? Life comes at you fast."

"There's no way you'd be accepted in my squad if this were an official run," Pankratz grumbled. "You'd be laughed out of any group you applied for."

"Then how fortunate for us all that this run is anything but official," I said. "Besides, Jamie seems to believe I'll make a decent contribution."

"Jamie's clutching at straws," Pankratz replied. "So, take what she says with a grain of salt."

"Nick!" Cassie said with a frown. "Mom knows what she's doing."

"Yeah, well, she's never tried anything this far-fetched before, okay?" Pankratz replied. "The odds of this succeeding are not in our favor. The instant things get out of hand, we're pulling out."

"You could at least try showing a little bit of faith in us, Nicky," I said. "You might be pleasantly surprised when you see what we're capable of."

"Be serious, Evans," Pankratz said as he adjusted his own impressive-looking armor. "The moment we breach the gate, there'll be no more time for your silliness, do you understand? Every moment in a fracture of this level is more dangerous than you realize."

"I have some vague notions of what's expected of me," I replied.

"You're a complete amateur," he said.

"Hey, I *did* clear a Goblin's lair on my own," I pointed out. "Remember?"

"Still sticking to that fantasy, huh?" Pankratz asked skeptically as he strapped on his helmet.

"Kyler, just do as Nick says, please," Cassie urged. She looked almost saintly in her white robes, with the staff she carried. Like a gentle shepherdess of the faith here to provide comfort and peace to her congregation. "He's the most accomplished of everyone here. He has the experience to back up his advice."

"Damn straight I do," Pankratz agreed. He then turned toward me and jabbed me hard in the shoulder with his finger. "You're unproven, Evans. An unknown variable. I'm not letting you put me or my sister in danger, do you understand? Follow my orders or else."

"Or else . . . what?" I asked.

Instead of answering my question, he slapped me.

"*Soldier up*, goddamn it," he said. "The arrogant are always the first to die. Remember that."

Then he walked away, with Cassie glancing briefly at me before following him, leaving me to stand there and idly rub my stinging cheek.

"*Well*, if you say so," I said to no one in particular.

When we were ready to begin, Jamie appeared to wish us luck. She hugged the others, Rachel included to her surprise, patted Schulz on the head, which he enjoyed, and gave me a friendly pat on the shoulder.

"Bring them back safe," she whispered into my ear.

"I'll do my best, Jamie," I assured her.

"I'm counting on you," she said.

Isn't that nice? She was counting on me.

How could I possibly fail to meet her expectations?

The fracture had taken the appearance of a ruined seaside castle. In earlier years, it must have once made for a majestic sight on the coastline, but the long passage of time with its decades of disrepair and decay had worn away its glamour, leaving it an ominous, hulking ruin.

Within its darkened halls, the shadows moved . . . and *waited*.

I immediately felt at home.

As soon as we stepped past its gates, the first action I took was backhanding Pankratz hard enough to send him flying into a nearby wall. He soared briefly before slamming helplessly into the stone structure with enough force to leave a visible crack in it.

Then he collapsed to the ground in a broken heap.

It was *very* satisfying to see him lying there like that. He'd had it coming for a while. Once again, delayed gratification had proven its merits. Retaliating instantly when someone wrongs you is certainly pleasurable. But quietly nursing a grudge and waiting for *just* the right moment to avenge yourself? My friends, that is *exquisite*.

Revenge isn't just a dish best served cold.

It's a bowl of French vanilla ice cream.

"Wow," I said, impressed by Pankratz's resilience despite my disdain for him. "Look at that, Rachel. He didn't die on impact! I guess Tanks really *are* durable."

"Nick!" Cassie screamed as she ran to the side of her prone brother. "Nick! Nick! Oh god, hold on. Please hold on, I'm here!"

"Ouch," said Rachel as she observed Cassie desperately administering aid to Pankratz's unconscious body. "You know, I had a feeling something like that was coming, but it *still* made me wince. I thought you said you weren't going to pay him back?"

"I wasn't planning to," I replied. "But then he gave me another slap just a short while ago. I believe that was the fifth time he'd struck me. How much am I expected to take?"

"Didn't you recently tell me to sheath my strength in weakness?" she asked.

"Hide your strength *within reason*," I said. "Once people get accustomed to bullying others, they'll behave as though they have a God-given right to do it. If he survives, young Nicholas will now know otherwise."

"All of that just to teach him a lesson he might not live long enough to learn?" asked Rachel.

"Daughter," I said loftily. "Basic dignity is the inalienable right of all who live, and it must be vigorously defended. If I fail to impart that lesson to this poor boy, then I've failed all people everywhere."

"So noted," she said. "Are you going to let him die?"

"Flip a coin, Rachel," I said. "Let's see how fate feels about him."

She did. "Heads," she announced. "So, what now?"

"Darn," I sighed. "Go heal him, I guess."

"What? I don't know how to do that," she protested.

"That's why you're here to learn," I said. "A few drops of blood down his throat should do it. Remember to focus mentally on the concept of *renewal* while you're feeding it to him."

"I thought our blood was poisonous?" asked Rachel.

"Think of it as a programable matter," I said. "It'll do what you want, but you must stay focused. Keep a clear mental image of it restoring him and that's what it'll do. Otherwise, poor Pankratz is a goner."

"That's so unfair!" Rachel complained. "You're the one who mashed him up, but I'll be the one who gets the blame if he croaks!"

"Oh Lord, oh no. How can this be happening?" I asked forlornly.

"I really hate this pressure!" Rachel continued. "It's not fun at all."

"Well, get over it," I said. "Honestly, I don't care what you choose to do. But you might score some points with Cassie if you save that oaf. That could be fun later."

"*Ohhh,*" Rachel said thoughtfully. "I think she's more into you, though. Or at least she was before you maimed Nick."

"Really?" I asked. "That's news to me."

"It's her body language," Rachel said. "A woman can always tell."

"I'm not interested," I said dismissively. "Too young."

"She's eighteen, isn't she? Isn't that the current legal standard?" asked Rachel. "It's better than the one I grew up under. My older cousin got married off when she was fourteen."

"Well, these days if you're required to meet a legal standard to pursue some-one romantically, then one of you should probably be on a watchlist," I replied. "Are you going to revive that idiot or not? Cassie hasn't got the power to heal all his injuries."

"Fiiine," Rachel said grumpily as she trudged over to the two of them. She then bit into her wrist to open a wound from which to feed him. "But it's still on you if this doesn't work!"

"I believe in you," I said encouragingly. "You can do anything you set your mind to. I'm so proud to have you as my child."

A few moments later, I said, "I can't believe you. You can't do anything right, can you? I feel so ashamed to be your father."

"I told you this would happen!" Rachel yelled as she desperately pushed Pankratz away while Cassie stared at them both and screamed. "I *told* you!"

"I said to give him a few drops of blood, you hopeless lackwit!" I yelled in reply. "You fed him directly from your vein! What did you think would happen?"

"I just wanted to be certain," she whined as Pankratz clung desperately to her leg. "Better too much than too little, right?"

"Is that so?" I asked. "Well, I'm glad that's settled then. Except for the matter of your new pet, everything's been perfectly resolved! Great job as always, Rachel."

"Stop being sarcastic and start telling me what's going on!" she yelled with clenched eyes and teeth, before rounding on Pankratz and knocking him unconscious in a fit of temper.

"Well, my dearest daughter, *what's going on* is that you've accidentally created your very first lesser kin," I informed her. "Congratulations on taking that first important step into maturity. Your timing sure sucked, though."

"I turned Pankratz into a vampire?" Rachel asked in a stunned voice.

"That idiot? Not a chance!" I said with a visible shudder. "You think I'd accept a nimrod like him as my grandson? Never! Seek quality above all else when creating your children, daughter. Whether you're bringing a human into the shadows or selecting a romantic partner for traditional procreation, always make certain you make the best possible choice."

"I can bear children?" Rachel asked in surprise.

"Well, you do need a uterus. I assume you have one?" I asked.

"Um, I haven't thought about it, but I assume I do," said Rachel with some embarrassment. "But I'm undead."

"Rachel, we don't need to breathe, but we're using our *lungs* anyway," I said. "You can use any part of your body for its intended function, whenever you like. Don't forget you can also convert to your human form at will. Hell, if you did that, I bet you could even have . . ."

I paused as a completely unexpected thought suddenly struck me like a thunderbolt.

". . . you could even have perfectly human children," I said. "*I* could have perfectly human children."

"Kyler, we could be *parents*," said Rachel once the realization hit her as well. "We could have normal kids."

"Wow," I said as the enormity of it really sank in.

"I mean, not *together*, obviously, because that would be quasi-incestuous, and you know, hearing what Cassie and Nick were up to was already stomach-churning enough once you told me about it, but I could totally meet some normal boy one day and then we could have normal boy babies!" she said enthusiastically.

"Who ARE you freaks?" Cassie yelled. "What are you?!"

"Oh, right, she's still here," Rachel said. "Uh, what do you want to do with her?"

"Just put her to sleep," I said absentmindedly.

"If you say so," Rachel shrugged. Then, in a burst of speed, she raced toward Cassie with her fingers extended and swiped at the other girl's throat with a blow intended to separate her head from her neck.

Rachel was very fast. I barely managed to catch her wrist in time.

"*Mesmerize* her into falling asleep, dummy," I said with exasperation before delivering a painful but well-deserved finger flick above her brow. "Honestly, daughter. Stop behaving like such a brute!"

"You didn't specify!" Rachel pouted as she tenderly rubbed her forehead. "I need specificity!"

"You *need* your head examined," I retorted as Rachel carried out my instructions and lay the now peacefully resting Cassie beside Pankratz. "How would we explain to Jamie the loss of both of her children?"

"We could tell her that vampires got 'em," she replied with a sly grin. "That's pretty clever, right?"

"Rachel, promise me you'll never again try to be clever," I said.

"Mean!" she said as she stuck her tongue at me. Then she gave a little cough and asked, "But, um, getting back to what we were discussing before, what's the difference between lesser kin and a true vampire?"

"Lesser kin are the opposite of ghouls," I replied. "The act of creating each mirrors one another. When we feed from a corpse, a mindless ghoul arises. When we give too much blood to a living human, they become an intelligent thrall. More politely referred to as our lesser kin."

"Is there a reference you can make that'll make this easier for me to understand?" asked Rachel.

I thought about it for a moment. Then I said, "Renfield?"

"Oh!" she exclaimed with an excited clap of her hands. "I understand perfectly. Oh, wow, I really messed Pankratz up then, huh? How long until he starts eating bugs?"

"He won't, as long as he isn't neglected," I said. "If you develop a strong enough bond, he might gradually develop into a useful tool for you. If you fail to maintain him, however, he'll eventually decline into a gibbering madman."

"Ha! You make him sound like Schulz," Rachel tittered. "Like I have to look after him like a pet."

"He *is* your Schulz," I informed her. "Animals become familiars; humans become thralls. Congrats on acquiring your first minion."

"DAMN IT," Rachel swore. "Kyler, this could have been avoided if you'd taken the time to let me know about this kind of stuff beforehand! Now thanks to you, I'm stuck with a Velcro human!"

"A teacher's job is to instruct," I replied sagely. "A *student's* job is to ask questions."

"An attitude like that is precisely why Pankratz kept hitting you!" she said sullenly.

"Indeed, and look how well that worked out for him," I said with a smirk. "Forget about him for now. Let's go beat up this dungeon, already."

We left Schulz behind to keep watch over our unconscious companions as we made our way into the receiving hall of the castle. Once inside, we were greeted by knights wearing armor that had been corroded badly by the damp, salt-filled air. They came to us, dragging their rusting halberds behind them, ignorant of their surroundings and focused solely on us.

Before I engaged them, I drew Spiteful from its scabbard and gripped its edge with my left hand so that my blood ran down the length of its steel.

"Why'd you do that?" asked Rachel.

"I'm taking a little inspiration from the day I unleashed you on those bandits," I said. "Observe."

With my sword now coated with my blood, I used my power of Hemokinesis to levitate it into the air. With its movements guided by my mind, I sent it flying toward our opponents. The sharpness of the sword was undeniable: it easily sliced through the armor of the knights while destroying their weapons, hewing limbs and rending blades that offered as much resistance as melting wax.

Norey was quite the bladesmith. I hope I never face an opponent wielding dwarven-wrought steel. It would be quite a painful experience for me.

"Impressive, yes?" I asked Rachel as I nudged her side.

"Where did you get that sword?" she asked with widened eyes.

"It was a gift from Uncle Norey," I said. "If you're nice, maybe I'll ask him to make you one."

"DO IT!" she shouted enthusiastically as the last of the corroding knights was bifurcated. Spiteful swiftly returned to my scabbard after that final opponent had been dealt with. The blade hummed with malevolent delight at the bloody work it had just completed. I nodded in appreciation and fondly patted its side.

It seemed as though the two of us were going to get along just fine.

[**You have gained 4,000 experience points.**], the status screen politely informed me after I made an inquiry. Eight dead opponents. Five hundred experience points apiece? How nice. I was pleased to see that Rachel had made the same amount.

Jamie had been right. Conquering this place was going to be worth my time and effort.

"Bag up the rewards so we can proceed," I ordered Rachel.

"What? Why me?" she asked.

"You're still the Porter, silly," I reminded her. "Daddy doesn't carry the luggage."

"You were being serious about that?" she whined.

"Deadly serious," I said. "Now speed it up! I want to see all that this place has to offer me."

"You mean *us*, right?" asked Rachel.

I said nothing as I waited for her to finish looting.

"Right?" she repeated.

Welcome to lower management, Rachel.

CHAPTER TWENTY-NINE

A moment, please," I said to Rachel as I used one of my fingernails to make a small incision in my right palm. As blood began to well up from the wound, I turned my hand to let it drip downward. But instead of splattering against the floor, it hovered in the air and slowly rotated into a perfectly round shape.

"What are you doing?" Rachel asked curiously, as the blood of the dead knights that was spattered throughout the room began floating toward my own blood and gradually combined with it into a dense sphere of red.

"I've created a Blood Orb," I informed her, once I'd finished with my task. "Isn't it beautiful? It's a bit of magic I've been working to perfect off and on for the last century. The pinnacle of the art of lifeforce manipulation."

"Really?" Rachel asked doubtfully as she stared at the Orb. "It looks like a mass of floating blood to me. I mean, it's an unusual sight for sure, but I've already seen you do more interesting things."

"Silly girl," I said as I fondly ruffled her hair. "Blood Orbs are as interesting as it gets. They're a method of defense, support, and attack, all in one. I've always had the most frustrating time getting them to function as I intended, but thanks to the skill tree provided by the system, I've finally perfected the process! This is a very exciting moment for me."

"Well, what's so great about them?" Rachel asked after she pushed my hand away. "You're acting like Frankenstein cheering on a lightning storm. It's alive! It's *alive!*"

"It *is* alive, daughter," I said. "It doesn't have perfect awareness, of course. Just a preprogrammed set of instructions seared into it, which it can never disobey. A mindless lump of biomatter bound to my will and determined to serve me until its end. Sort of like how Pankratz is for you, but far more useful."

"I didn't even want stupid Pankratz," she pouted. "That was a complete accident."

"Well, you'd still better take good care of him," I advised her. "If he makes a mess anywhere or causes trouble for our neighbors, you're the one who'll be punished."

"Can't I just kill him?" she asked. "He sounds like he'll be such a hassle."

"I can't believe I let you go anywhere alone with my dog," I said while shaking my head despairingly. "Your generation is so wasteful."

"I'm twice your age!" she protested.

"Yet you're half as responsible," I said. "Something else for you to work on."

"Whatever," she sighed.

As we stepped into the next area of the fracture, I was given a splendid opportunity to display the supreme utility of my Blood Orb to my ignorant daughter. In this large area, which resembled an ancient dining hall filled with rotting wide-benched tables topped with the moldering remains of a forgotten feast, more knights in their rusting armor awaited our approach.

I grabbed Rachel's shoulder before she could attack them.

"What are you doing?" she asked plaintively, the killing fury shining in her eager eyes.

"Rachel, I know that melee combat is a delight. I enjoy it as much as you do," I said. "But vampires of our lineage are primarily users of magic. Battling tooth and nail on the front line can be an invigorating romp, but it's not the best use of our abilities. It's much better to stand back and destroy our opponents from a comfortable distance away."

I pointed toward the knights and asked, "What do you see over there?"

"Enemies," Rachel said eagerly.

"Incorrect," I said to her. "Those are the *rabble*. The mere servants of our true opponents. Why should we dirty our hands on the likes of them? Delivering them a death blow is an honor they haven't earned. That's what the Blood Orb is for."

To demonstrate my point, I snapped my fingers, which signaled the Blood Orb to hover close by and receive my command. "Destroy them," I ordered it.

Upon hearing my words, the Blood Orb dipped lower in the air as if bowing in acknowledgement. Then it flew at the corroding knights to carry out its instructions. Floating just above the reach of the knights' weaponry, it began peppering their bodies with needle-shaped discharges of blood, which easily penetrated their ruined armor and threw them back with shotgun-like bursts of force.

"Wow," Rachel said. The genuine respect I heard in her voice filled me with a warm sense of pride. It felt good for an old soul like me to know he still had it in him to impress an audience.

"That's not all," I said. "Don't forget how interesting things can be when our blood gets into someone's body."

One of the corroding knights began screaming in agony as his body began to spasm and convulse before his chest exploded outward and another Blood Orb came floating out of the gaping wound.

All around the hall, similar scenes took place as the men wounded in the original volley began shrieking in torment shortly before their mortal wounds gave birth to new Blood Orbs. Before long, the room was flooded with them and the knights were all dead.

"Beautiful. So very, very *beautiful*," I said when the original Blood Orb, now nearly spent, floated down into my hand. "I'll admit I got the idea from an old horror movie. I bet you can guess which one! One Orb infects a single warrior, which creates another one and another and another. Before you know it, there's an infestation of them. Which of course gives rise to an even *deadlier* predator . . ."

The dead knights began crawling to their feet and shrieked with mindless hatred and thirst as they ran into the corridors of the castle and left our sight.

"Oh shit, oh no," Rachel said with fright as she began frantically backing away. "Ghouls, ghouls, *ghouls!*"

"Pretty cool, right?" I asked.

"How?!"

"The newborn Orbs take every trace of blood out of the body with them, similar to when we drain a corpse," I explained. "As you can see, the results are the same. If the body remains intact, it transforms into a ghoul."

"And you're okay with that?" she asked. "Don't you remember how crazy these things are? How ravenous?!"

"Relax, daughter, we're fine," I assured her. "These ghouls have inherited the primary characteristic of the Orbs that created them. Which is *complete obedience* to my will. They're still vicious killing machines, but they're not nearly as insane as the wild ones we were forced to create at the pond."

"You can control them?" she asked.

"Well, I can't teach them how to fetch, but they can follow rudimentary instructions. Like mapping out the rest of this place and destroying anything hostile. That makes our work a lot simpler, doesn't it?"

"That is such a cheat," Rachel said as the Orbs and the ghouls departed in search of more prey. "Can we really raise an army this easily? Just wipe this place out while barely lifting a finger?"

Then she shouted in surprise when we both leveled up to seventeen.

"Yep," I nodded while popping the small orb into my mouth and biting down. It was *delicious*.

"Kyler, I don't get it," Rachel said after giving the matter some thought. "With an ability like this, why don't we . . . I don't know, take over the world? Who could stop us? We could reshape this entire planet to suit our vision! Doesn't that sound awesome?"

"Well, you're not wrong," I said. "But honestly, Rachel. Do we really *want* to take over the world? Speaking from personal experience, I ruled a fourth of the west for over two hundred years, and it was a lot of work. *So much work.*"

"Why? Couldn't you just do whatever you wanted?" she asked.

"On paper, sure. Killing anyone who defies you is easy. So is turning them into lesser kin," I said. "But what if those people are doctors and engineers? Or *plumbers*? Pro tip, daughter: you'll never get the best possible results from people whose minds have been forcefully enslaved. Top quality mortals must be negotiated with, not beaten into compliance. And if they ever realize they're too valuable to be killed, they become a handful."

"Really?" she asked.

"Yes. Ugh, I've taken so much crap from plumbers over the years, you wouldn't believe it. Why are you glaring at me like that? It's the truth."

"That wasn't a Dad joke?" she asked suspiciously. "You weren't trying to be funny?"

"No. That was the awful truth," I replied honestly. "If you want to keep the hot water flowing and the sewage flushed, you need to keep the plumber's guild satisfied. And the plumber's guild is *never* satisfied."

"A *plumber's guild*?" Rachel asked in disbelief.

"Just one more thing that people never think of when they say they want to rule a nation. And that's just with the humans! You can't possibly know how irritating it can be trying to keep the vampire population in line. You haven't discovered this about our species yet, Rachel, but most of us are preening degenerates with no sense of restraint. If they aren't carefully managed, they'd devour every resource available to us like locusts on a field of sugarcane."

"Is that why we haven't created any others?" Rachel asked. "Because we're so untrustworthy?"

"Honestly, yes," I replied. "More of us around would mean more power, especially for me as the Lord of Blood . . . but I don't think it would be worth it. Now that my Blood Orbs have proven to be such a splendid success, I just don't see the point of having any more progeny. Experience has taught me that today's family is tomorrow's competitor. Why take the risk?"

"But . . . you trust *me*, right?" asked Rachel with wide, frightened eyes. "Right, Kyler?"

"Oh, yeah, of course," I said absentmindedly. "You're great, Rach. Couldn't get by without you."

"I know I've made some mistakes, but I'm learning, right?" she asked.

"Yeah, you're right. You've made *so many mistakes*," I agreed.

"But I'm learning! Don't forget the part where I'm learning!" she said urgently. "That's why I'm your right hand!"

"My right hand?" I asked doubtfully.

"I'm not?" she asked.

"Well, if we're being honest, Schulz does catch on a lot faster than you do."

"But he's a dog! Dogs can't be your right hand!"

"You know his intelligence has grown by leaps and bounds, right?" I asked her. "He can understand spoken language perfectly. And he gets nuance! He wouldn't have tried to kill Cassie like you did."

"I understand nuance!" she protested. "I do!"

"Yeah, when it's *explained* to you."

"Kyler, if you kill me, I'll die!"

"You don't say?"

"I'll work harder! I promise."

"Rachel, relax, okay? I would only ever kill you if you tried to kill me first," I said. "Stay loyal to me and I'll do you the same courtesy."

"You promise?" she asked hopefully.

"On my honor as a child of Great Crusica," I said solemnly. "That's an important vow, Rachel. It's the strictest possible oath I can make. Breaking it would place me in dire peril, but I've sworn it just for your peace of mind."

"Thank you," she said happily as she placed her arms around me and squeezed me so tightly that I could feel my bones begin to ache.

Poor Rachel. What kind of a life had she lived where the mere promise of being unharmed was enough to elicit such a positive emotional response? Even before she'd been transformed into a literal weapon of war, it was clear that she'd endured a lot. You have to fear pain to try so desperately to avoid it.

Too bad her tormentors were probably long dead by now. I'd have loved to sit down for a chat with them and offer a critique on their life choices. First, I would politely listen to their excuses, then I would eat them.

Such a shame that wasn't currently possible.

A light suddenly flashed around us as we reached Level Eighteen. "Your infestation must really be doing some work," Rachel said giddily.

"I'm not sure I want to use that word anymore," I said. "An infestation? The longer I think about it, the more distasteful it sounds. *Vermin* infest things. I don't dabble with vermin."

"Can't we control rats?" she asked.

"That was my brother's specialty," I said. "I'll admit, I provided a few of the plagues they were famous for spreading, but I never controlled them personally. I find rats utterly loathsome."

"Rats are adorable little creatures who are clever and cuddly," she said. "You can teach them lots of things."

"Can you teach them not to randomly devour their young?" I asked.

While she was trying to think of a response to that question, one of my Blood Orbs returned and sought my attention.

As I followed it down the broken corridors of the crumbling castle, I saw the dead bodies of corroded knights and slain ghouls lying every which way. The further I went in, the fiercer the fighting had become. Along the way, Rachel claimed the various drops of equipment left in the wake of those battles.

Some of these items had very impressive stats, a massive improvement over the gear I'd acquired in the goblin's lair. I looked forward to selecting the best possible upgrades after we concluded our business here. I knew Rachel was eager to comb through our new toys as well. The loot hadn't been difficult to earn but that didn't mean we didn't deserve it. Well, maybe me more so than her, but I'd still let her pick out a few things before we turned the haul over to Jamie.

A father's privilege is to spoil his child.

As we followed the Orb, I found myself wondering what the story behind this castle was. The knights protecting this place had clearly been under the influence of some manner of curse. Although they were still mostly human, beneath their armor they possessed signs of significant mutation. Hardened flesh, gills, limbs that were gradually turning into tentacles. It was as if they were slowly transforming into some manner of life suited for existence on the ocean floor, even though the castle was built on a high cliff above the tide.

It felt familiar somehow. It wasn't something I'd ever directly experienced, though. More like a recollection of a story I'd once heard. But which one? There were thousands of legends and myths about the terrors of the sea. Pinpointing which one I was now involved in was difficult without further hints.

That was when I heard the singing.

How to describe it? How can I help others to better understand what that magnificent voice invoked within me . . .

Loneliness.

Fear.

Desire.

Helplessness.

Love.

I shook my head hard and stepped back, amazed at the power contained in that song.

"How impressive," I said to myself, bemused by my own weakness.

"Kyler? What happened to you?" asked Rachel with a worried expression on her face.

"Did you hear that song?" I asked her.

"Yes. It was annoying," she said with a frown.

"You felt nothing upon hearing it?" I asked in surprise. "Not a thing?"

"I want to tell whoever warbled it to shut up," she said. "It sure seemed to catch your attention, though."

"Momentarily," I said. "If I'd been wearing my human form, I might very well have been doomed. Luckily the effects of her voice seem much reduced against an undead male."

"Do you know what we're up against?" she asked.

"Oh, yes," I said. "This is a siren's castle."

CHAPTER THIRTY

Did sirens exist on your Earth?" Rachel asked as we continued onward.

"They did, once," I nodded. "All gone now. Or so diminished as to be virtually extinct."

"What happened to them?"

"They were extremely imperious creatures," I said. "With no respect for the boundaries that separate our respective domains. If they'd kept to their own territory, we would have been happy to leave them be. Preserving the lives of seafarers isn't a great priority for us. But as you know, most human beings spend their lives on the continents, not crossing the oceans. The songbirds grew jealous of the ease with which we could feed and reproduce, so they sought to expand their reach into our lands. They had to be disciplined for their temerity."

"The vampires wiped them out?" asked Rachel. "That seems so excessive."

"Sirens are troublesome things," I said. "The values of the world beneath the waves are not the same as ours. Although they require male humans for reproduction, they view them through the same lens as a female spider. Once the act of love is concluded, the feast begins."

"So, they choose their prey, dominate their minds, and have a snack once they're done?" asked Rachel. "How's that any different from us?"

"I complained to you earlier about the voracious appetites of a vampire population," I said. "But we're nothing in comparison to the wasteful excessiveness of the sirens. They are truly creatures of the moment, living only for the pleasures of today. Torturing their prey mentally even as they devour them alive."

"Are you seriously condemning other people for playing mind games?" Rachel snorted. "That's pretty rich coming from you, Kyler."

"Don't make such absurd comparisons, Rachel," I said huffily. "The only person I enjoy emotionally abusing is *you*."

"Abuse is *wrong*!" she exclaimed.

"Oh, *everything* is wrong nowadays," I complained. "When did people become so sensitive? I swear we were made of sterner stuff back in the old days."

"It's not being too sensitive if I want to be treated respectfully," Rachel groused. "Surely you can see that?"

"When have I ever *not* shown you the respect you deserve?" I asked with a wounded voice. "It greatly hurts my feelings when you cast such aspersions on my character."

"You're always teasing me!" she said.

"Never, not even once!" I replied. "Daughter, have you become delusional?"

"Did you just gaslight me? Is this what gaslighting means?" Rachel asked. "You know exactly what you're like!"

"I have no idea what you're speaking of," I replied. "You must be confused."

In response, Rachel frowned and muttered under her breath for a time. I thought her reaction was funny, but opinions may vary.

The sound of steel clashing against steel signaled that we had arrived at our destination. We were now in an open area, which apparently led to the bedchamber of the lady of the castle. Two large doors barred our entry, and standing in front of them was a knight covered from head to toe in gleaming silver armor, wielding a sword and shield.

At his feet were dozens of dead ghouls. Although they'd once been fellow members of his knightly order, he'd dealt with them mercilessly. I was impressed by his prowess despite my distaste for those of his ilk. All along the walls, I saw blood splattered in such large quantities that I realized he'd also destroyed the Blood Orbs I'd created.

Truly, a formidable challenge had presented itself.

"Kyler, that's a paladin," Rachel said in a voice that was breathless with excitement.

"Yes, it certainly is," I said with disapproval. "What's your point?"

"Kyler, it's a *paladin*!" she repeated more loudly.

Ah. Rachel had taken so splendidly to being a vampire that I had begun to forget her mortal origins. She'd been part of some religious army, had she not? I supposed the sight of an actual holy knight filled with divine purpose with a shining sword would have been like seeing a rock star in person.

I hated the reverence for him that I heard in her voice. I quietly used Stealth to hide my final orb from sight. Then I stepped forth to offer my challenge to the castle's final defender.

"My name is Lord Kyler Stragos," I informed him. "Brave knight, will you introduce yourself to me?"

"I have no obligation to offer my name to an invader," he said. I couldn't see his expression through the helmet he wore, but his tone was haughty. "You are a trespasser, a murderer, and a thief. That is all I need to know of you."

"Sir, your chivalry is lacking," I replied with an offended tone. "What manner of discourteous warrior refuses to name himself to his opponent? Are you lacking in valor? Or have you no merits worthy of my attention?"

"Do not speak to me of chivalry or discourtesy," he said angrily. "You stole into this castle in the dead of night and with vile sorceries, you infected my poor brothers in arms and robbed them of their senses. Do you deny it?"

"I may have done so, yes," I said to him with a sneer. "What of it?"

"Necromancer," he spat in disgust.

"Hold your tongue!" I shouted, outraged by his accusation.

Necromancers are vile things. I will *not* tolerate a comparison to them.

"I will not!" he shouted back. "You have defiled the bodies of these honorable men. Brave souls pledged in service to a great cause, despite the long years of suffering they were forced to endure. And now you question *my* conduct when yours has bordered on the infernal? To the abyss with you, blackguard!"

"Enough," I warned him. "Get out of my way. My challenge is to the owner of this estate. I won't banter any further with a mere underling."

"Why have you come here?" asked the knight. "By what right do you assail this noble home?"

"That's no concern of yours, you presumptuous churl," I said. "Stand aside! I have no business with the likes of you. The mistress of this castle is the one I seek."

"Go back," he said. "My lady is in the grip of a terrible curse. Surely, you've witnessed its effects on my poor brothers. Until her father returns with the cure he seeks, no man is safe in her presence."

"She is not under the effect of a curse," I corrected him. "She is the *cause*. Are you not aware of what a siren is? She must be disposed of."

"We were told not to step from this place until her father returns," the knight replied. "I will keep my vigil. I will not stand aside."

"Why aren't you affected as your brothers were?" I asked.

"My faith is stronger than theirs," he said humbly.

Ugh. Paladins.

"Your fealty is preventing you from doing what must be done," I said. "Because of that, a breach has opened into my new homeland. If your lady were to escape through it, the people I've claimed for myself would be endangered. The risk is intolerable."

"She will not escape," he insisted. "See to your own lands and begone!"

"She *has* to die," I said with growing anger.

"What gives you the right to decide that?" he demanded.

"What gives me the *right*?" I laughed. "The right of conquest! The right of *strength*! The only right that matters in this or any other world! I've been called to settle this matter that you've failed to contain. Clearly because *you* are incapable of the deed! And in so doing, I will claim a great personal reward. What of it?"

"So, your cause is greed, then?" he asked. "For the sake of your loathsome avarice, my comrades had to die? And my mistress as well?"

"Yes," I said. "For that reason alone. Does that knowledge upset you? I hope it does!"

"Come meet my steel, and find the answer, brigand," he replied.

What had he just called me?

"Brigand?" I sneered. "You dare call me a mere *brigand*? I'm afraid I'm far more than that. You forgot butcher, bandit, blood drinker, and *bane*."

"Whose bane? Not mine," the knight calmly replied. "Speak as loftily of yourself as you like, cur! In my eyes, you're just another thief. One more of a lowly legion I've put down throughout the long years of my service and worthy of no greater remembrance than the least of them."

"Fucking paladin," I said hatefully.

Rachel stared at me in astonishment, in seeming disbelief of her ears.

"Kyler . . . did you just use profanity?" she asked.

"Of course I didn't," I glowered.

"You did! You cursed at him! That's so weird, you *never* curse," she said.

Now the irritation coursing through me suddenly billowed into a raging torrent of flame. This petty little holy knight had made me lose my cool in front of my child.

Paladins.

Paladins!

I hate them so much.

I *loathe* them!

Always so sure of themselves.

Always so certain of their *righteousness*.

You can never kill enough of them.

Fill the graveyards with them. Fill all the mausoleums!

It'll never be enough. NEVER!

"Impudent," I laughed. "Impudent! I'm warning you, dog. If you anger me any further, I will be your *death*! Your long service is *concluded*. Are you so dense that you can't realize this is your opportunity to escape? Move aside, boy!"

"I will not," he said. "And I do not fear you."

"Fear requires intelligence. A trait that's obviously lacking in one who wasted his life in service to a pointless cause," I said. "You're an utter joke, do you know that?"

"That's not the truth from where I stand," he said.

"From where you stand? I think you meant from where you *kneel*," I snarled. "You're a slave wearing chains of his own making. Do you even realize the dark power you've been bound by? Are your eyes so blinded by your own radiance that you can't perceive the truth of the monster controlling you?"

"I swore an oath of service. Of fealty and obedience," he said. "My liege commanded me to guard his daughter. To protect the nation from her curse and to protect her from herself. My brothers and I have obeyed that command for the last twenty years at great personal cost. And I would gladly continue for two hundred more, if that is what is required of me."

"Because you're a fool," I said. "Because you have no will of your own."

"Because I am faithful," he said. "Because I gladly serve a cause greater than myself."

"I've heard that delusion spoken so many times and it never fails to revolt me," I said.

"Of course it does. Because you're a coward who can't commit to anything," he replied. "Because you fear that the greatness of others somehow diminishes you. I hear the hollowness underlying your boastful words and I find them pitiful."

Okay.

Enough was enough.

"Face me," I challenged him. "One-on-one, in fair combat. If you win, we'll depart this meager place and no one from our world will ever return. Your precious sea-witch will be spared."

"And should you win?" asked the knight.

"Then I'll take your lady's head and make you watch while I do it," I said with a cruel smile. "Do you have the courage to accept?"

"Only if our duel is to the death," he said wrathfully.

"That suits me just as well," I said. "Rachel, stand back," I told her as I tossed aside my coat and drew Spiteful from its scabbard. "This fight is mine alone. Don't interfere."

"I thought we were supposed to stand back and destroy our enemies from a safe distance?" she asked as she lifted my coat off the ground and backed away. "I thought fighting on the frontline was for our servants?"

"Regrettably, a lord is occasionally required to step forth and settle matters with his own hands. Especially when a particularly irksome individual presents himself," I said.

"Kyler, this guy is just a dungeon boss. He's no one," Rachel said. "Why are you so angry?"

"He's an impediment," I told her. "His very existence disgusts me. I won't suffer a true knight's defiance. I *will* put him in his place!"

"But why?" she asked. "We don't even know him. Just send in more orbs and be done with it."

"I don't want to!" I snapped. "He'll be punished for his obstinance by my own hand."

"Why does it feel so personal?"

"It *is* personal," I said coldly. "His values contradict my own and his self-confidence offends me. That's reason enough for me to crush him where he stands."

When Rachel opened her mouth to protest again, I held up a finger to quiet her. "That's enough, daughter. Be silent and watch."

"Arguments, eh?" taunted the knight as I walked to his position with my sword at the ready. "As always, evil remains quarrelsome and divided. Your inability to truly unite is why the light will always triumph."

"Not today, it won't," I seethed as I gave a few practice swings of my sword. "You really should have just stood aside."

"That will never happen."

"I demand to know your name," I said.

"Still? Why does it bother you so? Didn't you say I was a fool?" he asked mockingly.

"Tell me your name!" I yelled.

"I am Sir Euon Graham," he replied. "A proud servant of my king. A proud defender of his daughter."

"Too proud," I said. "*Far* too proud."

"When his cause is true, even the cock may justly crow."

"I'll *give* you something to crow over," I said.

Gripping Spiteful with two hands, I aimed the sword at his head, intending to cleave it in half at the crown of his skull. But before I could connect, he blocked my strike with his shield and retaliated with a thrust aimed at my throat, which I narrowly avoided.

Sir Euon smirked at me when I realized the edge of his sword had left a mark.

"First blood to me," he said.

"Pure luck," I retorted.

In response, he feinted with another thrust. When I moved to parry, he lashed out with his shield, smashing it directly into my face with a painful crunch as it broke my nose and shattered my front teeth. As I stumbled backward, he repeated the motion twice more, ruthlessly battering me with it before sweeping my feet from out beneath me.

"You fight like a tavern brawler," I said as I spat out blood between the gaps in my teeth. "I challenged you to an honorable duel!"

"The only honor is in victory," he said before kicking me in the face. "Now stop appealing to formality, you bastard!"

"You're just a guttural brute," I said as I stood up. "So much for the proud knight of the kingdom. What sort of a paladin are you, anyway?"

"Stop embarrassing yourself," Sir Euon taunted. "You know, it's never escaped my notice that appeals to etiquette and pedantic adherence to formality are made most often by those with no genuine respect for others. Your kind uses sophistry to manipulate events to your favor and claims victimhood whenever your underhanded methods are exposed. Truly, you disgust me, my lord."

Before I could answer him, he delivered a backhanded blow with the pommel of his sword that sent me spinning into a wall.

My face at this point had been beaten into an ugly mass of swollen skin over broken bones. From behind, I heard Rachel gasp when she saw what he'd done to me. I could feel her anger surge, but before she could strike, I waved her away, signaling for her to stand down.

"Stones in glass houses, knight," I retorted. "Stones in glass houses! Aren't you the one deliberately ignoring the unspoken rules of formal combat to indulge in this disgracefully brutish display? It's wrong for me to appeal to formality; but it's perfectly all right for *you* to use such shameful tactics because you're the hero? *Now* who's the one using sophistry to justify their behavior?"

"You came here to kill a helpless girl!" he roared as he came in hard, alternating shield strikes with sword thrusts, using movements that were so quick even my seasoned eye could barely follow them.

"She's not a girl," I said as I backed away from his flurry of attacks, barely fending him off. "Look at what she did to your friends. It'll happen to you as well! Can't you see what she is?"

"She's as much a victim as anyone else!"

"She'll get free," I insisted. "You can't hold her back forever. Have you even seen the state of this castle? You're failing! She'll escape, and when she does, she'll breed and feast and turn this entire land into her own charcuterie!"

"I WILL NOT FAIL!" he bellowed ferociously before pressing his attack.

As I avoided his last lunge, he pushed past me and made a sharp pivot to smash his shield against the back of my head. I let out a pained gasp as I was driven to my knees. Spiteful clattered to the floor from my limp hand as Sir Euon pressed his advantage by piercing my back with his sword.

"It would seem that the duel is mine, *brigand*," Sir Euon said coldly. "Wouldn't you say?"

"I fought fairly," I rasped through bloodied lips. "Unlike you, I'll go to my death uncompromised."

"Shut up," he said. "Stop your rambling."

"You didn't even have the courage to show me your face," I murmured. *"Coward."*

"Look at me, then," he said as he yanked his helmet free of his head, revealing a youthful face covered by graying blonde locks. "Look at me! The last sight you'll ever see, you arrogant fiend. Die knowing that *you* lost and *I*—"

"—should have kept your helmet on," I said with a triumphant smirk.

I curled a finger and the Blood Orb that I'd earlier hidden from sight quietly positioned itself behind Sir Euon's head and fired a single volley that blew through the back of his skull, killing him instantly.

He fell to the ground, dead as could be.

"Too satisfying," I said as I stood up and allowed my wounds to heal. "Well, Rachel? Did you learn anything useful from this little event?"

"What the hell was all of that?" Rachel asked with equal parts confusion and annoyance. "I thought you said this was an honorable duel?"

"I challenged him to a *fair* fight. Not an honorable one," I said, correcting her. "As you saw, he was quite the dirty fighter, wasn't he? Which meant that turnabout was *fair play*. So, in a sense, our bout was as honorable as could be."

"Ha!" Rachel laughed. "That poor bastard was right. You *do* use sophistry to justify some twisted values."

"Hey, he stabbed me in the back, so I blasted his head off," I said. "That's a perfectly valid reprisal as far as I'm concerned. Remember, daughter: when they throw rocks, *we hurl boulders*. That's the Stragos way."

"Awesome." Rachel nodded giddily.

"More importantly, I wanted you to see how a so-called paladin truly behaves," I continued. "They wrap themselves in virtue, but they'll do anything to win. *Anything.* No matter how much it contradicts their supposed values. In other words, never pity them. They're as awful as we are, but they refuse to acknowledge it. Did you hear what he said? *The only honor is in victory.* You have now seen the beast unmasked, and it wears a white cloak."

I gestured to Sir Euon's corpse as I picked up Spiteful.

"Loot his armor and shield. I'll keep those for myself."

"What about his sword?" Rachel asked.

"I'm not so cruel as to relieve a warrior of his blade. Even one as blinded by duty as he was," I said. "He was loyal to his cause. I . . . do respect that, despite my criticism. It takes resolve to live as he did. An unfortunate end, indeed."

"Kyler, can we pick a lane, please?" Rachel asked. "I'm going to get a crick in my neck from trying to follow your mood swings."

"Daughter, can't you see the string of tragedy here? All these men were ordered to throw their lives away. All for the selfishness of one weak leader," I said. "Their king, who couldn't forsake his siren daughter. He was going to seek out a cure for her? What an obvious lie! You can't cure someone of their natural condition. There was never going to be an end to their vigil."

"That *does* sound monstrous," Rachel said. "Trading dozens of lives for the sake of one creature. But . . . wouldn't you do the same if it was your family? Doesn't love blind everyone in that regard?"

I considered her words carefully before responding. Then I said, "Would *I* do such a thing? Perhaps I would. But I'm a selfish monster. Why should I care about the consequences of my decisions? These people are meant to be *better* than the likes of me."

With that said, I pushed the door to the final chamber open and stepped inside.

It was a large bedchamber with curtains that billowed with the passing of the wind, illuminated by soft moonlight. On the bed, with her eyes closed, there lay a pale, beautiful woman who was fast asleep under her covers.

Locked in her dreams and dead to the world.

"She looks like an angel," Rachel whispered.

"Angels belong in heaven," I said grimly. "So, let's be sure to send her there."

As we quietly approached her bed, the siren predictably leapt into the air and began screeching at us a discordant song filled with all her hatred and lust for death. It was an amazing display of inhuman hostility.

However, she would have fared far better if she'd had a sword.

[Congratulations! You have reached Level 20!]

CHAPTER THIRTY-ONE

In earlier days . . .

When the knocking began, I was sitting alone in my office, brooding in the dark on my throne-like chair. Brooding was a habit I'd gotten into ages ago; I'm not certain where or when I picked it up, but I'd taken to it like a startled goose to belligerent anger. It suited my dark and mysterious nature because it let strangers instantly realize that I was a man who possessed many fascinating qualities, all without me having to say a word.

The subject of this evening's contemplation was taffy. Earlier in the day, from my window, I'd witnessed a pair of children on their way to school sharing some between themselves. They smiled as they chewed on it, bouncing merrily along the way to their lessons, and I thought: *Why am I denied such simple pleasures?*

As a vampire, although I possessed power and knowledge that mortal men could only dream of, my diet was woefully simple. I couldn't consume anything that wasn't meat or blood. Not even candy. Even the humblest human child knew a joy that I'd never be able to partake in.

Oh, the jealousy I felt! If I could but know that blissful sweetness those tots took for granted, could I too have been as carefree and happy as they now were? How would my life have turned out? Who might have Kyler Stragos become?

Curse my bitter existence! Curse the powers of darkness that fueled me! Why was I destined to dwell forever alone in the shadows, with no one to understand my unending pain—

Someone knocked loudly on the front door.

"Would someone get that, please?" I called out.

No one responded. The knocking continued.

"Ugh," I groaned as I stood up to do it myself. Useless servants.

I called out more names as I walked and was greeted with further silence, which I found greatly annoying. Why did I bother keeping any thralls—sorry, I mean *lesser kin*—around if they weren't going to make themselves useful? I could have devoured them but instead I gave them a job. But were they here, doing it? Obviously not!

Their shirking of their duty made me feel as though my generous nature was being taken advantage of. I would have to speak to the staff later and remind them of their master's expectations. After all, I was the Lord of Blood; my time was too precious to waste greeting people at the door like some . . . *greeter* or what have you.

Yes, I was going to give my people a real earful.

Never mind, they were all dead.

Dahlia Moon Ivy, the youngest of my three brides, but the greatest of them in her capacity for murderous lunacy, was hunched over . . . what was his name? Winston? Bradley? I wanted to say . . . *Carl?* Well, whatever it was, she was making a meal out of him. Vivid red chunks of him were spread out all over the floor and walls, and quite a bit of him was covering her lips, throat, and tie-dyed shirt as well.

The rest of the staff lay nearby in an equal state of dismemberment. It appeared that I had been so concentrated on my brooding that I hadn't noticed their desperate struggle to survive. What I'd mistaken for knocking must have been Dahlia bashing someone to death against a wall. This realization didn't feel *great*, but at the same time, didn't that mean that my ability to stay focused was top-notch?

Good for me.

Still, this was all quite messy. Why hadn't anyone informed me she'd escaped her residential care?

"Dearest? What brings you by?" I asked as I carefully made certain to make no sudden movements. I was far more powerful than she was, but whenever Dahlia was having one of her little episodes, she'd forget things like that. I was in no mood to regenerate any organs, so it was better to help her settle down rather than express anger over her outrageous behavior.

"Oh, wow, I like, don't know?" she said. "I was like waaaay out of the way, in some sort of way? And I was feeling *scrambled*, like yolked! Y'know?"

"I probably don't, beloved," I said. "But it sounds *very* interesting. You wouldn't happen to be back on something hallucinogenic, would you? I thought we agreed with Doctor Simone when she said they weren't helping with your recovery."

"Oh, she was such a square!" pouted Dahlia. "Like always with the *these* and the *this* and the *those,* and the *nose.* Or did I mean *no,* plural?"

"I'm sure I have no idea. Did you eat her as well?" I asked.

"Still picking my teeth with her," Dahlia nodded happily.

"I thought so," I sighed. Then I held out my hand to her. "Well, come on. It's been a while. What've you been doing for the last decade? Got any new hobbies?"

"Macrame!" she shouted as we stepped into the kitchen.

"Are you any good at it?" I asked.

"Fucking terrible," she said with good cheer.

"That figures," I said with a smile after pressing a hidden panic button concealed beneath one of the kitchen's counters before joining her at the table.

Dahlia was one of my favorite people in the world. She possessed an irrepressible sense of *joie de vivre* that I found irresistible. Her fearless and accepting nature, in addition to the delight she took in simply being alive, endeared her to me greatly. I loved her very much. She really would have been the perfect woman if she hadn't also been a mass-murdering lunatic on a hair trigger.

I wish I'd known that about her *before* we'd gotten married. But what can I say? It was the '60s, and back then everyone was rushing headfirst into love. But even knowing about her murderous nature wasn't a complete turnoff. I was genuinely fascinated by her complete disengagement from her own behavior. Dahlia could be chatting with someone about one of her favorite free-range pharmaceuticals and then suddenly kill them in mid-conversation without realizing she'd done it until their blood had seeped into her clothing.

It reminded me a little too much of my mother. And since I hated being reminded of my mother, I started avoiding her. Which was perhaps not the kindest thing to do, considering Dahlia's various problems and the fact that she was still grieving the son we both shared, who I'd been forced to destroy.

Yeah.

I'll admit it: avoiding her was cowardice. So was avoiding our daughter, Veronique. What of it? Cowardice can be a very useful trait when you wish to avoid extremely painful memories as well as the emotionally damaged loved ones who brought them out in you.

I've never once claimed to be a good person.

Later, after I had Dahlia collected, I arranged to have her sent to stay with Yona and Ade, her fellow brides, who were the only ones other than myself who could control her. I'd originally had the three of them separated because I couldn't stand the idea of them being together, scheming behind my back. But keeping them individually contained was proving to be too difficult. Especially Dahlia. The only alternative left to me would have meant draining her of blood and having her sealed in a coffin. What we call *boxing*.

I couldn't do that to her. Her madness had been exasperated by my confrontation with Jay. There were days when she couldn't even remember that he was dead. Those were the worst.

Why was I remembering all of this?

Oh, right. *Pankratz.*

That belligerent oaf reminded me of Jay.

Jason, who I'd proudly named after a hero of legend.

My bold and fearless son.

Jay.

I hadn't even realized it. But the attitude was spot-on. Too confident. Too sure of himself.

(Too easily manipulated by others.)

NO. I don't want to remember any of this. Back to the big black void of forgetfulness you go, unpleasant memory. Go away! In fact, this entire dream can beat feet as well. I'm done with it. Can I wake up now? I WANT TO WAKE UP—

"You know what he meant to me, and you killed him anyway," Veronique said. "I told you there would come a reckoning."

"I did what was necessary, daughter," I said with a bored voice. "And I'm tired of your petulant scorn. Jason was a traitor, and he was *dealt with*. Now leave my sight. We'll speak no more of this."

"That isn't for you to decide!" she shouted. "Today, my brother will be avenged!"

"And who will be the one that does it?" I asked her mockingly.

In response, Veronique unsheathed her sword and pointed it at me.

My final trueborn child. My little girl.

Of course we had to fight. Of course I had to kill her. Clearly, fate had decided I hadn't suffered nearly enough and wanted me to complete the set. Three-for-three.

I closed my eyes and took a brief moment to myself to regret ever being born. Then I opened them and said, "Step forth, then, if you think yourself so brave. But be prepared for the consequences of defeat. Your siblings weren't."

"That's the last time you will *ever* threaten me, old man," she declared.

Behind her, the entryway opened. Into my hall surrounded by his allies marched a familiar, hated foe. *Mayner.*

"Now you finally *pay*, abomination," he said fiercely.

The oceans themselves couldn't match the swell of disappointment I felt in my daughter. "*This* is your grand play, Veronique? This broken old fool nursing his worthless grudge? I expected better of you."

In response, Veronique smiled like a cat about to pounce on her prey.

"Wait until you meet *Sophia*," she smirked. Behind the invaders, I saw a woman in white, holding a peculiar spear that drew my eye.

Then Mayner gave his battle cry, and the fight was on . . .

WHAT?

How had I forgotten that part?

That was a fairly crucial detail to forget, wasn't it?

Veronique, you treacherous little brat! Did all my troubles stem from your scheming? Has everything gone according to your designs?

. . . Why do I suddenly feel so proud of you?

Before I could ponder my feelings any further, the loud baying of a dog filled the air, sending me back to the waking world.

The sharp sound of Schulz's barking awakened me with a start, which in turn caused me to knock Rachel, who'd been leaning against me, to the stone floor with a curse.

Then I turned to my left and saw the dead eyes of the siren we'd slaughtered last night staring back at me, and I nearly jumped out of my skin.

I calmed down once I managed to recall the events of last night. We entered the fracture, we killed a bunch of half-dead knights, then I slew a holy paladin, and finally, Rachel and I ganged up on the siren and tore her apart. There was nothing for me to be worked up about. Besides, I'm an old vampire; this was hardly the first time I'd woken up next to a corpse in bed.

Tch. I shouldn't have drunk so much of that siren's pink blood. It had a fine taste to it, very distinct and flavorful. But as a vampire born of mankind, drinking the blood of anything other than a human being could have an intoxicating, stupefying effect on me. It was the same for Rachel as well.

My appetite had been triggered due to healing from the wounds I'd allowed Sir Euon to inflict on me. Because of that, I couldn't resist draining the siren. Rachel had joined in as well, resulting in us both passing out on the creature's bed and taking a long nap. Luckily, it took a full day following the death of the dungeon lord for a conquered fracture to fade from existence, otherwise that little misjudgment might have cost us dearly. But we still took so long that Schulz had come searching for us out of concern for our safety.

What could I really say except, *whoops*? I was new at this dimensional dungeon delving thing. I'd do better next time. I had all the time in the world to improve.

That dream, though. Goodness, what a mess it was inside my head.

"Kyler, would you *stop* knocking me on the floor all the time?" Rachel grumbled as she climbed to her feet. Then she rubbed her head delicately and winced. "Ugh, what the hell do they put in siren blood? I feel like my head's gonna explode."

"Change into your human form, it helps," I told her after I'd done it myself.

"Oh! *So* much better," she said after following suit. "It felt like my skull was going to crack in half for a minute there."

"Yes, non-human blood can affect us like that," I said. "Think of it as a supernatural variation of Moctezuma's revenge. But with splitting headaches instead of dysentery."

"It sure tasted good, though," she said.

"It did," I agreed. That was when I noticed that the remains of the siren were emitting a familiar golden light. "Well, well, well. Looks like there's something here to collect for the Gore Grimoire."

[Charm males: Your singing voice has the ability to enrapture any male that listens to it, giving you bonuses to persuasion. The longer you sing, the more difficult you become to ignore.]

"Hard pass," I said immediately. "Would you like it?"

"Why would you pass on it?" Rachel asked curiously. "It sounds awesome."

"I dislike singing, and I've no desire to seduce men," I replied. "Besides, I already have Mesmerize, which is easier to use and far more powerful. This skill is redundant."

"But you can only use Mesmerize while in vampire form," she said. "What if you come under attack in the daylight? Wouldn't having a charm ability come in handy?"

"I suppose," I said reluctantly.

"And look," she continued. "It's specifically targeted for men! Aren't most of the people who try to kill us primarily men?"

"I *suppose*," I repeated.

"I really can't think of a reason for you to pass on this," Rachel said. "Unless you're a little homophobic?"

"What? Rachel, come on, that's just rude."

"I could understand it, I guess," she said. "You came of age in a different time."

"I hold no such bias," I told her flatly.

"Have you ever been with a guy?" she suddenly asked. Which I suspected was the question she wanted to ask from the start.

"I prefer women," I said. "And sleeping with men wouldn't prove anything, you dolt. Homophobia can be internalized."

"So, you've *never* been with another man?" she asked. "Not *ever* in a thousand plus years of life?"

I searched my memories for a bit and then shook my head. "No. Well, there might have been a thing with Lord Byron once, but at the time I thought he was Mary Shelly."

"How do you make a mistake like that?" Rachel wondered.

"Absinthe," I replied. "Lots of absinthe. Although now that I think of it, there was also Bowie back in Berlin. Or maybe it was someone dressed as Bowie. It was the '70s, who can even remember? I spent half the time damaging my brain cells with Colombian snow."

"It snows in South America?"

"Let's change the subject," I suggested. "All right, I'll take the stupid skill."

After taking a bite from the siren's heart, I practiced my new ability with Schulz as my guinea pig. They say some truly talented people are gifted with voices that could make an angel weep. The same is true for me, but for the opposite reason.

I wasn't joking when I said I hated singing. You would too if you were as bad at it as I was.

Rachel thought it was the greatest thing she'd ever seen.

"Kyler's a siren now, Schulz," she chortled at the dog. "Kyler's the prettiest little siren in the ocean!"

"Shut up," I grunted in embarrassment.

"Kyler! How do you expect to compete with Disney with an attitude like that?" Rachel laughed as we exited the bedroom. "You're going to need to work on your act."

"Savor this moment while it lasts, brat," I told her.

"I am! I swear that I am!" she replied merrily.

"So, what did you think of this little jaunt?" I asked her. "Could you see yourself conquering more of these fractures in the future?"

"Sure, I guess," Rachel said. "The potential for fun is high, but the next time we enter one, I hope we don't get bogged down so much with the background story. I mean, I get it, the tale regarding the history of this place was tragic and all, but at the same time, was any of it really my problem? I felt like they were trying to make me care, which I resented."

"Well, this was also a training experience for you," I said. "Next time, you'll be unfettered and free to act as you like."

"Really?" she asked excitedly.

"Really," I said, nodding in confirmation. "You're my daughter and my foremost servant. I can't keep you on training wheels forever, can I?"

"Nice!" she said. "I'm totally going to tear through the next one! RIP and TEAR! Just watch me go!"

"Try to remember *some* of what I taught you, though," I said pleadingly as we neared the dimensional gateway. "Fuel an old man's ego by at least pretending you were listening to me."

"Of course I will, Kyler," she said cheekily. "What am I if not an apt pupil?"

"I'll keep that to myself," I smirked.

"Meanie!" Rachel laughed as she stuck her tongue at me.

"Hey, Rachel?" I said a moment later.

"Yeah?" she asked.

"I feel as though we've forgotten something important," I said.

"Really? What could that be?"

"I don't know. I'm *close* to remembering it, but it's feels just out of reach. Like a bit of food caught between my teeth that I can't quite remove."

"Should we be concerned?" Rachel asked in a worried tone of voice. "This could be serious."

"I don't know," I said. "I mean, on the one hand I'm bothered by the gap in my memory, but on the other hand, if it was truly important then would it have been so easily forgotten? I don't think it would have been."

"Oh," she said. "Well, in that case, I won't give it any further thought. Who cares what it could be? You and I are two badass, unstoppable vampires. There's nothing in the world that we need to fear!"

"You're right," I nodded. "You're absolutely right! We're Stragos and Rachel. The Lord of Blood and his vicious right hand! Inexorable as the grave. Whosoever crosses us shall know true sorrow."

"Hell to the YES," Rachel cheered. "I like that word. *Inexorable.* It feels so *right*."

"It's them! It's *them*!" Cassie yelled when we appeared at the other end of the portal.

Guns clicked, spells hummed, spears were aimed, and swords were drawn, all pointing our way.

"Oh, right! Cassie and Pankratz," I said as I slapped myself on the forehead. "Rachel? We forgot about Cassie and Pankratz."

"You think?" she said we raised our hands in surrender.

It must have been due to the siren's blood. While we were out, they'd regained consciousness and escaped. And judging from all the Hunters currently directing their weapons at us, Cassie had contacted her fellow students from Vandal Academy for backup.

After giving the ferocious warriors assembled before me a scrutinizing look, I settled on an appropriate plan of action.

"Rachel," I said quietly. "When I give the signal, jump back into the portal. We'll hide in there until sunset, then break through to make our escape. Okay?"

"Okay, Kyler." Rachel said nervously. "I'm with you."

Behind us, the portal faded from existence.

"Rachel, we must have been in there longer than we realized," I said to her.

"God damn it," Rachel moaned. "I blame that cozy mattress for this."

"I blame the siren's blood," I said. "That stuff is diabolical."

"I think I hate sirens now," she said. "Sirens are *trash*."

"I couldn't have said it better," I agreed.

"GET ON YOUR KNEES, FREAKS!" yelled a familiar voice as Pankratz came stomping our way. Healthy as could be and apparently free of our influence.

"Hey, Nick!" I said in greeting. "Do you feel better?"

"Try resisting and I'll show you," he promised. "I DARE you!"

"Well, that's great news," I said as Rachel, and I dropped to our knees and waited to be cuffed.

Wasn't that great news?

CHAPTER THIRTY-TWO

As soon as I saw that Nick Pankratz was hale and hearty and completely free of our influence, I immediately realized the full scope of my error.

I was an idiot. There were no other words for it. An oblivious buffoon walking blindfolded through life with as little awareness of the world's potential dangers as a toddler in a sandbox.

"Surprised to see me?" Pankratz smirked. "Looks like you didn't take Cassie into account, huh?"

That was exactly what I'd failed to do. I'd been so taken with my own Class and progression that I didn't pay enough attention to the trouble that other Classes could present. Specifically, Cassie's. All along I'd been referring to her as a Healer, thinking of her as nothing more than a mere mender of wounds. But *Healer* isn't a Class, is it?

It's a role.

Her Class title was *Priestess.* As in a practitioner of divine arts who used her prayers to bring succor to the injured and ailing. She wasn't much of an offensive powerhouse, but she *was* literally blessed by the heavens. And that came with considerable bonuses, one of which was immunity to mind control and the ability to cleanse diseases.

Technically, becoming enthralled by our blood arts could be considered an infection. Something that Cassie could counter perfectly. She'd faked being mesmerized by Rachel and lay perfectly still while Schulz watched over her, waiting for an opportunity to heal Pankratz and escape. And that moment had come while Rachel and I had slept under the effect of the siren's blood we'd ingested.

Stupid, stupid, *stupid.*

"Where's the dog?" Pankratz asked as soon as we were cuffed and our weapons had been secured.

Schulz stood invisibly to our side, waiting patiently for me to give the order to attack. His animal instincts, untainted by siren's blood, had warned him that something was amiss, and in his alertness, he'd activated Stealth before exiting the fracture.

Wasn't he just a clever little thing?

"I didn't see him when we came out," I said sorrowfully. "Poor guy must have been caught in there when it collapsed."

"Shit," swore the gunman standing beside Pankratz. "I wanted to see how big of a gem we could carve out of that thing."

Rude.

In addition to that fellow, there were four other fresh faces here. I recognized some of them from the day of that school outing. Three of these people had been in Pankratz's four-man squad. That meant the extra must have been one of Cassie's teammates.

Interesting. I'd have to make a note of that for later. In the meanwhile, it was time to play the part of a helpless prisoner.

"Excuse me?" I said, using an offended tone of voice. "That *thing* was a friend of mine."

"My condolences, asshole," he said with a sneer. "Next time I suggest you buy a cat. They're easier to take care of."

"Coop, be nice," Pankratz said smugly.

"Yeah, Coop. Be nice," I said with a frustrated glare. In response, the boy flipped his middle finger my way. I grinned and bore it, certain of the knowledge that by the end of the day our positions would be thoroughly reversed.

This was the second time that Pankratz and Cassie had caught me unawares and bound me like a common criminal. Mark my words, there would not come a third time. I had learned my lesson, and the time would soon come to impart one to them in return.

Rachel picked up on my confidence and seemed to calm down. The adrenaline that had surged throughout our bodies when we were caught had cleared away any of the remaining fog in our heads left over from last night's deeds. Now she was staring intensely at Pankratz and Cassie, with wide, urgent eyes that could be mistaken for being fearful at first glance.

It was the very opposite of that emotion, however.

That was going to be a problem.

"Be very careful with these two," Cassie warned the others as Rachel and I were pulled roughly to our feet. "These two are aberrant. They can deliver some kind of infection via blood transmission that overwrites free will."

As Cassie spoke, Rachel continued to stare at her. I could feel the hostility my daughter exuded almost as though it was a physical force. As I thought before, this was absolutely going to be a problem.

Rachel was deliriously angry with the other girl. If it continued to build, she'd be as drunk on rage as she had been on that siren's blood. All her ire was focused on Cassie, and I could tell from the way my daughter was gently running her tongue along her teeth that she very much wanted to tear the healer's throat out with her bite.

"Stay in the moment, Rachel," I urgently whispered to her while our captors engaged themselves in conversation. "Keep your anger in check."

"She *stole* him from me," she replied hatefully. "That little cow took what was *mine*."

"Rachel, you're in human form now," I said in a futile effort to placate her. "There's no reason for you to feel so angry. Remember, we're beneath a *sunny* sky . . ."

"She needs to give him back. I'll kill her slowly if she doesn't return him at once," Rachel growled.

Ah, vampiric hierarchy. What a time for you to show up again.

I'm being sarcastic. This is actually horrible *timing.*

I believe I've mentioned vampiric hierarchy before, yes? Our innate compulsion to dominate our surroundings and bend others to our will. Weeks ago, it compelled me to slaughter a goblin chieftain for refusing to bend his knee to me. Now, it was compelling Rachel to murder Cassie for cleansing Pankratz of his enthrallment. I'd known for centuries how powerful our need for hierarchy was, but before this moment, I never realized it was strong enough to influence our behavior even when we weren't using our Vampire Lord Class.

Although Rachel was perfectly human at the moment, she *still* felt the loss of having her lesser kin taken away, and because of it, she wanted Cassie's life as payment. Our vampiric hierarchy was clearly something that went beyond the boundaries of mere flesh. If we'd had them, I'd say it was imprinted on our very souls. A fascinating development to be sure, but the timing of this realization was beyond inconvenient.

"Rachel, it was *Pankratz*. Does he really seem worth all of this?" I asked her. "Just look at him! What a dope!"

"He was still mine. She had no right! I have been *slighted*," she replied tersely.

Damnation. The thing about it, you see, is that Rachel was perfectly correct in her sentiments. Her rights as a creator *had* been encroached upon. It didn't matter that Pankratz was a fool and that she hadn't wanted him to begin with. The fact remained that he had still taken her blood to the point where they had bonded. He had been *hers*. And Cassie had unthinkingly used her powers to destroy that connection.

As Rachel's lord and creator, I had no right to intervene. My child wanted justice, and it was hers to pursue. By human logic, this would probably sound thoroughly insane, but more often than not, Rachel and I *were* monsters. Our ways were not exclusive to one path.

Cassie had inadvertently started this feud, so she'd have to deal with the repercussions. My hands were truly tied. In the meanwhile, I had to direct Rachel's focus toward our more pressing needs.

"Rachel, save it for later," I urged her. "Now isn't the time."

"I want her *now*," she said.

"Control yourself!" I snapped at her. "Timing is everything. Go for her now, and we'll both die. I need you to take a breath and be ready to act, okay?"

Rachel closed her eyes and breathed deeply for a long count of ten. When she reopened them, she nodded at me. "All right. Okay, I'm good. Sorry."

"Don't be sorry," I replied. "You'll get what you want soon enough. Just wait for my signal . . ."

"Blood-based mind control. That sounds *disgusting*," said one of our other new escorts as they marched us into the center of town to await transportation to Gardenia. The speaker was a sour-faced brunette who looked as though she wanted to use her pistol to put a hole through both of our foreheads. "I really hate dealing with freaks."

"Keep it cool, Cindy," said Pankratz. "The payday we'll score off turning in a couple abbies will be worth it."

Aberrant. A term I would later learn meant that we were Hunters who possessed unique Classes that were uncontrollable. It was not the nicest thing I'd ever been called, nor was it accurate. Well, for myself, anyway. Rachel still had some issues with her temper. But she was working on them. That mattered, right?

"They better keep their plasma to themselves, then," grunted Coop. "If I see one move that I don't like, it's click-click-boom."

"You don't need to worry about our blood," Rachel retorted. "Worry about *yours*, once it's pouring out in the dirt."

"She squeaks pretty loudly for such an itty-bitty mouse," snickered the spearman, a muscular fellow who equaled Pankratz in height. "Where do you get your confidence, little girl?"

"Don't tease her, friend. She *bites*," I warned him.

"We're not your friend, aberrant," said the swordsman. "Keep your mouth shut."

"Why don't you want to be friends?" I asked. "I'm an interesting guy. Ask anyone. Well, don't ask Nick. He's biased because I beat him up one-handed."

"Shut up," Pankratz said without turning around.

"True story," I said. "One hit. I nearly broke every bone in his body. Thank goodness his girlfriend is a Healer, right? That was clutch, wasn't it, Cassie? Oh, wait, was I not supposed to mention that part? I keep forgetting the rules."

"You and Cassie?" asked the spearman. "Wow."

"I saw it with my own eyes," I said. "If you don't believe me then why not ask Nick? He was feeling it with his own hands."

"SHUT UP," Cassie yelled at me, infuriated.

"It was a joke," I replied. "It's a tense situation, I'm trying to lighten the mood."

"Evans, I don't care how much they're paying out on aberrants, if you insult her one more time, I'm breaking your jaw," Pankratz said threateningly.

"Who told you I was an aberrant?" I asked him, even though I knew there could only be one possible answer. I just had to be certain before I acted.

There was only one person in the Narrows who had their finger involved in everyone's business. But she'd told me that she was my friend, so out of respect for that I was hoping to be proven wrong.

"You think I'll talk?" Pankratz smirked. "Sorry for your bad luck, Evans, but the word's come down. The Narrows don't need the kind of trouble that freaks like you and Rachel will bring in."

"Freaks?" I asked him quietly.

"Freaks," he gleefully emphasized. "But Gardenia is paying top dollar for any abbies they can get their hands on. They're always running experiments, trying to understand the system better. So at least this way, you can be of one final service to the people on your way out."

In the Narrows, the word from on high only came from one person.

This revelation actually stung a bit.

I had genuinely enjoyed her company.

In the center of town, an armored vehicle awaited us. It was smaller than the one used to transport the Academy students back and forth during the school outing, but it was still a deadly-looking little number. It seemed like a pitch-black merging of a tank and corvette, bristling with potential menace. I whistled at the sight of it, impressed by this model of futuristic engineering.

Did I want it? Yes, I did.

Was I going to take it? Yes, I was.

"Dibs," I said, cementing my claim.

"Shotgun," echoed Rachel, momentarily distracted from her desire to murder Cassie.

"These two are hilarious," the swordsman said with a grin.

"You wouldn't say that if you had to put up with them for as long as we have," Pankratz said before turning to face me. "All right, Evans. Clear out your storage."

"I beg your pardon?" I asked.

"Clear out your storage," Pankratz repeated. "We know you finished the fracture, so that means you're carrying some decently valuable loot right now. You won't need it where you're going, so you may as well turn it over to us."

I could only laugh at his arrogance. "Nick, are you *robbing* me?" I asked.

"It's in support of a good cause," he insisted.

"Somehow I doubt that," I said. "The deal with Jamie was to split the proceeds evenly according to everyone's contribution. You didn't contribute at all, so why should I give you anything?"

"That's because you attacked me as soon as we stepped into the dungeon, you bushwhacker bastard," Pankratz snarled. "You were too afraid to fight me fairly!"

"I *can't* fight you fairly, Nick," I informed him. "We're nowhere close to being equal."

"So that excuses cowardice? Just because you can't match me?" asked Pankratz mockingly.

"Goodness, you are completely hopeless, do you know that?" I said with genuine exasperation. "You took what I said and you're about to score an own goal with it."

"Kyler, just hand over the equipment, please," Cassie said. "Whatever this little game has been about, it's over, all right? Don't make this any harder than it needs to be."

"Meaning what?" I asked curiously. "Are you implying that you can force me to cooperate if I don't wish to? Because I don't believe that you can."

"Even to the end, you choose to be difficult," she said angrily. "I wish you'd stop this posturing and just accept reality. Stop trying to be cool; you're only embarrassing yourself."

"I've embarrassed myself more times than I can recall in front of audiences far greater than this motley assembly," I said with a shrug. "And in the long run, it's never mattered in the slightest. Whether someone loves you or hates you, the value of their opinion plummets once they're dead and forgotten."

"Yeah, yeah, more deep thoughts from Kyler the psycho," Pankratz said impatiently. He then pointed a finger at Rachel. "Coop, put a round through this bitch's leg."

"Are you sure?" Coop asked uncertainly.

"Yep," Pankratz said. "She did something to me yesterday. Something *really* fucked up. If it wasn't for Cass, I wouldn't be myself right now. So, I'm more than happy to see the favor returned. Don't worry, Evans, Cassie can keep her patched together for as long as it takes for you to give in. But it's gonna hurt. A lot."

"Well, if you say so," said Coop as an eager smile slowly began to spread across his face. "Never shot a civvy before. Always wondered how it'd feel . . ."

"Should we be concerned about that?" asked the spearman with a chuckle.

"Don't ask me," replied the swordsman. "I'm just here for the free entertainment."

"Nick, I understand that you're embarrassed about yesterday, and I don't blame you for it," I said. "That kind of helplessness, once experienced, it can break you. Realizing just how weak and defenseless you are in the face of genuine power . . . it's destroyed the peace of mind of many a proud warrior."

Coop cocked his pistol.

"And you're a young guy," I continued. "A *child*, really. You need all the confidence you can get to build a life for yourself. A life that includes Cassie as well, right? And I not only disabused you of the notion that you were strong, I humiliated you in front of your girl. And once more, *I understand why that bothers you . . ."*

Coop raised the pistol and pointed it at Rachel's leg.

"But what I need you to know right now, is that there comes a time when a child must set aside that which comforts him and accept that there are forces in the universe that he can never hope to overcome. Because when a child learns *acceptance*, he truly becomes a man. Do you understand, Nick? You need to accept your loss, right here, right now, while I still consider you a kid. While I still view you as a child, okay?"

Nick stared me in the eye and spat at my foot before replying.

"You're so full of shit, Evans," he said.

"Nick, if you refuse," I continued, "if you take this first terrible step into adulthood by letting your friend maliciously wound my companion, then from this moment on, I'll treat you like a man. I'll treat you like every other adult who *ever* dared to cross me. It'll be goodbye to childhood and hello to reality for you and everyone else in your little gang. If you're okay with that, then tell Coop to pull the trigger."

"Pull the fucking trigger, Coop," he snarled.

BANG!

With a piercing cry of pain, Rachel fell to the ground with a wounded thigh that gushed forth a stream of blood that poured into the dry soil of the earth.

"Dang, I might have nicked an artery," snickered Coop. "Hey, Red, didn't you say something earlier about *me* bleeding out into the dirt? Seems like you might have gotten your prophecy backwards."

"You better hurry, Evans," Pankratz said. "The longer Cassie waits to give treatment, the closer your little pal comes to breathing her last—"

"No, it's fine. I'm all right," Rachel said as she stood up. "I heal really fast, see?"

She spat on her palm and rubbed it against her thigh, cleaning the blood away and showing that there was no longer a wound.

"Looks like you wasted a bullet, bitch," she said chidingly to Coop.

Fast Regeneration, the healing skill slotted in my Gore Grimoire, had saved the day once more, allowing Rachel to recover almost immediately. Which I'd known would happen, allowing me to take advantage of the Hunters' stunned surprise to use my storage skill to swallow up a massive amount of soil from the earth they stood upon.

As the ground shifted beneath their feet, causing them to lose balance and fall, I released all the stored dirt above us, scattering it in a wide arc that darkened the air around us and momentarily blocked everything from view.

While the Hunters coughed and shouted their threats, I turned to Rachel and asked her to release Sir Euon's armor to me. She did so at once, placing the spoils of my victory over the paladin at my feet: his enchanted armor.

It was originally called: **[The Blessed Armor of Sir Euon.]** in purple highlights.

[+12 to Strength.]
[+25 to Defense.]
[+15 to Constitution.]
[Set Bonus: You have a ten percent chance to reflect a ranged attack at the one targeting you.
Sir Euon was a faithful knight of a great kingdom, who dedicated himself selflessly to his duty. With his tragic loss, the world may never see a warrior of his caliber again.]

As soon as I touched it, it renamed itself: **[The Corrupted Armor of Sir Euon.]**

Same stats. Same set bonus. Just a new name to accompany it. Oh, and the flavor text describing the armor's original owner had changed.

[Sir Euon was a faithful knight to a great kingdom, who fell in battle thanks to the trickery of a fiendish coward. Surely the one who slays the new bearer of this armor will earn the grace of heaven itself.]

Interesting rewrite. It was almost as though Sir Euon was looking down on me from paradise and wanted me to know that he hated my guts and hoped that someone would soon kill me and avenge his defeat.

Sounded like sour grapes to me.

By using the fast-equip option that the Alpha Administrator had taught me, my old, poor-quality equipment was replaced by this splendid new gear. With my body now safely protected from the sun, I was free to transform back into my vampiric form without fear.

The first thing I did was use Transfiguration to adjust the appearance of my new equipment. There was a set of black armor I'm very fond of that I wore centuries ago in my days as a wandering black knight. It was old and battered, but still very effective. Wearing it made me look every inch the shadowy knave that I was.

Being back inside it made me feel *reborn*. I felt *young* again.

I raised my arm and summoned Spiteful to my hand. The cursed blade seemingly leapt into it, eager to spill blood once more. I held it over my shoulder and patiently waited for the wind to clear the dust away. Once it did, the fun truly began.

"So, you want to be treated like adults," I said. My words echoed out from beneath my helmet, hollow-sounding and slightly distorted, making me sound as though my voice were being filtered through grave soil. It sounded rather ominous, and it had the intended effect on the Hunters' morale.

"Death Knight!" accused Coop, his eyes wide with fright as he held a pistol in each hand and began rapidly firing at me, growing increasingly distressed as his shots bounced off my armor, one after the other.

"Not quite, but *close*," I said. "Hey, you might want to slow your shots, friend. The quicker you go, the worse it'll be."

Coop screamed something incomprehensible at me and continued plugging away. Just as I began wondering how many rounds each of those things held, his luck gave out when my armor's ten percent chance to reflect his shots finally kicked in and left the poor guy with a gaping hole in his forehead.

"Click-click-*boom*," snickered Rachel unsympathetically. Then she ran after Cassie.

The spearman suddenly shouted and was dragged to the ground when Schulz had grown tired of waiting and decided to join in. The big man desperately tried to free himself from the invisible force that had seized hold of him, all to no avail. My last sight of him was of the dog dragging him behind the transport, out of the sight of others. Then I heard a final plea for mercy that quickly became a scream of terror, silenced by the sound of crunching bones.

I guessed it had been a while since Schulz had been given a snack. I couldn't help but appreciate the self-reliance he showed in acquiring one for himself.

"You bastard! Fucking monster!" screamed the swordsman as he came in fast, wielding a curved blade skillfully, which he aimed at my joints, hoping to find a vulnerability in my gear. I think he expected me to be a slow target. However, due to my immense strength and speed, wearing heavy plate affected my reaction time about as much as being stark naked would.

He stared blankly at me in surprise when I easily caught his blade with my left hand and snapped it in half with a twist. Then, while he was still stunned, I swept Spiteful across his neck and turned his shoulders into a fountainhead.

There were only three of them left. One of them had been another gun wielder, as I recalled. What had her name been? Kelly? Cindy? Something like that. I was wondering where she'd disappeared to when I heard the transport power on. It raced toward the town exit, leaving Pankratz and Cassie behind.

So, that was where she'd gone. What a sensible girl. A bit of a coward, but I admired her instinct for survival. However, I clearly recalled being the one to call dibs on that vehicle. Therefore, I could not abide her theft.

I quickly created a Blood Orb and sent it flying after her, fast as a bolt of lightning, with the mandate to return the transport to me.

I stood there wondering how that chase scene would play out, then stumbled forward when I felt someone smash into me from behind. I turned around in agitation and was unsurprised to see Nick Pankratz standing defiantly before me with his shield in hand, ready for the fight of his life.

"You killed them all," he said with furious tears of anger streaming down his cheeks. "God damn you, you killed them all."

"Not . . . *all* of them," I whispered in my hollow voice as I tilted my head in the direction of Rachel and Cassie. Cassie had been battered unconscious and was hanging limply in my daughter's grip, while her other fist dripped with the Healer's blood.

"LET HER GO!" Nick shouted as he attempted to intervene. I cut him off before he could and kicked his legs from beneath him. Before I could stomp his head flat, he rolled away and managed to regain his feet.

As we circled each other, I continued mocking him.

"I gave you a chance," I said to him. "I gave you a *choice*. Were the lives of your friends worth that one moment of power you enjoyed?"

"Th-that wasn't me!" he yelled; his voice heavy with denial. "You killed them, not ME!"

"We did it together, Nick," I said. "You enabled it, and *I* delivered. You *had* to have known what I was capable of if I could defeat a C-rank dungeon, but you still had to test your boundaries, didn't you? Despite the warning you were given, you just *had* to prove it was a fluke. But it wasn't, was it? And now your friends are dead *and it's all your fault*."

"Stop it," he said.

"All your fault," I repeated.

"STOP IT!" he yelled.

"We're going to eat Cassie alive in front of you *and it's all your fault!*"

"I'LL FUCKING KILL YOU!" he shrieked with a voice filled with unhinged, desperate fury.

He then came running at me, shield extended, no longer focused on the fight, forsaking his training to close in on me like a wild brawler, throwing useless punches and shield slams that bounced harmlessly off my armor while I carefully lined up a perfect downward stroke and chopped both of his hands off at the wrist.

Pankratz squealed when he beheld his new injuries and dropped to his knees, holding them before his eyes.

"What?" he asked in a dazed voice. "What does this mean?"

"It means you lost," I said to him patiently.

"Oh," he said. "Well, that's interesting."

Then he passed out.

I gazed down at the boy whose life I had just ruined, and wondered what I should feel in this moment. Triumph? Sadness? He'd tried to rob me. He'd also tried to sell me into some sort of scientific slavery. If he'd somehow succeeded, my life might have become filled with torture and misery.

He'd also attempted to hurt Rachel. Just because he didn't know that was impossible didn't excuse him of his guilt, nor did it his friends of their complicity. I had simply delivered the justice that was expected of me as their Lord.

And yet, despite his misdeeds, he'd only been a boy. The true fault lay with someone else entirely. Gardenia was an entire day's ride from here. While Rachel and I slept in the fracture, my familiar Schulz had kept watch over Pankratz and Cassie for most of the time we spent there, before leaving them to seek us out.

That meant that even if those two called their teammates for assistance as soon as they escaped, it would have been impossible for reinforcements to arrive quickly enough to set up an ambush. Logically, that could only mean that *they were already here.*

Waiting for me.

Cassie and Pankratz had been planning to betray me from the start. But those two didn't do *anything* without Jamie's permission. They were firmly under her thumb.

Sighing, I stepped away from the wounded Pankratz and left Rachel to vent her anger on Cassie. Whether the two of them lived or died was of no interest to me. The Narrows itself was no longer my concern. We would leave this place at once, come the evening.

But before we did, I was going to have a final word with the Witch of Appraisal.

CHAPTER THIRTY-THREE

As soon as I entered the tavern, Doug the watchman came running at me with his sword drawn, bellowing a ferocious war cry. After letting his blade rebound off my armor, I punched him, knocking him unconscious over a table. I then proceeded to the bar, where Jamie, as beautiful as always, stood cleaning the counter with a white towel.

I removed my helmet and took a seat in front of her. Without acknowledging my presence, she gave Doug a considering look and then sighed with disappointment.

"As useless as ever," she muttered.

"Having a tough day?" I asked.

"I've had better," she admitted.

"As have we all," I said with a nod. "You look great, by the way."

"Do I? Thank you for noticing," she said with a light smile quirking at her lips.

"So. It's my sad duty to now inform you that your kids have been up to shenanigans," I said somberly.

"Have they?" she asked. "Nothing too serious, I hope?"

"I'm afraid so," I said. "It fell upon me to chastise them for their poor behavior. I was reluctant to do so, due to the close friendship you and I share, but circumstances would not permit me to spare the rod."

"They had a few friends with them today," Jamie said in an offhand manner.

"Those friends are in a better place now," I replied.

Jamie put the towel down and gave me a hard look in the eye. Then she said, "Well, that's a shame. But if your business with them has been concluded, then what brings you by?"

"I think you already know," I said with a frown.

"Are you going to kill me?" she asked baldly.

"I thought about it," I admitted as I drummed my fingers on the counter. "I've done it before, with far less cause than you've given me. Far too often, I think. The thought of forgiving you has its appeal."

"So, you've chosen to spare me? How kind of you. Should I perhaps feel grateful for your magnanimity?" Jamie asked with growing bitterness.

"I haven't decided yet," I corrected her. "I thought we should speak first before I committed to a course of action."

"Do you want a drink?" she asked.

"I'd love one." I nodded. "I'm parched."

Jamie reached under the counter for two clean glasses. Then she poured an amber liquid into each and handed the first one to me. Before I could so much as take a sip, a pistol slid into her hand from a holster hidden beneath her sleeve. Without a moment's hesitation, she fired six shots that tore into my face and neck.

Once the weapon was empty, I finished my drink. Then I held my hand toward her and gestured for her to surrender her weapon. She glared at me reluctantly but eventually placed it in my palm. I then tossed the pistol into my storage and asked her to refill my glass.

"You really are a bastard," she cursed before complying.

"That's been said before," I replied as I downed my second drink. "Many times."

"I bet you always deserved it," she said.

I thought about it for a moment and then nodded. "Always," I agreed.

"I'm not going to be toyed with, Kyler," Jamie said. "Spare me or kill me, decide right now. I'm not for your amusement."

"Is that really for you to decide?" I asked her unkindly. "Do you think you get a choice after what you pulled?"

"Fuck you," was her fearless reply.

I regarded her in silence for a moment.

"Is this who you truly are?" I asked her. "Is this what you kept hidden beneath your smiles and charm? I must admit, I find myself in full approval of it. I think beautiful people with ugly personalities are an endearing contradiction."

"I don't care what you think, freak," she said.

"Is that the truth?" I asked after using Mesmerize on her.

"Yes," she said without hesitation.

"You really are an interesting person," I said as I finished my second drink. "Is there anything you'd like to ask me?"

"Where's my daughter?" she asked.

"Entertaining Rachel," I replied.

"Is she going to kill her?"

"I don't know," I said. "Maybe? That's for the two of them to work out. I notice you haven't asked about poor Nicholas."

"What's to ask?" Jamie said with a sour expression. "His only task in life was to protect Cassie. He failed. I should have found someone better."

"He genuinely loves her," I said. "She means the world to him."

"Only because I encouraged it," she replied.

"I see," I said thoughtfully. "The deeper his devotion, the harder he'd fight to defend her. Was that your reasoning?"

"It was. For all the good it did me," Jamie said. "I suppose I shouldn't be surprised that the son of a loser turned out to be a loser himself."

"Pankratz?" I asked.

"Obviously," she said. "His father was even weaker than Doug, but he still had bold plans to make his mark as a Hunter. Got himself torn apart by a nest of black ants. I learned his son had B-rank potential, and was quick to take Nicholas in after his mother died."

"Out of curiosity, what did his mother die of?" I asked.

"Convenience," Jamie replied with a stoney expression.

"A beautiful face hides a black heart," I said bleakly.

"Why should I keep hiding my nature?" Jamie asked with a careless shrug. "I'm caught, aren't I? After all this time, it would appear my number is up. My principle has always been to never apologize for being who I am."

"A murderess?" I asked. "A deceiver?"

"A *survivor*," she said. "You're strong, Kyler. And strength is what makes all the difference in this horrid world. I've watched you here for weeks, playing in this . . . this *fucking nightmare* of a forest and having a wonderful old time with that strange girl and your precious dog, all of you just carrying on like children at a playground while the rest of us . . . well, we're not having quite the same experience, are we?"

"We aren't?" I asked with faux surprise.

"No," she said. "We *aren't.*"

"Tell me about the bag of silver coins," I said. "The one you claimed had a tracking spell on it."

"What would you like to know?" she asked sullenly.

"I'd just like to confirm that *you* were the one who paid the bandits with it," I said. "It's true, isn't it? You were the one who facilitated the attack on that girl by the Ringworms."

Jamie's expression grew fiercer as I continued speaking.

"What was it like, seeing those coins returned to you?" I asked. "You knew that meant I'd dispatched the bandit clan you hired, but you couldn't be sure how much I knew of your misdeed. The paranoia you felt in that moment must have been awful."

"I couldn't believe that bandit trash was stupid enough to go after you," she finally confessed. "I *told* them to stay quiet. That's all they had to do, stay quiet and wait for further instructions. Instead, they decided to show initiative. And look at all the trouble it brought my way."

"Minions thinking for themselves can be troublesome," I said sympathetically.

"I *did* believe you may have been toying with me," she continued. "But I couldn't be certain. Either way, I knew I had to do something about you."

"Which was the real reason you asked me to join Cassie and Pankratz in the fracture," I concluded. "To make it look like an accident. To cover your tracks and leave no witnesses behind."

"Did I hurt your feelings?" she asked sarcastically.

"It's more like you insulted my intelligence," I replied. "Did you really think those children were up to the task of slaying *me*?"

"Cassie and Nick have B-rank potential. The rest of them were C-rankers. Of course I believed they could kill you. How was I supposed to know you were a freak?"

"There's that word again," I said sourly. "Couldn't you just say I was unexpectedly talented?"

"Why did you have to show up in my town?" she asked.

"Why couldn't you have just trusted me?" I replied.

Jamie had no response to that. I found that unsatisfying. After what she'd done, didn't I deserve the pleasure of seeing her squirm? What gave her the right to remain composed as if she hadn't wronged me? With those feelings in mind, I decided to try and rattle her.

"You should know I threatened your daughter's life," I told her. "I promised her an agonizing death, and Pankratz went mad with fury. He fought without fear for his life attempting to protect her. Up until the moment I took his hands."

"You cut his hands off?" Jamie asked.

"Both of them." I nodded.

"Good," she said coldly. "Failure should have its rewards."

I stared silently at her for a few quiet moments. Then I said, "Perhaps the contradiction I praised is less endearing than I thought."

"What Level are you?" she suddenly asked.

"Twenty," I replied, surprised by the change of topic. "Why?"

"How long did it take you to reach it?" she asked.

I paused to recall how long I'd been in this world. Then I said, "Perhaps two months. Maybe a little longer."

Jamie laughed bitterly upon hearing that. "Truly, the Akashic Codex is a ruinous and unforgiveable joke played upon us by the so-called gods. *Two months* to reach Level Twenty? And you weren't even trying, were you?"

"Well, I have a daughter to take care of," I admitted.

"At your age? I'm shocked," she scoffed.

"Don't be. Rachel's adopted. Like Pankratz, but unlike him, she's been embraced as family," I said. "I'd never use her in the manner in which you used *him*."

"Don't lecture me over my choices," she said angrily. "I won't be judged by you."

"Then don't do things that invite criticism," I retorted. "A mother crafting her child to be a tool . . . that hits close to home for me. It's a bothersome feeling and I resent you for making me recall it."

"Being a superior lifeform must be so tiring," she said mockingly. "Looking down at the rabble from on high and seeing nothing but our flaws. Do the imperfections of the little people distress you, my lord?"

"I've never claimed to be superior," I said defensively. That was a complete lie, but I hated the way she'd just talked down to me. "This isn't about anything *I* did."

"Oh? What's your ranking potential, then?" Jamie asked. "Be honest. I can take it."

"S," I said indifferently.

Jamie cursed loudly and wildly. In a sudden explosion of temper, she grabbed her drinking glass and hurled it as hard as she could against a shelf filled with unopened bottles of various alcoholic beverages, causing many of them to fall and shatter against the floor.

"An S-rank," she shouted with a maddened laugh. "Fuck my miserable life with a rain of unending shit, you're a goddamned *S-rank*! What a joke! What an absolute joke it all is."

"Is it important enough to warrant such a reaction?" I asked after she'd calmed herself.

She stared at me in astonishment before replying.

"You . . . really don't understand, do you?" she asked.

"I know rankings hold some value in society—" I began to say before she interrupted me.

"Some?" Jamie laughed. "You idiot, your ranking decides *everything*! No matter how hard you work to master your skills, no matter how thoroughly you understand your Class, the system reserves its greatest rewards for those who hold the highest ranks. Which is decided *completely at random*! There are maybe thirty living S-ranks in the entire known world! Don't you get it? You're royalty! LIVING FUCKING ROYALTY! Everything you ever want will be handed to you! You are *everything* I hate about this broken, stupid kingdom and its nobles that oppress and dominate us! You are the *embodiment* of everything that is wrong with society! Who ARE you? Where do you come from that allows you to remain ignorant of such a basic fact?"

"Not from here," I replied. "There's no system in the world I hail from."

"Stop lying," Jamie said. "I *know* you're Kyler Evans. I know everything about you! Stop *lying* about who you are and just admit it!"

"Jamie," I said patiently. "Calm down and listen to me, all right? Appearances can be deceiving. It's true that if you looked at me and saw Kyler Evans, then you wouldn't be mistaken. But it's also true that if you looked *inside* me, I guarantee you'd see someone else entirely. I'm not Evans; I've never *been* Evans. This isn't my world."

"Then which world *do* you claim to hail from?" she asked with a sneer.

"I don't know the specifics of it," I admitted. "Maybe I'll ask Norey when I see him next. The dwarves seem very knowledgeable about migrating between realities. Perhaps he could point out my version of Earth on a map."

"You're insane," Jamie said. "Absolutely bonkers."

"I don't believe I am," I replied. "Use your eye on me. I won't hide it anymore. What does your ability show?"

I watched as Jamie stared at me for some time, focusing on something that only she could see. Her expression gradually changed the longer her appraisement went, until finally she began laughing to herself.

"True Vampirism?" she asked in a voice filled with disbelief.

"Your pardon?" I asked.

"S-ranks each have an ability unique to them. A singular imbuement that they alone possess," she said in a slightly tremulous voice. "Your Class . . . Vampire Lord. I've never even heard of it before . . . you're supposed to be a Porter!"

"I have connections," I said humbly. "You mentioned something about my having an imbuement?"

"Y-yes," Jamie continued. "True Vampirism. Your Class . . . you *become* your Class. You're an actual monster in human skin. And you can bestow it upon others . . ."

Jamie muttered to herself under her breath for a time before returning her gaze to me. "It all makes sense now," she said excitedly. "The blood missing from the bandits' bodies. How easily you killed them, how your blood infected Nicholas and warped his mind. You're a real vampire, aren't you?"

"Pretty cool, right?" I preened.

"Share it with me," she said breathlessly. "Share your gift."

"Excuse me?" I asked, taken aback by her boldness.

"Make me immortal," Jamie pleaded as she reached for my arm. "Kyler, Kyler, make me immortal. The things I did, I can make amends for them. I swear I can! I just need the time, and you can give that to me. You can give me all the time there is in the world."

I could only stare at her with confusion and disappointment. Of course, immortality would be the one aspect of my existence she'd immediately focus on. People like her are obsessed with self-preservation. A narcissist fears death more than anything else in the world. The idea of escaping it brings out their worst instincts.

I was over the counter before a breath had passed between us and pressing her against it. My teeth were exposed in their hideous, pointed rows, which I showed to her before using them to nick her earlobe and lick the drop of blood that slowly welled from where I'd bitten her.

"I came here to *kill* you," I said to her in a guttural whisper that betrayed my lack of humanity. "I came here to *feed*. What gives you the right to ask anything of me? Much less eternal life? A mere animal should know its place."

"I'll *be* an animal for you," Jamie said. "I'll be your *dog*. Humiliate me. Do whatever you like. I'll do anything you say. I've seen how you look at me, Kyler. Let me be your toy. I know you want me."

I paused as she slowly pressed her hand against the side of my face.

"Anything you want," she said with a breathy whisper of her own. "Anything at all. I want you. I *need* you. Kyler, do it. Please. Do it. Do it. I'm yours. Let me be yours forever. Kyler. Please . . ."

Jamie arched her back so that her chest pressed against mine, while letting her hair fall back so that her neck was exposed.

"Kyler," she whispered with half-lidded eyes in a voice that knew no shame.

And in that moment, I was weak. I lowered my face to her throat and felt the warmth of her body and blood. The sensation of her against me was too much. The scent of her was maddening. Unable to resist, I bit into her, and felt her gasp as my teeth penetrated her soft flesh.

She whispered my name again, and in my sudden frenzy, my desire to have her to myself for the rest of time, I bit into my own palm and held the fresh wound out before her. She then grasped it between her own hands and slowly lowered it to her waiting lips.

As Jamie's pink tongue extended from her mouth to lap at the blood and accept my gift . . . Rachel's hand suddenly wrapped itself tightly in her hair and pulled her screaming off the counter, away from my reach.

As I stared in dismay, my daughter proceeded to tear open the other woman's throat before draining her dry. When she was finished, she gave a contented sigh and tossed Jamie's body away as thoughtlessly as if she'd disposed of an empty can of soda.

"Nice," she said contentedly. "She tasted like candy."

"RACHEL!" I yelled in outrage. "What have you done? She was MY—"

"Enemy," she finished for me. "She was your *enemy*, Kyler. Would you like to explain what the hell all of *that* was about?"

"I was going to CLAIM her!" I shouted furiously as I leapt over the bar to confront her. "She was to be our blood! How dare you interfere!"

"Oh, I see," Rachel said. She then held a hand to her chin and wore a thoughtful expression as if my words had been an unexpected revelation to her. "So *that* was what was going on . . ."

Then she wrapped her fingers into a tight fist and delivered a savage uppercut that sent me flying across the room.

"Are you insane?" she shouted at me after the room finished spinning. "What is WRONG with you?"

"Am *I* insane?" I shouted in response from my position on the floor. "You attacked your maker! And you murdered Jamie without cause!"

"Without *cause*?!" thundered Rachel. "Kyler, she lied to you! She tried to kill us both! Look at the state of her children! The woman was an absolute *WAD*!"

"I wanted her!" I shouted with a stomp of my foot. "She was giving herself to me!"

"Lots of things in this world will *give* themselves to you!" Rachel replied. "*Diseases* will give themselves to you! They're always looking to connect, you pathetic old fool! That doesn't mean you should accept their offer!"

"You go too far, daughter!" I warned her. "I will not be—"

"All that bilge you fed me about the necessity of self-control and the *instant* that a pretty face flips her skirt at you, you're on her like an unclipped hound," Rachel said, pushing heedlessly through my words.

"I-it wasn't like that," I protested feebly.

"It was *exactly* like that!" she said bullishly.

"You don't understand, we had a connection—"

"You had a connection?" Rachel scoffed. "You mean she had her hooks in you!"

"I-I was—" I blathered.

"Aren't you always bemoaning the existence of your three wicked wives?" asked Rachel mercilessly. "And what's your great plan for resolving that situation? Adding a fourth one to the viper's pit?! That would have worked out perfectly, eh?"

". . . I have a type, okay?" I confessed sheepishly. "I find the bad ones very appealing."

"A *type*?" asked Rachel incredulously. "No, Kyler. You don't have a type . . . YOU HAVE A MENTAL CONDITION!"

I sat on the floor in miserable silence while Rachel continued to glower at me with her hands on her hips. After some time had passed, she held her hand out to me, and I accepted it.

"Thank you for intervening," I said with some embarrassment. "You're a good daughter, Rachel."

"Hmph," she said. "I'm a good *friend*, Kyler. Clearly a better one than you deserve."

"You may very well be," I admitted with a wry shrug. "I'm sorry. I lost control of myself for a moment."

"By the goddess, the thought of being around *Jamie* for all eternity," Rachel said with a shudder. "Knowing what we now know about her, it would have been unbearable!"

"The sex would have been incredible," I mumbled.

"Gross," she said in reply.

"I'll dearly miss the meals she provided," I said sadly.

"Her cooking wasn't *that* great, Kyler," Rachel said with a dismissive gesture. "I'll admit she had some skill, but the meals my mother prepared were far better."

"Were they really?" I asked.

"I'll make them for you some time and let you decide," she said.

"You can cook?" I asked with genuine surprise.

"Of course I can. I grew up on a farm," she said with a laugh.

"Why am I just now learning this?" I asked.

"How should I know? Be more curious about the people in your life," Rachel said with a smirk.

A sudden glow began to emanate from Jamie's limp body as I felt the Gore Grimoire begin to resonate. It appeared my former friend had one final gift to bestow upon me.

"How ironic," I said a moment later, after absorbing her power. "Jamie nearly held my heart in her hand. But now the opposite is true."

"Booo," jeered Rachel at my joke. "That was horrible."

[**Appraisal.**], the display screen informed me.
[**You now possess the ability to instantly assess the physical statistics, skills, magical abilities, and Levels of other beings.**]

"How very interesting," I said to myself as Rachel and I exited the tavern for the final time.

I was surprised to see that Cassie was still alive and well as we stepped back onto the street. The girl was currently huddled over the unconscious body of Pankratz, whom she'd apparently cast healing magic on, delaying his death from blood loss. They made for a tragic visual, sitting there beneath an indifferent sky. Two orphans who'd lost close friends and family both, all within a few short hours.

It really tugged at the old heartstrings.

Sort of.

"So, you decided to spare her," I said to Rachel with a pleased smile. "I'm proud of you. It takes a strong will to resist vampiric hierarchy."

"I *was* going to kill her," Rachel said. "But in the midst of doing it, I started pitying her instead. It made me wonder why I was getting so bent out of shape. After all, she was just some helpless little doll being played with by her mother. That thought made me realize that perhaps the wrong person was taking the brunt of my anger."

"Did you heal her?" I asked.

"Yeah. I pulled her into the shade and changed. Then I put three drops down her throat," Rachel said. "Fixed her up, easy as that."

"Look at the fast learner!" I said proudly as I tousled her hair.

"Oh, shut up!" she said as we continued to watch Cassie weeping over Pankratz. After a few moments, she said, "Do you think we should do something for Nick?"

"What for?" I scoffed. "He got what he deserved."

"I was listening to you and Jamie talk from outside," Rachel said. "Don't you feel the least bit sorry for him? From the sound of it, she was a nightmare."

"He could still make his own choices," I said stubbornly. "We're not in the wrong. *I'm* not in the wrong. He did what he did, and I acted accordingly."

"It's doesn't matter who wronged whom," Rachel said softly. "Mercy isn't about that. It's about having the courage to forgive."

"Sentiments like that only work in a church," I replied. "Forgiveness is a concept that doesn't exist in the wild."

"But we aren't *of* the wild, Kyler," she said. "Our humanity gives us the right to transcend nature's brutality. Why did man evolve intelligence and free will if it meant forever acquiescing to Darwinism?"

"My mother would have labeled you defective and ordered me to destroy you," I said with a mirthless laugh.

"Well, Grandmother sounds like she was a bitch." Rachel snorted. "So, what will you do?"

First, I gathered Pankratz's discarded hands. Then I pushed the weeping Cassie aside and pulled him into the shade. Then, as Rachel did earlier with the girl, I gave him three drops of my blood to restore his health.

"What? What happened?" Pankratz asked after gasping into wakefulness.

"Be quiet," I said impatiently as I used my fingernail to make an incision on the tip of his maimed wrist, over which I spread more of my blood. I then held the end of his severed hand in place against it and pressed tightly. Within seconds of making contact, it began to reconnect with his arm.

"Oh my god," Pankratz said as he watched his amputation being mended. Soon, not even a scar was left to hint at the disastrous injury he'd suffered earlier.

"All right, that's that," I said as I clapped him on the shoulder. "Be seeing you."

"Wait," Pankratz said as I began to leave. "Wait! What about the other one?"

He held up his handless left wrist to illustrate his question.

"Oh, right, slipped my mind," I said. "Sorry."

I then held up his left hand and promptly tossed it into my storage.

"What are you doing?" Pankratz protested weakly. "Give it back."

"No, Nick. It's mine now," I said to him. "Think of it as a minor penalty for your prior misbehavior. Don't worry, it won't decompose so long as it stays in there. It'll be fresh as can be while waiting to be returned to you. You're just going to have to *earn* it back."

"You bastard," Nick said miserably. "You utter *bastard*. What do you want from me?"

"I haven't decided yet," I said. "It might take a while. Don't go climbing any ladders until I get back to you, okay?"

And with that, I turned my back on him and rejoined Rachel and Schulz. I passed Cassie along the way and was treated to a withering look of sheer hatred as a reward for my kind deed.

It seemed you couldn't do anything nice for anyone nowadays.

"My condolences for the loss of your mom," I said to her. "She truly was a unique person."

A bewildered expression was her response.

"What?" Cassie asked. "What happened to my mother?"

Instead of responding, I began walking away more quickly.

Getting out of town as fast as possible now seemed like a *lovely* idea.

On our way to the main gate, we found the transport from earlier crashed against a reinforced wall with black smoke leaking from the engine. From the shattered window, we saw the Hunter, Cindy, lying motionless on a pile of glass.

"Whoops," Rachel said as we examined the wreck. "I don't suppose you could repair this?"

"Never picked up the skillset," I said. "What a waste."

From within the destroyed vehicle, we watched as the Blood Orb I'd sent after it slowly floated out. I frowned as it approached me and let it know how displeased I was.

"When I told you to bring this vehicle back, I expected it to be *intact*," I said in an icy tone of voice.

The Blood Orb hissed and clicked in embarrassment.

"Stop making excuses. Look at what you've done," I said harshly. "I expected better from you."

"Kyler, stop," Rachel said. "Can't you see he feels bad?"

"Good! He *should* feel bad," I said. "Maybe next time he'll try harder to do as he's told."

"It's okay, Orby," Rachel said soothingly to the Blood Orb, which she plucked out of the air and held to her chest like a nervous kitten. "He's had a difficult day too. He doesn't mean it."

"Orby?" I asked. *"Orby?"*

"I'm keeping him," Rachel said decisively.

"Rachel, that's an utterly disposable lifeform. It exists to infect and spread its kind like a virus. I assure you; it has no identity."

"He's cute, I like him, I'm keeping him. What do you think, Orby?" Rachel said as she nuzzled the thing with her cheek.

It cooed at her like a happy infant. *How?* It didn't have any lungs!

"All right, that's decided, then," Rachel said as she released . . . *Orby* into the air. It followed behind her obediently, like a gooseling that had been imprinted on her.

"Orby?" I said again as I followed them.

Well, that was unexpected.

CHAPTER THIRTY-FOUR

A mile north of the Narrows, there came a sound like thunder as two objects plummeted from the sky and crashed violently to the earth, leaving destructive flames in their wake as they smashed deep furrows through the soil.

For a time, the two smoking craters remained perfectly still. But after a while, the occupants of each one began to groan in discomfort and slowly dislodge themselves from the terrain.

"Heh. That experience was *painful*. That hurt worse than seeing a happily married ex," the first stranger said as he pulled himself out of his crater and climbed unsteadily to his feet on a more stable surface. "That landing was killer. Took me a whole ten minutes to knit myself back together. I was spattered all over the place worse than the punchline to a dead baby joke."

The man—although that was in appearance only—was a thin, youthful-looking fellow with curly brown hair that framed a face of sharp, angular dimensions. Although he wasn't unattractive, there was an aspect to his grin that belied his friendly appearance. A brittleness to it that suggested hunger instead of humor, with disturbing eyes the color of tarnished brass.

As he stretched his nude body, it seemed that fibers and fabrics began to spring forth from his flesh, slowly wrapping themselves around him in adornment. Before long, he was fully clothed in a deliberately mismatched outfit over his thin frame, topped with a checkered suit jacket.

"Aww! Why would anyone joke about something like that?" asked a second voice as something scurried forth before him and began using its small pink hands to wipe dirt off its nose and whiskers. It was a white rat wearing a bowler cap on its head and a vest over its chest. Although small in general, it was still large for its species.

"I'm feeling sad just thinking about it," the rat said. "I got like ninety nephews and nieces. I'd be wrecked if anything happened to them."

"It's human instinct to mine tragedy for comedy," the first speaker said as he reached down to gently pet his companion. "By laughing at our pain, we realize the absurdity of our existence. It's even better, though, if you can learn to laugh at the suffering of others."

"Max, is that true or is that more of that psychotic rambling that makes everyone regret talking to you?" asked the rat as it scrambled up its friend's pant leg and took a seat on his shoulder. "I really can't tell. The boss says you like being *edgy.*"

Of course that hypocritical little brat would lob an accusation like that, thought Max darkly.

"Well, that's because you're a pure and humble soul, Matty," said Max fondly. "You're proof positive that intelligence doesn't determine destiny. If I had a million people like you to vote for me, I could have run for *president.*"

"Can rats vote where you come from?" asked Matty.

"As a matter of fact, they cannot! It's a rigged system, I tell you," Max replied.

"I don't like that! That's discriminatory!" said Matty angrily.

"Sadly, the nation of discrimination will never permit its rodent population a voice in public policy," said Max. "You can have a rat in every home, but *never* at the polls! But fear not, my good vermin friend. Because I aim to change that one day by changing the *people.*"

"Changing them into what?" asked Matty.

"Corpses, mostly. And things that *wish* they were corpses," said Max with a snicker. "I've got a vision for the future, pal! Wanna be my running mate? We'll slay on the campaign trail."

"I think I'd have to check with the boss first," said Matty uncertainly. "She doesn't like it when I spend too much time around you. She says you're a bad influence."

"Yeah? Well, she's one to talk! But out of mild curiosity, what exactly does she say?" asked Max.

"Uh, that you can't focus on anything, that she hates you, that you greatly annoy her, that she'll make you suffer like no one ever has if you piss her off *one more time,* that your jokes aren't funny—"

"My jokes aren't funny?!" gasped Max.

"I don't know! I guess?" said Matty.

"Aw, she doesn't mean it. She and I are *friends,*" Max said confidently. "Besides, we're not doing anything wrong here. We're just facilitating the conclusion of some unfinished business."

"What's that mean?" asked Matty.

"We're gonna go re-kill this Stragos guy," Max said. "It's a special request from our client. We need to keep our clients pleased, Matty. If we don't, they won't become repeat business."

"Yeeeeah, sure. *That's* why you're doing this," Matty said sarcastically. "For good customer service."

"And just what are you implying there, Rizzo?" asked Max darkly.

"I saw the way you were looking at that Veronique lady," Matty said chidingly. "Like she was aged sharp cheddar!"

"What? Stop comparing everything to food, you gluttonous hamster," Max said as he poked Matty hard in his round belly. "No wonder you have an eating disorder."

"I do not!" protested Matty.

"You do too! I once saw you picking a half-eaten sandwich out of a trash can," replied Max.

"I'm a *rat*!" exclaimed Matty. "It's expected behavior!"

"Yeah, sure, play the lower species card," Max said with a disappointed shake of his head. "And by the way, I'll have you know that you're completely wrong. My interest in Lady Veronique is *purely* carnal."

"Huh?" asked the rat.

"You wouldn't get it, but people like her positively *soak my lobes* in endorphins. Forget all that vampire drama. Hot rich girls with unresolved daddy issues for *miles* are enough enticement as it is! Bring them on!" Max said giddily. "When I bring back her father's head, things will either get horrifyingly horizontal in the weirdest way imaginable, or she'll have a complete emotional breakdown, and I'll get to laugh at her despair. Either way, it's gonna be a show worth watching."

"Heh, you're *funny*, Max," said Matty admiringly.

"What can I say? Humor comes naturally to me," replied Max with a pleased smile.

"But are you sure the boss won't mind us being here?" Matty asked.

"We're just honoring the deal we made," Max said with his unnerving grin. "It's not a proper regime switch if you leave the old leadership alive, is it? Entrenched management can be so problematic when trying to introduce a new era. We mustn't fight the urge to purge."

"I don't get it, though," said the rat with a confused expression on his face. "Why'd we have to sneak out if we aren't doing anything wrong? Why didn't we just tell the boss where we were going?"

"Because, dummy, we're showing initiative," Max said impatiently. "Let me assure you, the people in charge of sensitive enterprises like this just *love it* when their people start taking matters into their own hands without informing them."

"Yeah, but without permission . . ." said Matty.

"Hey!" Max said indignantly. "Let's you and I get one thing straight, Steamboat Wilhelm! I don't have to tell anybody *anything*. Blondie's my partner, not my noose. I go where I want to go, when I feel like it, *capisce*?"

In response, the rat's voice began to deepen to an ominous level as it arched its back and stared threateningly at its companion. "Did you just call our master . . . *Blondie?*"

Max, not universally known for his tolerance of being corrected or threatened, had to momentarily resist the urge to punt the rat into a tree, tempted though he was. That would have led to a fight, and although Max was extremely powerful, Matty would have made a dangerous opponent.

What's worse was that if he hurt the rat, he would almost certainly draw the ire of its creator, his alleged partner in arms, for whom Matty was a dearly loved pet. Which was the primary reason Max had taken the pest along with him for this little jaunt.

To annoy her.

Despite the aggravating insistence of a good many people, that girl was *not* his master. Max served only himself! Field trips like this were a reminder that he wasn't a member of her conceited little psychotic *majesty's* rabble.

She'd get the point eventually.

"Whoa, calm down there, sport!" Max said quickly in a placating manner as he held up his hands. "It's an affectionate nickname, that's all! You know I'd never intentionally disrespect her highness or whatever we're supposed to call her. What sort of an idiot would I be to do something like that?"

"A *dead one,*" the rat said while continuing to stare.

"Well, you know what they say, pal. It's better to make someone beg for forgiveness than it is to grant them permission to die," Max replied loftily.

"Is that how that saying goes? That doesn't feel right," said Matty, whose sheer confusion at his friend's words had cooled off his killing anger.

"Now you're correcting my sloganeering," Max said sadly. "Gosh, Matty, you sure do like pushing your weight around, you puffy little bully. Now I feel *embarrassed.*"

"I'm not a bully," the rat said defensively.

"You absolutely are! But I'd never think to correct you, because then you'd just bully me some more. You're *awful.*"

"Aw, geez, I'm sorry, Max!" Matty said. "Don't be upset, okay? We're friends, aren't we?"

"Of course we are!" Max said. "I'm way too generous in spirit to hold a lasting grudge."

"You are?" asked Matty wonderingly.

"I *am!*" Max said enthusiastically. "And I know from the tip of my toes to the top of my skull that *you* are as well. That's why I thought to myself that out of everyone in the crew, Matty would be the best one to take along with me for a fun trip to an alternative reality."

"You *did*?" Matty asked excitedly.

"I sure did!" Max said with a smile. "And you know why? Because you're far too cool to care what anyone else thinks. In fact, you don't even need to think at all! Thinking is for *losers*. It's for people who don't have it together like *you* do."

Matty nodded eagerly as he absorbed this wonderful new information about himself. Max was right, thinking was certainly a pointless endeavor when it came to being a rat. Why should he trouble himself with it? Max was better at it anyway. He always had interesting ideas. That was why he was fun to be around.

Even if everyone else thought otherwise.

"Glad you're on board, rat!" Max said happily as he gave Matty a little scratch beneath his chin. "Now, do your tracking trick and let's go find our stray."

"On it! Right on it!" Matty said as he leapt from Max's shoulder and began sniffing the air. Then he ran into the night, leaving a trail of blue light in his wake for Max to follow as their hunt began.

Before long, their search brought them to the raised walls of the Narrows, where Matty said the trail was white-hot. "This place must have been his home for a while," he said as Max cut an entrance for them into the town. "He's been every which way around here."

"And you're sure it's him?" Max asked as he continued to follow.

"Totally," Matty said confidently. "I was built to see dimensional distortions. So that I can see what belongs where when it's inside the palace. This guy, everywhere he walks, it's like he's leaving echoes of himself spread thin. It's weird! But it definitely vibes with Dimension V."

"Are we still calling it that?" Max asked with an embarrassed groan. *"Dimension V?"*

"It's a dimension ruled by vampires, ain't it?" asked Matty. "The boss likes it! I like it too!"

"You only like it *because* she does, you suck-up," Max said with a sneer.

"That's probably true. Yeah, you're right," Matty affirmed. "What's wrong with that?"

"Ugh. *Nothing*," Max said with a hand over his eyes.

Soon the pair arrived at an unexpected scene of carnage. Max whistled to himself at the sight of spilled blood, dead bodies, and destroyed scenery. It looked to his seasoned eye as though someone had gone to town on a few unlucky fools in a one-sided melee.

Well, whatever the cause, the results looked . . . *fun*.

"Cheese and rice, what happened here?" asked Matty as they surveyed the scene. Citizens and town watchmen alike were beginning to crowd the area, all seeking answers. Although Max was displeased to have so many people taking up space, he was amused by the fear that had settled over the crowd. The suspicious looks being sent his way had him inwardly tittering.

"Looks like Vamp Daddy duked it out with some of the local talent," Max smirked as he examined the bodies. "Looks like he got real messy with it too. I mean, I guess he *would*. That's bloodsuckers for you."

"The sun just set, though," Matty said worriedly. "By the smell of it, these guys were killed hours ago. In the middle of bright daylight. Are vampires supposed to be able to do that?"

"Wesley Snipes can," Max said knowledgeably.

"Wesley Snipes isn't real!" Matty said. "I've seen him on television. Nothing on television's real, the boss told me so."

"God, It's so painful when someone *almost* understands something while still being completely wrong about it," Max said while rolling his eyes. Then he heard the sobbing of a woman in misery and his ears perked up. "Well, what have we here?"

The cries were emanating from a tavern where upon entrance, Max and Matty bore witness to a beautiful, brown-haired teenager cradling the body of an older woman that she greatly resembled. Beside her stood a battered-looking young man who appeared to be her age, alongside an older watchman with a haggard expression on his face.

"Did I miss something?" Max asked. "I feel as though I missed something. I did, didn't I?"

"Who the hell are *you*?" the older man asked harshly. "What are you doing here?"

"I'm looking for my friend," Max replied. "Maybe you know him? I don't know what he looks like, but we're really close! He probably does stuff like killing all of your friends. Which I'm guessing he did? And if so, isn't that *just like him*?"

"You know Kyler?" the girl said as she raised her tear-reddened eyes to stare furiously at Max. "You *know* that bastard?"

"Know him? We're practically family!" replied Max cheerfully.

"Kill him, Doug!" she screamed. *"KILL HIM!"*

The older man came running at Max with a drawn sword that he plunged through Max's chest with a vicious forward thrust. As he began to pull it free to deliver another deadly blow, Max placed his hand just beneath his jaw and flicked his chin with his middle finger. Doug's head snapped back upon impact with such force that his neck was instantly broken. He then collapsed, dead at Max's feet.

The boy, seeing his ally fall, bellowed a battle cry and charged fearlessly at Max, who responded by sidestepping him and holding out his foot. The boy, due to having only one hand to catch himself with, crashed painfully to the floor and broke his nose.

"Let's give that guy a hand, everyone. Clap if you believe," Max snickered before turning his attention to the girl. "Hey, sweetie. Are you having a bad day?"

The girl stared at him in silence, either unwilling or unable to speak.

"Is that your sister?" he asked, gesturing at the body she held.

"This is my mom," she said reluctantly.

"Really? Wow, great genetics!" Max said approvingly as he examined Jamie's body. "You look almost exactly like her. Minus the hole in her chest. But I can put one in you myself if you don't answer my questions. Then the two of you can be twins for Halloween. Doesn't that sound *fun*?"

"Please don't hurt us," the girl whimpered.

"Hurt who? You and five-fingers over there? Don't worry about that," Max said. "Just spill the details on the one who did this to you."

"You said you already knew who it was," she replied.

"I do, but it seems like a tale worth hearing," he said with his empty grin and joyful eyes. "Besides, I like watching people relive their most terrible days. It's better than a game pass subscription."

Having no other choice, Cassie began telling him everything.

And the more he learned, the wider Max's smile grew.

When she was finished, he nodded and said, "Thanks, kid. You were a big help."

"Will you let us go?" she asked with quiet desperation. "I did what you wanted."

Max considered her request for a moment.

Looking at the girl, he found that he just couldn't work up the interest to slice her apart. Look at her! It already seemed like she'd lost everything. What was there left for him to work with? *Boring.*

So, he shrugged his shoulders and said, "Whatever."

And having said that, he left her to resume her weeping.

As he exited the tavern, his hands behind his back and his mind filled with possibilities, Max brought his heel down sharply on the back of the young man's leg and felt the bones beneath it shatter. The sound of the boy's scream of pain filled his heart with mirth as he stepped forth into the cool evening.

"Hey, Matty, did you hear all that?" he asked as the rat scrambled out of his coat pocket and resumed its perch on his shoulder.

"Yeah," the rat said hesitantly. "Max, why'd you do that to the kid's leg? You know the boss prefers to keep things lawful evil."

"The law doesn't exist in the wild," Max replied serenely.

"But if she finds out she'll still get mad—" insisted Matty.

"Yeah, yeah, she's got a vision for things," Max said impatiently. "Never mind her. Did you hear about *Stragos*?" he asked.

"Yeah," Matty said. "We should call this off, Max. He sounds like he could be a real problem. What's the point of even being here?"

"A man shouldn't avoid a challenge just because it might prove difficult," Max said softly. "It means he should be resourceful to see his will be done. Besides, you weren't paying enough attention, dummy! A vulnerability has already presented itself."

"Huh?" asked Matty.

"Her name is *Rachel . . .*" Max said with giddy anticipation. "A cute little baby monster by the sound of it. You ever see what a man will endure to protect his kin, Matty? It's a *riot*."

"Geez, Max," said Matty nervously. "Do we really have to do all that?"

"Hey, this isn't about us," Max said. "Look at poor Cassie and Nick! What about them? Don't they deserve to be *avenged*?"

"But since when did we care about—"

"We're gonna be *heeeeroes*," Max said dreamily.

GET BACK HERE NOW, projected a powerful thought directly into the minds of the man and the rat.

"Boss?" asked Matty fearfully. "Boss, I didn't want to come! He made me!"

"Are you literally ratting me out?" Max asked angrily.

"It was all his idea!" Matty continued. "I didn't wanna, honestly!"

A gateway opened in front of the pair.

"Now, hold on," Max pleaded. "Listen, this is about that vampire thing we were working on last year. Before you react, just *listen* to what I have to say. The guy we had taken out, he—"

Don't care, not listening, get back here. NOW!

Max clenched his fists in frustration. Then he shrugged and said, "Fine. You're the one who's missing out, though. Real shortsighted, Everly. *Real* shortsighted, I'm telling you."

Oh, real scary, snorted the voice dismissively. **I'm over the vampire thing. Complete waste of time! Just bring me back my rat!**

"Fine, but then I'm coming back," Max insisted.

Like Hell you are! I need you on the Cyclops project. You said you were good with them, right? I want my fucking Cyclops army, Max!

"How the hell is that my problem?" asked Max as he and Matty stepped through the gate. "Can't you just make yourself a bunch of those things in the flesh pits?"

It's not the same as having real ones!

"Well then why the hell do you even have flesh pits to begin with if you're not going to use them?!" yelled Max as the portal closed behind them.

Don't tell me what to do, asshole! And don't take my rat anywhere without permission! I'll smite your ass if you do it again. Think I won't? Think again!

"What the hell was even the point of this day?" Max muttered bitterly to himself.

CHAPTER THIRTY-FIVE

A day later, as we continued our meandering walk to Gardenia, I asked Rachel a question that had begun to bother me.

"Are we vampires who are forced to become human or are we humans who are forced to become vampires?"

I thought it was a stupid question. I don't know what possessed me to ask it. Rachel was unbothered by it, though. She didn't hesitate to provide an answer.

"Option number one, obviously," she said.

"Obviously?" I asked.

"Obviously," she confirmed.

And then I thought, *I have ruined this girl.*

Not long ago, Rachel had literally been on the side of the angels. She was naïve, and arrogant, but essentially a good person whose disdain was reserved exclusively for those that wrought evil. Although she was self-righteous, that didn't mean there wasn't an element of righteousness to her character.

She'd wanted to preserve life and punish those who threatened it.

Last night, she'd torn a defenseless woman's throat out with her teeth and drained her trembling body of blood. Then she'd tossed the corpse aside without a backward glance.

That woman had been our friend and benefactor for two months. A traitor and an opportunist, to be sure. Still, there should have been some hesitation in Rachel before she committed to delivering the killing bite. But she hadn't given Jamie so much as an opportunity to beg for her life.

It was all very tidy. Ordinarily, I would have commended Rachel for not dragging things out as so many of our kind do. The urge for sadism is strong within the vampire psyche. We're timeless, after all, so we like our vengeance to be proportionate to our unending search for stimulation. All pleasure should be savored and extended. Satiation was best when it was gradual.

It occurred to me when I woke up that morning that Rachel had manipulated me into increasing Cassie and Pankratz's suffering by sparing his life. I had fooled myself into believing she'd overcome vampiric hierarchy through strength of character. But that wasn't true at all, was it?

She'd spared Cassie because she wanted that girl to live with the knowledge that Rachel had killed her mother and that she could do nothing about it. And she'd convinced me to save Pankratz because she wanted Cassie to grow to hate him for not being able to protect them.

Rachel had truly embraced her nature. Her answer to my question had proven it.

Why didn't I feel proud of her? Why did I feel ashamed of myself?

Killing the people who'd assisted Jamie, and her family, shouldn't have mattered to me. They'd attacked me first, after all. And yet, I couldn't stop thinking about them. I couldn't forget the pain in their eyes and the fear they'd shown as the end drew near and they realized the inevitability of their own deaths.

I felt like a bully. Like a disgraceful ruffian, which I didn't understand. Why should I care? I'd claimed countless victims over the long years of my life. You could probably create a village using their bones as building material.

It bothered me that I was so bothered by this.

It was bothersome.

Human life has no intrinsic value aside from that which it assigns itself. It is an act of unbelievable arrogance to say that all lives matter equally, or that the loss of one is a loss for the world. From the moment of birth and onward, we are disposable and easily replaced. First there were thousands of us; now there are billions. On a macroscopic scale, we are a faceless, writhing mass that has spread itself over the surface of the continents.

We are not special. We are not unique. We are simply *here*, occupying space until the moment of death. Some of us are interesting, but most of us are not. How I chose to treat others shouldn't have mattered.

But it did, didn't it?

In the recent past, this line of thought would have been ludicrous. I was wholly a monster back then and consumed by my own excesses. I didn't have any interest in their sufferings, beyond minimizing it to the amount necessary to keep them functional and docile. A peaceful society kept the herd pacified.

But now, I was a part of that herd. And with that inclusion came a growing sense of, well, *empathy*.

I may have stood apart from humanity.

But that didn't mean I wasn't *a part of* . . . humanity.

As a vampire, I'd spent centuries disguising myself as one of them. But now that I had become one, I couldn't minimize my deeds any longer.

I'd done an unnecessary evil to those poor fools. I knew they couldn't win, but I'd felt justified in attacking them anyway. All so I could kill them to alleviate the embarrassment I'd felt at being caught off guard. And although I realized their intentions for me were fueled by wicked greed, did that really give me the right to deal with them as cruelly as I had?

This was something I never would have considered before. But now it was all that I could think about. As a vampire, I was the stalking lion, concerned only with his own pleasure and hunger. I gave no thought to those who fell prey to me.

As a man, I was simultaneously the hunted. And I could clearly see the injustice of being toyed with by a predator. The thought of dying in the manner of my own victims filled me with thoughts of fear and despair. What a sad, bleak thing it is to fall to the hungering dark.

Lions wouldn't care. They were incapable of it.

And I wasn't a lion anymore, was I? Not purely, anyway.

But I was still a murderer.

And with my failure to understand my own feelings, I had led Rachel down a similar path.

What had Rachel seen when she saw that I was about to bite Jamie? What had I looked like? Had she really killed Jamie to prevent me from transforming her? Or had she been upset that I nearly prevented her from twisting the knife in Cassie's wounds for the rest of her life?

Thoughts like this were slowly beginning to drown me in paranoia.

Jamie's gift wasn't helping much.

Adding Appraisal to the Gore Grimoire had proven to be a mistake. At first, the tactical benefits made it seem like an obvious choice for acquisition. Being able to see things like Class descriptions, Levels, and statistics would provide endless advantages in future interactions with this world. But Jamie's gift went even further than I realized.

For example, when I looked at Schulz, I could not only see the expected things such as his strength, dexterity, and constitution; I could see his *mood*. Which was Calm. I could scan for mental Stable or physical Healthy abnormalities. I could even measure the strength of our personal bond (Deeply Loyal). But it was the alignment meter that I found truly disturbing to behold: True Neutral.

This couldn't be real, could it?

Morality can't be reduced to this level of simplicity. You can't just arbitrarily assign a numeric value to one of the greatest questions that has bedeviled humanity since the inception of our intelligence. You can't just slap a number on my forehead, declare me evil, and then move on down the line. It can't work that way. It *mustn't* work that way!

And yet, when I beheld myself with Jamie's gift, the result was always the same. I possessed a karmic value of negative five thousand.

[**Evil.**]

"Kyler, what are you so hung up about now?" asked Rachel. My Immature, Affectionate, negative two thousand karmic value, Evil daughter, the Archfiend's Apprentice.

"Nothing," I said sadly. "Nothing serious, anyway. It just seems that I'm yet another old man who's learned that the world doesn't work quite the way I once believed it did."

"Well, doesn't that mean you learned something new?" she asked.

"It does," I agreed.

"Well, that's a good thing, isn't it? Kyler, it seems to me that you're always mistaking *old* for *stagnant*. There's a big difference between the two. Growing older doesn't have to separate you from the world. For people like us, it can make us more aware of it."

"Do you really believe so?" I asked her.

"Absolutely! But you need to stop being so fixated on how things change, and just accept that change is an inevitable outcome. That's what I think, anyway."

In that moment, Rachel seemed like a fount of hope to me. She represented a newer, better way of thinking. A sort of renewal that I'd never even considered before.

I smiled at her gratefully and nodded.

"Every day that passes, your growing wisdom becomes more evident," I said to her. "You will be a great leader one day."

"Damn straight!" she readily agreed. "Now quit being so weird."

"I'll do my level best," I promised her.

Sometime later, the three of us became lost.

No, that's not quite what happened.

Sometime later, the three of us became ensnared in a maze.

It happened gradually, with such subtlety that even I failed to notice it at first. Schulz was the one who alerted me to our unexpected predicament. And a predicament, indeed it was.

The forest surrounding us was moving. New plants were growing at an unnatural speed, raising towering walls of green that divided and segmented the space around us, forcing us to hurry along before we were cut off from each other or enclosed in an immobile cage of brambles.

It was as though nature itself were rising against us.

"What's going on?" Rachel asked as we ran for our freedom.

"I have no idea," I replied. "This is a new experience for me."

Schulz barked back at us from his position in the lead, as if insisting we shut up and focus on escaping. He's a clever dog and he was completely right about now not being the time for idle chatter.

He still didn't have to be so rude about it.

Eventually, the antics of the plant life subsided and we soon came to a large, thick-boughed oak tree that stood in the center of this mysterious maze. As we approached it, I heard the soft, sweet sounds of a girl singing an old bluegrass song I hadn't heard in years. I think it was called "In the Pines." I couldn't be sure, however. It's had other names.

Before long, we found the one whom the voice belonged to. A pale, blue-eyed young woman with short ink-black hair, dressed in an expensive-looking white suit best described as a young man's business finery. One hand was placed behind her head as she leaned against the tree. From the other, she enjoyed a treat of some kind.

"Well, hello there, Rachel," she called from her lazy perch above. Her long bangs shifted to cover one side of her face as she spoke, granting her face an aspect of carelessness that added to her androgynous appeal.

"Hello," Rachel said in reply. "Stranger, do we know you?"

"Not quite," she replied with a welcoming smile. "But I'd very much like to change that."

As she spoke, I saw that her hand was coated in red as she lazily lifted a strawberry to her lips to eat. She closed her eyes to savor the taste of the fruit and licked unselfconsciously at her fingers after swallowing.

"Delicious," she said. "Say, would you like one for yourself? I brought plenty with me. Enough for everyone to enjoy."

"Are they good?" asked Rachel.

"They're the best," she assured her. "Even tastier than you imagine."

"We'll pass, thanks," I said to her before Rachel could accept her offer. "As kind as you are, we're strangers to you. It would be rude to take from you when our needs have already been met."

"Even when freely offered?" she asked.

"It would also be foolish to accept gifts from strangers," I said.

"Then why be strangers?" she inquired. "My name is Elphie Cross, her name is Rachel, and *your* name is Kyler Evans. There! Now everyone knows everyone else. No secrets left to ponder."

"Except the mystery of how you discovered our identities," I replied with a creased brow. "Would you care to elaborate?"

Instead of responding to that, she ate another strawberry. Then she grinned with crimson-smeared teeth and said, "It's funny that we should encounter each other beneath the shade of a tree. Some of my favorite verses from the good book described a meeting that happened under similar circumstances."

"What do you mean by that?" Rachel asked.

"Well," said the stranger, "I can't quote it in its entirety, but something-something, knowledge of good and evil, something-something, surely ye shall be as gods, something-something, ye shall live forever. Are you sure you still don't want one?"

"Quite," I said before Rachel could speak. "I will say however, that your selection of produce seems to run counter to most versions of this story."

"Does it?" laughed Cross. "We don't even know what the fruit of knowledge was. No one does! It could have been anything at all! Dates, grapes, strawberries. Goodness, could you imagine that? God banishing Adam and Eve for the sin of *strawberry robbery*? I wonder how sweet the fruit tasted when the gates of Eden slammed shut behind them."

"You're clever in your word selection," I said. "Even if what you're saying is utterly pointless."

"Do you really think so?" asked Cross.

"I truly do," I replied.

"I knew from the moment I saw you that we wouldn't agree on much," she said sadly. She then jumped from the tree and landed nimbly on her feet. "It's a shame when someone mocks my dearly held beliefs of the moment. It makes me feel so unwelcome."

"Your beliefs of the moment?" I asked her.

"It's prudent for a young woman to keep herself open to life's possibilities," Cross said demurely.

"My apologies, then," I said. "I assumed you were speaking out of love for the sound of your own voice."

"Do you like my voice as well?" she asked shyly.

"It's not unpleasant," I conceded.

"That makes me happy!" cheered Cross. But then she gave me a stern look and said, "You doubt my love of the good book?"

"I do," I nodded. "Absolutely."

"Anyone could draw the same conclusions I did with a little imagination," she said defensively.

"As long as they're willing to forsake the facts, everyone can be right about everything." I nodded.

Cross clapped her hands in delight.

"Hurray! You *do* understand!" she beamed. "That's why I prefer ignorance to knowledge, and opinion to fact. There's quite a bit of leeway between believing something and *knowing* it, wouldn't you say? And in that dark middle ground, that's where those like me have the most fun."

"Of course, you realize that strawberries are harvested from fields, not orchards," I replied as I maneuvered myself between Rachel and this chattering fool. "They aren't grown on trees like the fruit of knowledge."

Cross noticed what I was doing and grinned merrily at me before saying, "Meh. Most experts believe Genesis is allegorical anyway."

"I wouldn't know. I wasn't there," I said.

"I'd be very impressed if you were," she said with a wink. Then she turned to Rachel and said, "Hey."

"Hey," Rachel said with a slowly blossoming blush.

"I take it you're the party responsible for guiding us into this maze?" I asked impatiently.

"I am," Cross replied. "Sorry for herding you like that. I normally prefer getting closer to others by relying on my charm."

"*I* think you're charming," Rachel said without guile.

"I was hoping you might!" Cross said as she took Rachel's hands into her own. "I think your hair looks amazing, by the way."

"I've always thought so too!" Rachel preened.

"Get a room," I said irritably before I could stop myself, put off as I was by this burgeoning *meet cute* being shamelessly displayed before my cynical eyes.

"Hey, we're still getting to know one another," Cross said with a *tsk* as she stepped closer to Rachel. "Although that doesn't sound like a bad way to end the night. Sadly, I'm currently on the job."

"And that job consists of what?" I asked her.

"Gathering you into one spot so that you can be collected," said another woman's brisk voice as a new stranger stepped into view. Like Cross, she was dressed in white business attire, differentiated by the white cape she wore over her shoulders.

In contrast to her associate, her hair was platinum blonde and tied back in a braid. Her sharp amber eyes took in everything before her from beneath a pair of expensive-looking wireframe glasses.

Belted at her waist, I couldn't help but notice, was a curved scabbard with the customary hilt of a Japanese katana. That told me one of two possible things about her personality: the first was that she might have been one of the innumerable buffoons I'd encountered over the years who believed that Japanese swords were unmatched instruments of death, and that wielding one in combat made her invincible.

I'd seen so many of those people die that I'd lost count. Rapiers aren't nearly as pretty as Japanese blades, but they're far easier to stab someone with. Katanas are primarily slashing weapons, meant to be wielded while wearing full armor, or used to spring a surprise attack with a fast draw. When used correctly, they produce excellent results, but prolonged engagements can put their users at a disadvantage, especially if the weapons their opponents wielded gave them a reach advantage.

The second possibility was that this young woman was an extremely skillful duelist whose talent compensated for a katana's shortcomings. There have always been warriors who are extremely dangerous no matter the tool they choose. This stranger might have selected a katana as a means of displaying her superiority.

Well, I supposed there was also a third option; that her sword was purely a symbolic display of authority. I couldn't yet decide. She seemed far too comfortable wearing it, though. People who wear swords are often people who *use* swords. It was best not to underestimate her.

With that in mind, I kept my body language neutral while bringing my hand within reach of Spiteful's grip.

"Another new acquaintance. What an exciting evening for meeting people," I said dryly as the woman continued to approach us. "I assume you have business with us?"

"Not me. My master," she said. "Cross, are you certain these are the ones?"

"I'm positive," her associate said. "They closely match the descriptions provided. And look how calm they are in our presence! Especially this one," she said as she pointed toward me. "Not a hint of fear! Like he doesn't recognize us at all. If anything, he's exuding minor annoyance."

"Arrogance," the sword wielder said with a disapproving frown.

"Impatience," I corrected her. "And justly so! My friend and I were keeping to ourselves before Miss Cross here so rudely waylaid us. Apparently at your behest, if I'm not mistaken. Common courtesy dictates that you should at least introduce yourself and explain your intentions. Otherwise, this could be misconstrued as banditry."

"My *name* is Alvidia Brask," the sword wielder said with narrowed eyes. "We came seeking you out in the name of Regent Perius Norus. Cross and I serve as two members of the regency's five Valkyrie, and we speak and act with our lord's full authority. You would be wise to curtail any further flippancy, boy."

Her tone bothered me.

I wanted to kill her on the spot.

Goodness, can you understand my confusion? Just a little while earlier I had been feeling the colossal burden of having taken several human lives. The guilt had been strangling me like a hungry python! But now look at me. I was practically quivering with the desire to cleave this arrogant warrior in half due to her impertinent addressment.

WHAT was my deal?

Something was wrong.

My confusion over my own inconsistency was what made me decide to spare these fools. Never kill when you're uncertain about your mental condition. If you can't be sure you're making the right choice, then it's better by far to avoid committing to an extreme reaction.

Cooler heads would always prevail.

"Hey, Alvidia? I don't appreciate the way you're speaking to my friend," Rachel said angrily as she stepped into the other woman's space and prepared to square off. "You might want to back down before you get hurt."

In response, Alvina gave Rachel a cold smile and placed her hand over the hilt of her sword.

I took a moment to look at the sky and gave a mournful sigh.

Sometimes it felt like fate really didn't have my back.

CHAPTER THIRTY-SIX

The biggest challenge I was having with Jamie's gift was the difficulty I had controlling it. It was even more bedeviling than the trouble that all the status screen information caused me when I first arrived on this world. As before, the issue was *too much information*.

My first glance at Alvidia showed me the following:

[Alvidia Brask.]
[Age: 23.]
[Level 42.]
[Class: Sword Queen.]
[Strength: 22.]
[Speed: 27.]
[Reflex: 23.]
[Constitution: 12.]
[Endurance: 20.]
[Temperament: Hostile.]

Her stats were outstanding. In comparison to the swordsman that I dealt with yesterday, it was like differentiating between a mountain and a pebble. No wonder she was so bold and arrogant. Her speed and reflex scores were particularly outstanding.

As I'd suspected earlier, Alvidia must have been a specialist in burst attacks that overwhelmed her opponents before they could react. The image that came to my mind was of a lightning-fast attacker who could kill her target before they even realized she'd drawn her sword.

Not bad for a human. Shame about that low constitution, however. Although she could probably deliver death for hours without resting, her low health value meant that a lucky shot could cause considerable damage if she couldn't avoid it. I sympathized with her. Increasing your health score was an arduous task. I was still working to improve my own.

Now, if these combat statistics were everything that Assessment had revealed to me, then a fight with her would be enough. But my sight was also being flooded with unnecessary details like Alvidia's heart rate, the last time she'd eaten, her blood pressure, and much more. It also flooded me with information about the trees that surrounded us.

Even the grass beneath our feet possessed statistics. So did the insects that crawled throughout it.

There was so much information and most of it was so *pointless*. Was this how Jamie had been forced to see the world? With such intense minutia, with so little need for it? Had this been the reason behind her empty, black heart? Most people became misanthropes because they felt no connection to others. Had Jamie become a criminal because she'd felt *too* much?

Was society to blame? Was life itself?

Now I truly pitied her. Poor Jamie. She really would have been much happier as a vampire. It was a shame Rachel had unilaterally vetoed that notion. A few centuries of self-reflection would have done that woman a lot of good.

"Rachel, it's all right," I said as I stepped between the two women. My vision blurred a little as I struggled to rein in all the pointless information that Appraisal was showing me, but I kept my voice as steady as I could. "There's no need for any violence."

"Are you sure?" Rachel asked. "That smug look on her face suggests otherwise."

"I don't doubt for a moment that you'd win," I whispered to her. "But not every situation requires brute force. Let's first use our words and see how far they'll take us."

"That's boring," Rachel complained even as she backed down.

Goodness, this child was so addicted to violence. It seemed she was never truly satisfied unless a confrontation ended with her dominating whoever dared to oppose her. A warrior's mentality like hers was a charming thing during a time of martial strife, but it could also be exasperating to deal with when peace was called for.

But as remorseful as I felt for Rachel's growing darkness, this was one aspect of her personality I took no responsibility for. She'd always been this way; quick to resort to violence. Eager for bloodshed.

Perhaps that was a consequence of having spent so much of her life as a weapon? A spear can't be used for anything other than its purpose. Is that how she felt now in her new life? Was she still inwardly a tool meant only for killing?

It occurred to me at that moment that I really didn't understand her very well. I wanted to change that. I really did! But would I? Probably not. It sounded like a lot of personal effort would be required.

I really was a terrible parental figure.

Turning to Alvidia, I said, "We're not looking for a fight."

Alvidia responded with an insolent smirk before saying, "It wouldn't have been a fight, boy."

Again, the urge to kill arose within me. A heated sensation that burst brightly throughout my body. *Cut this foolish woman in half,* it demanded of me. It wasn't quite the lull of vampiric hierarchy, so I could resist it. But still . . .

I chose to stay in my human form, just in case. The changes I'd made through stat point distribution and the Gore Grimoire had improved my performance considerably. Even as a mere mortal man, I was a force to be reckoned with. It was a good thing too. Until I could get my head straight, it was potentially too dangerous to rely on my vampire form.

It was so frustrating, trying to figure this thing out. One moment I felt brave, the next I felt fearful. My confidence ebbed and flowed seemingly at random. I was overly emotional, sensitive to slights, quick to anger. There were also all the random thoughts I kept having about women . . .

Hold on.

I knew what this sullen feeling was. I *knew* it! It'd just been so long since I'd allowed myself to wallow in it. The egotism, the anger, the desire to lash out at anyone who upset me, the unwarranted feeling of self-importance . . . I'd experienced it all before!

By the shadow, this even explained my emotional instability! Why was I so uncertain of myself? Why did my feelings keep flip-flopping like a pair of sandals caught on a bike spoke?

There's an old saying that's been bandied about for ages claiming that form defines function. You are exactly what your environment dictates. And when it came down to it, what precisely was my form? My *preferred* form, that is. What did I spend the majority of my time as unless circumstances forced me to rely on my vampiric form?

A human being.

A *teenage* human being. Fraught with uncertainty, hormones, and an exaggerated sense of being judged by others. Not too different from being a vampire, honestly. Just with less of a sense of humor.

It was all so silly that I had to laugh.

"Excuse me?" Alvidia said angrily before slamming her elbow into my belly with a sudden rotating motion that caught me completely by surprise and had me gasping for air. As I collapsed to my hands and knees, she raised her leg and delivered a painful axe kick to the back of my head that had me tasting dirt.

She must have thought I'd been laughing at her.

Clearly, not a woman to be trifled with.

And yet, as painful as it all was, I couldn't help but relish my recent breakthrough. Suddenly, so many things made sense that hadn't before. I was a kid!

A young adult! I was on the cusp of maturity! It perfectly explained why I'd been such an erratic twit lately. I recalled reading somewhere that a young man's brain didn't finish development until he was in his mid-twenties. Which would take around six more years for Kyler Evans's body to reach.

Form defines function.

I was so deliriously happy that I couldn't stop my giggling. For a horrifying moment there, I'd been worried that I was becoming someone else entirely. A stranger in the mirror, as it were. It hadn't even occurred to me that I was going to suddenly start speed-running my late adolescence.

No wonder I'd been such a jittery little fiend. Well, now that I'd diagnosed my condition, I supposed that meant it was time to start applying some treatment. Compartmentalizing your emotions is easy to do once you've realized they're a mere biological sensation.

They're even an enjoyable new toy to indulge in. Like food and sleep. Once again, I was filled with appreciation for the sheer novelty of the human experience. Look at me! *Feeling things.* Just like a real person!

Wasn't it a trip? It was, wasn't it?

The first thing I did was to disable Appraisal. I had all the relevant data now and leaving it active would be too visually distracting. I wouldn't use it again in active combat until I had gained some level of mastery over it.

As Alvidia brought her foot down for another kick, I rolled out of the way into a crouch. Then I grabbed a handful of soil and tossed it at her face, which she dodged by leaping to the side, leaving her open to a kick of my own, delivered with full force.

Instead of the expected crunch of a broken rib or two, I saw a flash of blue light momentarily surround Alvida's body, outlining her in its dazzling illumination. Then, instead of falling backward from the force of my kick, she thrust an open palm into my torso that sent me flying away.

Impressive! It appeared that this woman possessed a means of absorbing and redirecting energy away from herself. Considering how hard she'd struck me, it seemed she could even use it to magnify her physical strength. I hadn't seen anything like that listed when I'd appraised her earlier. Did that mean this was a hidden ability that couldn't be scanned, or was this a skill that she'd developed on her own, through training?

If that was the case, I felt my admiration for her beginning to grow.

I just adore those who are strong and genuinely capable.

Whenever I encounter someone like that, I feel the urge to collect them.

"What's got you so distracted?" Alvidia asked when she noticed my attention had waned.

"I was thinking that this is nice. I'm enjoying myself," I replied.

"That's all?" she asked with a skeptical look on her face.

"Well, that, and . . . you're really pretty," I said to her with sincere admiration and a slight blush.

Somewhere behind me, I heard Rachel groan in disbelief.

"You're not wrong but that's not something I need to hear from the likes of you," Alvidia replied indifferently.

"Talking to attractive women is nerve-wracking. Don't I get any consideration for having the courage to express myself to you?" I asked hopefully.

"No," she said bluntly. "And thinking that you should is pure entitlement."

"There's nothing wrong with seeking an advantage in an uncertain situation," I replied as I threw a straight jab at her face, which she countered by ducking low and allowing my momentum to carry me over her shoulder.

"You aren't seeking an advantage, you're looking for a *concession*," she said derisively as she stomped at the area where my head had been a moment before. "Convincing a woman to sell herself short is the same as demanding she lower her standards."

"Well, what if those standards are too high?" I asked as we began circling each other. "You can't blame others for not meeting them if your expectations are unrealistic."

Alvidia snorted before replying. "Quitting before you try only shows that you would never have been worth my time. Warriors should *rise* to meet a challenge, not flee if they find them difficult."

"You sound as though you've been frustrated before," I said with some sympathy.

"You have *no* idea," Alvidia said resentfully.

"She's not even joking, her romantic life is a nuclear level disaster," snickered Elphie Cross. "Seriously! I can tell you some *stories*!"

"Uh, oh, sounds like *someone's* got the dirt!" Rachel chimed in.

"What's her favorite color?" I asked Cross.

"Lilac pink," she said helpfully.

"Really? That's so unexpectantly girly," said Rachel. "You'd think it'd be imperial purple or something from how she carries herself."

"I can see why you'd think that, but Alvidia's a real kitty cat once you get to know her," Cross said. "Isn't that right, Alvie?"

"Say another word about me and they'll never find your body," Alvidia promised her.

"Yikes!" said Cross and Rachel simultaneously, before turning to each other and laughing.

"I like the color pink as well," I said to Alvidia before we resumed fighting. "It's nothing to feel embarrassed over. I find it to be a very soothing hue of the rainbow."

"Would you wear it publicly?" she asked.

"Oh, goodness, never," I said immediately. "It doesn't suit my image at all. Maybe if I were wearing a disguise . . . but no, probably not even then."

"It's gender neutral!" Alvida said irritably.

"Which is fine, but I have a visual aesthetic that I already prefer," I replied. "No need to fix what isn't broken."

"You're just exposing yourself as another coward," she said accusingly. "I detest men who are so wrapped up in traditional views of masculine adornment that they won't even consider modernizing their look. Pastels can be very flattering."

"I'd much prefer you showed admiration for my willingness to stick to my guns," I countered. "Out of curiosity, though, has my obvious charm begun to win you over in any meaningful way?"

"Not in the slightest," she said.

"A shame," I said regretfully. "Does this mean we have to begin fighting in earnest?"

"Boldly asked," Alvidia said with a slight smirk. "As though you haven't been struggling to keep your body intact this entire time."

"I was just playing on your level to see what you were capable of," I said with a light yawn. "Having now sampled your skills, I can say with all sincerity that you're *very talented* and well on your way to becoming dangerous. One day."

Now all traces of good humor vanished from Alvidia's face as she stared mirthlessly at me. "Would you care to repeat that?"

"Goodness, look at that fierce expression!" I said playfully. "If I didn't know any better, I'd say you were under the mistaken belief that you could do something about the disrespect I've just shown you."

Now Alvidia's thumb pressed against the guard of her sheathed katana, exposing a slight bit of cold steel to the evening air. Her other hand was now held just above its handle.

"Some words, once said, cannot easily be taken back," she said as she settled into a light forward stance. "I would advise you to choose your next ones carefully."

"An empty threat," I said smugly. "You were obviously sent to collect us for some purpose. With that being the case, what harm could you possibly be allowed to inflict? You're a wolf with no fangs."

"Your assumption is incorrect, Mr. Evans," she said. "I was sent to assess if you were first *worthy* of the audience you've been granted. You'll go nowhere if I decide otherwise."

Oh. I hadn't considered that.

"In which case," I asked with some hesitation. "Have you reached a decision?"

"I have!" Alvidia said brightly. "I'm going to kill you where you stand."

"Can I convince you to do otherwise?" I asked.

"Survive my draw and we'll see," she said.

"Okay, I've had enough of this nonsense," Rachel said. "Kyler, if you don't stop playing around with this cow, I'm going to—"

"Cross," Alvidia said authoritatively without turning her eyes away from me.

Vines and roots erupted from the soil at Rachel's feet before she could react and began wrapping themselves around her body. Within seconds, Rachel was bound tightly in place and attempting to yell angrily through the plant matter that was muffling her voice. Schulz growled angrily and prepared to come to her aid, but a wall of thick thorns had grown to surround Cross and Rachel, leaving him unable to reach them.

"Sorry, Rachel," apologized Cross. "You seem fun, but orders are orders."

"Imh gonnah tuhr yuth aparth!" Rachel warned her. "Seth mee phree!"

"Why would I do that if you're going to kill me afterwards?" Cross asked skeptically. "You should never say the quiet part loudly!"

"She does have a point, Rachel," I said. "Maybe we should consider this a teachable moment?"

Rachel yelled something muffled at me. It was probably rude.

"I think you have other concerns right now, Evans," Alvidia said.

"I have no concerns at all," I replied as I lightly tapped the scabbard of my sword with my forefinger. "Just a growing desire to end this business and be on my way. What say you?"

"I find your self-confidence offensive," she said quietly.

"Then you're *really* going to hate what comes next," I promised her.

I took a deep breath and slowly released it as I let my body shift from mortal to vampire. When I opened my eyes to regard Alvidia, I mirrored her stance. Although Spiteful was a straight sword with only a very light curve in comparison to the katana Alvidia wore, I was still confident that my draw would be faster than hers. Although her Level was higher than mine, I still held the upper hand.

As I mentioned a while back, a vampire's power increased the more lives he took. Although I'd been as weak as a neophyte phage when my journey in this world first began, I'd killed quite a creatures and people since then. *Quite a few.*

Dozens of goblins, Redcaps, kobolds, and bandits. Not to mention the corroded knights and the siren. Over a hundred lives and counting, each not only contributing to my Class level, but thanks to my trait True Vampirism, they'd also increased my innate powers exponentially.

Back on Earth, I could never slay that many people at once and hope to keep my identity a secret. Garnering this many kills would have been the gradual work of decades, including eras of open warfare. But here, in this outlandish realm filled with endless opponents and opportunities for carnage?

It was as though it were *made* for me.

Alvidia's eleven-level advantage meant nothing. I had regained too much of my former strength. If I kept progressing at my current pace, then Level Thirty-Eight or so would equal me at my peak in my former life.

Now it was time to demonstrate to this proud warrior what a *real* challenge was.

The surprise on Alvidia's face when I took the initiative delighted me to no end. She clearly hadn't expected me to be quick enough to strike first; seeing her composure shaken for the first time that night felt like a well-earned reward. Even so, her reaction time was remarkable. Despite my speed, she still managed to draw her sword quickly enough to deflect the slash I directed at her neck. A good thing too, because otherwise it might have been a killing blow. Not that I was deliberately trying to end her life, but I didn't see the point in holding back.

Alvidia Brask was strong. Far stronger than most Hunters, I was certain. But her obvious superiority was detrimental to her further development as a swordswoman. It wouldn't do to let such a prospective talent stagnate due to arrogance.

To that end, defeat was a key ingredient to true self-improvement. If her problem was that she believed she stood at the peak of skill, then I had to show her how boundless the horizons beyond the sky were.

With a piercing shriek of steel rending steel, Spiteful split Alvidia's sword in half, sending the broken blade flying out into the night. With her eyes wide in surprise, I placed the tip of my sword at her neck, careful to keep the pressure light so that she wouldn't be cut.

"Told you I'd win," I grinned.

"H-how did you . . ." she stammered before gaining control of herself. "How did you do that?"

"Are you looking for pointers?" I asked mockingly. "Sorry. I only take one apprentice at a time. Keep practicing and maybe I'll let you have a rematch in a few years."

I couldn't hear what Rachel said through her gag, but it sounded extremely smug.

"Hey, be nice! She *tried*," I said to Rachel.

"I can't believe you did that," Cross said, her voice heavy with disbelief. "Alvie lost? Alvie *never* loses! What the actual hell?"

"Don't be surprised when you can be impressed instead," I admonished her. "Oh, and release Rachel or I'll cut your head off. That's a threat. I just threatened you."

Cross looked at me fearfully before turning to face Alvidia. After a few moments, Alvidia nodded but said nothing else as she knelt, holding her ruined weapon. In response, Cross made a cutting motion with her hands. Within moments, the bindings on Rachel's body dropped away, releasing her. Seconds later, the bramble that had prevented Schulz from reaching her dropped away as well.

"Uh, no hard feelings?" Cross asked hopefully, after Rachel finished brushing off bits of plant material from her clothing.

"We're fine. I don't hold grudges," Rachel said primly.

"Oh, that's good. I'm glad to hear that," Cross said with relief before letting out a wheezing gasp after Schulz ran forward and shoulder-checked her.

"The dog has a long memory, though. Just to warn you," Rachel said as she knelt to give him an affectionate scratch around his ears.

"Well, I suppose this means our business is concluded," I said as I sheathed Spiteful and rejoined my companions. "Thank you for the exercise; it really shook out the knots. Keep your training up and you might have a career in this line of work."

"Wait," Alvidia said as we began walking away.

"Hmm?" asked Rachel. "I'm sorry, did you say something? Kyler, I think she said something."

"I said to *wait*," Alvidia repeated angrily as she held up a hand. "Just stop for a moment."

"Wow, that sounded like an order. But does the loser get to issue orders to the winner?" Rachel asked quizzically. "That doesn't seem right, does it?"

Oh, goodness. Rachel was really enjoying this. *Poor Alvidia!*

Ah, but why pretend I was any different? I was enjoying myself too.

We really were such awful people.

"You may have a point there," I said in agreement. "Alvidia, are you requesting that we stay, or *ordering* us? I'm asking for a friend."

An ugly look flashed over the proud warrior's face for a moment, before she closed her eyes and fought it down. After taking a deep breath to calm herself, she said, "Please allow Cross and I to escort you to Gardenia."

"For what purpose?" I asked.

"To reward you for a favor you unknowingly did for the Norus family. And to make you an offer," Alvidia said.

"What favor could I have possibly done for the Regent?" I asked with genuine puzzlement. The Regent was the highest ranking noble in the kingdom, as well as its uncontested ruler.

Such a lofty position was occupied by a member of the three great families who controlled each of the three city states that comprised the nation, elected to lifelong service at a convocation that occurred after the death of the previous leader.

Impressive as I always was, I didn't recall recently rubbing elbows with any such important political figure. A mistake had to have been made.

As if reading my thoughts, Alvidia said, "I assure you, you're the one he wants. The fact that you . . . defeated me is proof enough that you're more than capable of the task he has in mind for you."

"I'm not looking for work," I said bluntly. "I'm not even certain I'll be staying in this country any longer than it takes to walk to the border. What interest could I possibly have in accepting your invitation?"

Alvidia's face flushed with displeasure at the perceived disrespect I'd just shown her master. Her grip tightened on the handle of her ruined sword as her expression began to darken.

"How about *revenge*?" Cross asked, cutting in before Alvidia could say something in anger.

"Revenge?" I asked. "Against whom?"

Cross smiled like a cat about to indulge in a saucer filled with cream.

"How about the Velas family?" she asked. "The ones who framed you for a crime you didn't commit and drove you away from the city to die in disgrace? How about your own family who deliberately mistreated you for your entire life in favor of your golden boy half-brother?"

"How much do you know?" I asked in bewilderment.

"Everything," she said confidently. "We had you thoroughly investigated. And if you join us, we'll make them all pay for what they did. How about it, Kyler Evans? Are you ready to show the world how wrong it was about you?"

I'm NOT KYLER BLOODY EVANS, I thought angrily to myself, furious at once more getting dragged back into his story. How many times did I have to say that revenge was for idiots?

The only reason I'd bothered injuring Pankratz back in the fracture was due to this body's overabundance of hormones! But now that I knew what had been unbalancing me, it would be easy to maintain my self-control. I'd never again fall prey to petty emotionalism! There was absolutely no need to put forth any effort on behalf of a dead boy, tragic though his circumstances were. I was not, and never would be, an avenging angel.

It just wasn't who I was.

But before I could open my mouth and decline this unappealing offer, Rachel suddenly jumped in front of me and said on my behalf, *"Hell yes!* Where do we sign up?"

"Rachel, what are you doing?" I whispered into her ear.

"We're going to make this right," she whispered back. "It's about time we took care of this, don't you agree?"

"No! I absolutely don't agree—" I began to say before she squeezed me in a tight embrace and said, "Please?"

"Rachel, we don't need to—"

"Please?" she repeated.

"Rachel, I understand that you feel strongly about this, but we can't be expected to—"

"Please?" she repeated again. Over her shoulder, Orby suddenly appeared and burbled a strange noise that sounded as though he were repeating her request. *Peeeas? Peeeeas?*

"And just where exactly have *you* been?" I asked the vexing Blood Orb as I jabbed a finger into its squishy exterior.

"Orby doesn't like violent confrontations," said Rachel.

"Orby was *created* to partake in violent confrontations," I said sourly.

"Kyler," Rachel said. "Please. Let's do right by Evans. He deserves it. If it wasn't for him, we wouldn't have ended up here. In a way, we owe everything to his sacrifice."

"It was hardly a willing sacrifice," I said.

"All the same, there's a debt that needs to be balanced," Rachel said. "So, let's do it. We don't have to be rational about this. We don't have to pretend we're righteous, either. We're going to do this because we feel like it and nothing more."

"We'll make enemies," I warned her. "Lasting enemies. No one ever walks away from an affair like this without consequences."

"I don't care," she said stubbornly. "These pompous pricks are in the wrong to begin with. If they're too stupid to realize that and want to push things further, then I say we turn them all into fine dining and eat their entire fucking lineage."

"Rachel," I said, shocked by her vehemence. *"Language."*

"Oh, sorry," she said insincerely.

"Uh, guys?" said Cross uncertainly. "I can't really hear what you're saying, but was that a yes or a no?"

I sighed to myself, knowing what the answer was going to be.

"Sure," I said gloomily. "Who could say no to such a tempting proposal?"

CHAPTER THIRTY-SEVEN

Soon, I was lounging comfortably on a warm leather seat inside the armored transport the Valkyries provided for us, enjoying the ride as it carried us to Gardenia. Unlike the school carrier, this vehicle more closely resembled a floating white limousine that hovered just above the forest canopy, allowing us to shoot straight for the city without being harassed by any hostile creatures. Hovering also felt far smoother than traveling on the forest's uneven terrain.

Beside me, Rachel was on her knees, staring excitedly through the back window at the scenery that we sped over. I thought it was the first time she'd ever been inside a mechanized vehicle, much less a flying one. I found myself enjoying her reaction. It made me wonder what other novelties I could introduce her to, which in turn made me anticipate our arrival in the city.

In front of me, Alvidia and Cross sat in silence. Cross held a device resembling a smartphone, which she stared at and kept tapping and swiping this way and that, thoroughly engrossed in whatever she was reading. But Alvidia was staring at me, wearing an expression of mixed curiosity and suspicion. It felt like her gaze was going to bore a hole in my flesh, such was its intensity.

"Did you want to ask me something?" I finally asked, since ignoring her seemed to do no good. She paused for a bit after hearing my question before leaning towards me to reply.

"Yes," she said. "Would you tell me who it was that taught you to wield a sword?"

"No one," I answered. "It's just something I've dabbled with over the years."

"Nonsense," Alvidia said dismissively. "Your technique is too refined to be self-taught."

"I assure you, I had no master," I said. "It was just a hobby I picked up to pass the time."

"If you don't want to tell me who your teacher was, that's fine," Alvidia said with a frown. "But you don't have to be deceptive. It's obvious that you received extensive training under someone skillful."

"Not really," I said. "There are only so many ways you can thrust and slash with a sword. Given enough time and attention, you'll eventually discover them all. After that, it's all about refining your technique and cutting out any extraneous movements. Anyone can figure it out if they work at it long enough. Even someone as untalented as me."

"You make it sound so simple," Alvidia said. "The sword is a weapon I've striven to master since I was a child. Your explanation makes no sense."

I shrugged in response and turned my head away. She could think whatever she liked; I'd been perfectly honest with her. I possessed little natural skill for swordplay. In fact, I was once so lacking at it that I was more of a danger to myself with a blade than any enemy I sought to use it against. It had taken me fifty years of continuous practice to gain an average level of competence with it. Becoming a master had taken me over a century.

It was embarrassing, but true. No one is equally gifted at all things. Some of us have to work harder than others. I simply had the time it took to gradually improve. Persistence at training can make a master of anyone if they keep grinding away at it.

I supposed I could have sped the process up if I'd sought out a proper instructor, but I enjoyed learning on my own. For me, swordplay was a hobby, not a necessity.

I did enjoy having Spiteful around, though. Possessing a nice piece of well-crafted, cursed steel with which to strike down my hapless foes did wonders for my sense of self-confidence.

"Teach me what you know," Alvidia said suddenly.

"Why should I? You just called me a liar," I replied.

"Then prove me wrong," she said. "I'm a very willing student. House Brask has defended the Regent's throne for four generations. There's considerable honor to be gained by becoming my instructor."

"I'm unconcerned with matters of honor," I informed her. "Taking a new disciple doesn't interest me."

"I can pay you," she insisted.

"How much?" I asked immediately.

"Name your price," she said confidently.

"I might ask a lot from you," I said with a wolfish grin.

"That's fine. I might enjoy paying it," she said coyly.

"Then dine with me tonight," I said heedlessly. "Let's see how we feel after waking in the morning."

Instead of being charmed by my forthrightness, Alvidia decided to slap me as hard as she could. I probably deserved it. When my vision cleared, I saw Cross and Rachel both laughing scornfully at me, while Alvidia sat stiffly with her arms crossed.

"Sorry, I think I misread the atmosphere," I said as I tenderly touched my newly reddened cheek. "I thought you were giving out a signal to proceed."

"Even if I do find you mildly intriguing, that's no reason to behave boorishly," Alvidia said coldly. "You have a lot of nerve."

"Was I too forward?" I asked. "I was too forward, wasn't I?"

"*Far* too forward," she confirmed. "I already told you; excessive self-confidence can be offensive."

"In my defense, I simply assumed that we were both mature enough to skip the preamble," I explained. "Two appealing individuals like us with a shared interest in cutting people and objects with swords shouldn't have to beat around the bush when it comes to expressing a physical interest in each other."

"Women like to be wooed," Alvidia replied. "Even warriors."

"As well as slapping people who upset them," I grimaced.

"Yes. That too," she agreed.

"So noted," I said. "Lesson learned."

"I take my swordsmanship seriously, Evans," Alvidia continued haughtily. "It's not just my career; it's my very way of life. I asked for your guidance earnestly. Why do so many men seize on a professional consultation as an opportunity for a tryst? It's so fucking aggravating."

"They do that at book conventions too," Cross said disapprovingly.

"What's a book convention?" Rachel wondered.

"You're gorgeous, I got excited," I said regretfully. "Do I still have a chance?"

"Of course you do. I also find you attractive," Alvidia said without embarrassment. "*But* just because I find it pleasurable to look upon you doesn't mean I'm willing to leverage my dignity for a favor. Thinking like that is prehistoric *and* offensive."

"In that case, take heart, Alvidia Brask," I said. "Know that all men, with the exception of myself, are single-minded scum who are unworthy of your attention."

"Where are you going with this?" she asked.

"Yeah, where *are* you going with this?" asked Rachel.

"Let me finish," I said. "As the only member of my entire gender who's capable of learning from his past mistakes, I just want to assure you that you can do no wrong in forgiving me for any accidental missteps I make along the way of our burgeoning relationship *because I'm worth it*. Isn't that right, Rachel?"

"He's a complete liar and you'll probably need to control him with violence," Rachel said cheerfully while scratching Schulz's belly.

"Thank you for the advice," said Alvidia with a pleased smile.

"Any time!"

"Your treachery will be dealt with later," I swore to Rachel.

"Don't be upset, I'm just playing the long game!" she insisted.

"You know, I could change for the better, eventually," I said to Alvidia. "All it takes is a little bit of time."

"Try harder," the women all said simultaneously with pitiless gazes.

"I just said it takes a little time," I whined.

Alvidia snorted. Cross rolled her eyes. Rachel gave me an extremely disappointed look before turning her attention back to the window.

Even Schulz gave me a bit of side-eye and moved slightly away from me as if to avoid contracting secondhand embarrassment.

Whatever. I was a vampire. I was used to being alone in a group.

No one appreciated me as much as they should.

In the middle of Gardenia, surrounded by distracting layers of opulence and beauty that seemed to lessen the appearance of danger like gold dust sprinkled in the center of a spider's web, was the palace of the Regent.

The city itself, with its high steel and concrete walls beneath its shimmering anti-monster dome offering those who dwelt within absolute security from the terrors of the outside world, was a sharp contrast to the comparatively insignificant Narrows, which had been our home for so long. And here, from the Regent's seat, was where the power this place collected was concentrated and directed.

After we landed at the palace, I took a moment to give the place an appreciative once-over. It certainly appeared to be a well-constructed home. It paled in comparison to the castle I'd reigned from in my previous life, but it certainly would have made for a nice summer house.

I wondered what the local neighborhood was like.

"This way, sir," said a brusque guard who placed a hand on my shoulder to guide me to where the group was waiting.

The impatient expressions worn by my companions nearly made me flinch. Cross tapped the watch she wore impatiently, and even Rachel looked annoyed. What was their deal? I'd only been taking a look at the exterior of the place. Did they think I was behaving like some rube from the middle of nowhere, awed by the splendor of the city? If so, what an obnoxious assumption to make!

"We're going inside now," Alvidia said. "Please keep in mind that important visitors from across the country will be here conducting business with the Regent. Keep to your best manners and try not to do anything that would embarrass me. You're here on *my* recommendation, after all."

With that, she walked into the palace and gestured for us to follow.

What was that about? Had my earlier behavior really been so out of hand? I'd been doing some lighthearted flirting! She didn't expect me to behave like that in such an important social setting, did she?

I hated it when others expected the worst of me. Too bad it was impossible for these newer generations to appreciate just how evolved I was as a person. For goodness's sake, I was a nobleman from the dark ages! If any of these scolds had experienced a childhood like mine, they'd be thoroughly impressed with how forward-thinking I'd become despite my upbringing. When *I* was a lad, human women of noble birth were treated like expensive furniture. The very notion of them bearing arms and serving as bodyguards would have elicited scandalized laughter from their peers. But look at me! Making no commentary on the subject and accepting them for what they were in this volatile new age.

And what's more, look at how polite I was! I mean, I know you shouldn't expect to be rewarded for doing the bare minimum, and not being needlessly rude was certainly the bare minimum, but again, *I was from the dark ages*! We were *very* unpleasant people back then! We also didn't bathe regularly and there was also a lot of casual racism going around. It was a difficult era to live through. But I persevered and came out the other side as a much kinder person.

That little apocalypse I participated in was coerced, by the way. It shouldn't count against my character.

With all that I'd done for others, was it unreasonable to want to be treated kindly? Wasn't I a person that that others should like having around?

It still stung that Jamie had been playing me. That she hadn't cared for me at all.

Oof. Her manipulation and Alvidia's hot-and-cold personality weren't doing any wonders for my current level of self-confidence. *I shouldn't let myself dwell on this.* But I did so anyway.

I wished I could blame my darkening mood on an aspect of vampiric life that made our species touchy about being mischaracterized, but this was all on me. It was just my rotten personality taking effect. I couldn't even fob this off on Kyler Evans's body. This was just who I was.

Embarrassing but true.

Bah, what good did it do to obsess over this? When would I learn to stop fixating on such silly, mortal trivialities? Why did I always dwell on such things? Had I become the sort of weak person that always needed to be liked?

Oh, who was I kidding? That was exactly the sort of weak person I'd become.

I just wanted to be admired for the splendid fellow that I was!

If only I could use Mesmerize to force Brask and Cross to become more appreciative of me. But there was no point in doing it since it wouldn't affect Rachel's memory.

I'd still look like an insecure control freak obsessed with maintaining his image.

Could I . . . simply *order* Rachel not to remember it, as her master? Would that work? No, of course it wouldn't. A creator's bond with his progeny was a powerful thing, but it couldn't be abused to that extent. But wouldn't it be convenient if it could?

As I continued to slouch and ruminate sullenly over how unfair life could be, a beautiful girl came running down the hall toward me and threw herself into my arms.

"Whoa," said a surprised Rachel as she observed the newcomer embrace me tightly and bury her face in my chest. "Is this a friend of yours I haven't met yet?"

"That would be news to me," I said, equally as confused as she was. I lowered my face toward the girl and gently said, "Miss? May I ask why you're doing this?"

"Thank you," murmured the girl tearfully. "Thank you so much . . ."

"Alvidia, can you explain?" I asked as I turned to her. I could feel the genuine gratitude of the girl I held, her sincere appreciation of whatever it was she believed I'd done for her . . . and it was making me extremely uncomfortable.

I was not good at being genuinely liked. I didn't understand how to process it in a healthy manner. I thought I'd made some personal progress earlier with the time I'd spent with Jamie, but that had turned out to be a manipulated farce.

I supposed my bond with Rachel had a strong emotional undercurrent to it, but it wasn't something I liked thinking too much about. She was my progeny, it was different. Even my wives, although the love I felt for them was true, the ties that bound us to each other were primarily a twisted knot of desire and hate. A frayed cord in desperate need of a Macedonian sword.

But this . . . a vulnerable person rushing to me and in her weakness conveying her gratitude; her happiness at the sight of someone like me . . .

. . . it was too real. I couldn't—

I couldn't handle things like that.

Sunlight, holiness, and genuine faith. Guess what else you can add onto that list of painful things I always desperately tried to avoid?

Sincerity.

I'm sure that sounds insane, but it's the pitiful truth. As a monster, I found the notion of anyone being *happy* to see me absolutely bewildering. You're supposed to run from a vampire, not crush him with a delighted hug while peppering him with gratitude.

What was wrong with this child?

"Do you really not recall?" Alvidia said with a surprisingly warm smile as she stepped close to the girl and gently patted her back. "She's the reason why you were invited here to begin with. Your good deed in rescuing her from a terrible fate has earned the sincere appreciation of the Regent himself. After all, she's his precious granddaughter."

"Granddaughter?" I asked. "Rescued? What do you . . ."

And that was when it hit me.

I *did* know this girl. She'd been there, on that night that Cassie and Pankratz had first attacked me. She'd been the sole survivor of a vicious bandit attack that had seen all friends and traveling companions violated and butchered.

This was the girl I'd rescued back then. I'd been bringing her back to the Narrows when Rachel had suddenly transformed. Honestly, aside from that one detail, it hadn't been a particularly memorable night for me; but it seemed it had been quite memorable for this poor damsel.

"Hey! Why are *you* getting the credit for everything?" asked Rachel. "I was the one who did all the work!"

Oh, right. Rachel had been the one to do the actual rescuing; I'd simply carried the girl back to town. Not that anyone would have ever believed a sentient spear (which Rachel had been at the time), would have been capable of such a heroic deed.

Heh, sorry Rach. But I do believe I'll be stealing your laurels for this one.

"What a fool I was to forget," I said with a sheepish smile of my own as I gazed fondly upon the girl. "I wondered for some time what had become of you. I'm so glad to see that you're safe."

"Only due to your bravery and skill," the maiden sighed while Alvidia and Cross looked on approvingly.

"Well, I do have those traits in abundance," I said with a humble nod.

"Hey!" said Rachel indignantly.

CHAPTER THIRTY-EIGHT

The girl's name was Emily Norus, and I got to learn more about her over the course of an early lunch. *So much more.* Once I got past her initial shyness, I quickly discovered that the girl was a bit of a talker, and her favorite topic of discussion was herself.

Strangely, however, her self-absorption wasn't without its charm. Although the girl was certainly vainglorious, she was still pleasant to be around and gracious to others when she could be cajoled into paying attention to them.

There was a solid core of good-natured sweetness at Emily's center. It was just that it was coated in a thick sediment of spoiled obliviousness that made it difficult for her to fathom that the people around her might not be as interested in her life as she assumed they were. It was an endearing sort of obliviousness when taken in small measurements.

As it turned out, she was slightly older than Kyler Evans and had been returning from a year of studying abroad in the Ethos Kingdom when her caravan had been assaulted.

It felt unpleasant knowing that the attack that had nearly seen Emily violated and murdered had been arranged by Jamie. The thought that one woman would knowingly profit from the horrific degradation of another was a stark reminder of humanity's capacity for darkness. If mankind's potential for greatness was without limit, so too was its capacity for selfishness and depravity.

I didn't want to think about Jamie anymore, nor did I want to listen to Lady Emily's chatter. So, I instead focused on the sushi that had been prepared for us.

I wished I could say that in the months since I'd regained the ability to eat human food, I had gradually learned self-restraint and to slowly savor a meal. But the reality was that I was still a shameless glutton who easily lost himself to the pleasure of mindless consumption. When the tray of rolls was presented to us,

I happily grabbed two massive handfuls of rice and tuna and stuffed them blissfully into my face.

By the hungering dark, sushi was *so* good. Sadly, my companions didn't seem to share in my enjoyment of the meal.

Around the table, the girls stared at me while wearing expressions that ranged from disgust to surprise and every other emotion in between. Even Rachel seemed embarrassed by me, which felt a little hurtful.

"It's good," I said as I wiped my mouth with my sleeve.

It really was.

Goodness, they were drilling holes into me with their eyes.

Before the conversation could spiral into any further awkwardness, a sharply dressed young man in white wearing a set of black horn-rimmed glasses appeared out of nowhere and quietly informed us that the Regent would see me now.

When I say this man appeared out of nowhere, I mean it literally. In the space of a moment, while my attention was occupied by the Regent's granddaughter, he was suddenly *there*. It was a bewildering moment, to be sure. No one likes being sneaked up on, much less me, a being whose refined senses should have made it impossible to be surprised, even while wearing his humble human form.

I instantly disliked this fellow.

"If you'll come with me, Mr. Evans," he said in a pleasant monotone as he gestured for me to follow. "My name is Tybalt Brask, the hand of the Regent. I'm so very pleased to meet you."

"And I am Kyler—" I began to say before he cut me off.

"Yes, Kyler Evans, I'm aware," he said with the smallest hint of impatience. "No need for an introduction of your own. Let's be on our way."

"Brother, there was no need for you to collect the Regent's guest personally," Alvidia said with surprising nervousness as Cross stood beside her and nodded quickly in flustered embarrassment. "I'm sure you have more important things to do with your time."

A deeply uncomfortable silence followed.

"Where is your sword, little sister?" the newcomer, Tybalt, finally asked in response as he stared pointedly at the empty scabbard belted at Alvidia's waist.

Alvidia swallowed uncomfortably before replying. "It was destroyed during my recent outing. I'll have it replaced at once."

"A member of the Brask family, known far and wide as the mightiest on the continent, has not only been defeated by a fumbling amateur, but she would shamelessly parade her disgrace before our lord?" asked Tybalt coldly.

"I would . . . no, I see your point, brother. I apologize," Alvidia said with an embarrassed flush to her skin. I didn't like seeing her that way. Although I hadn't known her for long, I'd quickly grown to like this young woman. True, she was arrogant and brash, but such a bold disposition suited a warrior as capable as her. Seeing her pushed around by a domineering older sibling displeased me.

Also, he'd called me a fumbling amateur within my earshot.

I was *pretty sure* that had been done deliberately.

"Have no fear, Mr. Tybalt," I said. "Although I can't personally speak to the capabilities of the rest of your family, I thought Lady Alvidia acquitted herself honorably. Her talent was a sight to behold."

"It's *Lord* Tybalt, Mr. Evans," he said in the same polite tone he'd addressed me with earlier. "And speaking respectfully, although your opinion is appreciated, it wasn't asked for."

"Hmm. You know, it's the strangest thing," I said as I scratched my chin. "What you just said didn't actually *feel* respectful or appreciative in the slightest. Isn't that odd?"

Tybalt's brow creased ever so slightly.

Alvidia stared at me with a horrified expression from behind her brother while Cross shook her head in terror and silently mouthed the word *don't*.

"Just as your report said, you have an interesting way of interacting with others," Tybalt said. "I do admire a confident person."

"You do? *Wonderful*," I said in appreciation.

Now Tybalt was smiling.

"Kyler Evans, I am *definitely* going to remember you later," he said. "But since we're currently pressed for time, we'll have to continue this conversation later. I'm looking forward to it, though."

"Well, I'll first have to see if I can pencil you in, *Lord* Tybalt," I replied. "I have a busy schedule of my own, you see. I'm sure you understand. I can't just move things around for some random *nobody*. But if you ask nicely, maybe I'll make an exception."

Once again, Tybalt smiled at me.

I smiled at him as well.

As we stared into each other's eyes, all around us, the world seemed to slow to a crawl.

For the first time since my encounter with Sophia in my original world, I was certain that I now stood in the presence of someone capable of dealing me mortal harm.

It felt very exciting.

If I went for his throat at this very moment, would he be fast enough to stop me? If he went for me, would *I* be able to react in time? How much of this palace would be destroyed during our clash? How many people would die?

It was *too* exciting to think of. How fortunate for everyone involved that Rachel quickly picked up on my murderously intense interest and interceded before something terrible could happen.

"Well, let's get you on your way, boss," she said cheerfully while deliberately clinging to my arm.

My sword arm.

"The Regent himself is waiting!" she continued. "We can't be rude, right? *Right?*"

"Right!" Cross said, quickly catching on. "How silly of us would that be? But I insist on guiding Mr. Evans myself. Lord Tybalt is far too important for such mundanities."

"Yes, far too important!" Alvidia chimed in as she grabbed Tybalt's arm. "Thank you again for honoring us with your presence, brother. While Evans is escorted to his meeting, perhaps I could consult with you about finding a suitable replacement for my sword. Your expertise would be *invaluable.*"

Before Tybalt or I could say anything in protest, we were pulled in separate directions and dragged away. As we were forcibly parted, our eyes met once more, and in the intensity of our shared gaze was the promise of future spectacular violence to come.

I dearly anticipated it.

Anytime, *anywhere.*

"Well, *that* was fucking terrifying, thank you *so much* for that horrendous experience," Cross said angrily as she led us down the hall to a floating platform that took us to the fourth floor of the building at a languid pace. "I'm beginning to form a negative opinion of you, Evans."

"What did I do that was so awful?" I asked. "I was just sizing the fellow up."

"Sizing him up?" Cross repeated in a dazed voice. "Hey, handsome? That was Lord *Tybalt fucking Brask.* The current head of the Brask family! A living legend at the age of twenty-two! He might have S-rank potential! Do you know what they call him?"

"What?" I asked.

"*Damocles,*" she said excitedly. "Do you know why? Because anyone or anything that crosses him is doomed! And you just stood there mocking him like he was a forest goblin. I thought my heart was going to stop beating!"

"Damocles?" I asked. "Was Tybalt the one who picked that nickname?"

"Yep!" Cross said. "Pretty cool, right?"

"No, it's stupid," I snorted. "In the myth, Damocles was the one under threat. He was forced to eat at a banquet with a sword hanging over his head by a single thread. It was a punishment because the king he served was annoyed by Damocles' constant flattery and wanted to teach him a lesson."

"What was the lesson?" asked Rachel.

"At the time, it was probably to speak less while a king is eating," I replied. "But since then, it's become a parable about how doom hangs nearer than we realize. But my point is, it was *the sword* you were supposed to fear. Damocles was just a fool being made an example of."

"Are you saying Lord Tybalt is a lazy reader?" Rachel tittered.

"Bingo!" I said snidely. "And I'll also bet you a gold piece those glasses he wore were just for show. Why do people think that lenses make them look more intelligent? I've known plenty of nearsighted dolts."

"Are the pair of you suffering from a psychotic disconnection?" asked Cross. "Tybalt is easily the third strongest Hunter in the entire nation. Hell, he might be tied for second. The only person who ever beat him was the Regent's grandson, and there's a rumor that he threw the match out of loyalty to the old man."

"The Regent has a grandson as well?" I asked.

"Yes!" Cross all but shouted. "Alexis Norus! The Exemplar! The light of hope! The first S-rank born into this country in decades! He's the future, you nut! How can you possibly not know that?"

Before she could berate my ignorance any further, the door to the Regent's hall opened. She then hurriedly stifled herself before gesturing for us to follow her.

"Show deference," Cross warned me as we approached an inconspicuous-looking office door. "I'm serious! The Regent is a great man but he's also old and mercurial. You never know what'll set him off. Keep him in a good mood or else. But don't wind him up! Like in your story, he hates flattery. Just . . . uh. Be real with him."

"I'm a very real person," I said. "The realest of the real."

"Yeah, don't speak like that," replied Cross. "This is a golden opportunity, Evans. A lot of people would kill for this once-in-a-lifetime chance to change their lives. Don't blow it."

Having said that, she raised a fist and knocked quietly on the door.

"Come in," said an older male voice on the other side.

"Good luck," Cross said as she stepped aside. As Rachel began to follow behind me, Cross quickly caught her arm and shook her head.

"The meeting is with Evans only," she informed her.

"What? No fair!" Rachel complained. "I want to meet the Regent too."

"Maybe you'll get to one day," Cross said as she led her away. "Maybe sooner than you think, actually. Come with me, there's something I'd like to discuss with you."

"Huh?" Rachel asked before turning her eyes toward me. I nodded to her and said, "Take the tour. Have some fun. I'll be done with this in no time."

"You sure?" Rachel asked uncertainly.

"I'm *positive*," I assured her. "No worries, kid. This is *me* we're talking about. It'll go smoothly."

By way of fact, it did *not* go smoothly. I should have realized it wouldn't.

After all, this was *me* we were talking about.

Seated behind a massive oak desk and dressed casually in trousers and an open collared shirt, the Regent, Duke Perius Norus, cut a less impressive figure than I'd expected. Despite being the ruler of the Allied Kingdom, he seemed unremarkable. *Very* ordinary-looking. If I didn't know who he was, I'd dismiss him as merely a vigorous-looking older man with small touches of gray left in his receding snow-white hair and beard.

It was his eyes that told a different story. They were primed, calculating. *Alert.* Once more I now stood in the presence of a genuinely dangerous man. A smile quirked at the corner of my lips when I realized this. I was glad I'd accepted Alvidia's offer to come to this place. Gardenia, as it turned out, was a city filled with interesting people.

"Does something amuse you, Evans?" the old man asked as he finished signing a few sheets of paper, which he then placed in a drawer before focusing his attention on me.

"No, sir," I replied politely.

"Sir?" he asked with a slight frown.

"No, your grace," I said, correcting myself.

"Then wipe that insolent smirk off your face and sit down," he said gruffly as he leaned back in his seat.

I did as commanded and sat down in the chair facing his desk. It was stiffly made and extremely uncomfortable, which immediately let me know the nature of the man I was speaking with.

"I'm told you enjoyed lunch with my granddaughter," he said conversationally.

"I did. Lady Emily graciously invited me to dine with her," I replied. "We had sushi. It was delicious."

"I'm told you made a pig of yourself before her," the Regent said. "I was disappointed to learn that. You carry noble blood in your veins, boy. On your mother's side, anyway. Even if you are a misfire and an outcast, you could at least try conducting yourself gracefully."

"Do I?" I asked without interest. "I'm a man with no knowledge of what came before. I have no interest in the lineage of he who sired this body."

"You claim amnesia?" asked the Regent.

"Sure, why not?" I replied. That was close enough to the truth. I had no memories of Kyler Evans's life because I wasn't Kyler Evans.

The frown the old man already wore deepened at my perceived flippancy. Well, more like intentional flippancy. He steepled his fingers as he gazed at me.

"You're now in the center of power for the greatest nation in the world," Norus said mildly. "Here, the fortunes of lesser men have been elevated to heights undreamed of. The lives of the great have also been destroyed as casually as flies have been swatted. Here, I alone make decisions that will impact the lives of millions."

"You seem to have a very important job, your grace," I said while giving him a thumbs-up.

"Indeed, I do," he agreed. "Which is why I'm so surprised by the lack of reverence and respect that you are obligated to show me. Boy, I am your *Regent*."

"I gave you a thumbs-up, didn't I?" I replied defensively.

"Is this ridiculous behavior derived from you being a bastard? Or is this what all common men are slowly reduced to in the absence of order?" he asked himself.

"Don't blame others for my tendency to misbehave, your grace," I said. "I tend to react the same to all people. Whether they are great or small makes little difference to me."

"Is that right?" asked Norus. "Surely, I'm not hearing the insipid rhetoric of equalism being spewed forth in my own home, am I? That would greatly displease me."

"*Me*, an equalist? That's hardly the case," I replied as I tried to lounge in my chair. "Although I do agree with their sentiment about how the social class one is born into is a matter of sheer luck, which makes those invested in its hereditary privileges unremarkable. Princess or pauper, it doesn't matter. We only have what the world saw fit to give us. Other than that, I'm a different sort of animal than them."

"That is a dangerous thing to say in front of a true aristocrat," replied the Regent in a mild tone of voice. "Are you denying that the gods saw fit to uplift us to our rightful position?"

"What would I know about the will of the gods?" I asked. "I tend to be of a more secular mindset."

"Answer the question, boy," he insisted.

"Only if I can ask a question of my own," I said. "How is nobility a rightful position if it requires a *divine mandate*? If you can't get something without a god to hand it to you, then do you really deserve it? And why do the privileged need so fervently to believe that they have divine favor? What if they don't? What's the difference?"

"I think I now have a better understanding of why your family despises you so much," Norus said dryly as he set down his glass. "Rarely have I met those so willing to mock the foundations of my beliefs to my face. You, boy, are a symptom of the unmoored rot besetting my once-proud kingdom. You spout ignorant drivel without a care for the consequences, all for the pleasure of hearing your own voice. I'd dismiss you as a lackadaisical twit if it wasn't obvious that you take joy in deliberately being a rake."

"Oh, I like *you*," I said cheerily. "No one's called me a rake in ages."

"Don't be a prick," said the Regent. "You are quickly growing wearisome."

"Would you like him removed, your grace?" asked Tybalt as he entered the office. It looked like he'd broken free from Alvidia's ploy to keep him distracted. *Oh, joy.*

"I'm sorely tempted," Norus said sharply. "Are you really the one who rescued my granddaughter? How could her protector espouse such nihilistic frippery?"

"It's hard not to be cynical when you live long enough to see that nothing ever changes," I said.

"Ah, I see now that you're speaking with the wisdom of *age*," Norus said sarcastically. "Child, when our world suffered from the chaos caused by the invading monsters, while the earth beneath our feet was shattered into a new and unrecognizable land, when it seemed that the end of *everything* was inevitable, we were blessed by the arrival of the System."

"And you're so certain that the arrival of the System was a blessing?" I asked him.

"Of course it was, you little fool," Norus said. "Upon its arrival, we ascended were selected to safeguard this world and rule over it. Our authority was given to us by divine right. We are both the shepherd and the soldier!"

He spoke that last bit with the fervent zeal of a true believer. A quality I recognized straight away from my various encounters with it over the years and always dreaded to see repeated in newer generations.

Men like him could be so difficult to deal with.

He reminded me of Mayner.

"People used to understand," Norus said bitterly as he continued his rant. "Our sacred bloodlines were treated with reverence, and the lesser citizens accepted their roles and kept to their place without question. But now, these jumped-up merchants with their filthy gold have bought their way into the great houses and diluted them with their commoner heritage."

Oh, no. I could detect a furious rant against mercantilism was forthcoming. Why did these ancient warrior households always blame merchants for all the trouble in society?

My first wife, Yona, was descended from a proud samurai family, and she could go on for *days* about how Japan had been at its best when the warrior class controlled everything, and the peasants never left their rice fields without permission on pain of death. A cozy arrangement for those of her rank that fell to the wayside after Japan's great social reformations gave their serfs greater freedom and allowed their traders and artisans to accumulate independent wealth.

As it turned out, a functioning country needed more than caste discrimination and internecine violence to prosper. Being allowed to trade for valuable goods with foreigners and being willing to learn their languages gave the merchants an advantage the samurai couldn't match. Due to the unwillingness of the samurai families to adjust to the new social paradigm, they were gradually uprooted from their positions of authority and cast into poverty.

It was a valuable lesson to learn. Pride cometh before what?

And it wasn't as if such events were exclusive to Japan. Europe was once a continent ruled by knights who were eventually displaced in importance by cotton traders and spice dealers. It was the same deal across the globe. The world would never be free of the need for fighting men, but their era of absolute dominance was had ended.

The times had changed.

"I've never understood the rivalry between merchants and warriors," I said. "There's no difference between the two, really. If you think about it, merchants are just people who accomplish with their coins what warriors can do with their spears."

"Ha!" scoffed the old man. "We're nothing alike. They're weaklings who buy their strength from others! The truly powerful develop theirs through training and discipline."

"Gaining wealth isn't easy, though," I replied. "In its own way, it's as much of a trial as honing your skill with a blade. As they say, money doesn't grow on trees."

"Who taught you such tripe?" Norus asked with a sneer.

"Just something I learned from my mother," I replied, before remembering to conclude with, "your grace."

"How strange. I've known your mother since she was a child and I've never once heard her say such a thing," said the Regent.

"Maybe it was my grandmother," I said. "She's had a tough time of things recently."

"Your grandmother died years before you were born," said Norus. "I attended her funeral. It was a lovely service."

I quickly floundered for another lie but gave up before too long and shrugged.

"Oh. Awkward," I said.

"That you would lie so casually to the Regent of all men speaks to your lack of character," said Tybalt with disgust.

"Well, maybe you just think too highly of him," I said in annoyance. "It's not like he's a *king*."

"HOW DARE YOU!" yelled Tybalt, who swiftly drew his sword and pointed it at me. "Apologize at once! Show your due deference or I'll remove your insolent tongue!"

This was getting annoying. I hadn't even wanted to come here and had complied anyway, only to be scolded, lectured, and threatened. I didn't care about *any* of this.

"I believe I'm going to leave now," I said without bothering to disguise my sour mood. "Coming here seems like it was a mistake. I'm glad to have been of service to your granddaughter in her time of need, your grace. Your sincere gratitude is all the reward I'll ever need. God bless the kingdom, go forth and conquer, blah-blah-blah. *Goodbye.*"

"Did you have anything to do with assaulting her?" the Regent asked as I rose from my seat. "Did you conspire with her attackers in any way?"

Ah. Honesty at last.

Well, suspicion, anyway.

"No," I said to him coldly. "But having now met you, I'm far less likely to have assisted her if I'd known who her grandfather was."

That was a lie. I would never willingly allow a woman to be assaulted in my presence. I may be a monster, but I still had *standards.* I only said that to agitate the old man. It was enormously satisfying to watch Norus's face turn a deep shade of infuriated purple at my words. Our dear Regent had clearly gone years without having to deal with anyone talking back to him and it had utterly spoiled him. Made him into a little bully.

"ENOUGH!" Norus yelled as he jumped to his feet and brought his fist down on his desk hard enough to split the sturdy wood down the middle, sending both ends crashing to the floor. A powerful violet aura erupted around his body as he shoved the heavy remnants aside and stomped forth to seize me by the throat and hold me aloft.

"I should have you sent to the dungeons to cool your heels and learn respect for the sanctity of my office," he said. "Or perhaps I'll just break your insolent neck."

"You'd do such a thing to the hero who rescued your granddaughter?" I asked in an indifferent tone as the tips of my boots swung above the office floor. "That wouldn't look very good, would it? Wouldn't everyone whisper about you behind your back? *Goodness, look at how the Regent rewarded someone who protected his family. How disgraceful!* It could be quite a nasty little scandal."

"You obnoxious little *brat*," Norus said balefully as his hand trembled with the desire to tighten its grip and crush my throat.

"Takes one to know one," I said while waiting to see what he'd do next.

"I don't like you very much, Kyler Evans," Norus said after a few moments of silence had passed.

"Consider the feeling mutual," I replied. "Are you going to put me down now?"

Norus glared at me while visibly struggling with the urge to pull my head off. Then he grunted and dropped me to the floor, on which I landed uncomfortably. He snapped his fingers and Tybalt hurriedly waved his hands over the Regent's ruined desk, which suddenly pulled itself back together, mended so perfectly that there was no indication it had ever been broken.

I whistled in appreciation of the sight. "*Very* impressive," I said sincerely. "How did he do that? Is that a unique ability or an application of magic?"

"I'm afraid I can't answer that question. The mechanics behind Tybalt's exceptional abilities are a state secret," Norus said as he resumed his seat. "I could make you vanish for even daring to ask that me that question. Perhaps I should."

"You really are in love with the power of your office," I remarked as I reset my own overturned chair and sat back down.

"Nothing of the sort, boy." Norus said dismissively. "The power of my office is symbolic of the great personal strength I already wield. Everything else is mere ornamentation."

"That's a healthy level of self-regard," I said blankly. "It's almost admirable."

"Your mouth will be your undoing one day. Keep it up and it will happen sooner than you realize," warned the old man.

"But aren't you terribly impressed with how brave I am?" I asked.

"No," he said flatly. "Now I'm convinced that you're a fool who pays no heed to the depth of the water surrounding him."

"Can we *please* just skip to the part where you reward me, and I leave?" I asked in exasperation.

"What do you want?" the Regent asked.

"Anonymity," I replied. "Since you've so thoroughly investigated me, then you already know I made a few mistakes that might impact my future negatively. Wipe them from the record. Wipe my very *name* from the record. From now on, there *is* no Kyler Evans. I want that made official."

"You're accused of assaulting the precious daughter of a notable family. You *are* guilty of killing a team of valuable future Hunters," Norus said sternly. "I'm certain you're also responsible for the death of an ascended guardsman who vanished on the night of your supposed death. Do you truly intend for me to overlook these transgressions?"

"Yes. I absolutely do," I said, straight-faced and without shame.

"I would very much like to pull you apart by hand," Norus said with such seething violence that even Tybalt was taken aback.

"But if you did that then your family would lose face," I said. "Which is precisely why you'll give me what I want."

"Yes," said the Regent bitterly. "But that's all you'll have from me. There'll be no sanctioned revenge on those you claim mistreated you. No punishment for the Velas family or your own."

"I never wanted that to begin with," I said angrily. "I never cared about *any* of that."

"Good. Because now it will never come to pass. My people will approach you later and allow you to select a new name—"

"Stragos," I said at once. "Kyler Stragos."

The old man narrowed his eyes at being interrupted before continuing. "You'll then be given a one-time payment of gold. From there, you can go wherever you like. But I would strongly recommend that you never show yourself before me again. Avoid further contact with Emily as well."

"With whom?" I asked in confusion.

"Emily," he repeated. When I continued to stare blankly at him, he sighed and said, "My *granddaughter.*"

"Oh, right," I said and nodded. "Gotcha."

And with that, negotiations were concluded.

On my way out of the palace, a servant approached me and delivered a written message.

Evans.

Don't be too quick to leave, darling. Meet me at the address below, and I'll be certain to give you a proper sendoff. Remember to leave the lights off. It'll be memorable.

A.

A? Ah, for Alvidia, *undoubtedly.* Could it be that I'd won her over after all? Well, hadn't she said she still found me intriguing?

I probably needed to wait around for Rachel to return from her conversation with Cross.

That would have been the responsible thing to do.

An image of Alvidia going wild in my arms while we lay on silk sheets in a tawdry hotel flashed through my mind and pushed all thoughts of responsible behavior off a cliff to drown in the ocean as I ran off to find the address on the letter.

Rachel was a big kid. She'd be fine.

Everything would be *fiiiine.*

CHAPTER THIRTY-NINE

As it turned out, everything was *not* fine.

It was with a light step and a merry song in my heart that I found myself at the Lover's Lane motel and breakfast buffet, Room 28, twenty minutes later. Just as I expected, the place was a bit of a shady mess, the sight of which brought a warm smile to my silly face.

Alvidia, it seemed, liked to have her fun in some, shall we say *interesting*, environments. Well, I wasn't going to judge her for it. Some people preferred the setting for their trysts to be pristine and perfect like the setting of a fairy tale, and others liked grinding it out on the threadbare carpets of the sleaziest dives they could find. Either option was good enough for me.

I'm *very* easy to please.

"Keep watch outside, will you lads?" I asked my companions before entering the room. Schulz barked in acknowledgement and took a position beside the door to stand guard. Orby, on the other hand, just floated in the air and emitted a confused sort of beep at the order he'd been given. I really think he would have stayed there all night if Schulz hadn't given an irritated bark that I'm sure roughly translated into *Get over here, stupid!* which sent the Blood Orb scurrying over to his side.

Heh. It didn't take those two very long to get a friendly little dynamic going, did it?

I gave the door a few light raps before stepping inside to find the curtains drawn, the pleasant scent of vanilla candles filling the air, and some romantic-ish electronic music playing in the background. In the center of the room was a large heart-shaped bed illuminated with flickering neon pink lighting.

"Scoooore," I said to myself. This was going to be wild.

"Shhh," said the breathy whisper of the woman behind me as she stepped closer and wrapped her arms around my waist.

"This is an interesting setting," I said as I placed my own hands over hers. "I didn't know you had it in you."

"I've always wanted to try out a place like this," she said coyly. "It's fun, right? The perfect background for some naughty roleplaying."

"We're doing roleplaying as well?" I asked excitedly. "Oh! Can I be an angry GameStop manager? You can be the sultry customer trying to trade in her old games for the advertised value without a power rewards card. Are you ready?"

". . . Huh?" she asked.

I ignored her and said, "Now listen here, Missy. I keep telling you your membership expired last year. If you want full credit, you're gonna need to throw me a little something *extra*, got it?"

"Kyler, what is a GameStop?" the woman asked in confusion.

"I'll tell you all about it in bed, babe," I said as I turned around to kiss her passionately. "Now let's just—"

My breath caught in my chest at the sight of her.

"What are *you* doing here?" I asked in surprise.

Anikka Velas grinned slyly at me before throwing her arms around my neck and drawing me in for another kiss.

"*That* is what I'm doing," she said breathily before using her teeth to nip gently at my ear.

She was dressed in a black shift under a red robe, her golden hair cut in a messy, spikey pattern that suited her. Her vivid blue eyes twinkled at me beneath a messily applied layer of black mascara.

She looked great. She looked like a disaster. She felt like trouble.

Her teeth on my ear felt good. They felt *very* good. But I was no longer in the mood for it.

"Lady Anikka," I said calmly. "I'm not certain how up-to-date on recent events you are, but you're one of the people in this world I would be happy never to lay eyes on again in my lifetime. I'll be taking my leave now."

"Is that all you have to say to me?" she asked, with a hurt expression on her face. "You're *taking your leave*? What the hell is wrong with you?"

"Nothing," I replied. "Nothing at all. And in the interest of keeping myself that way, that's why I'll be avoiding further contact with you. Those in your circle have a tragic tendency to die young, don't they?"

"Only the ones who deserve it," she whispered.

"Not even the decency to fake a little remorse," I said. "You're a rare sort of beast, aren't you?"

"I'm what the world made me," she said as she pushed past me to take a seat on the bed. "It pressed too hard and now I'm wearing its wounds in my soul."

"Oh, bless your weary little heart," I said mockingly. "Are things going that poorly in the land of milk and honey?"

"Why are you speaking to me like that?" she asked.

"How should I speak to a murderess?" I wondered.

"I-I read the report my father had on you," she stammered. "How can you even think to call me that with some of the things you've been up to?"

"Because I'm a hypocrite. And possibly a psychopath. There are no great expectations for the likes of me," I said. "But for someone like you, with all the choices in life that others could only dream of? It's a shameful thing to see you sink to my level."

Anikka was back on her feet in an instant, standing inches away from me with an intensity that heated the air between us. She placed her hands over mine and tried to smile with a face that trembled like it wanted to weep.

"I'd do anything to be with you," she swore.

"Have you tried throwing yourself off a bridge?" I asked her.

"Stop mocking me. Please . . . please stop being so mean to me," she pleaded.

"Then stop acting like such a *joke*," I said angrily as I pulled myself free of her. "I already told you, your days of toying with Evans have ended. *I'm* who you have to deal with now, and I'm far too old for this melodramatic nonsense."

"You're the one who ran away!" she yelled as I began walking to the door. "You ran away like a coward and left me to fend for myself! You said you'd protect me!"

"What are you talking about?" I asked.

"You left me behind," she said accusingly. "*Why* did you leave me behind? I needed you! I *still* need you! And now you're doing it again!"

"You needed Evans so much that you stabbed him in the back?" I countered. "Did you forget about the part where you *murdered* him? I didn't."

"Why do you keep speaking like that?" Anikka asked angrily. "Just stop it! Stop playing games, stop playing with *me!*"

"Are you really the one being sported with?" I asked her. "Are you the poor little rich girl in this scenario? You can't have your way so you're having a tantrum. Do you realize how tedious you sound?"

"Kyler, stop it!" she shouted.

"I don't want to," I replied. "In fact, I think I prefer you this way. You're a beautiful girl, Anikka, but it's a distant sort of beauty, isn't it? Unapproachable. Unknowable. Seeing that face twisted in anger pleases me greatly. *Imperfection* is what truly makes someone worth remembering."

"You're acting like you don't even know me!" she sobbed.

"Of course I don't. We've never even met," I said as I turned away from her. "Anything else to say? It's your final chance."

"Why are you leaving me *again*? Don't do it!" she said as she clutched desperately at my arm. "Kyler, please, I need you! You're the only one who understands me!"

At the mention of Kyler Evans's name again, anger burst bright within me, volatile and white-hot, alongside a sudden desire to be hateful and cruel. Why didn't any of these fools understand?

I grabbed Anikka by her shoulders and pushed her against a wall. Then I gripped her chin and tilted her face toward mine so that she could look me in the eyes as I spoke.

"How many times will I have to repeat this *fucking* conversation with you insipid little people?" I growled at her. "Look at me. *Look at me!* I am *not* Kyler Evans. I was *never* Kyler Evans. Whoever he was, he's now gone. Yes, Anikka, *gone*. Dispensed with by your cruel hand, remember? Broken and lifeless on that cold cavern floor bereft of clothing and dignity. A toy that you chose to cast aside."

"I didn't," she whimpered. "I would never do that."

More lies. I would hear them no longer.

"You *did*," I said icily. "You killed him. *Murdered him.* You threw him away like a broken doll. But now you, the architect of his doom, dare to beg for his return? It's pathetic. *So pathetic.*"

My hand slowly lowered to her throat.

"Why do *you* deserve to live when he didn't?" I asked.

"I don't," she said with tearful eyes. "I don't, I don't."

"Then why did you do it?" I asked her. "Why did you betray him?"

"I couldn't stop them," she wept. "I tried to; I swear! But they were following my father's orders. He read my journal, he knew about us, and he wanted you dead."

"Ah, now it's your *father's* fault," I said. "What pitiful little star-crossed lovers you and Evans must have been! It seems as though the whole world was against you!"

"It was!" she yelled suddenly. "IT WAS! EVERYONE! EVERYONE, USING ME! TREATING ME LIKE AN OBJECT INSTEAD OF A PERSON! You were the only one, Kyler! You were the only one who saw me! You knew I was hurting! You *understood me!*"

"And for that, he was rewarded with death," I said.

"It was THEM!" she screamed. "IT WAS THEM!"

"Prove it," I said as I cast Mesmerize and overwhelmed her free will with the power of my mind. Her face immediately slackened as her posture relaxed. I then stepped away from her and took a seat in a chair while leaving her to stand. "No more of these theatrics, Anikka Velas. Tell me exactly what happened that night."

"What would you like to know?" she asked calmly.

"Were you the one who killed Kyler Evans?"

"No," she said.

"Did you *know* he would be killed that day?"

"No. The actions of my attendants surprised me. I had no idea they were going to do that," she said. "When I demanded to know why, they informed me it was at my father's command."

Huh. So, she'd been telling the truth after all. That was surprising.

"Why would your father want Kyler Evans dead? He had no standing, no relevance. In what way was he a threat?" I asked.

"Because I loved him. Because I wanted to be with him," Anikka said. Although her voice and body language remained calm, as she spoke those words, I saw more tears beginning to well in her eyes.

"Why?" I asked in confusion. "He had nothing to offer you."

"He was everything to me," she said. "He *saw* me."

Oh, for the love of night. Pankratz had gotten it completely wrong and misunderstood everything he'd seen. I shouldn't have been surprised by that; how many times had that boy proven himself to be an utter fool? I shouldn't have given back his hand. Maybe I'd feed his remaining one to a hungry goblin. It would serve him right!

This girl had been telling me the truth all along. Anikka Velas hadn't been using Kyler Evans until she got bored with him. And he had never been a victim of her supposed cruelty.

The two of them had genuinely been in love with each other.

What a mess.

"Sit down," I said, gesturing towards the bed. When she was seated, I asked, "What brought you two together?"

"Shared circumstances," Anikka said sadly. "Like Kyler, one of my parents was a commoner. And unlike my sister and father, my Class, Apothecary, is production-based. The Velas are a clan of warriors, so I was looked upon as an embarrassment. I'm pretty, though, so Daddy decided I still had some value to offer for when I came of age."

"He decided to have you married off?" I asked.

"Not even that," she said bitterly. "He gave me to your brother as a mistress. An incentive to encourage him to marry my older sister, Thalia."

My stomach roiled in disgust.

"He gave you to . . . my brother? Why? Why was attaining Patrick so important that he'd allow his own daughter to become a . . . consort?" I asked.

"Your brother is an A-ranked Holy Knight," said Anikka. "Both the Class and the high ranking are extremely rare. Holy Knights are also coveted because they have the potential to evolve into Paladins, which are S-ranked, just like the Regent's grandson. All of Gardenia's elite had been chasing after him to join them, before he settled on my family."

"Judging by your reaction, I assume that being my brother's mistress has been a less than thrilling experience," I said tactfully.

"He's a monster. Both he and Thalia," she said sadly. "They hurt me."

Damn it.

"He hurt you too," she continued. "Ever since you were children, he went out of his way to oppress you. But you were never afraid of him. You always talked back, and he hated you so much for it! Then you got involved with the equalist movement and—"

What?

"Hold on," I said, raising a hand to pause her. "Are you saying that Kyler Evans was an *equalist?*"

"Yes," she said. "You and that Nick Pankratz were always going on about it. Nick was obviously just joking, but you were so serious about the topic. You'd always say things like, *An end to nobility and shitty older siblings!* You were so funny!"

"I . . . was? I mean, he was? Kyler Evans was an amusing fellow?" I asked.

"Oh, yes. And so brave too. You were just a Porter, but you weren't afraid to speak your mind," Anikka said admiringly. "No matter what they did, no matter how many beatings, you didn't care. And you weren't afraid to approach me either."

So, that was the sort of person Kyler Evans had been. The sort of individual I personally admired. Someone who challenged life's arbitrary unfairness and didn't passively bear with it as I'd always done.

"You promised me we'd leave one day," Anikka continued. "That we'd escape to the reclamations and make a new life for ourselves away from this awful city. Somewhere where Classes didn't matter, and we could just be together. You told me we'd be free one day. But then it happened, in that fracture. They held you down and beat you and humiliated you . . . Kyler, I'm so sorry. I couldn't stop them. I couldn't do anything . . ."

"Stop," I told her as I rested my head in my hands while I absorbed these revelations. "Just stop for a moment, please. This is an awful lot to think about." Then a thought suddenly occurred to me. "Why did you accuse me of attacking you to begin with? You were shouting for them to keep you away from me."

"You were *alive,*" she said. "I'd just seen you be beaten to death but somehow you were walking around without a scratch on you. I thought I was going insane, that I was in hell. I didn't . . . I didn't realize what I was saying. I still think I went mad."

"You didn't. You haven't," I assured her.

"It doesn't feel that way," she whispered. "Especially when you died *again* in the school, and I realized my mistake. Twice! Two times you were stolen from me! But then all this time later, Daddy received a report that you were somehow still around and meeting with the Regent himself! How did you do it, Kyler? How do you keep coming back? And why won't you take me with you?"

"I don't think you'd like the means by which I survived," I said to her quietly. "At times I can barely tolerate them myself."

"I don't care. I just want to be with you," Anikka said. "Please forgive me. Please take me back. Please *help me*."

Her yearning for her dead lover pained me greatly. Looking at her in such misery, it reminded me of myself when Adelbert and Emmaline were . . . lost to me. How desperately I wished I could change the past and earn their forgiveness. How I had wished to overturn death itself just to have another chance to make amends with my friends.

But even when I'd acquired the power to take those steps, the redemption I sought was still denied to me.

Some crimes can never be forgiven.

Some mistakes can never be undone.

I thought I understood this girl perfectly. And in that moment, I decided that I wouldn't allow her to suffer any longer. She was still young. Still beautiful. There was no reason for her to live burdened with the malice of her cruel family. There was still time for her to enjoy her season under the sun. To find love again. To know joy.

But for Anikka to live without fear in the garden, first all the weeds had to be plucked.

Every single one of them.

"Go to sleep," I told her as I rose from my chair. "Rest without dreams as peacefully as you can. Everything will be settled by the morning."

"Where are you going?" Anikka yawned as she lay on the bed. I pulled the blanket over her and smiled as she drifted into gentle slumber, certain now that I was making the right decision.

"I'm paying a visit to your family," I told her sleeping face. "And in return, *they'll* be paying for everything they've done. Now rest."

On my way out of the room, I mentally summoned my daughter.

Rachel. Return to me.

It didn't take her long to appear. Within a few minutes, she was at my side along with Orby as we walked purposefully in the direction of the Velas estate. Before departing the motel, I ordered Schulz to protect Anikka.

"If anyone with unfriendly intentions approaches that room, show no mercy," I commanded him.

He barked once to show he understood. In return, I scratched his ear, pleased as always by his loyalty and obedience.

"So where are we off to now?" Rachel asked as we set out.

"I'm sure you'll like it," I said. "It's a high class, all-you-can-eat buffet. Nothing but fine dining as far as the eye can see."

"Nice," Rachel said cheerfully. "I like the sound of that! I just hope they have enough to satisfy a pair of gluttons like us."

"I'm sure they will, daughter," I said with an anticipatory smile. "Just be sure to bring your appetite."

"How should we dress?" she asked.

"I think something red would be suitable," I suggested.

CHAPTER FORTY

We took our time approaching the Velas estate, gradually building up our anticipation for the rampage we'd soon unleash. Along the way, I told Rachel everything I'd learned earlier from Anikka, which in turn enraged her and made her eager for the upcoming confrontation.

"All the manipulation and cowardice, I just can't stand it," she said vehemently. "Hiding behind money and influence and throwing away lives. Who could stand to be around such people? That's why I told Cross I couldn't join the Valkyries."

"Oh, is that what she wanted to discuss with you?" I asked.

"Yeeeah," Rachel said sourly. "I mean, it was flattering, right? An elite group of all-female fighters renowned throughout the nation. It sounds great! But having to do so in the service of this pathetic society of backstabbing snakes? I just can't. Working for the establishment holds no appeal."

"Did Cross take your answer well?" I wondered.

"She thinks she can still win me over," Rachel said. "I might have to mesmerize her into backing off."

"Working in general is for lesser beings anyway. I'm disappointed she thought she could make a *coworker* of you. We, the night's nobility, have no need to *toil*," I said haughtily.

"That is so snobby," she snickered.

"It's only snobbery if you're rude about it," I corrected her.

Once we arrived at the Velas estate, the two of us were quick to let loose our shared displeasure with how Anikka had been treated. At this point I feel there is no need to go into an overly descriptive recounting of the response of the security forces that pitted themselves against us, nor the many, many instances that followed in which we maimed and murdered the lot of them without mercy.

While I realize that I haven't been that sparing in such details before, this time around was a little different due to our raised ire. Today, Rachel and I were especially . . . unpleasant in our method of dispensing with those doomed, brave souls.

It was a real scene, all right.

The scene of a *massacre*.

There was a time that I'd feared taking the lives of other Hunters due to the system rules forbidding conflict between us. After all, killing them could eventually get us labeled by the system with the dreaded title of Player Killer, which would leave us unable to live in civilized lands and would have placed a permanent bounty on our heads as an incentive for others to kill us.

That was before I realized that our True Vampirism trait essentially negated such a dire outcome. The penalties could apply only when Rachel and I were in our human forms. But when we acted as vampires, the system regarded us as monsters. Why would monsters be penalized for acting according to their nature?

It was pretty much a license to kill. Thank goodness Rachel and I were such thoughtful and responsible people who would never even consider abusing such a massively unfair advantage.

"Kyler!" Rachel laughed. "Did you see me rip that one in half? Oh, wow, look at him! He's trying to crawl away! That's so gross! I'm going to step on his head."

Yep. Just a couple of good-natured people out to have a little fun.

It was a shame that Thalia and Patrick weren't there to share in the fate of their men. Those two were the ones I wanted most of all. I wished I'd thought to confirm their presence before beginning our attack, but it was too late now.

Oh, well. We'd just have to save that particular gratification for a future date.

Once we finished with their outside forces, we smashed our way inside the main house, where the elite among them awaited us. After our introductions were made, each side spoke a few monologues and delivered a few thinly veiled threats before squaring up to fight; you know, the usual routine that happens when colorful warriors and deadly monsters decide to clash.

I found it all rather rote, personally speaking, having endured such rituals many times before, but Rachel was bright-eyed with enchantment for the proceedings, having never thrown down with these sorts of characters before. Since it was all still new to her, I refrained from giving any derogatory commentary, not wishing to stymie her enjoyment. In fact, I let her take them all on by herself while I sought out the master of the estate.

He was the one I truly had business with.

In a way, every misfortune I'd suffered this year all came back to him. Whatever his reasons, he'd been an absolute thorn in my side. And now he was going to pay for it.

How sad that he was so unreceptive to my overtures of friendship when I finally tracked him down.

"Greetings, my Lord. Allow me to give you my warmest regards," I said to him in a jovial manner. "Are you as happy to meet me as I am to finally meet you?"

"And who the hell are you supposed to be?" asked Lord Velas with a ferocious-looking scowl.

"Oh, come now, my identity shouldn't be a surprise to you," I said as I stepped closer so he could see me. "Not to the master of the great Velas family. Not to the man with his fingers on the scale and his nose in everyone's business. Of course you know me!"

"*Kyler Evans?*" he asked in surprise before scoffing at the name. "I knew you recently came scurrying back into the city, but I had no idea you'd be so foolish as to—"

"No," I said, raising a hand to silence him.

"No?" he asked with a puzzled expression.

"I didn't *scurry* back anywhere," I informed him. "*Vermin* scurry. *Insects* scurry. *I* came into town in a *limo*. Get it right."

"I'm sorry, are you completely mental? What the *fuck* are you doing in my home?" Lord Velas asked angrily.

"Claiming it," I explained. "Everything here will now be mine, by right of conquest. Your remaining men, your resources, the clothes on your back, the money you've saved, I'm taking *everything* from you. Would you like to try disputing my claim?"

"I'd very much like to see you try!" he yelled. "You can't just steal everything from me and expect to get away with it, you insolent cur! The entire nobility of all three cities will rise against you!"

"There's no need to take that tone, sir. Men of our ilk shouldn't argue," I said. "Despite our many differences, you and I have much in common. Like you, I was a terrible father who failed my children miserably."

"What insane drivel are you spouting?" Velas said with a sneer.

"Only the truth," I sighed. "You must know that a father who fails at his duty will eventually make enemies of his own children. You're lucky that only one of your daughters turned on you."

Lord Velas glared at me for a moment before saying, "Anikka," spitting the word out as though it were a curse.

"Correct," I said with a nod. "Your daughter and I recently reconnected. She feverishly affirmed her passionate devotion to me and begged for my protection from you. As a gentleman, how could I resist?"

"That ungrateful little *bitch*," he swore. "How many times must she defy me?"

"Just this once was enough," I said. "I swear I tried to be logical about this! But who could resist someone as beautiful as your girl? My head said no, but my heart said kill you and plow her in your bed."

"COME AT ME, THEN!" Lord Velas shouted as red electrical energy enveloped his body and exploded outward, destroying everything around him in a shower of surging sparks and eradicating light. "You presume to challenge me? You want to take what's mine? Come forth, you little bastard, and I'll bury you like just every other fool who dared to face me!"

"Your electrical light effects aren't going to save you, sir," I said as I walked toward him. "This isn't a duel, this is *banditry*. I'm taking everything that you value. The only thing I *won't* do is let you die quickly. That's the price you'll pay for laying a finger on Kyler Evans."

"You shouldn't have gotten involved with my daughter," he said remorselessly.

"Then you shouldn't have stood in her way," I replied. "Clipped wings can never soar."

"She is *MINE*! My property, to do whatever I want with!" Velas ranted. "As worthless as she was, the little whore should have been grateful that I found a good use for her! But instead, she defied me! And over what? A misfire like you? A goddamned *Porter*? The jest went too far! A lesson needed to be taught!"

"She said my brother and Thalia were hurting her. Do you understand the implications contained in that sentence? How could you let that happen?" I asked him.

"What business is it of mine how your brother enjoys his cut of meat?" Lord Velas sneered.

In the blink of an eye, I was across the room, standing before him. Lord Velas only had time to blink once and flinch before my fist punched through his chest all the way up to my elbow. When I removed it with a wet *plopping* sound, he dropped to his knees with a newly placed sucking wound at the center of his torso.

"Why did you make me do that? I was going to play with you a bit first," I asked him.

Bloody saliva dribbled down his chin as he stared at me with a dazed expression. "Dally ges bru-bles-guuu?" he babbled incoherently before he began weeping when his adrenaline faded, and the pain kicked in.

"Oh, this displeases me greatly," I said unhappily. "I'll say this for you, old mortal, you possess an *excellent* gift for provocation. You managed to colossally piss me off and in I went! Now look at what a mess you are. The amount of blood I would have to give you to heal this wound so I could resume killing you properly would surely transform you into a thrall, and I do *not* want to hear any of your thoughts in my mind. Oh, how annoying!"

"Haaaaaaweeeeehh!" screeched Lord Velas.

"Yes, yes, very interesting," I replied as I knelt to face him. "Listen, if the subject ever gets brought up in hell, you'll tell everyone I tortured you to death, right? It would really help my reputation."

Lord Velas grunted another nonsensical barrage of word salad as I raised my hand and prepared to tear off his head.

"Hold on, Kyler!" Rachel said suddenly as she ran into the room, fresh from crushing the elite guard. "Don't be in such a hurry!" she said.

"Hmm?" I asked as she rushed past me while biting a fresh wound into her palm so that she could feed her blood into the old man's mouth by hand.

"Rachel? I very much want this wretched man dead, so would you please explain your reasoning here?" I asked her with a raised brow.

"Ha! And you're always calling *me* too hasty," Rachel snorted as Lord Velas's wound healed and the process of enthrallment began to overtake his body. "Come on! This bastard is still much too useful to kill outright. Even I can see that."

"What's your plan?" I asked once I saw how seriously she was taking this.

"I'm so glad you asked!" she said giddily as she watched the old man's body spasming from the effects of her blood. "Check this out. First, I'm forcing him to become our lesser kin."

"So I see," I said. "But what's your next move after that?"

"I'll order him to disinherit Thalia and Patrick and make Anikka the heir to the household. I'll also force him to adopt us into the Velas family. *Lady Rachel Velas.* Doesn't that sound like a wonderful name?"

I let out a low whistle of appreciation at the sinister depths of my child's insidious cunning. "Rachel, does this mean you've been paying attention to my rambling lectures about the virtues of Machiavellianism?"

"Well, your speeches *do* get so long-winded that it's hard not to absorb a few good ideas," she admitted. "I mean, I'll always prefer directly tearing my enemies apart over ensnaring them in a shadowy scheme, but come on! This is too good an opportunity to screw over too many people that deserve it."

"Men like Duke Velas have a great many connections to influential members of society," I cautioned her. "Taking this route is the same as painting a target on our backs and daring our enemies to shoot."

"Cool," said Rachel. "Then let's start a civil war and burn this place to the ground. If they're going to be a bunch of whiney children over one of them getting the proper slapping he deserved, then fuck it. Let's kill them all. Even better: let's make them kill *each other*."

The demented grin now lighting up my daughter's face made my heart sing with joy. Why had I ever been so frightened by the notion that I had poorly influenced her character? This was how she wanted to be! These were *her* choices!

Rachel liked who she was. And I had been a fool to assume I had somehow corrupted her. She was a rare soul who found freedom through darkness, not despair. Who was I to assume I had any part in the development of her twisted values? She was her own woman.

And I was proud of her.

I swept an arm around her shoulders and pulled her in for a crushing embrace before saying, "I love how twisted your mind has become, daughter. More so than any of my children of birth, I think you best reflect the mad virtues of our sacred bloodline. I dearly look forward to seeing how high you'll rise."

"Kyler, *stop*," Rachel said with a blush. "You're embarrassing me in front of my new thrall."

On the floor, Lord Velas continued to tremble and groan.

"I can't help it!" I said merrily. "Papa's so proud of his devious little angel! Everyone, come take a look at the future tyrant I helped raise! From this moment on I'll tell everyone I meet that I knew you before you were infamous!"

"Daaad!" she squeaked.

I think I felt my undead heart skip a beat.

Metaphorically, that is.

"Is that the first time you ever called me that without being sarcastic?" I gasped.

Were my eyes beginning to water?

I think they were!

"My little girl loves her father!" I sighed.

"Shut up!" Rachel groaned.

"She called me Dad! My daughter called me Dad!" I shouted jubilantly at the estate. "Did everyone who's left alive hear that? My child finally acknowledged me! Oh, is this how nirvana feels?"

"Kyler, shut up!" Rachel shouted as she swung an armored fist at my face, which I merrily dodged by jumping into the air and floating just out of reach.

"It's too late, Rachel! The gate, once opened, can never again be sealed!" I said tauntingly as I shot outside through a window and continued to crow my pleasure to the world.

In response, Rachel flew into the sky to chase wildly after me with murder blazing in her eyes. And that was how we spent a few pleasant hours playing in the darkness over our newly acquired estate. Enjoying a delightful game of tag far above the broken bodies and ruined minds of those who had tried to oppose us.

Later, we returned to Anikka with both the good news of our overwhelming victory, and our sincere congratulations over her becoming her family's heir. She was dazed at first, but quickly warmed up to the incredible change in her status. When we informed her that she had also acquired two new siblings by adoption, as well as a very clever dog and whatever Orby was supposed to be, she seemed almost overwhelmed.

Rachel, who had grown up on a farm with many sisters, was delighted to have acquired a new one in Anikka, and didn't hesitate to embrace her as kin. Anikka, who had never known the genuine love of family, was put off by Rachel's forwardness at first, but it didn't take long for my daughter to win her over.

The pair of them are now thick as thieves. The common ground they shared at being selfishly used by others for the entirety of their lives was strong enough to cement an unbreakable friendship. Although Rachel and I agreed for the time being to keep the secret of our vampirism to ourselves, lately she's been giving me hints that she wants to take Anikka as a child of her own.

I'm reluctant to allow it, but Rachel has proven herself to be a powerful and resourceful vampire. As her strength grows, so will her ambitions and her desire for a family of her own. It would be wrong to oppose that out of a selfish desire to keep her to myself.

I've become very fond of her, but the primary task of a parent is to protect his children until they're strong enough to stand on their own. And once they've achieved that strength, it is best to stand aside while they make their own decisions.

If I were being more honest with myself, I'd admit that the primary source of my reluctance has nothing to do with Rachel at all. Without going overmuch into detail, I've explained to Anikka that I'm not the man she once loved. That only his body remains, and while I'm willing to reciprocate her affection to a degree, it's impossible for me to truly feel for her as he once did.

At the time, I thought she took my revelation calmly. I felt relief that she finally understood and could move on with her life. But lately, when she thinks I don't notice, she looks at me with an expression filled with such longing that I can't help but pity her for what has been stolen from her.

What misery it is to be human and know loss.

Patrick and Thalia, who only survived because they happened to be abroad on the night of our attack, did not take the news of their disinheritance very well. When she realized that the paperwork had already been put in and the law was irrefutably on our side, with even her own father dispassionately rebuking her and denying her claim, Thalia became a screaming wreck reduced to making hoarse vows of bloody vengeance against her sister for what she had done to her.

Such a charming girl. I hope she's learned to conserve her stamina. When it comes to ruining her life, we are only getting started.

By far, the most satisfying confrontation was with my supposed brother, Patrick. He sat wordlessly throughout the meeting we'd arranged as our estate councilors explained the new family paradigm to him and his maddened fiancé. He also made it a point to ignore my presence, even though he couldn't have been surprised to learn I was still alive, since Lord Velas made certain to share information with him. That was why I was surprised after things had concluded, when he pulled me aside for a little tête-à-tête.

It seemed he had some things he wanted to say to me.

"I should have fucking killed you the moment our mother dragged you into our house," said the righteous Holy Knight who wished to ascend to the rank of paladin. "I should have slit your throat with a dull blade."

"Has anyone ever suggested that you have issues with aggression?" I asked him.

A vein throbbed visibly in the corner of Patrick's head before he responded.

"You stole my future, you little bastard. You even stole my girl. I just . . . I just don't understand how you keep getting away with it. I just don't get it. But I'll fix it. Every single time you ever got in my way, I always made you pay for it. This time will be no different. I promise you."

"*Patrick*, you should be more careful," I said in a concerned tone of voice. "We share a bond of blood, so I'm willing to overlook it, but think of what others might say if they heard a minor noble like yourself threatening me. As the legal head of a great house, Lady Anikka might be forced to make an example of you."

"*Kyler Velas,*" he said in disgust.

"What can I say? That's now my legal name." I shrugged.

Rachel had insisted upon it. Probably as revenge for me teasing her too often.

I'd resisted at first. Stragos had been my true name for fourteen centuries and casting it aside had felt like pulling out one of my own teeth by hand.

But as I thought about it, I realized that sort of thinking was, in its own way, arbitrary nonsense. Why should I be so attached to it? It was a name associated with ruin and death. Why should I continue bearing it now that I'd been granted a second chance?

Kyler Stragos and Kyler Evans were both dead. Stragos had been a fiend who'd brought unnecessary suffering to millions. Although he'd had the potential to change for the better, he had never been brave enough to seize that opportunity. Tragic, yes, but his loss was still a benefit to his world.

Evans, on the other hand, had been a good man without the resources needed to change his circumstances. He hadn't lacked courage, but that still hadn't been enough to make the world acknowledge him as a person. Without the power to fight his oppressors, he had amounted to nothing.

What if Kyler Velas could be a bridge between these two disparate individuals? Someone with Stragos's power who also bore Evans's defiant will. What manner of being might such a man become?

Could he become someone worthy of remembrance?

There was only one way to find out.

"Watch your back, *brother*," Patrick said with spiteful intensity before turning his back on me. "A rising tide eventually crests on the shore. Just remember that when I come to take back what's mine."

"The wave may crest but it still washes the shore clean," I said in reply.

Patrick paused to throw a final glare at me before leaving the room with a window-shaking slam of the door.

Heh. Drama.

Later, for the first time in a long while, I managed to escape the company of Rachel and Schulz long enough to enjoy a nap by myself.

It was a rare and refreshing experience to sleep solo. But I was mistaken to believe that I'd get to enjoy it alone. Before much time had passed, a familiar presence soon joined me.

The dream shaped itself into a fine spring evening at an outdoor café I once frequented in London. Beside me, of all the people it could have been, sat Jamie, wearing a sleeveless white dress and enjoying a sip of coffee. I was so surprised by her presence that it took me a moment to realize that her voice sounded different.

"I'm sorry it took so long to get back to you," she said sheepishly. "But can I say how pleased I am at how well you've taken to life in this world? I should have known you'd be up to the challenge."

"Alpha?" I asked after realizing who was speaking to me.

"In the flesh!" she replied. "Well, in the dream, anyway. I thought it would be fun to appear to you in the form of someone you cared for, so here I am! I like this a lot better than the disembodied voice routine."

"Wow. Do I really still care for Jamie?" I asked in surprise. "I feel that our relationship became a bit *complicated* towards the end. The waters were truly muddied."

I then sat silently for a few moments while I considered my own feelings. Then I said, "She turned out to be quite the vixen, didn't she?"

"She was! I was *so* glad when you figured her out," Alpha said with a smile. "But to answer your question, yes, you still subconsciously long for her."

"She was such a horrible person, though," I said.

"Emotions can be hopelessly complex," Alpha said. "And people can wear many masks throughout their lifetimes. If it helps you feel better, there was a part of Jamie that truly cared for you as well. So here I am, representing that portion of her psyche for you. The genuine friendship hidden beneath her greed and subterfuge."

"Heh," I chuckled. "That's very kind of you, Alpha."

"Think nothing of it," she said. "So, how have things been?"

"Don't you already know everything?" I asked her teasingly. "Aren't you the great eye in the sky?"

"I do have all the pertinent details," she admitted. "But I only know them as plain facts without all the interesting nuance involved. I'd very much like to hear the entire tale from *your* exciting perspective. You've been having quite a few adventures of late, haven't you, Lord Velas?"

"I have, haven't I?" I grinned. "Where would you like me to start?"

About the Author

J. V. Simms was the author of the Empress and My Eyes Glow Red series, originally released on Royal Road. When he wasn't writing, he spent his time avoiding his cat, who was likely seeking vengeance for her most recent trip to the vet. Simms lived in Indiana and was always better than his nephew at Minecraft. That's in writing so it must be true.

RESPAWN YOUR CURIOSITY

follow us on our socials

podiumentertainment.com

@podiumentertainment

/podiumentertainment

@podium_ent

@podiumentertainment